Mary Pickering Nichols

Gudrun, a Mediaeval Epic

Mary Pickering Nichols

Gudrun, a Mediaeval Epic

ISBN/EAN: 9783744746267

Printed in Europe, USA, Canada, Australia, Japan

Cover: Foto ©Andreas Hilbeck / pixelio.de

More available books at **www.hansebooks.com**

Ditz puech ist von Chautrun

s wuochs in
verlanndt.
ein reicher
kunig her.
gehayssen
was er Ger
em guter
die hieß Ute.
vnd was ein
kuniginne. durch ir hohe tugende
so gezam dem reichen wol ir mynne.
Ger dem reichen kunig das ist
wol erkannt. dienten vil der Burge
Er hette siben fursten Lanndt. dar
ynne hett er lehen. Viertausent oder
odermere. damit Er taglichen moch
te erwerben baide gut vnd ere Den
iungen Dyebande man gey hofe ge
pot. da ihr solte lernen ob in des
wurde not. mit dem Sper reiten.
schirmen vnd schiessen. so in iuden
vemden kame daz ers dester bas moch
te geniessen Er wuochs vntz an die
stunde. daz er waffen trug in helde
achte erkunde alles des yenig des
in solten preysen man vnd wayb

Fac-simile of the Ambrasian manuscript of Gudrun, reproduced from Koenig's Deutsche Literatur Geschichte.

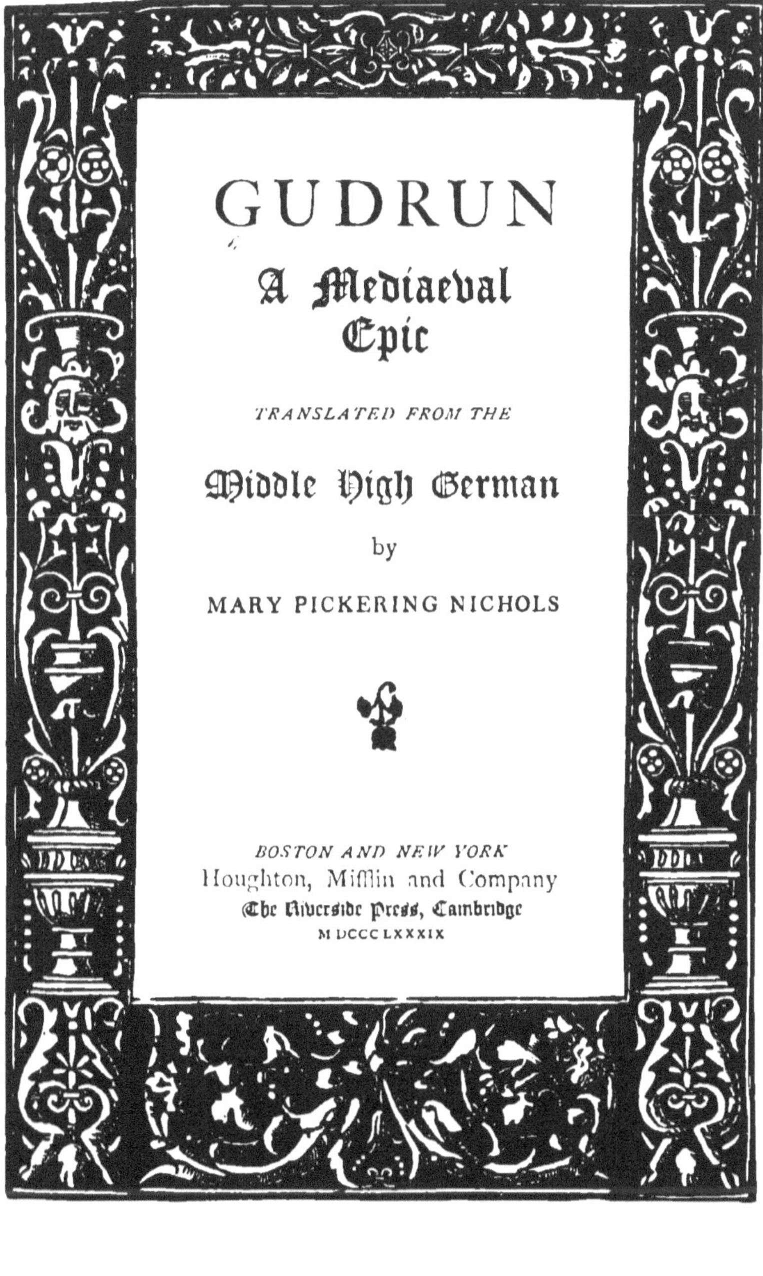

GUDRUN

A Mediaeval Epic

TRANSLATED FROM THE

Middle High German

by

MARY PICKERING NICHOLS

BOSTON AND NEW YORK
Houghton, Mifflin and Company
The Riverside Press, Cambridge
M DCCC LXXXIX

Preface.

THE epic poem of Gu-drun is one of the most important early literary works of the German race. It is attributed to the latter part of the twelfth or the beginning of the thirteenth century, and to a date a little subsequent to that of the Nibelungen Lied. It was first brought to the notice of the modern world in the year 1817, the only original manuscript now known to exist having been discovered about that time in the castle Ambras in the Tyrol, among other manuscripts which had been collected by the Emperor Maximilian I. (1493–1519). The manuscript is now in the Imperial Library at Vienna. It has been several times edited and printed in the original Middle High German, with critical annotations; various translations into modern German have also been published : but so far as I can learn, no complete metrical version in the English language has been made public.

The name of the author is unknown; it is generally thought to have been constructed, in great measure, from earlier legends which had been repeated by wandering singers. According to the late Karl Bartsch, the distinguished critic and editor of Mediæval German literature, the tale shows affinity to legends of the Scalds of Norway and Denmark, and to those of the Shetland Isles. Traces of resemblance are said to be found among the relics of Anglo-Saxon literature. The supposition that the poem was constructed from various early legends explains some of the marvellous incidents of the tale, and those chronological inconsistencies where the rude habits and ideas of earlier times are combined with the later knightly usages of the Middle Ages and with Christian belief.

The scene of the poem is laid principally on the shores of the North Sea, and includes Ireland and Normandy, as well as Holland, Denmark, and Friesland. Very vague ideas of geography were, however, entertained by the poet. Some names of places are thought to be fabulous, and critics disagree with regard to the modern countries designated by other names used.

The poem is founded upon the themes of love and war, and properly consists of three parts. The first portion, embracing four tales, relates the adventures of Hagen, the grandfather of Gu-drun; the second part gives the story of the wooing and abduction of Hilda, his daughter, the mother of Gu-drun. The proper story of Gu-drun begins only with the ninth tale.

The narrative gives a vivid picture of the ideas, manners, and customs of the age of the author; of the dwellings, dress, and ornaments in use; of the weapons and warfare; of the ships and sea-life; and of the tournaments and court festivities. From it we see the nature of the intellectual amusement enjoyed by the northern nations, at that period of their mental development when literary entertainment in the modern sense was yet unknown, and its place was supplied by listening to the recitals of wandering bards.

Modern German critics agree in assigning a high literary value to the poem of Gu-drun, and compare it not unfavorably with the Nibelungen Lied. Bartsch, the critic above named, says: "The general impression which the poem gives is one of greater beauty, though not always of equal grandeur with that of the Nibelungen; it is a worthy companion-piece. The two are justly compared, as are the Iliad and the Odyssey. In the Nibelungen as in the Iliad the fate of a whole people is decided by the sword, and the ruling house, consisting of noble heroes, meets destruction before our eyes; but the conquerors do not fully rejoice in their success. The whole breathes a tragic spirit, even more than the Greek epic. '*Nach Freude Leid*' — 'after joy comes sorrow' — is the earnest tone throughout. Gu-drun, like the Odyssey, closes more tenderly and in a spirit of reconciliation. Although pitiless fate has destroyed the happiness of those for whom the poet has awakened our sympathy, and we see a noble being suffer in the most shameful manner, yet we are sustained by hope, and a happy end compensates for woes endured. '*Aus Leid Freude*'— 'sorrows end in joy' — is the final conclusion. . . . All the characters are worked out in the most

minute and careful manner, and are developed consistently.
. . . The best traits of the German nature, fearless bravery,
unfaltering fidelity, and unswerving integrity, are presented.
The nobility of a feminine soul which, inspired by pure
love, in the distress of a hard captivity, preserves its fidelity
to its beloved, perhaps in no poem of the German middle
ages is so strikingly shown as in the character of Gu-drun.
. . . The descriptions both of battle and scenery are mas-
terly, and are painted with a few decisive strokes."

The metrical form of Gu-drun is similar to that of the
Nibelungen. In both, the accentuation is determined by
the logical sense, as in prose, and not always by the number of syllables, as in most modern verse. In both, the lines
are metrically divided, giving three accents to each half-line
of the stanza, except in the fourth line, in which Gu-drun
differs from the Nibelungen in having five accents instead
of four on the concluding half-line.

The translator has adhered to the original rhythm, and
has endeavored in each stanza to convey strictly the ideas
of the author, being careful not to introduce anything, in
thought or simile, foreign to the poem, and, as far as the
verse would permit, to give a verbal rendering.

The translation has been made from Bartsch's edition
of the original Middle High German (Brockhaus, Leipzig,
1874). He, like the other editors, has supplied some
omissions in the manuscript, an instance of which may

be seen in the sixth line of the fac-simile given. The drawings introduced are copied from mediæval German printed books.

I wish to acknowledge my obligation to my brother for careful revision and for many important improvements throughout the translation.

M. P. N.

Boston, 1889.

Contents.

Names of Persons.

GER, — an early king of Ireland, grandfather of Hagen.

U-TE, — wife of Ger.

SIGEBAND, — son of Ger and U-te.

U-TE, — a Norwegian princess, wife of Sigeband.

HAGEN, — son of Sigeband and the second U-te, and grandfather of Gu-drun.

HILDA, — a princess of India, wife of Hagen.

HILDA, — daughter of Hagen, wife of Hettel.

HETTEL, — king of the Hegelings, husband of Hilda, and father of Gu-drun and Ortwin.

GU-DRUN, — daughter of Hettel and Hilda.

ORTWIN, — prince of Ortland, son of Hettel and Hilda.

WA-TE,
FRU-TE,
HORANT, } vassals of Hettel.
MORUNC,
IROLD,

LUDWIG. — king of Normandy.

GERLIND, — wife of Ludwig.

HARTMUT, — son of Ludwig and Gerlind, a suitor for Gu-drun.

ORTRUN, — daughter of Ludwig and Gerlind.

SIEGFRIED, — king of Moorland, a suitor for Gu-drun.

HERWIC, — king of Sealand, betrothed to Gu-drun.

HILDEBURG, }
HERGART, } maiden companions of Gu-drun.

Names of Places.

ABAKIE, — an imaginary Eastern land, subject to Siegfried.

ABALIE, — an Eastern land, noted for gems and cloths.

ALZABIE, — a fabulous Moorland city, the residence of Siegfried.

AMILE, — an imaginary Eastern land, the home of mermaids.

ARABY, — a land whence came fine clothes and treasures.

BALLIAN — Ballyghan, Hagen's chief city in Ireland.

DANELAND, — not the present Denmark, but, in the ninth century, the seat of the Danes in Friesland, near the mouth of the Scheldt.

DIETMARSCH, — a province subject to Hettel.

FRIESLAND, — subject to Hettel, and held in fief by Morunc and Irold.

GALEIS, — a land whose people are friendly to Herwic.

GALICIA, — Portugal, the home of Hildeburg.

GARADIE, — an indeterminate country, near Ireland.

GIVERS, — a fabulous land, subject to Horant.

GULSTRED, — a place in the West.

HEGELING, — the name of a people on the North Sea, in Holland, governed by Hettel.

HOLSTEIN, — variously mentioned as subject to Fru-te, to Irolt, and to Ortwin.

ICARIA, — a fabulous land whose people are allies of Siegfried of Moorland.

IRELAND, — The situation seems sometimes to correspond with the modern Ireland, and sometimes to a part of Holland. There is a place in Texel, at the present day, named Eijerland.

ISERLAND, — the home of one of Gu-drun's maiden companions.

KAMPALIA, — a fabulous land noted for rich clothing.

KAMPATILLE, — Hettel's castle, also called Matelan.

KARADIE, — a land belonging to Siegfried of Moorland.

KASSIAN, — the chief city and castle of Normandy.

MATELAN, — see Kampatille.

MOORLAND, — the kingdom of Siegfried ; owing to the love of the marvelous in antiquity, regarded by the poet as the land of the Moors, but probably a low country near the North Sea.

NIFLAND, — "the land of fogs," on the lower Rhine, the home of the Nibelungen.

NORMANDY or ORMANIE, — may be the country now known as Normandy,
or is perhaps a region near the mouth of the Scheldt, where the name
Ormaus-kapelle occurs in an ancient map.

ORTLAND, — probably Jutland, under the rule of Ortwin.

SALME, — a fabulous country.

SEALAND, — Herwic's kingdom, not the Danish Zealand, but probably the sealands of Friesland.

SCOTLAND, — spoken of as belonging to Norway.

STURMLAND, — subject to Wâ-te, adjoining Herwic's kingdom.

WALEIS, — the western limit of Hettel's kingdom, by some supposed to be
Wales, but generally thought to be the country near the mouth of the
river Waal in Holland.

WULPENSAND, — an island at the mouth of the Scheldt.

Tale the First.

HOW HAGEN WAS CARRIED OFF BY THE GRIFFIN.

IN olden days in Ireland   a king to greatness came
Who bore the name of Sigeband;   Ger was his father's name.
Queen U-te was his mother;   she of a king was daughter;
High was her worth and goodness,   and well her love beseemed
                        the lord who sought her.

The sway of Ger was mighty,   as unto all is known;
He many lands and castles   and lordships seven did own:
Four thousand knights or over   he thence was often leading,
And wealth, and name yet greater,   he daily won, with those
                        who did his bidding.

Now the youthful Sigeband   to his father's court must go,
That he might there be learning   all he had need to know, —
To bear the spear in riding,   to thrust it, and to shield him,
That when he met the foeman,   the better fame thereby
                        the fight would yield him.

That age he now was reaching   when he the sword might bear;
Of all that a knight befitteth   he learned a goodly share.
This from kin and vassals   praise unmeasured brought him;
For this he still was striving,   and of the toil it cost he
                     ne'er bethought him.

A few short days thereafter   death came among them all,
As even to men the greatest   sadly doth befall.
In every land and kingdom   the truth of this we 're meeting,
And we, with heavy sorrow,   such news ourselves must every day
                     be waiting.

Sigeband's mother, U-te,   the widow's seat must take;
Her son, so high and worthy,   left all things for her sake.
No whit he cared for wedlock,   and had no heart for wooing;
Many a queenly lady   at this was sad, young Sigeband's
                     sorrow ruing.

A worthy wife to find him   his mother him besought;
So might he and his kingdom   to greater name be brought;
And he with all his kindred,   after their bitter sorrow
For the death of the king, his father,   might for themselves
                     no little gladness borrow.

The teaching of his mother   he heard in kindly mood,
And began at once to follow,   as that of a friend one should.
The best of high-born maidens,   'mong those in Norway dwelling,
He bade his men to sue for: to help in this he found
                     his kinsmen willing.

She soon to him was wedded,   as hath of old been said.
With her, among her followers,   came many a lovely maid,
And, from over Scotland's border,   seven hundred warriors fully ;
They came with her right gladly,   when the worth of the king
                     was known to them more truly.

Proudly their way they wended,   as beseemed the maiden's birth ;
With all the care they led her   befitting his kingly worth ;
Hidden were the roadways   by gazers without number,
Who hasted to behold her ;   for three miles and a half the
                     throngs the ways did cumber.

Where'er along the roadside   the path with green was spread,
Flowers and grass were trampled,   by crowds, with heavy tread.
It fell upon that season   when the leaves are springing,
And in every copse and thicket   all the birds their best
                     of songs are singing.

Of simple folk and merry   there rode with her enough ;
While many loaded horses   bore much costly stuff,
Brought there from her birthland   by followers of the maiden ;
They came with her by thousands,   with gold as well as
                     clothing heavy-laden.

On the shore of two wide marches,   the dwellers by the sea,
As they saw the west wind waft her,   gave her welcome free ;
They found a seemly lodging   for the lovely, well-born lady,
And brought her all things needful,   by the youthful king,
                     before, for her made ready.

The fair young maid they welcomed   with knightly tournament ;
Not soon their games they ended,   when on the spear-fight bent.
To the land of Ger his father   they bore her to be wedded ;
She there was loved and mighty,   and men to sound her name
                         she never needed.

All, as they were able,   waited on the maid ;
The gaudy cloth for her saddle   down to the grass was spread ;
The horses' hoofs were hidden   by the housing, heavy drooping.
Aha ! In mood how gleeful   was Ireland's lord, once more
                         a blessing hoping !

When now the time was fitting   that he the maid should kiss,
All crowded thick about him,   in haste to see their bliss.
The bosses of their bucklers   were now heard loudly clashing,
Struck with blows together ;   each strove to shun the throngs,
                         in uproar crashing.

Now with the dawn of morning,   they sent out, far and wide,
To give to all the tidings   of the coming of the bride,
And that, with their master,   they erelong would crown her.
His queen she was thereafter,   and well she earned from him
                         the honor shown her.

It was not deemed becoming   that he his love should plight,
Since she by birth was queenly,   and he not yet a knight :
He first, before his lieges,   must the crown be wearing ;
To this his kinsmen helped him,   and later of his worth
                         were all men hearing.

He, with knights five hundred,   then was dubbed with the sword:
Whatever they could wish for   was given them at his word, —
Both shields, and, for their wearing,   every kind of clothing.
The youthful king so dauntless,   thro' life, of fame and honor
                 wanted nothing.

For many a day thereafter   his sway did Ireland bless,
And never did his greatness   at any time grow less.
To all he freely listened;   the poor man's wrongs he righted;
Widely known was his goodness;   no truer knight than he
                 his word e'er plighted.

His boundless acres yielded   a full and ready gain;
His wife was known for wisdom,   and worthy to be his queen.
To hold her as their mistress   full thirty lords it booted;
As long as the sway she wielded,   her hand to each his lands
                 and home allotted.

She bore unto her husband,   within the next three years,
A child to see most comely;   (such is the tale one hears.)
When later he was christened,   and they were told to name him,
They gave the name of Hagen;   and never since, the tale
                 of his life doth shame him.

He had most careful breeding,   and kindly was he nursed;
Should he be like his fathers,   he would of knights be first.
Watched over by wise women,   and by maidens of early age,
His father and fond mother   found in his face their glad
                 eyes' pasturage.

When now the boy, well fostered,   to his seventh year was bred,
'T was seen that he by warriors   by the hand was often led.
He was happy in men's teaching,   but was with women wearied;
All this he knew no longer;   for, torn from them, he far away
                     was carried.

Whene'er to him it happened   weapons at court to see,
He understood them readily,   and their wearer longed to be;
The helmet and ringed armor   would he have put on gladly:
Alas! not long he saw them,   and all his hopes of fighting
                     ended sadly.

While the kingly Sigeband,   beneath a cedar-tree,
One day on the turf was seated,   the queen said earnestly:
" Although good name and riches   we share with one another,
At one thing yet I wonder,   and this from you I dare to hide
                     no further."

He asked of her: " What is it?"   Then said his helpmeet kind:
" It me doth sorely worry   in body and in mind,
And my heart, alas! is heavy;   to my wish you give no heeding,
To see you 'midst your vassals,   my beaming eyes with pride
                     upon you feeding."

The king to her thus answered: " How should it ever be
That you have had such longing   me with my knights to see?
I will strive thy will to follow,   of this think not so sadly;
Ever to meet thy wishes,   both care and toil will I give
                     myself most gladly."

She said : " No man is living   who owns such wealth, I trow,
Who has so many castles   or lands so wide as thou,
With silver and gems so costly,   and gold so heavy weighing ;
For this are our ways too lowly,   and nought there is in life
                       to me worth saying.

" When erst I was a maiden,   and on Scotland's soil drew breath,
(Chide not, my lord, thy helpmeet,   but list to what she saith,)
I there was daily seeing   the liegemen of my father
For highest prizes striving ;   but here such games we never
                       see together.

" A king so rich and mighty,   as you in name have been,
Before his followers often   should let himself be seen ;
He oft should ride in tilting   with other champions knightly,
That both himself and his kingdom   should seem more fair,
                       and hold their rank more fitly.

" It shows, in a lord so noble,   a most unworthy mind,
When he has heaped together   riches of every kind,
If he with his faithful warriors   to share them is unwilling :
When men in the storm of warfare   deep wounds have had, how
                       else can they find healing ? "

Then said to her King Sigeband :   " Lady, you mock at me ;
In all these warlike pastimes   I will most earnest be ;
And for the strife so worthy   my wish shall never waver :
No man shall find it easy   the ways of well-born kings
                       to teach me ever."

She said : " You now for warriors   must send throughout the land ;
Stores of wealth and clothing   must be given with open hand.
I too will send out heralds   my kinsmen all to rally,
And to show them my good wishes ;   we then shall find our life
           to pass more gaily."

At this the king of Ireland   unto his wife thus said :
" I yield to you most willingly,   for men are often led
By the wishes of fair women   great feastings to make ready;
I therefore now will gather   my brave and hardy kinsmen,
           and those too of my lady."

To him the queen then answered :   " Sorrow no more I wear ;
Five hundred women's garments   I will give, to each her share ;
To four and sixty maidens   gay clothes to give I 'm willing."
Then the king did tell her   high times he soon would hold,
           his word fulfilling.

The sports were then bespoken :   he bade his men to send,
In eighteen days or sooner,   to liegeman and to friend,
To say to all in Ireland,   who would in his games be riding,
That, after summer was ended,   they should spend the winter,
           with him abiding.

He bade his men make benches,   so our tale doth run,
And for these, from out the wilderness,   timber must be drawn ;
For sixty thousand warriors   seats must they make ready.
His henchmen and deft stewards,   to do this work for the king,
           were skilled and speedy.

Thither men then hastened   on many a winding way;
All were kindly cared for   throughout their lengthened stay.
Now from Ireland's kingdom,   as the king had bidden,
Full six and eighty thousand   of warriors strong there
to his court had ridden.

From the store-rooms of the castle   clothing now was borne,—
All the gear they wished for,   and all that could be worn.
Shields were also given,   and steeds of Irish breeding;
The proud and queenly lady   bedecked her guests with all
they could be needing.

She gave to a thousand women   costly clothes enow,
And likewise to fair maidens   what one to youth should allow, —
Broidered bands and jewels,   and silk that glistened brightly;
The many lovely ladies,   together standing there, were fair
and sightly.

To every one who wished it   were given clothes well-made.
Horses were there seen prancing,   by the hand of foot-boys led;
These light shields did carry,   and their spears were seizing.
U-te, the queenly mother,   was gladly seen, as she on the leads
sat gazing.

The guests by the king were bidden   freely in tilts to meet:
The glitter of their helmets   grew dim in the dust and heat.
The ladies, held in honor,   near by were also seated,
Where they the deeds of the warriors   saw full well, and with
words of wonder greeted.

As oft before has happened,   the show had lasted long ;
The king was not unwilling   to be looked on by the throng.
This, meanwhile, to his lady   happiness was giving,
As she, amidst her women,   sat on the roof, and saw their
earnest striving.

When now her lord had ridden,   as doth beseem a king,
He thought to end their onsets ;   some rest to them to bring
He deemed not unbecoming ;   to stop the games he bade them.
And then before the ladies,   after their skill thus shown, he
proudly led them.

U-te, the high-born lady,   began her friends to greet,
With those from far-off kingdoms ;   them as guests to meet
The queen was truly willing ;   on them her glad eyes rested.
The gifts of Lady U-te   were not on scornful friends
that evening wasted.

Knights and lovely ladies   together there were seen.
The good-will of the master   to all well-known had been ;
In all their games and tilting,   his kindness was not hidden.
Once more the guests, that evening,   to ride in warlike strife
by him were bidden.

Their games and sports had lasted   until nine days were gone ;
They, as knights befitteth,   their skill to the king had shown.
By the many wandering players   the show was liked the better,
And they plied their work more briskly,   and hoped that their
reward would be the greater.

Sackbuts loud and trumpets   there might all men hear;
Fluting too and harping   fell upon the ear.
Some on the rote were playing,   others in song were vying;
They, by their jigs and fifing,   soon would better clothes
                 for themselves be buying.

On the tenth morn it happened,   (now hark to my sorry tale,)
That, after all their pastimes,   there rose a bitter wail.
About these days so merry   new tales were told on the morrow;
And tho' they now were mirthful,   they came to know deep gloom
                 and heavy sorrow.

When the guests were seated   beside their kingly host,
There came to them a player,   and proudly made his boast
That he, before all others,   (who should indeed believe him?)
Was far more skilled in playing,   and even the greatest lords
                 their ear must give him.

Outside, a lovely maiden   was leading by the hand
The little son of Sigeband   who swayed the Irish land;
With him were likewise women   who to the boy gave heeding,
And friendly kinsmen also,   who carefully taught the child,
                 and oversaw his breeding.

Within the great king's palace   was heard a din and shout;
All were there heard laughing,   the roomy walls throughout.
The guardians of young Hagen   crowded up too nearly,
And thus lost sight of the maiden,   together with the child
                 they loved so dearly.

The evil luck of their master   to him that day drew near,
And brought to him and U-te   sudden woe and fear.
Sent by the wicked devil,   from afar his herald hasted
To them in their happy kingdom ;   they were by this with
                               sorrow sorely wasted.

It was a strong, wild griffin   had quickly thither flown ;
From the little boy of Sigeband,   who ever care had known,
Came ill luck to his father,   who soon of this was tasting.
His son, so well-belovéd,   to him was lost, with the mighty
                               bird far hasting.

A shadow now came o'er them,   from wings that bore him fleet,
As if a cloud had risen ;   great strength had the bird, I weet.
The guests, in pastime busy,   no thought to this had given,
And the maid, with the child she was leading,   was standing
                               now alone, unheeded even.

Beneath the weight of the griffin   forest trees broke down ;
And now the trusty maiden   looked where the bird had flown ;
Then she herself sought shelter,   and left the child forsaken.
Hearing a tale so startling,   one truly might the whole
                               for a wonder reckon.

The griffin soon alighted,   and in his claws he held
The little child, gripped tightly,   while with fear it quailed.
His ghastly mood and anger   the bird was harshly showing ;
This must knights and kinsmen   long bewail, with sorrow
                               ever growing.

The boy was sorely frightened,   and began aloud to shriek;
Higher the mighty griffin   flew, with outstretched beak;
To the clouds above them floating   he his prey was bearing.
Sigeband, lord of Ireland,   loudly wept, his outcries never
sparing.

His friends and all his kinsmen   the sorry tale soon heard;
They, in the death of his offspring,   his bitter sorrow shared.
Downcast were he and his lady,   and all their loss felt nearly;
Sorely they wept together,   mourning the boy, now torn
from them so early.

In this their mood so gloomy,   the happy, merry plays
Must now be sadly ended.   Before their frightened gaze,
The griffin so had robbed them   that all for home now started,
Sober, and filled with sadness.   They truly felt forlorn,
and heavy-hearted.

The king was bitterly weeping,   his breast with tears was wet;
The high-born queen besought him   his sorrows to forget,
Thus wisely to him speaking :   " Should all in death be stricken,
There must be an end of all things ;   it is the will of God
their lives hath taken."

Now all would hence be faring,   but the queen to them did say :
" I beg you, knights and warriors,   longer with us to stay ;
Our gifts of gold and silver,   that here for you are ready,
You should not think of meanly ;   our love for you is ever
true and steady."

The knights to her bowed lowly,   and then began they all
To say how they were thankful.   The king, thereon, did call
For silken stuffs, the richest,   for all who there yet tarried ;
They had ne'er been cut nor opened ;   and from far-off lands had
                  erst to the king been carried.

He gave them also horses,   both palfreys and war-steeds ;
The horses out of Ireland   were tall and of hardy breeds.
Red gold was likewise given,   and silver without weighing ;
The king with care had bidden   outfit good for his guests,
                  no longer staying.

Soon as the queen was willing,   each her leave now takes,
Both lovely maids and women ;   each one herself bedecks
With gifts that made her fairer ;   all new clothes are wearing.
The high times now are ended ;   Sigeband's land they leave,
                  and are homeward faring.

Tale the Second.

HOW HAGEN SLEW THE GRIFFIN.

OF how their stay was ended   I will speak no longer here ;
  Now I tell you further   of the rushing flight in the air,
That the child with the angry griffin   far away was bearing.
For this his friends and kinsmen   long in their hearts were
                                heavy sorrow wearing.

Because the Lord so willed it   the child was not yet dead ;
But, none the less, he later   a life of sadness led,
After the harsh old griffin   back to his nestlings bore him.
When on their prey they gloated,   hard toil enough the boy
                                had now before him.

Soon as the bird that bore him   did on his nest alight,
He dropped the boy he carried,   and in his claws held tight ;
One of the young ones caught him :   that he did not devour him
Thanks to God thereafter   were given, far and wide, for the
                                watch kept o'er him.

Else the birds had slain him,   and with their claws had torn.
Now listen all with wonder,   and his bitter sorrow learn :
Hear how the king of Ireland   then from death was shielded ;
Him a young bird now carried,   strongly clutched, and naught
of his grip he yielded.

From tree to tree in the forest   he with the boy took flight ;
The bird a little too boldly   trusted his strength and might.
Upon a branch he lighted,   but now to the ground must flutter,
For he was much too heavy ;   in the nest to have longer staid
had methinks been better.

The child, while the bird was falling,   broke from him away,
And hid among the bushes,   a little, lorn estray ;
Well-nigh was he to starving,   't was long since food he tasted.
Yet on a day long after   the hopes of women in Ireland
on him rested.

God doth many a wonder,   truly one may say.
By the craft of the mighty griffin,   it came to pass one day,
Three daughters fair of princes   had been taken thither,
And now near by were dwelling.   No man can tell how there
they lived together,

And how, thro' days so many,   their lives to them were spared,
Were it not that God in heaven   for them in kindness cared.
Hagen now no longer   need live without a fellow ;
Those good and lovely maidens   soon found the little waif
in a rocky hollow.

When, crawling to his hiding,   they the child did see,
It might, so thought the maidens,   a dwarfish goblin be,
Or perhaps it was a water-oaf,   from out the sea up-driven;
But when the boy came near them,   at once a welcome kind
                        to him was given.

Hagen was ware of the maidens,   as into their cave they stole,
While with fear and sadness   their little hearts were full,
Before they yet had knowledge   that they a Christian greeted.
But the care they later showed him   lifted the pain from
                   many hearts o'erweighted.

First spake the eldest maiden: "How darest thou in our cave,
Where from the God of heaven   we home and shelter have?
Go, seek again thy playmates,   the billowy waters under;
Enough ourselves we sorrow,   and on our bitter lot in sadness
                       ponder."

The high-born child then answered: "I pray you let me stay;
I truly am a Christian,   you must not say me nay.
One of the griffins seized me,   and to the cave did carry;
I cannot live all lonely,   and here with you would I
                   most gladly tarry."

Then to the child so friendless   they loving welcome gave;
But they of his worth thereafter   did better knowledge have.
They now could ask him only,   whence he had been stolen:
But, such was then his hunger,   in telling his tale, his heart
                   was full and swollen.

Then spake the little foundling: "Food I sorely need;
Give to me, in kindness, a little drink and bread.
'T is long since I have had it, and now three days I 'm fasting,
The while the griffin bore me, and full a hundred miles

was hither hasting."

Then answered one of the maidens: "Our lot it so hath been,
That we our wonted cup-bearers never here have seen;
Neither our lordly steward, who should food to us be giving."
Still they praised God's goodness; altho' their years were few,

they were wisely living.

A search they soon were making for roots and herbage wild,
Wherewith they hoped to strengthen Sigeband's darling child.
Such food as they had lived on they gave to him most freely;
To him 't was a meal unwonted, but such as they long time

had eaten daily.

Yet he needs must eat it, for hunger sore he hath,
And hard it is to any to meet with bitter death.
Thro' all the days so dreary, while with the maidens dwelling,
To them his help most willing he ever gave, his thankfulness

thus telling.

They, too, had him in keeping, that can I say for truth;
He there grew up in sadness, throughout his early youth;
Until, one day, the children, to make them greatly sorrow,
Before their cavern-dwelling saw wonders rise, that

threatened more to-morrow.

I know not from what border,   tossing o'er sea to land,
Came to those shores so rocky   a holy pilgrim band.
The ground-swell it was heavy,   and rocked the bark full sorely;
Thereat the banished maidens   felt their care and sorrow
                growing hourly.

Soon the ship was shattered;   not one his life could save.
Quickly the stern old griffins   came down beside the wave;
Seizing many drowned ones,   back to their nest they hurried.
Many a woman was mourning,   soon as the sorry tale to her
                was carried.

When to the hungry nestlings   the food they took in haste.
Back again the griffins   came from their offspring's nest;
From what far spot I know not,   along the sea-paths flying.
Their young they left on the hillside,   with a neighbor grim.
                while they were hither hieing.

One day the goods of the sailors   Hagen saw near the sea.
For many had been drowned there;   holy men were they.
He thought, among the wreckage,   food might still lie hidden:
But, through fear of the wicked griffins,   he softly crept
                to the shore, by hunger bidden.

No one could he find there,   but a body in armor alone;
Thereby the wild old griffin   hard work would give him soon.
Out from his armor he shook him,   nor did he spurn to wear it:
He found a bow and weapons,   by its side, on the sandy shore.
                lying near it.

With these himself he girded,   that simple little child;
When in the air above him   he heard a rushing wild.
He wished that he had loitered,   the sorry little master;
But quickly came the griffin;   to the sheltering cavern fain
                     would he flee the faster.

The bird swung down in anger   to the sandy beach and foam;
The little playmate and fellow   of the young it left at home,
Would by the angry griffin   have at once been swallowed;
But now the bold young Hagen   the ways of a daring foeman
                     bravely followed.

He with strength but youthful   the tightened string drew out,
And arrows swift and many   from the well-bent bow he shot.
Alas! he did not hit him;   what hope of his ill-luck turning?
Then he of the sword bethought him;   he heard the maids
                     bewailing him and mourning.

Tho' his years were not yet many,   he still was brave enough;
A wing from the angry griffin   he struck at the shoulder off,
And in the leg he smote him   a heavier blow and stronger;
So that his wounded body   the bird away from the spot
                     could drag no longer.

The boy was now the winner;   one of his foes lay dead;
But quickly came another,   who sorrow for him made.
All at last were slaughtered;   nor old nor young were living;
God in heaven helped him;   but truly against such strength
                     't were hopeless striving.

When he that feat of wonder   had done, with heart so brave,
He called the friendly maidens   from out their rocky cave.
He said: " Let air and sunshine   your sorry hearts be filling ;
Since now the God in heaven   to grant to us some bliss
at last is willing."

His call they kindly welcomed,   and many times, forsooth,
The boy by the lovely maidens   was kissed upon the mouth.
Their keeper now lay lifeless ;   and none there was to hinder
Their roaming o'er the hillsides,   and, far or near, at their
good-will to wander.

By help of the boy, from sorrow   they now were wholly free ;
The little childish wanderer,   so skilled with the bow was he,
That birds his well-shot arrows   could never shun by flying.
He shot them now for pastime ;   but to get them soon for food
must he be trying.

He in heart was daring,   he was mild, but also brave ;
Hey ! from the wild beasts learning,   what nimble leaps he gave !
As doth the strong young panther,   over the rocks he scrambled :
Himself was his only teacher,   and, far away from kin, alone
he rambled.

While on the shore, by the waters,   his time he often spent,
He saw, among the sea-waves,   live fishes, as he went ;
To catch them it were easy,   but yet he did not get them,
For with fire his kitchen smoked not.   Daily his sorrow grew
that he could not eat them.

Oft from his rocky shelter   to the forest he would roam ;
Many wild beasts saw he,   strong and grim in their home.
One there was among them   greedy to devour him ;
But with his sword he slew him,   and let him quickly feel
                         the hate he bore him.

Unto a wild chameleon   this dreadful thing was like ;
Its skin the boy drew from it,   (for that was he not too weak ;)
Now for its blood he thirsted,   and, when of this he had taken,
He felt great strength come o'er him ;   and many thoughts began
                         in him to waken.

Then with the skin of the monster   he wrapped himself around ;
When soon to him it happened   hard by a lion he found.
To shun him it were hopeless,   for he quickly rushed upon him ;
But the boy was yet unwounded ;   his foe from the daring child
                         warm welcome won him.

When he the lion had smitten   to death, with many blows,
He to the cave would take it,   as homeward thence he goes.
At all times had the maidens   been by his care upholden,
But now this food unwonted   did raise their waning strength,
                         and their hearts embolden.

Of fire they yet knew nothing,   but wood they need not seek ;
From out a stone he quickly   many sparks did strike.
The food they long had wanted   he soon was on them bestowing,
And, since there was none to do it,   themselves the flesh must cook
                         on the coals now glowing.

When they of food had eaten,   at once they grew more strong;
Their boldness, too, grew greater,   (to God their thanks belong.)
And now their bodies also   as healthy were, and comely,
As if they still were living,   each in her father-land,
on fare more homely.

The wild young Hagen also   the strength of twelve did own;
And for this, thro' all his lifetime,   praise by him was won.
But both to him and the maidens   't was pain and sorrow only,
To think that they forever   must pass their lives in a waste
so sad and lonely.

They begged of him to lead them   down to the watery flood.
Shame they felt in going,   for the clothes were none too good
The maidens now were wearing;   they themselves had sewed them,
Ere yet the youthful Hagen   them in their banishment found,
and his kindness showed them.

For days full four and twenty   they fared thro' the piny wood;
At last, on a morning early,   down they came to the flood,
And saw a laden galley,   that came from Garadé.
Then did the lonely maidens   sorrow and pain at the sailors'
plight betray.

Hagen shouted loudly;   he was hindered none the more.
Altho' the winds were boisterous,   and wild the waves did roar.
Now the ship was groaning;   and the sailors, landward steering,
Felt dread of water-nixes,   on seeing the maids, as they
the shore were nearing.

The ship it had a master,   a lord from out Salmé;
Hagen, as well as his kindred,   had he known on a former day.
They before were neighbors,   but Ireland's child, here roaming,
The youthful son of Sigeband,   was to the pilgrims unknown,
                 who now were coming.

The earl forbade his steersman   nearer to sail to the shore ;
But now the childish outcast   but begged of them the more,
For love of God, to take them   away from that shore forsaken.
The sailors felt emboldened,   when by the boy the name
                 of Christ was taken.

The earl, with eleven others,   into a boat now sprung ;
Ere he the truth was learning,   the time to him seemed long.
Whether the maidens as goblins   or mermaids must be treated
He knew not; such beings never,   in all his life before,
                 his eyes had greeted.

He first began to ask them,   before he reached the strand:
" Boy, have you been baptized?   What do you in this land?"
Dight with fresh green mosses   he saw those lovely daughters,
Who earnestly begged the sailors   that they would deign
                 to take them o'er the waters.

Tale the Third.

HOW HAGEN SAILED TO HIS HOME.

ERE they went on shipboard,   the pilgrims them besought
  Kindly to take the clothing   they with them had brought.
However shy were the maidens,   to wear them they were ready ;
They donned the clothes with blushes,   and now their sorrow
                                        had an ending speedy.

Soon as the lovely maidens   embarked upon the wave,
They heartily were greeted   by knights both good and brave,
Who to the high-born daughters   welcome to give were heedful ;
Tho' they at first mistook them,   and thought them wicked elves,
                                    or mermaids dreadful.

That night the maidens rested   with friends upon the sea ;
So wondrous was their dwelling,   from fear they were not free :
Wiser it were in the children   to think this home a blessing.
Soon as the earl had bidden,   their food upon the maids
                                      they all were pressing.

After they had eaten,   and while with them he sat,
The lord of the land of Garadie   the maidens did entreat
To say by whom such fair ones   were brought unto that shore.
The children, at his asking,   only felt their sorrow grow
                 the more.

First answered him the eldest   of those who with him sat:
"I come from a far-off kingdom,   (my lord, now hear my fate;)
I was born in the land of India,   a land wherein my father
Was king while he was living,   but I, alas! the crown
                 must leave to another."

Then spake the maid next younger: "I too have come from far;
Erewhile a strong old griffin   did me from Portugal bear.
A king in the land was my father;   none than he was prouder,
Nor for a mighty ruler,   far or near, were ever
                 praises louder."

Then the youngest maiden, who by the earl sat near,
To him spoke low and modestly,   and said: "I pray you hear;
From Iserland I was carried,   my father there held power;
But from those who hoped to rear me,   alas! afar was I borne
                 in an evil hour."

The high-born knight then answered: "By God 't is ordered well,
Since you among your kinsfolk   not long were left to dwell;
Now, at last, by his kindness   you are freed from dangers,
For I within these borders   have found you living here,
                 such lovely strangers."

However much he asked them,　they yet to tell were loath,
How unto them it happened　grim death had spared them both,
When erewhiles the griffin　unto his nest had brought them.
Many had been their sorrows ;　no more to speak of these
　　　　　　　　　　　　　　　　the maids bethought them.

Then said the worthy leader,　turning to the youth ;
" My dearest friend and fellow,　now let me hear the truth ;
Since unto me these maidens　their sorry tale have given,
From you would I hear gladly,　and learn the land and kin
　　　　　　　　　　　　　　　　whence you were riven."

To him wild Hagen answered :　" That will I tell to you ;
One of those dreadful griffins　bore me hither too.
Sigeband was my father ;　in Ireland once was I living ;
But long with these lovely maidens　I since have dwelt,
　　　　　　　　　　　　　　　　with many sorrows striving."

Then they all besought him　to say how it befell
That, living with the griffins　he had come off so well.
To them young Hagen answered :　" To God it all was owing ;
But now I have cooled my anger ;　no more for them my heart
　　　　　　　　　　　　　　　　with hate is glowing."

Then spake the lord of Garadie :　" I fain would learn from you
How you were freed from danger ?"　He said : " I quickly slew
Both the old and the young ones ;　not one of those is living
By whom my life was threatened,　and who to me such fear
　　　　　　　　　　　　　　　　were daily giving."

Then said all the sailors: "Your strength indeed was great;
For every man and woman   to praise you it were meet.
A thousand of us truly   'gainst them in vain had striven,
Nor ever could have slain them;   truly to you have blessings
great been given."

The earl and all his followers   were of the boy afraid;
His strength was past all measure,   and sorrow for them made.
They would by craft his weapons   have taken from him gladly,
But these he sternly guarded,   and soon, thro' him, it ended
for them sadly.

Then spake the earl yet further: "It now has happened well,
After our toilsome wanderings,   and all that us befell.
But since you are a kinsman   of my foeman, Sigeband,
And here have come from Ireland,   I as a hostage hold you
in my hand.

"You come to me most fitly,   as you shall know ere long,
For many of your kindred   have done to me great wrong.
In Garadie's fair kingdom,   which lies too near their border,
In a heavy fight, my warriors   were seized upon and murdered
by their shameful order."

Then answered him young Hagen: "Of all the wrongs they did
I am wholly guiltless;   if me to them you lead
I their hearts will soften,   and so will the strife be ended.
Let hope to me be granted   that I on my kinsmen's shore
may soon be landed."

Then said the earl to Hagen : " For a pledge must you abide,
And I shall keep these maidens   to live at court by my side ;
They will swell my greatness,   and I shall be their owner."
Then thought the youthful Hagen,   such words to be to him
a wrong and a dishonor.

He quickly said in anger :   " No bondsman will I be ;
That may no man ask for,   who would unscathed go free.
And now, my worthy sailors,   you needs to my land must bear me ;
I will reward you gladly,   and to give you clothes and gold
will never spare me.

" The earl has thought my maidens   his own shall ever be ;
But they shall yet be happy,   and shall of him be free.
Whoe'er is blest with wisdom,   let him my bidding follow ;
Look to your sails, and turn them,   and guide the ship
to Ireland, o'er the billow."

The men, as the earl had bidden,   to seize the boy now dared,
But boldly did he meet them,   and for their lives they feared.
He by the hair caught thirty,   and into the water flung them ;
Soon the strength of his body   was known to all, and dreaded
much among them.

Had not the kindly maidens   sought to end the fight,
Soon the earl of Garadie   he would have killed outright.
'Gainst neither low nor mighty   did his anger falter ;
These warriors and sailors   now to Ireland's shores
their way must alter.

They began at once to hasten,   lest he their lives might take;
For now the wrath of Hagen   made them with fear to quake.
For seventeen days the sailors   from toiling never rested,
And sorely were they frightened;   whene'er he seemed unkind
                         they ills forecasted.

When he now drew nearer   unto his father's shore,
He saw the roomy castles   he well had known before;
Soon a lofty palace   he spied at the edge of the river;
Three hundred towers fully   he there beheld, as strong
                         and good as ever.

In it dwelt King Sigeband,   with his proud and queenly wife.
Again each pilgrim sailor   thought to lose his life;
For should the lord of Ireland   aught of them be learning,
They feared that he would slay them;   but Hagen stood between,
                         his anger turning.

Then spake unto the pilgrims   that brave and warlike man:
"Your peace will I make gladly,   altho' I do not reign;
I hold no sway in the kingdom,   but thither will I be sending,
And 'twixt yourself and my father   of the hatred old I soon
                         will make an ending.

"Would any now be doing   what wealth to him will bring,
Let him my errand carry.   Whoever to the king
Shall say what I shall bid him,   gold will I give him truly:
And also, very gladly,   my father and my mother will reward
                         him duly."

Twelve of the stranded pilgrims   he bade to ride away:
" Now ask of the king, my father,"   thus the youth did say,
" Whether to see young Hagen,   his son, he still is yearning, —
Him who erst by the griffin   was stolen far away, heart-sorrow
learning.

" I know that what you tell him   the king will not believe ;
Then ask you of my mother   if she her faith will give,
And if for her child to own me   she will at last be willing,
If I upon my bosom   will show a golden cross, the proof
fulfilling."

When those he sent had ridden   farther into the land,
They found, in the palace seated,   Queen U-te and Sigeband.
Then knew the king that the riders   from Garadie came thither,
And that they to him were foemen ;   at this both he and his men
were wroth together.

He asked of them how dared they   to come within his land?
Then one among them answered :   " We are sent here at the hand
Of your son, the youthful Hagen.   If any fain would meet him,
He now is here, so near you,   that you ere many hours, in truth,
may greet him."

Then spake the kingly Sigeband :   " To cheat there is no need :
The loss of my dear little one,   who hath so long been dead,
Still my heart's deep sorrow   doth too oft awaken."
" Ask, then, the queen, your lady,   if for a falsehood should
our word be taken?

" The little boy so often   in her fond care has been,
She knows if on his bosom   a golden cross was seen.
And if upon this wanderer   be found the self-same token,
You as your child can own him ;   you then will grant that
                       truth by us is spoken."

Then to the Lady U-te   the tale was quickly told ;
Glad was she of the tidings,   yet mourned she as of old.
She said : " Now let us hasten,   that the truth no more be hidden."
Her lord then bade to saddle ;   and steeds for himself and his
                       bravest knights were bidden.

Straightway one of the pilgrims   to the fair Queen U-te said :
" I will tell you, if you listen,   what now to do you need.
You first must carry clothing   for each young lovely maiden
Whose coming does you honor ;   as followers of your son
                       were they hither bidden."

Soon brought they richest clothing,   and tiring-women, too ;
The queen was also followed   by men both brave and true.
They found the youthful Hagen,   who on the shore was standing ;
And many men from Garadie,   who with the wandering boy on the
                       beach were landing.

Tale the Fourth.

HOW HAGEN WAS MET BY HIS FATHER AND MOTHER.

SOON both men and women   riding there were seen ;
   Then the brave young Hagen   went forth to meet his kin.
Who 't was that came to greet him   he now to know was seeking ;
The throng grew ever thicker   of friends who came in haste,
their kindness speaking.

The king a friendly welcome   into his land soon gave ;
He said : " To send men hither   did you the boldness have,
To say that our queen beloved   is in truth your mother ?
If the words are true you 've spoken,   so glad as now I am
there 's not another."

His queen, the lovely U-te,   with lofty breeding, said :
" Bid that for these new-comers   lodgings now be made ;
I shall know right easily   if he for the crown is fitted."
She found, in truth, the token,   and, full of bliss, her
youthful son she greeted.

With eyes all wet with weeping,　she kissed him on the mouth:
"Though I before was ailing,　I now am well in sooth.
Welcome be thou, my Hagen,　my only child, loved dearly!
All in the land of Sigeband　right glad shall be for him
　　　　　　　　　　　　they lost so early."

The king to the youth came nearer;　his happiness was great.
For the hearty love he bore him　his manly cheek was wet;
With tears that hot had risen　his eyes were overflowing.
For the child, from him erst stolen,　rightly the father felt
　　　　　　　　　　　　the love he was showing.

The queenly U-te welcomed　the homeless maids that day;
Many clothes she gave them,　both bright in hue and gray,
Of silk, with downy linings,　that much the maidens wanted.
Their sorrows now were lightened　by all the gifts the wife
　　　　　　　　　　　　of Sigeband granted.

Well they clothed the maidens,　as their loveliness became;
This they long had needed,　and oft had blushed with shame;
But, decked with gaudy trimmings,　now they came less shyly.
The king and all his followers　soon to the maidens gave
　　　　　　　　　　　　a welcome freely.

Hagen asked that friendship　to the men of Garadie
Should by the king and his lieges　be granted speedily;
Beseeching his forgiveness　for all their foul misdoing.
Soon, at the wish of Hagen,　kindness to the pilgrims he was
　　　　　　　　　　　　showing.

When the king had kissed them   and soothed his angry mood,
He to the shipwrecked pilgrims   made their losses good.
To them it was a blessing,   and praise to Hagen carried;
The lands of the men of Ireland   never since have they
                        as foemen harried.

Then their food and clothing   the guests took out, for use,
And up on the sands they bore them,   trusting in Hagen's truce;
To take their rest for a fortnight   them did he embolden.
The band of haughty pilgrims   to give to him their thanks
                        were now beholden.

Then, in the midst of uproar,   they rode away from the shore;
Up the castle of Ballian   came also many more,
Led by a tale of wonder   that the son of the king was living, —
Of their king so rich and mighty;   a thing so strange was
                        to many past believing.

The water-weary pilgrims,   long-tossed upon the sea,
When fourteen days were ended   to leave the land were free.
To them by the host were given   gifts of gold, bright shining:
By the help of his son's great kindness   he hoped a lasting
                        friendship to be winning.

Hagen his maidens never   henceforth unthought-of leaves:
Kindly doth he teach them   ofttimes to bathe in the waves.
He showed himself most loving,   ever for them caring;
Rich clothes to them were given,   and wise beyond his years
                        was all his bearing.

Now was the youth beginning to be a man well-grown.
He ever showed his kinsmen the skill to warriors known ;
Whate'er a knight befitteth with hand and weapon doing.
In the land of his father, Sigeband, his mighty sway he soon
           to all was showing.

Hagen was ever learning what doth a king beseem.
He who of knights is leader must ever free from shame
And every stain be living ; this earns fair women's praises.
So gentle was he truly that every one with wonder on him
           gazes.

Brave he was and daring, (such is the olden song,)
And ever was he ready to right his neighbor's wrong.
He high upheld his honor in all things, never fearing ;
Throughout the land, his praises were spoken and were sung
           in all men's hearing.

In a waste he grew to manhood, that youthful son of a king,
Wild beasts his only fellows ; but none so quick could spring
That they to flee were able, if he for them was striving.
I ween both he and his maidens had wonders seen, while by
           the waters living.

Rightly his name was Hagen ; but later men did own
He was " of kings the Devil ; " so came he to be known
In every land and kingdom, such was his strength in fighting.
The bold and wild young Hagen well did earn his name,
           his foemen smiting.

He oft was begged by his kinsmen   that he a wife would take ;
One so fair was near him   that none had need to seek
A fairer or a lovelier,   all earthly kingdoms over.
He himself had taught her ;   with her in sorrow grown, and now
her lover.

She bore the name of Hilda ;   from India she had come,
And love she oft had shown him   under their wretched doom,
Since, in their early childhood,   he in the cave had found her.
None better need he wish for,   or seek in any land
the heavens under.

His father bade him hasten   to be knighted with the sword,
With a hundred of his vassals.   He gave, with kindly word,
To him and to his maidens,   for clothes and horses needed,
A thousand marks of silver.   Hagen said that the will of his
father should be heeded.

The news of this was bruited   through many a prince's land ;
And the day when it should happen   all did understand.
Soon the king's great kindness   from all won praises golden
In a year and three days after   the festival of knighting them
was holden.

For this the knights made busy,   glad to be bidden there.
Soon they made them bucklers,   bright and painted fair ;
In making showy saddles   the workmen were not idle ;
With gold both red and shining   the breastplate was bedecked,
as was the bridle.

Upon a broad green meadow   the guests of the mighty king
Were bidden then to gather.   He left not anything
That they from him could ask for ;   seats were spread in order,
And many guests soon after   were seen to ride to his land
                         from every border.

To those from far now ready   the sword with him to bear
Fighting-gear was given,   that beseemed them well to wear.
They who from other kingdoms   into his land were faring
A thousand men were reckoned ;   to give them clothes and steeds
                         he was not sparing.

Unto his friends then said he :   " If now you deem it fit
That men a king should call me,   it therefore seemeth meet
That she my heart holds dearest   a crown with me be wearing ;
Never shall I rest happy   until, for her love to me, she this
                         is sharing."

Then asked of him his followers   who might the lady be,
Who, riding proudly before them,   they at court should see ?
He said : " Her name is Hilda,   in India once living ;
To me and to my kindred   she, as our queen, no shame will e'er
                         be giving."

Well pleased was now his mother,   when she the tidings had,
That they thought to crown the lady ;   his father, too was glad.
Of them was she so worthy,   that high in heart they set her.
With him the sword was taken   by full six hundred ; the number
                         e'en was greater.

As is the way of Christians,   both of them were bid
First for the crown to be hallowed ;   this at once they did.
King Hagen with Queen Hilda   in state were soon seen riding ;
Many games of knighthood   were played at court by his men,
at Hagen's bidding.

Sigeband, too, rode with them ;   high rose his heart as he went ;
He reckoned very little   the wealth that must be spent.
When in jousts they had ridden,   in ways most true and knightly,
Then were pages busy   to make the halls for the guests
all fair and sightly.

Seats were brought together,   strong, and broad, and long,
With stools besides, and tables.   After the mass was sung,
U-te, his wife, came riding,   with women round her thronging ;
These the youthful warriors   to gaze on, as they rode, right
earnestly were longing

While the great King Sigeband   sat by U-te's side,
And Hagen next to Hilda,   all looked on with pride ;
And said, in his child-belovéd   happy was their master.
Before them, while at table,   the throng was great ; the clash
of spears grew faster.

After the king of Ireland   at the meal his fill had eat,
By riders the grass was trodden ;   flowers to dust they beat
With rude and heavy trampling,   while in uproar riding.
The men best known for bravery,   before the fair, in knightly
jousts were leading.

Four and twenty warriors,   bearing well the shield,
Over the plain came riding;   bold were they in the field,
And now in many a struggle   all their strength were spending.
'T was done in sight of the ladies,   and hard it was of their
                          games to make an ending.

The brave young son of Sigeband   himself in the onset rode.
Not loth was she to gaze on him   who her with hope had wooed;
That she to him was friendly   in a far-off land forsaken,
For this would he reward her.   No truer knight the sword
                          had ever taken.

Amid the throngs here riding,   one thro' the dust might see
Men whose birth was princely,   in number twelve and three;
The Christian and the heathen   to him their fiefs were owing,
And honor now, right heartily,   to Sigeband and Hagen
                          they were showing.

Long those high times lasted;   their mirth, how loud it rose!
With crowding and with shouting   great the bustle grows.
The king now bade the champions   to end the strife so heated;
And leave to them was given   that they beside the ladies
                          should be seated.

Before his friends and kinsmen   then spake King Sigeband:
" Unto my dear son Hagen   give I now my land,
With the dwellers and the strongholds,   be they far or nearer.
Let all my trusty liegemen   have him now for their lord,
                          and hold none dearer."

As soon as his father, Sigeband,   his sway did thus forego,
Hagen his lands and castles   began in fief to bestow ;
This he did right freely,   and to those to whom he gave them
He seemed so true and worthy   that they indeed from him
would gladly have them.

As by feudal law is rightful,   many stretched the hand
To the youthful king in fealty.   To all, from every land,
Or far or near, then gave he   clothes and riches hoarded.
A feast so freely given   would now the poor not harm,
and with thanks be rewarded.

At court now dwelt the maidens   who had before been brought
With him within those borders ;   of these one now was sought,
And sent to the king and Hilda ;   there she soon was dwelling.
The maid it was from Iserland ;   of one more fair to see
none e'er was telling.

A princely youth soon wooed her,   who saw the maiden fair
Beside the king's fair daughter.   Soothly might he swear
That she by right was worthy   to be of a crown the wearer.
She had erst been Hilda's playmate ;   of widespread lands
she now became the sharer.

At last the guests were scattered,   and all now left the king.
That high-born lady also   men did straightway bring
Into the land of Norway,   to her youthful lord's kind keeping.
After her heavy sorrows,   blest with hope, she knew no more
of weeping.

Now, throughout all Ireland,   did Hagen his sway begin.
If ever among his lieges   a deed of wrong was seen,
At once for this the doer   must pay with pain well dreaded;
Of such, within a twelvemonth,   eighty or more were for evil
                                       deeds beheaded.

An inroad made he later   into the lands of his foes.
He spared the poor, and brought not   flames, to add to their woes;
But if with pride and rudeness   he was by any treated,
He quick laid waste their strongholds,   and deadly wounds
                                     in bitter wrath he meted.

When it came to fighting,   he was a goodly knight.
Of heroes high in breeding   he soon brought low the might;
To all he showed his bravery,   whether far or near him.
Of kings was he the Devil;   in truth his many foes
                                     might greatly fear him.

The life he led was happy,   nor of gladness asked he more.
His wife, from far-off India,   to her lord and master bore
A fair and lovely daughter;   she also, like her mother,
Bore the name of Hilda;   well known is her tale to us, and to
                                     many another.

Wild Hagen bade his maidens   so to rear the child,
That the sun ne'er shone upon her;   nor were rough winds wild
Oft allowed to touch her.   She was by ladies guarded,
And cared for by her kinsmen;   most wisely was the trust
                                     to them awarded.

Before twelve years were ended   the fair and well-born maid
Was comely more than any,   and her name was widely spread;
Rich and high-born princes   gladly would have sought her,
And earnestly were thinking   how they could win wild Hagen's
lovely daughter.

One of these same princes   in Denmark had his home,
Within the land of Waleis.   When the tale to him had come
About this lovely maiden,   his longing ne'er would leave him;
But he was scorned by Hagen,   who swore of life and name
he would bereave him.

Whene'er to seek the maiden   men were by wooers sent,
In his pride, wild Hagen   upon their death was bent.
He to none would give her   who than himself was weaker;
Of the tale of the mighty Hagen,   far and near, was every man
the speaker.

He bade that more than twenty   of those sent there be hung;
None might wreak his anger,   though sore his heart was wrung.
When all had done their errand,   for Hagen's daughter suing,
" Enough," soon went the saying: " 'T were best that none should
go for her a-wooing."

But still by high-born warriors   the maid was not unsought.
Let pride be ne'er so lofty,   as we have long been taught,
There always is another   with just as high a bearing;
While to win her kindness   his yearning grows, and his toil
he is never sparing.

Tale the Fifth.

HOW WÂ-TE WAS SENT TO IRELAND AS A SUITOR.

HETTEL was lord in Daneland;   to be its king he rose ;
'T was in the Sturmisch marches,   as many a one well knows ;
There abode his kindred,   who ways of honor taught him.
Ortland also served him.   His might and worth high fame
       with all soon brought him.

One among his kinsfolk   the name of Wâ-te bore ;
He for his lands and castles   fealty to Hettel swore.
As kinsman of his master,   he careful teaching gave him
In all things good and worthy,   and in his watchful care did
       ever have him.

A landed knight in Daneland   was Wâ-te's sister's son,
The brave and upright Horant.   Later his faith was shown
Unto his lord, King Hettel,   who for his worth did crown him.
This to him he grudged not,   but ever for a prince was glad
       to own him.

Hettel, rich and mighty,   at Hegeling held his seat,
Not far from the lord of Ortland ;   this is true, I weet.
He there owned many castles,   eighty at least or over ;
They who these strongholds guarded   in truest faith and honor
held them ever.

Lord he was of Friesland,   its waters and its land ;
Ditmarsh, as well as Waleis,   were swayed by his kingly hand.
Hettel was truly mighty ;   his kinsmen they were many ;
Bold was he and daring,   and 'gainst his foes he plotted,
well as any.

Hettel was an orphan,   and so he felt the need
That he a wife should find him.   To him, at last, were dead
Father as well as mother,   who their lands had left him.
He friends in truth had many,   yet found he much in life
that of bliss bereft him.

The best of these besought him   some maiden's love to seek,
Who of his birth was worthy.   The knight did answer make :
" I here know none who fitly   should be o'er the Hegelings seated,
Nor is there any lady   who, brought from far, should as
my queen be greeted."

Then spake a knight of Nifland,   Morune, a youthful lord :
" I know of a lovely maiden,   of whom I oft have heard ;
She in truth is fairer   than all on earth now living.
Her will we gladly sue for,   that she her troth to you may
soon be giving."

Then quoth the king: " Who is she? her name I pray you tell."
Then said Morunc: " 'T is Hilda, in Ireland she doth dwell;
Her father's name is Hagen; King Ger was her forefather.
If to this land she cometh, your life will then be blissful
altogether."

Then spake the young King Hettel: " I oft have heard it said,
Whoever woos this maiden her father's wrath must dread.
Many a worthy suitor his life for her has ended;
But none among my vassals must meet his death for having
me befriended."

Morunc quickly answered: " Then send to Horant's land,
And bid that he come hither; he well doth understand
The ways and moods of Hagen, for often has he seen them.
Unless his help he gives you, 't will come to nought, howe'er
your friends demean them."

He said : " Your will I follow, since she is so fair ;
But if my friends shall seek her, yourself the suit must share :
And if unto your friendship the task I 've trusted fitly,
Wealth shall you have and honor, when as the Hegeling's queen
she 's greeted rightly."

He quickly sent out riders through the Danish land to haste ;
By them was the mighty Horant, his nephew, found at last,
And to the court was bidden; to come must he be speedy,
Within seven days, not later, if he to help his lord in truth
were ready.

When Horant met the heralds,   and did their errand hear,
Then for friendly service   himself he would not spare.
Right gladly did he listen   to the bidding of his master ;
But this, on a day thereafter,   to him brought sorrow great,
and sore disaster.

To the court he soon went riding,   with sixty of his men ;
Of friends at home young Horant   to take his leave was seen.
He then made haste the faster,   when now the tale was told him
How he must help his master,   if for a faithful knight
he now would hold him.

Upon the seventh morning   he came to Hettel's land ;
Decked in finest clothing   was he and all his band.
The king to welcome Horant   rode forth, most glad to greet him,
And saw that with him Fru-te,   another Danish knight, was there
to meet him.

Good news it was of their coming,   of which all men now spoke ;
Glad was the king to see them ;   from him a share it took
Of the deep and heavy sorrow   which his heart was filling.
" Welcome, Cousin Fru-te ! "   cried he, the while he looked
upon him smiling.

When Horant now with Fru-te   before the king did stand,
Then he asked for tidings   of their home in the Danish land.
Both of them now answered :   " Not many days are ended
Since we in stormy battle   with many deadly blows our lives
defended."

He asked whence they had ridden   from off the stormy field.
They said : " It was from Portugal,   where the strife was held ;
There the mighty ruler   from fighting would not spare us ;
Daily within our borders   he did us wrong, and much ill-will
did bear us."

The young King Hettel answered :   " Now cast all care away ;
I know that the aged Wâ-te   will never yield the sway
He holds o'er the Sturmisch marches ;   he of the land is owner ;
Who wins from him a castle   will earn high praise and long
be held in honor."

Within the roomy palace   the guests then took their seats.
Both Horant and Sir Fru-te   with thoughtless, merry wits,
Of the loves of high-born ladies   began to gossip gaily.
To them the young king listened,   and costly gifts he gave
unto them freely.

Hettel turned to Horant,   and thus to ask began :
" If aught hath reached your hearing,   then tell me, if you can,
How 't is with Lady Hilda,   King Hagen's lovely daughter ?
To her would I send most gladly,   and would that words of love
from me were brought her."

The youthful knight then answered :   " She is to me well known ;
A maid so fair and lovely   my eyes ne'er looked upon
As she, that maid of Ireland,   Hilda, the rich and stately,
The daughter of wild Hagen ;   to wear a crown with you
would befit her greatly."

On this King Hettel asked him :   "Now think you, can it be
That ever her lordly father   will give this maid to me ?
If I deemed he were so friendly,   I would seek to win her,
And would reward him ever   who gave to me his ready help
                to gain her."

"That can never happen,"   to him young Horant said :
" No rider with this errand   to Hagen need be sped.
To hasten thither boldly   I feel, myself, no longing ;
The man sent there to seek her   is either slain with blows,
                or dies by hanging."

Then spake again King Hettel :   " Not so for her I care ;
To hang my trusty vassal   should Hagen ever dare,
Then he, the king of Ireland,   himself must death be facing.
Be he ne'er so boastful,   he 'll find his rashness is to him
                no blessing."

Then spake the knightly Fru-te :   " If Wâ-te deigns to go
Unto the king of Ireland,   to woo this maid for you,
Lucky will be our errand,   and we shall bring the lady ;
Or wounds throughout our bodies,   e'en to the heart, to take
                shall we be ready."

Then said to him King Hettel :   " My men I now will send
With word to the lord of Sturmland ;   I do not fear the end,
For Wâ-te will hasten gladly   wherever I shall bid him.
Bring Irold, too, from Friesland,   with all his men, for sorely
                do I need him."

His riders then went quickly   into the Sturmisch land,
Where the brave old Wâ-te   they found among his band.
Then the word they gave him,   now to the king to betake him;
But Wâ-te felt great wonder,   to know for what the Hegeling
                           king did seek him.

He asked if it were needful   to bring, when he should go,
His breastplate and his helmet,   and any followers, too?
One of the heralds answered: " We did not hear it spoken
That he had need of fighters;   for you alone did his words
                           a wish betoken."

Wâ-te would be going,   but left behind a guard,
To care for lands and castles.   Then taking horse, at his word,
Twelve of his followers only   with him from home now started;
Wâ-te, the brave old warrior,   at once on his way to court
                           in haste departed.

He reached the land of the Hegelings.   When he now was seen,
As he came near Kampatille,   but little sorrow, I ween,
Was felt by the kingly Hettel;   with speed he went to greet him,
And thought of the kindly welcome   he would give his friend,
                           old Wâ-te, when he met him.

Right glad was he to see him;   with hearty speech he says;
" Sir Wâ-te, thou art welcome;   many are the days
Since I have looked upon you,   when on our horses sitting,
Side by side together,   we proudly met our foes with blows
                           befitting."

Then answered him old Wâ-te : " Ever should good friends
Be glad to be together ; that fight the better ends
Where, before the foeman, friends as one are fighting."
Then by the hand he held him, to him his love and friendship
warmly plighting.

They took their seats together, nor place to other gave.
Hettel, he was mighty, and Wâ-te, he was brave ;
He yet was also haughty, and proud in all his bearing.
Hettel now was thinking how Wâ-te could be brought
to Ireland to be faring.

Then spake the knightly Hettel : " For this I bade thee come :
Need have I of riders, to send to Hagen's home.
Truly I know of no one whom I would send the sooner
Than thee, my good friend Wâ-te, or who in this could bring me
greater honor."

Then said the aged Wâ-te : " Whatever I can do
To show my love and fealty, I 'll gladly do for you.
Herein I may be trusted, to be for you bold-hearted ;
And to bring about your wishes, unless in this by death
I should be thwarted."

Then quoth the kingly Hettel : " Many friends have said
That if the mighty Hagen will my wooing heed,
And give to me his daughter, she, as my queen, would honor
Me and my kingdom also ; my heart is bent as a wife
and queen to own her."

Angrily spoke Wâ-te :   " Whoever this has said
Would truly feel no sorrow   if I this day were dead.
'T is Fru-te, he of Denmark,   I know it is no other,
Who to this has stirred you,   to send me to the maid,
your suit to further.

" This young and lovely maiden   is guarded now with care ;
Horant and Fru-te also,   who say she is so fair,
And speak to you her praises,   must go with me to seek her.
Never shall I rest easy   unless they strive with me your own
to make her."

Both these faithful vassals   King Hettel sent for soon ;
To others good and trusty   they also made it known,
That by their king and master   they at court were wanted.
No more their thoughts men whispered,   but freely spoke
of the coming raid, undaunted.

When Wâ-te, the brave old warrior,   did on Horant look,
And on the Danish Fru-te,   how sharply then he spoke !
" Brave knights, may God reward you,   to me you are so friendly,
And of my fame so careful,   and my trip to court this time
you help so kindly.

" You are, forsooth, most willing   that I this errand do ;
But both of you are bounden   with me thereon to go,
To serve the king, our master,   even as our duty calleth.
He who my life endangers   himself the risk must share, whate'er
befalleth."

" For this I now am ready,"   answered Horant the Dane ;
" If leave the king will grant us,   I then will shun no pain,
Nor aught of toil will grudge me.   Only to see this lady,
For me and for my kinsman,   were happiness enough, and bliss
already."

" Then we ought," said Fru-te,   " to take upon our way
Seven hundred warriors.   No man doth honor pay
To Hagen without grudging.   He is overweening, truly ;
If he thinks that he can crush us,   he soon must lay aside
his boasting wholly.

" Sir king, you should bid your workmen   a ship of cypress-wood
To build upon the river ;   strong must it be and good,
So your band of warriors   shall shipwreck ne'er be ruing.
From timber white as silver   the lofty masts your men must
soon be hewing.

" Also food for your fighters   you must now bespeak ;
And bid that men be busy   helmets for us to make,
And hauberks strong for many ;   when we these are wearing,
Then wild Hagen's daughter   we shall the easier win by craft
and daring.

" Also my nephew Horant,   who is shrewd and wise,
Must go with us as a shopman ;   (I grudge him not his guise)
There must he to the ladies   be clasps and arm-bands selling,
With gold and costly jewels ;   thus greater trust in us
will they be feeling.

“ For sale we also must carry   weapons and clothing, too ;
And since wild Hagen’s daughter   it is such risk to woo,
That only now by fighting   one can hope to wed her,
Let Wâ-te choose the warriors   to go with him, and home
to the king to lead her.”

Then spake the aged Wâ-te :   “ A shop I cannot keep ;
Not often doth my money   in coffers idly sleep ;
My lot I ’ve shared with fighters,   and that I still am doing ;
Therein I am not skilful,   that I to ladies gew-gaws
should be showing.

“ But since my nephew Horant   on me this task has laid,
He knows full well that Hagen   will never yield the maid :
He prides himself on owning   the strength of six and twenty ;
If he shall learn of our wooing,   our hope to leave his land
will be but scanty.

“ Good king, now let us hasten,   but bid that first our hull
With a deck of deal be covered ;   let it, below, be full
Of knights both strong and doughty,   who shall help be giving,
If ever the wild King Hagen   forbids that we shall leave
his kingdom, living.

“ Of these brave knights a hundred,   with outfits good for war,
Unto the land of Ireland   we in our ships must bear ;
There shall my nephew Horant   in his shop be seated,
Keeping two hundred near him ;   thus shall the ladies’ coming
be awaited.

" Your men must also build us   barges strong and wide,
To carry food and horses,   and to sail our ships beside :
Enough for a year or longer   we must take to feed us ;
And we will say to Hagen   that to leave our land King Hettel
did forbid us,

" And that our lord and master   great wrong to us hath wrought.
Then with our gifts so costly   we often shall be brought
To Hagen and to Hilda,   where they their court are keeping ;
Our gifts shall make us welcome,   and kindness from the king
shall we be reaping.

" We then the tale will tell him,   we wretched outlaws are ;
And thus at once the pity   of Hagen we shall share.
To us, poor homeless wanderers,   shelter will be granted,
And in his land King Hagen   thenceforth will see that nought
by us is wanted."

Hettel asked his warriors :   " My friends, I pray you tell,
Since you to go are willing,   how soon you hence will sail ? "
" So soon as comes the summer,   and May with gladsome weather,"
They said, " we shall be ready,   and, riding again to court, will
we come hither.

" Meanwhile must men be making   whatever we shall need, —
Sails and also rudders,   well-made, and that with speed,
Barges wide, and galleys,   to bear us to our haven ;
So the swell of the waters   shall stir us not, nor make us
sick or craven."

King Hettel said : " Ride quickly,   now, to your land and home.
For horses and for clothing   no cost to you shall come ;
For you and all your followers   such outfit shall be ready,
That you no shame shall suffer,   whenever you are seen by any
lady."

When he his leave had taken,   Wâ-te to Sturmland rode ;
Horant and with him Fru-te   followed in hurried mood,
Back to the land of Denmark,   where they held the lordship.
To help their master Hettel   they thought could never be to them
a hardship.

Then, in his home, King Hettel   let his will be known ;
Of shipwrights and of workmen   idle was not one.
While the ships were building   to do their best they hastened ;
The beams that met together,   were with bands of silver
strongly fastened.

All the spars and mast-trees,   they were strong and good ;
Red gold, and brightly shining,   was laid on the rudder-wood,
And like to fire was glowing :   wealth their master blesses.
When time it was for leaving,   the men their tasks had done,
and won high praises.

The ropes that held the anchors   came from a far-off strand,
Brought from the shores of Araby ;   never on sea or land,
Before that day or after,   had any man seen better :
So might the men of the Hegelings   easier make their way
o'er the deep sea-water.

They who the sails were making   worked late, and early rose;
For the king had bid them hurry.   For making these they chose
Silken stuff from Abalie,   as good as could be brought them.
Truly far from idle   were, in those days, the busy hands that
                          wrought them.

Can any one believe it?   They had the anchors made
Of purest beaten silver.   The heart of the king was led
Strongly now to wooing;   no rest would he be knowing,
Nor of his men was sparing,   until the day when they should
                          thence be going.

Well-framed, with heavy planking,   now the ships were seen,
Sound 'gainst war and weather.   Then word was sent to the men,
That to seek the lovely lady   they must soon be faring.
This was told to no one   but those who the trust of the king
                          were rightly sharing.

Wâ-te to meet King Hettel   from Sturmland held his course;
With silver gear and housing,   heavily went his horse.
To court went, too, his followers,   four hundred men undaunted;
And now the doughty Hettel   brave knights enough, for guests,
                          no longer wanted.

Morune, the brave and daring,   from Friesland thither went,
And with him brought two hundred.   Word to the king was sent
That now, with helms and breastplates,   they were thither riding;
In haste came Irold also;   thus gladly Hettel's kinsmen did
                          his bidding.

Thither rode from Denmark Horant young and brave;
Hettel to do his errand did trusty liegemen have;
A thousand men or over might he for this be sending;
Only a prince so mighty of such a task had ever made
          an ending.

Irold, too, of Ortland, was ready now to go:
E'en though on him King Hettel should never clothes bestow,
Yet, for himself and his followers, he had of these so many,
That wheresoe'er they were going, they never need to beg for
          aught from any.

The king, as well beseemed him, greeted all the band;
First, his liegeman Irold he kindly took by the hand;
Then he turned to Wâ-te, to where he found him seated:
At last, his hardy warriors, ready to leave the land, his word
          awaited.

To all it now was bidden that they should give good heed,
And everything make ready that knights could ever need.
Now were seen by the warriors the ships so fair and stately;
To woo the lovely Hilda the king in all things showed
          his forethought greatly.

Two new and well-made galleys they had upon the flood,
With two broad ships of burden; both were strong and good.
A ship of state went with them; than this had ne'er a better,
By any friend or foeman, on the shores of any land, been seen
          upon the water.

To start they now are willing;   already on the ships
Were the clothes and horses loaded.   Then from Wâ-te's lips
Came kindly words to Hettel;   he begged him to feel easy,
Till they should again be coming,   for to do his bidding
                                  they would all be busy.

The king to him said mournfully: " I give into your care
The knights, untaught and youthful,   who such risks will dare,
With you upon this errand: most earnestly I pray you
That, for your honor, daily   you teach these youths with care,
                              and make them to obey you."

Him thus Wâ-te answered: " To that give not a thought;
Keep a brave heart, I beg you,   that here at home, in nought
You fail of being steadfast,   where'er your honor reaches:
Watch well, too, o'er our holdings: these youths shall learn
                         from me what wisdom teaches."

The good and trusty Fru-te   the wealth of the king did guard, —
The gold and costly jewels,   and of many things a hoard.
The king was free in spending   whatsoe'er was wanted;
If Fru-te aught did ask for,   thirty-fold to him he gladly
                                  granted.

A hundred men were chosen,   and now within the ship,
Wherein to woo the maiden   his friends must cross the deep,
All craftily were hidden,   to help them, if 't were needful.
Gifts both rich and worthy   the king to give these faithful
                                men was heedful.

With these, among the followers,   every rank was seen ;
Of knights and squires also,   thirty hundred men,
Who, for toil and struggle,   from far-off lands came riding.
Then said the king to his lieges :   " May God in heaven to you
       give careful guiding."

To him thus Horant answered :   " From fear now be you free ;
When you shall see us coming,   you then with us will see
A maid so fair and lovely,   you well may wish to greet her."
This the king heard gladly,   but far was the day when he
       at last should meet her.

They took their leave with kisses,   the king and many a guest ;
For these the king was feeling   wearisome unrest.
While they for him are toiling,   each hour he fear must borrow ;
He forsooth was downcast,   and nought could cheer him,
       in his mood of sorrow.

This was for his welfare,   that a wind from out the north
Now their sails was swelling,   and briskly helped them forth.
The ships were wafted evenly,   as they from land were turning ;
But hardships they had known not   the youths, upon their way,
       erelong were learning.

The truth we cannot tell you,   nor can it e'en be guessed,
For nights full six and thirty   what lodgings gave them rest,
While upon the water.   The youths they with them carried,
Bound by oaths of fealty,   swore again to keep them, where'er
       they tarried.

However willing were they   to sail on the tossing sea,
Yet sometimes it befell them   in great unrest to be.
Ease they took but seldom,   as the waves would spare it;
But he who ploughs the waters   pain must often feel,
and yet must bear it.

After the waves had borne them   full a thousand miles,
They came to Hagen's castle,   where, as was said erewhiles,
He, the master of Ballian,   shamefully had lorded:
This was a wicked falsehood,   the deeds were never done
as the tale was worded.

When now the men from Hegeling   over the sea had gone,
And neared wild Hagen's castle,   their coming soon was known;
Much the folk there wondered   from what far kingdom sailing
The waves had borne them thither;   how finely they were clad
all men were telling.

First the ship with an anchor   was fastened on the strand;
To furl the sails then quickly   each gave a ready hand.
It was not long thereafter   before the news was bruited,
Throughout King Hagen's castle,   that ships, with unknown men,
in his harbor floated.

Now on the shore they landed,   and did their goods unlade;
Whatever could be wanted   on the sands, for sale, they spread,
And all that any asked for.   In wealth they were not lacking;
But tho' their men had silver,   't was little that they bought,
or for themselves were taking.

Clothed in the garb of tradesmen,   on the shore did stand
Sixty men or over,   well-dight, a goodly band.
Fru-te, the lord of Denmark,   was busy as their leader;
His clothing was far better   than there was worn by any other
trader.

The worthy lord and master   over Ballian town,
When he heard of their coming,   and the riches they did own,
Rode down with many followers   to where those crafty sellers
He found, himself awaiting.   Kind was the mien of all
who there were dwellers.

First the master asked them : " Whence their way they had made,
And over the sea come thither ? "   To him then Fru-te said :
" God have you in his keeping ;   we from afar are sailing ;
Tradesmen truly are we ;   our masters rich, near by, in ships
are dwelling."

" Let peace with us be plighted,"   old Wâ-te then began ;
But from the master's grimness,   the truth to see was plain,
That, where he was the ruler,   stern and harsh was his bearing.
Straightway then to Hagen   they led the guests, who with
their tale were faring.

Hagen said, as he met them :   " Safeguard to you I give ;
My peace I pledge you willingly.   He shall no longer live,
But hang upon the gallows,   who these guests shall harry :
Let them not be fearful ;   them shall nothing harm while in my
land they tarry."

Rich and costly jewels   they to Hagen gave,
In worth, of marks a thousand.   From them he nought did crave,
Nor even so much as a penny ;   but what for sale they offered
He begged of them to show him,   such as to knights and ladies
                           might be proffered.

For all he thanked them warmly ;   he said : " If I should live
Not more than three days longer,   for all that now they give
My guests shall be rewarded.   If my liegeman do not heed me,
And these for aught be lacking,   all shall then for this
                           with right upbraid me."

Now the gifts they gave him   the king with his men did share ;
Among them there were necklaces,   fit for ladies fair,
With finger-rings and arm-bands,   as well as ribands dainty,
And head-gear, to bedeck them :   these the king to many gave
                           in plenty.

His wife and lovely daughter   now most rightly thought
That never to their kingdom   had gifts for them been brought,
That were so rare and costly,   by sellers or by traders.
Horant and Wâ-te also   in sending gifts to court were now
                           the leaders.

Sixty silken garments,   the best that e'er were sold,
Up to the shore were carried,   and forty wrought with gold.
They would have prized but lightly   cloths from Bagdad even ;
Of linen suits a hundred,   the best they had, now to the king
                           were given.

Beside the handsome clothing,   made of silken stuff,
Of richest inner garments   they also gave enough ;
There might perhaps be forty,   or more, if reckoned fully ;
Could ever man buy praises,   they by their costly gifts had
                              gained them truly.

Twelve Castilian horses,   all saddled, were brought, I trow ;
Also many breastplates,   and well-made helmets, too,
Men were bidden to carry ;   twelve bucklers likewise bore they,
Rimmed with golden edges.   Kind were Hagen's guests ;
                              free givers were they.

Then, too, with gifts came riding   Horant the brave and bold ;
Irold the strong came with him ;   this to the king was told :
'T was said to him, moreover,   that those now thither faring
Of lands were the lords and owners.   This might well be seen
                              by the gifts they were bearing.

After these came riding   four and twenty men
Whom they were thither leading,   well-bred were they, I ween ;
Such also was their clothing,   they seemed as if well fitted,
And now in truth were coming,   that very day to be by Hagen
                              knighted.

Then unto King Hagen   one of his friends thus spake :
"The gifts the men now bring you   't is best you deign to take :
Never must you leave them   unthanked for all their treasure."
Hagen lacked not riches,   but yet his thanks he gave them
                              without measure.

He said: "I thank you kindly,   as I of right should do."
Then he bade that his stewards   to see the gifts should go;
And also that the clothing,   piece by piece, be shown them.
Glad were they to see them,   and wondered greatly as they
                                        gazed upon them.

Then said one of the stewards: "Hear now the truth I tell:
Chests there are of silver,   and filled with gold as well,
With many costly jewels,   rich and kingly even:
Marks fully twenty thousand   the goods are worth, which they
                                        to you have given."

Then the king thus answered: "Blessings on my guests!
I now will share with others   the riches in these chests."
Then to his knights was given   whate'er of these they wanted:
To every one among them   all that he might wish by the king
                                        was granted.

The king now seated near him   both the two young men, —
Irold and also Horant;   he began to ask them then,
"Whence to his kingdom sailing,   they to come had striven?
Gifts so rich and worthy   have ne'er before by guests to me
                                        been given."

Then spake the knightly Horant: "This shall you know full well;
My lord, now hear us kindly   while we our sorrows tell.
Outlawed wanderers are we,   and from our homes were driven;
A king most rich and mighty,   to wreak his anger, woe to us
                                        hath given."

Then spake again wild Hagen :   "What may be his name,
From whose rich kingdom driven,   outcasts you became ?
You of wealth are owners,   and, if not by his wits forsaken,
To keep such worthy lieges   within his land he would
                 some pains have taken."

He asked "Who them had outlawed,   and what name he bore ?
Of what misdoings guilty,   had they to this far shore
Made their flight in sorrow,   to ask the help of strangers ? "
To him then answered Horant :   "To you will we make known
                 our woes and dangers.

"He bears the name of ' Hettel,   Lord of the Hegeling land ';
Brave and mighty is he,   and sways with a heavy hand.
We of all our happiness   have been robbed and plundered ;
Of right are we embittered,   since from our land and home
                 we now are sundered."

To him spoke Hagen kindly :   "This to your good shall turn ;
I will in full repay you   the losses that you mourn.
If I make myself a beggar,   by thus so freely giving,
Yet from the king of the Hegelings   you need not ask for help
                 while I am living.

"If you, good knights," he added,   "here with me will stay,
With you will I share right gladly   the lands I own to-day ;
Such guerdon by King Hettel   ne'er to you was given.
The wealth from you he has taken,   that give I you, and more
                 by tenfold even."

"To stay with you we are ready,"   then said Horant the Dane,
" But we fear that when King Hettel   shall learn that we were seen
Within the Irish borders,   he will find a way to reach us;
And I am ever dreading   that we can nowhere live,
and this he 'll teach us."

Then to the band of wanderers   the lordly Hagen said :
" Do what now I bid you,   and a home for you is made.
Never will King Hettel   dare for your harm to seek you
Within my land and kingdom;   it were a wrong to me from hence
to take you."

He bade they should be sheltered,   at once, within his town ;
Then to his men and lieges   he made his wishes known,
That now unto the wanderers   all honor should be granted.
The water-weary sailors   soon found the rest that they
so long had wanted.

Then the townsmen freely   did the king's behest ;
To do it they were ready :   houses, the very best,
Forty, or even over,   were empty left, to be taken
By the Danish sailors;   their homes, by the king's good lieges
were willingly forsaken.

Up on the beach were carried   the wares, full many a pile,
That in the ships lay hidden.   Their owners thought, the while,
That they would rather struggle   with storms upon the water,
Than to seek their luck and welfare   in wooing Hilda, Hagen's
lovely daughter.

Hagen bade his followers : " Now ask these guests of mine
If they will deign most kindly to eat my bread and wine,
Till they, within my kingdom, on lands they hold are living."
The Danish Fru-te answered : " To take your food would shame
            to us be giving.

" If erst the great King Hettel had been to us so good,
That he both gold and silver would give to us for food,
We in our houses had them, and might of them be wasteful ;
We e'en could stay our hunger, and feed thereon, if this to us
            were tasteful."

'T was bidden then by Fru-te that his booth should be set up.
To see for sale such riches men ne'er again could hope.
Never within their borders did any trader offer
Fine goods at such a bargain ; they easily were sold before
            the day was over.

All could buy who wished them, gold and jewels rare.
The king, by greatest kindness, was to his guests made dear.
If any, without buying, still these treasures wanted,
The traders were so friendly that they, as gifts, the goods
            to many granted.

Whate'er of Wâ-te or Fru-te was said by any one, —
Of all the deeds of kindness that here by them were done, —
The tale might not be trusted, how they for these were ready ;
They strove to gain high praises, and this at court was told
            to many a lady.

Of the poor nor man nor woman   for clothes was seen to lack;
To those in need among them   they gave their pledges back,
And from debt they freed them.   To the princess, morn and even,
Oft by her faithful steward   the tale of these guests from far
was truly given.

To the king she made her prayer: " Dearest father mine,
Ask that these guests so worthy   to ride to court will deign.
They say that one among them   hath charms beyond all measure;
Should he to your bidding listen,   the sight of him ofttimes
would give me pleasure."

To her the king thus answered: " That shall quickly be;
His well-bred ways and bearing   I soon will let you see."
But still the great King Hagen   never yet had known him;
Long the ladies waited   till Wâ-te came, and they could
look upon him.

Word to the guests was carried;   to them 't was kindly said,
That if it e'er should happen   that they of aught had need,
They should to the king betake them,   and his food be sharing.
To Fru-te this was pleasing,   for wise he was, not less
than he was daring.

Those who came from Denmark,   when at court, took care
Ever to be blameless   for the clothes that they should wear:
'T was so with the men of Wâ-te,   from Sturmland thither faring,
And than himself no sword-knight   in any land could show
a finer bearing.

Those who came with Morunc   wore mantles over all,
With robes from far Kampalia.   Fiery red, as a coal,
Gold and gems that sparkled   on their clothes were shining.
Irold, the daring champion,   came not alone, young Hilda
bent on winning.

Thither came brave Horant ;   all others he out-vied
In rich and costly clothing.   With mantles long and wide,
Gay in hue and gaudy,   his men were decked out brightly :
Those brave men from Denmark   proudly came, and had
a look most knightly.

Tho’ Hagen’s birth was kingly,   and lordly was his mood,
He yet went forth to meet them.   His daughter, fair and good,
Rose up before old Wâ-te   from where she now was seated.
Such was Wâ-te’s bearing   as if with smiles his friends
he never greeted.

She said, in way most seemly :   “ Welcome to you I give ;
Both I and the king, my father,   must from your looks believe
That you are weary warriors,   and sorely have been fighting.
Good-will the king will show you,   and soon his faith to you
will he be plighting.”

To her they all bent lowly ;   their ways, they were well-bred.
The king then bade to be seated,   as hosts are wont to bid.
Of drink to them was given,   wine the best and rarest ;
Better ne’er was tasted   in the home of any lord, albeit
the fairest.

In talk and fun and merriment   seated were they all.
Soon the queenly maiden   was seen to leave the hall:
But first she begged her father   the kindness now to show her
To bid the knights so worthy   to come to her, for pastime,
                                                to her bower.

Her wish the king then granted,   (so to us, 't is said);
His young and lovely daughter   at this was truly glad.
Soon fair clothes and jewels   the maidens all were wearing;
And earnestly were watching   the many knights from far,
                                                to see their bearing.

When now the elder Hilda   sat by her daughter fair,
Each one of her lovely maidens   demeaned herself with care;
So that all who saw her   high in breeding thought her,
And nothing else could say of her,   but that she was indeed
                                                a king's fair daughter.

Now bade they that old Wâ-te   should to the maids be brought;
Though he was gray and aged,   none the less they thought,
To guard against his wooing,   they must as children meet him.
Then to the aged Wâ-te   stepped forth the youthful queen,
                                                right glad to greet him.

She was the first to do so,   but wished she might be spared
When she now must kiss him: broad and gray was his beard,
And the hair of the aged Wâ-te   with golden strings was braided.
He and the Danish Fru-te   the queen's behest to seat them
                                                slowly heeded.

Both the well-clad heroes   before their seats now stood ;
Well they knew fine breeding,   and made their teaching good.
In many a bitter struggle,   in their manhood early,
They gained a name as warriors ;   and men to them gave praises
for it fairly.

Queen Hilda and her daughter,   in lively, merry mood,
Began to ask of Wâ-te,   whether he thought it good,
Thus with lovely ladies   to sit in ease and pleasure,
Or if to him 't were better   his strength in stormy fight
with foes to measure?

The aged Wâ-te answered :   " To me the last seems best ;
Altho' among fair ladies   glad am I to rest,
Never am I happier   than when with knights most daring,
Wherever that may happen,   upon the stormy field the fight
I am sharing."

At this the gay young maiden   broke into laughter loud ;
Well she saw, with ladies,   his stern, uneasy mood.
With this in the halls yet longer   were the maidens merry ;
Queen Hilda and her daughter   to talk with Morune's knights
were never weary.

She asked about old Wâ-te :   " Say, by what name is he known ?
Has he any liegemen ?   Doth he lands and castles own ?
Has he a wife and children   in the land whence he is roving ?
There, as I am thinking,   at his home and hearth, there must be
little loving."

Then answered one of the warriors: " Both children and a wife
In his home and land await him.   His riches and his life
He risketh for his duty ;   a hero brave he has shown him.
A bold and daring champion,   throughout his life, both friend
                    and foe have known him."

Irold the tale was telling   about this fearless knight,
That never worthier liegeman,   or bolder man in fight,
A king need e'er be seeking,   his lands and castles over :
Though mildly now he bears him,   there ne'er was found a stronger
                    or a braver.

The queen then said to Wâ-te :   " Give heed to what I say ;
Since in his Danish kingdom   Hettel forbids your stay,
I here, within my borders,   a home will gladly give you ;
There lives no lord so mighty   that he would ever dare from
                    hence to drive you."

Then to the queen he answered :   " I too, myself, own land ;
There give I clothes and horses,   at will, with open hand.
To wait on you as liegeman,   would make me sorry-hearted ;
And from my lands and castles,   more than a year, I never
                    can be parted."

At last they all were going :   then begged the lovely queen,
That when at court they waited,   they always might be seen
Seated among the ladies ;   no shame by this were done them :
Then said to her brave Irold,   that in their home this seat
                    was ever shown them.

To load with gifts these wanderers   the king was ever bent.
But in a mood so haughty   had they been thither sent,
To no man were they willing   to be for a mark beholden.
Hagen, the king, was lordly,   and took it ill that their pride
should them embolden.

To the king they now betook them ;   many were they who came ;
There they found, for pastime,   for each some merry game :
Draughts were many playing,   or spear and shield were trying ;
For these they cared but little,   but ever were in Hagen's
praises vying.

As happens oft in Ireland,   with every kind of fun
Forthwith the men made merry.   In this old Wâ-te won
A friend for himself in Hagen ;   but to win the ladies' praises,
Horant, the knight from Denmark,   his time in lightsome frolic
with them passes.

Fru-te and also Wâ-te   were knights full brave and bold ;
When standing near each other,   both alike looked old.
Their locks were gray and hoary,   and with gold were twisted ;
But where the bold were needed,   to show their bravery
earnestly they listed.

The followers of King Hagen   wore their shields at court,
With clubs as well as bucklers ;   there they strove in sport,
In the sword-play slashing ;   thrusts of spears they parried ;
Well themselves they shielded.   The youthful knights in games
were never wearied.

Then asked the brave King Hagen   of Wâ-te and his men,
"If, where they erst were living,   such fights were ever seen,
Or such heavy onslaughts,   as his good knights were dealing,
Here in his Irish kingdom?"   A smile of scorn o'er Wâ-te's face
                            was stealing.

Then quoth the knight from Sturmland: "The like I never saw;
If any here could teach it,   from here would I not withdraw
Till a year was fully ended,   and I had learned it rightly.
Whoe'er should be my master,   for his care and pains would I
                            not reward him lightly."

The king to him then answered: "For the love to you I bear,
I will bid my best of masters   teach you his art with care,
Till the three strokes are easy,   that, in field-storms raging,
Men give to one another;   by this will you be helped
                            when battle waging."

Then came a fencing-master,   and began his craft to show
To Wâ-te, the daring fighter;   in him he found a foe
Who fear for his life soon gave him.   Wâ-te his onset parried,
With all the skill of a fencer.   The face of Fru-te the Dane
                            a smile now carried.

To save himself, the teacher   gave a spring as wide
As doth an untamed leopard.   Wâ-te his weapon plied,
And in his hand it clattered,   until the fire-sparks glistened
Upon his foeman's buckler;   he well might thank the youth
                            who to him had listened.

Then said the king, wild Hagen: "Give me the sword in hand.
I will take a little pastime   with him of the Sturmisch land;
I will be his teacher,   and he my four strokes be learning.
He for this will thank me."   Soon was the king high praise
                         from Wâ-te earning.

To him old Wâ-te answered: "A pledge I now must hear
That I from you, great Hagen,   no guile soe'er may fear;
Should I by you   be wounded,   with ladies' scorn shall I redden."
In the fight was Wâ-te nimble;   such quickness to believe
                         should none be bidden.

The simple, untaught fencer   smote Hagen many a blow;
Till, like a wet brand steaming,   was the king before his foe.
The learner outdid his teacher: well his strength he boasted.
The host laid strokes unnumbered   upon the guest, who
                         in his skill had trusted.

Many looked on gladly   to see the strength of both.
To own the skill of Wâ-te   the king was nothing loth;
He might have shown his anger,   and brought no shame upon him.
Great was the strength of Wâ-te,   but yet 't was seen that Hagen
                         had outdone him.

To the king then spake old Wâ-te: "Let each no favor show,
While we together struggle.   Well have I learned from you
Your four strokes to be plying;   my thanks be you now sharing."
Such thanks he later showed him   as doth a fighting Frank
                         or Saxon daring.

No more a truce was thought of   by Wâ-te and the king;
With strokes that loud were crashing,   the hall began to ring.
Harder blows than ever   they gave, as now they battled;
All their thrusts were sudden;   the knobs upon their swords
snapped off and rattled.

The two sat down to rest them;   then Hagen said to his guest:
" You fain would be a learner,   but you in truth are the best
That ever I was teaching   the skill that the foeman dazes.
Wherever you are fighting,   you in the field will win most
worthy praises."

Then to the king spake Irold: " My lord, the strife is done
That you so well were waging;   such fights have we seen won,
In the land of our king and master.   Oft, at home, we freely
Try our skill with weapons;   knights and squires there meet
in matches daily."

Then again spoke Hagen: " Did I this understand,
I never a fighting weapon   had taken in my hand.
No youth have I ever met with   who was so quick at learning."
When to these words they listened,   the face of many a one
to smiles was turning.

Now by the king 'twas granted   to his guests to pass the day
As they might all be choosing.   Glad of this were they,
The men from out the Northland.   When the hours grew weary,
They vied huge stones in hurling;   or else in shooting arrows
made them merry.

Tale the Sixth.

HOW SWEETLY HORANT SANG.

IT came to pass one evening, good luck did so befall,
  That Horant, the knight of Daneland, sang before them all.
His singing was so wondrous that all who listened near him
Found his song well-pleasing ; the little birds all hushed
                                their notes to hear him.

King Hagen heard him gladly, and with him all his men :
The song of the Danish Horant friends for him did gain.
Likewise the queenly mother hearkened with ear befitting,
As it sounded thro' the opening where she upon the leaded
                                roof was sitting.

Then spake the fair young Hilda: " What is it that I hear ?
Just now a song the sweetest was thrilling on mine ear,
That e'er from any singer I heard until this hour.
Would to God in heaven my chamberlain to raise such notes
                                had power ! "

Then she bade them bring her   him who so sweetly sung ;
Soon as the knight came forward,   thanks were on her tongue.
For her with song the evening   blissfully was ended ;
By Lady Hilda's women   the minstrel-knight was carefully
befriended.

Then spake the lovely Hilda :   " Once more you must let us hear
The songs that you this evening   have made to us so dear.
Truly it were blissful   every day, at even,
To hear from you such singing ;   for this would great reward
to you be given."

" Since you your thanks, fair lady,   have thus on me bestowed,
Every day will I gladly   sing you a song as good ;
And whoso listens rightly   shall find his pains departed,
His cares shall all be lessened,   and he henceforth will
feel himself light-hearted."

When he his word had given,   forthwith he left the queen.
Great reward in Ireland   did his singing win ;
Never in his birthland   had such to him been meted.
Thus did the knight from Denmark   give his help to Hettel,
as him befitted.

Soon as the night was ended,   with the early dawn of day,
Horant raised his carol ;   the birds soon stopped their lay,
And to his song they listened,   while in hedges hidden.
The folk who yet were sleeping   rested no more, by his sweet
tones upbidden.

Horant's song rose softly,   higher and yet more sweet;
King Hagen also heard it,   while near his wife was his seat.
From out their inner chamber   drawn to the roof, they waited;
Their guest of this had warning;   and Hilda the young gave ear,
                            where she was seated.

The daughter of wild Hagen   with her maids around her heard
From where they sat and listened;   and now each little bird
Wholly forgot his singing,   and in the court-yard lighted;
The warriors hearkened also,   and well the song of the Danish
                            minstrel greeted.

Thanks to him were given   by women and by men;
"But," said the Danish Fru-te,   "would that I ne'er again
Such songs might hear him singing. ·   Whom would he be pleasing?
To whom is my witless nephew   such worthless morning-hymns
                            so bent on raising?"

Then spake King Hagen's liegemen: "My lord, let him be heard;
There's none so sick is lying   but would in truth be cheered,
If to the songs he listened   which fall from him so sweetly."
Said Hagen: "Would to Heaven   such skill to sing were mine;
                            't would glad me greatly."

When the knightly minstrel   three songs to the end had sung,
No one there who heard him   thought they were too long.
The turn of a hand, not longer,   they had thought it lasted,
E'en if they had listened   while for a thousand miles
                            a horseman hasted.

When his song he ended,   and to leave his seat was seen,
The youthful, queenly maiden   more blithe had never been,
Nor decked, at early morning,   in gayer clothes or better ;
Forthwith the high-born lady   sent to beg her father now
to meet her.

Then came her father quickly,   and on the maiden looked,
While, in a mood of sadness,   her father's chin she stroked ;
With her hand she coaxed him,   to make her word the stronger,
And said : " My dearest father,   bid that he at court may sing
yet longer."

He answered : " Best loved daughter,   if again, at the hour of eve,
His songs he deigns to sing you,   a thousand pounds I 'll give.
But now a mien so lofty   these guests of ours are wearing,
To us 't is not so pleasant   here, at court, to give his songs
a hearing."

However much she pressed him,   would the king no longer stay ;
Then strove again young Horant,   and never on any day,
Had his knightly song been better.   Sick and well together
All lost their wits in hearing,   and none could leave who
to listen once came hither.

The wild beasts in the forest   let their pasture grow ;
The little worms that creeping   through grass are wont to go,
The fishes. too, that ever   amidst the waves were swimming,
All now stopped to listen ;   the singer's heart with pride
was overbrimming.

Whatever he might sing to them,   to no one seemed it long ;
Ill vied with his song the choral   which by priests is sung.
Even the bells no longer   rang as of yore so sweetly ;
Every one who heard him   was moved by Horant's song,
                 and saddened greatly.

Then begged the lovely maiden   that he to her be brought ;
Without her father's knowledge,   she slyly this besought.
From her mother, Hilda, also   must the tale be hidden
That unto her, in her bower,   unknown to all, the minstrel
                 had been bidden.

It was a yielding chamberlain   who did the wages gain,
That, for his help, she gave him ;   red gold it was, I ween,
Glittering and heavy,   with armlets twelve, full-weighted.
'T was thus within her bower   the maid, at eventide, the singer
                 greeted.

By hidden ways he did it ;   Horant was glad indeed
That such good-will and kindness,   at court, had been his meed.
To win her love for his master   from far had he been faring :
To his tuneful skill he owed it   that she such friendly will
                 to him was bearing.

She bade her faithful chamberlain   to stand before the house ;
That so there might be no one   who could the threshold cross
Until the songs were ended,   soon heard with praises truthful.
None went into her bower   but Horant only and Morunc
                 the youthful.

She bade the bard be seated : " Now sing to me once more,"
Thus spake the high-born maiden,　" those songs I heard before.
For this I feel sore craving ;　than aught beside 't is sweeter
Unto your lays to listen ;　than any gem or pastime
　　　　　　　　　　　　　　　　　　　　't is far better."

" If I might dare to sing to you,　most fair and lovely maid,
And never need be fearful　for this to lose my head,
Thro' your father's anger,　never will I falter
In any wise to serve you,　if in my master's land you 'll
　　　　　　　　　　　　　　　　　　　seek a shelter."

He then began a ditty　of a mermaid of Amilé,
Which never man nor Christian　had learned to sing or say,
Although he may have heard it　on some wild, unknown water.
In this the good knight, Horant,　gave honor meet at court
　　　　　　　　　　　　　　　　　　　to Hagen's daughter.

At last, when he the love-song　had sung unto the end,
Then said the lovely maiden :　"Thanks I give, my friend."
She drew a ring from her finger,　nought of gold were fairer,
And said : " I give it gladly ;　be this of my good-will to you
　　　　　　　　　　　　　　　　　　　the bearer."

Now her word she pledged him,　and with it gave her hand :
" Should she of a crown be wearer,　and ever sway the land,
That ne'er by the hand of any　need he be further driven
Than unto her in her castle ;　there to live in honor would
　　　　　　　　　　　　　　　　　　　leave be given."

Of all she pressed upon him   nothing would he take
Unless indeed a girdle.   He said : " Let no man speak,
And say that I the maiden   e'er for myself was wooing ;
I will to my master bring her,   and for this his heart shall be
with bliss o'erflowing."

She asked : " Who is thy master ?   By name how is he known ?
Have e'er his liegemen crowned him ?   And any lands doth he own ?
For love of thee, most truly,   good-will I bear him ever."
The knight from Denmark answered :   " A king so rich and mighty
saw I never."

He said : " To none betray us,   most fair and lovely maid ;
To thee will I tell most gladly   what our master said,
When from his land we started,   hither to come at his bidding ;
For thy dear sake, fair lady,   unto thy father's land
and castle speeding."

She said : " Then tell me freely   the errand on which you 're sent
By him you call your master ;   if my will that way is bent
I shall let you know it truly,   before we yet are parted."
But Horant feared wild Hagen,   and began at court to feel
himself faint-hearted.

To the lady thus he answered :   " To you he sends this word, —
That his heart for you is longing ;   his love alone is stirred.
For him, I beg, fair lady,   let now your kindness waken ;
He from other women   has for your sake his love and longing
taken."

She said : " May God reward him ;   such love for me he shows.
If he in birth is my fellow,   I fain would be his spouse,
If you will deign to sing to me   every morn and even."
He said : " That will I gladly ;   to this no care by you need e'er
be given."

Quoth he to the queenly Hilda :   " Most fair and high-born maid,
There daily live with my master,   and long at court have staid,
Twelve minstrels who, before me,   earn much higher praises ;
But, though sweet their singing,   my lord, the king, in song
still better pleases."

She said : " If your loving master   in song so skilful be,
Of longing for him, truly,   I never can be free ;
My best of thanks I give him   for the love he now is showing,
And, dared I leave my father,   gladly from here would I
with you be going."

Then spake the knightly Morunc :   " Lady, with us there are
Warriors full seven hundred :   our weal or woe they share,
And each for this is ready ;   if once in our hands we have you,
Know you nor fear nor sorrow   lest we to meet wild Hagen's
wrath should leave you."

He said : " From Hagen's kingdom   we wish forthwith to go ;
Therefore beg your father   the kindness to us to show,
Youthful, high-born maiden,   that he and your queenly mother
Will deign our bark to look on ;   and you must also come,
e'en if no other."

" That will I do most gladly,   if my father's leave you have ;
Of him and those about him   this boon you now must crave,
That I and my maidens also   may ride to the shore some morning.
If he shall grant your wishes,   three days before, of the time
                       you must give us warning."

The first of all the chamberlains   was wont, and had a right,
Often to be with the maidens.   Just then, this very knight
There had come for pastime,   and to give to them his greeting ;
There found he Horant and Morunc ;   well might they fear some
                       harm was their lives awaiting.

He said to Lady Hilda :   " Who are they sitting here ? "
From the lord so hot and hasty   was never such wrath to fear.
He said : " Whoe'er allowed you   to come into this bower ?
Whoso in this hath helped you   ne'er showed you falser
                       friendship to this hour."

She said : " Now soothe your anger :   in peace pray let them live.
If to yourself great evil   you do not wish to give,
You must unseen by any,   them to their rooms be bringing ;
It else hath helped but little   that his knightly songs
                       the minstrel here was singing."

" Is this the knight," he asked her,   " they say so well can sing ?
E'en such a minstrel know I :   never hath any king
Had a braver fighter.   My father and his mother
Were children of one father ;   worthier knight than he there 's
                       not another."

The maid began to ask him :   "Tell me, then, his name."
He said : " Men call him Horant ;   from the Danish land he came.
Although no crown he weareth,   he yet for one is fitted :
We now know not each other,   but once at Hettel's court
                          our love we plighted."

When Morunc, too, was telling   that erst, in his fatherland,
He also had been outlawed,   his heart was sorely pained.
His eyes with tears were welling,   and now were overflowing ;
Then the queenly lady   kindly looked on him,
                          her sorrow showing.

Then saw the chamberlain also   how that his eyes were wet.
He said : " Most worthy lady,   these friends whom here we meet
I know to be my kinsmen ;   help now that all goes rightly
With both these worthy champions :   most careful will I be
                          to keep them fitly."

Much for them he sorrowed,   and felt heart-pain, forsooth ;
" Durst I before my ladies,   I would kiss upon the mouth
Each of these knights so worthy.   The days indeed are many
Since tidings of King Hettel   I could from a Hegeling ask,
                          or learn from any."

Then spake the maiden further :   " Since these thy kinsmen be,
Now so much the dearer   are they as guests to me.
Known unto my father   thou should'st quickly make them ;
They will not then so hastily   to their homes afar across
                          the sea betake them."

A busy talk began they,   those two young heroes brave ;
Morune unto the chamberlain   his mind most freely gave.
He said for Lady Hilda   they came within those borders ;
And that their master Hettel   to bring her back had sent them,
                             as her warders.

Then said to them the chamberlain :   " A twofold care I feel,
As liegeman of my master,   and to help you, too, as well.
How could I turn his anger,   if he knew you now were seeking
To win his maiden daughter ?   Never from here could you
                             your way be taking."

Then spake the knightly Horant :   " Hear well what now I say
In four days' time to Hagen,   we will come, and him will pray
That we may leave his kingdom,   if such may be his pleasure.
The king will then make ready   gifts for us of clothes,
                             as well as treasure.

" We will ask for nothing further,   (help you here must lend,)
But that Hagen shall be willing,   as well beseems a friend,
To come to the shore to see us,   my lady with him riding, —
His wife, the high-born Hilda ;   there to see the ship in which
                             we 're biding.

" Might we in this be lucky,   our toil we well shall spend ;
And, with a happy outcome,   our sorrows have an end.
If only to the seashore   he will ride with his daughter,
We well shall be rewarded   at home by our master Hettel,
                             for whom we sought her."

Then from out the castle   they were led by the crafty man,
So that the kingly Hagen   mistrusted not their plan.
When, for their floating shelter,   they the courtyard quitted,
All they had done for their master   should not, I ween, by him
at home be slighted.

They told the aged Wâ-te   what yet to none was known:
They said the high-born maiden   her love did freely own
Unto their master, Hettel,   for whom they now had sought her;
They talked with wise old Wâ-te   how best to bring her home
across the water.

Then spake the aged Wâ-te: "Were she once outside the gate,
And I the lovely maiden   there might only meet,
However hard the struggle   that there we had with the foeman,
To cross her father's threshold   none again should see that
lovely woman."

Their plot, well-laid and crafty,   to no one did they break,
But slyly made them ready   their homeward way to take.
This they told the warriors   on board their ship there lying;
Not loth were they to hear it,   for now to sail the weary men
were sighing.

They quickly brought together   such goods as they did own;
Then, in stillness whispered,   their hidden thought made known.
Later, throughout Ireland,   it was mourned, with bitter wailing;
Though woe it brought to Hagen,   the Hegeling's greatness
would it soon be telling.

Upon the fourth day's morning   to court they bravely rode,
With new and well-cut clothing;   none better ever showed.
Then the guests there gathered   were their wishes speaking;
Of the king and all his liegemen   they asked that they their
                         leave might now be taking.

Then spake to them King Hagen :   " Why will you leave my land ?
So far as I was able,   I have striven for this end, —
That you within my kingdom   should meet with kindness only ;
Now would you hence be sailing,   leaving me here, to lead
                         a life all lonely."

To him old Wâ-te answered :   " The Hegeling king, our lord,
Has sent to call us homeward ;   he will not hear a word
Of aught but our forgiveness.   Then, too, for us are mourning
Those we left behind us ;   we therefore soon must back
                         on our way be turning."

Then said to him wild Hagen :   " Your loss my heart doth break ;
Horses and fine clothing   deign, for my love, to take,
With gold and costly jewels.   Right well it doth beseem me
For all your gifts to pay you ;   in this shall no one ever
                         dare to blame me."

Then said the hoary Wâ-te :   " Too rich am I to-day
That I the gold you give us   should wish to take away.
Our master, whose forgiveness   our friends have lately won us,
The rich and mighty Hettel,   in such a deed would truly
                         never own us.

"One thing we have yet further,   my lord, to ask of thee ;
(If you this kindness show us,   a worthy boon 't will be.)
It is that you shall witness   how well we can be feasting ;
Of food for hearty eaters   we have in store what might
                 three years be lasting.

"To all who ask we give it,   for hence we sail o'er the deep ;
May God long give you honor,   yourself may He ever keep.
We now betake us homeward,   we here may bide no longer ;
Now may you and your kinsfolk   ride with us to our ship ;
                 no guard were stronger.

"If but your lovely daughter,   and with her my lady, your wife,
Shall look upon our riches,   glad will it make our life,
And dear to us forever.   If this to us be granted,
Great and good King Hagen,   from you no other gifts
                 shall e'er be wanted."

Then to his guests he answered,   with seemly, well-bred mien :
"Since you are now so earnest,   at early morn shall be seen
A hundred mares made ready,   saddled for woman or maiden ;
I, too, will ride down with them ;   right glad am I that to see
                 your ship I 'm bidden."

Then for the night they left him,   and rode away to the shore.
Then up on the beach was carried   of wine a goodly store,
That in the bark was lying ;   for food they were not lacking.
By this the ship was lightened ;   wisely had Fru-te of Denmark
                 his plans been making.

𝕮ale the 𝕾ebenth.

HOW THE MAIDENS CAME TO SEE THE SHIP, AND WERE CARRIED TO HETTEL'S KINGDOM.

EARLY on the morrow,   after the mass was said,
   To don their richest clothing   strove each wife and maid :
A throng of these King Hagen   to the sandy shore was leading ;
And with them riding gayly   a thousand stalwart Irish knights
                                        were speeding.

Within the town of Ballian   the guests had heard the mass.
Of all the woe and sorrow,   that soon would come to pass,
Hagen as yet knew nothing :   little honor was left him
By his guests' withdrawal ;   this of his fair and well-born
                                        child bereft him.

When now they all had ridden   to the ships upon the strand,
Queen Hilda and her ladies   were lifted down on the sand.
The young and lovely maidens   to see the ships were taken :
The traders' booths were open,   and the goods did wonder great
                                        in the queen awaken.

Many fair-wrought jewels   lay in sight in the shops,
Such as men prize highly;   King Hagen to see them stops,
And many with him also :   soon as the goods were shown them,
The maidens, too, must see them,   and rings and bands of gold
                             were pressed upon them.

To see the sights King Hagen   into a boat had gone:
Not all the booths were open,   nor all the goods were shown,
When Wâ-te's men heaved anchor   up from the sea-sands deftly,
And Hilda with her maidens   was borne away from the land
                             of her fathers swiftly.

For no one's hate and anger   Wâ-te greatly cares;
Little he recks what happens   to the shops of costly wares :
Hilda, the queenly mother,   was sundered from her daughter;
The men, in the ship long hidden,   up-sprang and sorrow made
                             for Hagen on the water.

Then the sails were hoisted,   and 't was seen that they were set :
From the ship they threw the foemen,   who thoroughly were wet,
Like sea-birds on the water,   when near the sands they flutter.
For her daughter dear-belovéd   sorrow and anger the queen
                             aloud did utter.

When the weaponed fighters   by Hagen there were seen,
Then, in truth, how scornful   and wrathful was his mien !
" Now bring to me my long-spear,   to feel it I will teach them ;
They all shall die full quickly   when my strong right arm
                             with that shall reach them ! "

Boldly then spoke Morune: "Be not so much in haste!
Though now you think to fight us,   and to rush on us so fast
With a thousand well-armed foemen,   we yet will overthrow them,
And fling them into the water;   a damp, cold lodging we will
           quickly show them!"

Still, brave Hagen's followers   the fight would not give o'er;
The water shone and glistened   with the armor that they wore;
Then they drew their long-swords,   spears were thickly flying;
But oars were dipped full quickly,   and fast the boats away
           from the shore were hieing.

The bold and daring Wâ-te   from the sands had given a bound
Into a well-manned row-boat;   loud did his mail resound,
As he, with fifty warriors,   after Hilda hasted:
Hagen's careless followers   now must rouse themselves,
           no time they wasted.

Onward came King Hagen;   his fighting-gear he wore,
And a heavy sword, the sharpest,   he proudly with him bore;
But now the aged Wâ-te   almost too long had waited;
Wild and grim was Hagen,   and high his spear he raised
           'gainst his foe belated.

Loudly then he shouted,   and bade his men make haste;
None of all his followers   would he allow to rest,
Hoping these guests, now fleeing,   who had been such traitors,
Might be with speed o'ertaken,   and either should be slain,
           or bound in fetters.

The king had now about him   fighters many and brave,
But yet he could not follow   across the wild sea-wave;
His ships were all unready,   and many of them leaking,
When now he would be sailing;   of Hagen's blame for this were
                all soon speaking.

On the gravelly sea-shore standing,   no other way he knew
But that more ships be builded   for him and his liegemen true,
And workmen called together,   who must therein be speedy:
All came who now were able,   and these he found to be both
                skilled and ready.

Upon the seventh morning,   there left the Irish land
The men sent forth by Hettel   to ask for Hilda's hand,
And bring to him the lady.   They were a thousand barely;
Hagen brought against them   thirty hundred men, if reckoned
                fairly.

The daring knights of Denmark   sent men home before,
To carry word to Hettel   that Hagen's child they bore,
And to his land would bring her,   with honor him befitting.
Though now they little thought it,   still harder work erelong
                must they be meeting.

To them their master, Hettel,   in happy mood then spoke:
" My sorrows now are over.   Great toils my liegemen took
For me in Hagen's kingdom,   and now have brought me gladness;
Since they on their errand left me,   fear for their doom has filled
                my heart with sadness.

“ Dear friends, if with your tidings you have not me betrayed,
And do not tell me falsely that you have seen the maid
Near to my land and kingdom, and in my friends’ safe-keeping,
For your tale will I reward you, and gladly will your praise
be ever speaking.”

They said : “ No lie we tell you, that we the maid have seen ;
But when we miles had measured, the daughter of the queen
Sadly said, for our welfare she feared, and was heavy-hearted,
Lest the king, her father, to follow with his ships e’en then
had started.”

For the tidings, Hettel gave them a hundred marks in worth ;
For all his knights there gathered, men at once brought forth
Swords as well as helmets, and shields for them were bidden :
Thus from Hettel’s castle they went, as if to court, to bring
the maiden.

All the men he was able Hettel for this now sought ;
Greatly was he hoping, and much thereof he thought,
So great a host to muster, and these so well outfitted,
That never to king’s fair daughter so fine a welcome might
again be meted.

In haste were all then bidden who ought with him to go ;
They still made ready slowly, till gifts he should bestow
Of all things that they needed ; they for this were waiting.
At length by him were gathered a thousand men or more,
for Hilda’s greeting.

Gay were they in clothing, —   'gainst this could none say nay, —
Poor as well as wealthy   were shining in war-array :
To bring the lovely ladies   to their new home and dwelling
Were Hettel's lieges earnest ;   with lofty hopes of this
their hearts were swelling.

Soon as they left the castle,   shouts the land did fill,
As they their way were making   thro' lowland and o'er hill ;
Men saw upon the pathways   crowds still thronging nearer :
Hettel hastened forward,   to see the maid, than every other
dearer.

At last the aged Wâ-te,   the knight from the Sturmisch land,
Had reached the Waalisch marches   and stepped upon the sand.
There on the shore were gathered   the sailors, water-weary ;
Shelter they sought for Hilda,   and in a friendly land were
glad to tarry

Stakes for tents were driven   near to the broad sea-flood
By the followers of Wâ-te ;   they were in happy mood.
Erelong the news was bruited,   and soon to them was given,
That Hettel, king of the Hegelings,   had left his home, and now
was near them even ;

And that he with many liegemen   was riding down to the shore,
To meet his well-belovéd.   Now hoped the maids the more
That she with greatest honor   should, as her birth befitted,
Be brought into his kingdom.   No more the thought of strife
their hearts affrighted.

The guests for nothing wanted,   they had both wine and food;
Those who were living near them   freely on them bestowed
The best that they were able;   the wants of all they heeded;
Whate'er they had they gave them,   and left them not to lack
               for aught they needed.

Hettel now drew nearer   to those who had reached his land;
And with him, gathered hastily,   the strong and goodly band,
Drawn from his father's kingdom.   They came bedecked so gaily,
And in such glittering armor,   the guests looked on full glad,
               and praised them freely.

Then the men of the Hegelings   came down upon the plain,
And soon the rushing riders   a tilting-match began;
All with youthful boldness   for knightly prizes striving:
Then came the Danish Fru-te,   and with him Wâ-te, wise as any
               living.

They were seen from afar by Hettel;   happy in heart was he.
His horse he set a-prancing;   right glad was he to see
Two of his bravest liegemen,   sent by him o'er the water,
With fighters bold to Ireland,   in hopes to win for him wild
               Hagen's daughter.

On him, too, looked they gladly,   their worthy king, so good;
Each day they spent there with him   found them in happy mood.
Wâ-te with all his fellows,   while far away they were living,
Had known much bitter hardship: for this would Hettel now
               reward be giving.

As he met his friendly liegemen,   King Hettel wore a smile ;
Then said he to them kindly :   "Much have I feared erewhile
For you, my faithful helpers,   and a heavy heart was bearing,
Lest in Hagen's castles   my men were held, and all were
                                 bondage sharing."

Then for love he kissed them,   both those gray old men ;
His eyes had never rested   on so glad a sight as then,
Nor on a fairer pasture   had fed, with longing fonder.
I ween that never to Hettel   was aught so full of bliss
                                  and sudden wonder.

Then spake the aged Wâ-te :   "No harm to us was done ;
But yet a sway so mighty   I ne'er before have known,
As this that wild King Hagen   over his lands now wieldeth :
His followers bear them proudly,   and he himself in strength
                                  to no one yieldeth.

" It was a day as happy   as ever could be thought,
When we to you sent tidings   that we had Hilda brought,
The loveliest of maidens   (no falsehood have I spoken,
Believe the tale I tell you)   that ever in this world
                                  my eyes did look on."

The high-born knight then added :   " Belike with greatest speed
Will come these daring foemen :   for this should you take heed
Lest the angry Hagen   soon shall overtake us
Here within your marches ;   if so, his hatred bitter woe
                                  will make us."

Then Wâ-te and Sir Fru-te   down to the shore did bring
Many worthy followers,   knights of Hettel, the king,
There to see fair Hilda,   and there must they await her.
Upon their shining bucklers   many a spear-shaft crashed
                         in battle later.

Now came the fair young maiden,   under a comely hat;
Then all the men of the Hegelings   who on their horses sat
By the side of the king, their master,   upon the grass alighted.
With merry hearts then gladly   the well-bred throng their love
                         and friendship plighted.

Irold, he of Ortland,   and Morune of the Frisian land,
Both of those brave champions,   one on either hand,
Came with lovely Hilda,   and Hettel soon were meeting;
Worthy was she of praises.   Now thought the maid to give
                         the king her greeting.

With her there came young maidens,   twenty or even more,
All clad in fair white linen, —   whiter none e'er wore, —
Or best of silken clothing,   that could be found by any:
Proud were they to wear them,   and, gaily decked, they there
                         were seen by many.

The king, both good and stately,   then began to greet
With well-bred, seemly bearing,   the maid he thought was meet
To wear the crown hereafter.   He gazed on her with yearning;
Her in his arms he folded,   and fondly kissed the maid,
                         her face upturning.

Then one by one he welcomed   all the maidens fair ;
But one there was among them   so lofty in her air
She might of birth be kingly :   in nought her kin were lacking.
She was one of the maidens   who with the griffin long
                        her home was making.

She bore the name of Hildeburg :   from Hilda, Hagen's wife,
She ever had won the honor   befitting her worthy life ;
Born in the land of Portugal,   thence had she been taken.
She now saw many strangers :   a longing sad for her friends
                        did this awaken.

Hettel to all the maidens   gave a welcome free,
Yet was their lot no brighter ;   for when they thought to see
An end of all their sadness,   upon the coming morrow,
Soon as the day was dawning,   there came to them again
                        as great a sorrow.

Her throng of high-born followers   were greeted on every side :
Near to Hagen's daughter   on a flowery meadow wide,
Under silken awnings,   many there were seated.
But Hagen was now too near them ;   to them from him must
                        many ills be meted.

Tale the Eighth.

HOW HAGEN FOLLOWED HIS DAUGHTER.

WHEN the day was dawning,   there was seen full well,
    And known by Horant of Daneland,   a cross upon a sail,
With other emblems blazoned,   that pilgrims did betoken.
For such a band of pilgrims   in Wâ-te's heart was little
                                love bespoken.

Loudly Morune shouted   to Irold brave and true:
" Now ask our lord, King Hettel,   what he thinks to do?
A sail with the arms of Hagen   comes to our shore too nearly:
Too long have we been sleeping,   and well to be rid of this
                                will cost us dearly."

To Hettel the tale was carried   that the father of his bride,
Hither from Ireland sailing,   with ships broad-built and wide
As well as many a galley,   now their shore was nearing.
From Wâ-te and from Fru-te   their wisest thoughts the king
                                was bent on hearing.

Both those knights of Denmark   could hardly this believe,
Had not their eyes beheld it,   that Hagen, with followers brave,
Seeking his daughter Hilda,   to the river Waal was steering.
The men who came from Ortland   lay happy on the beach,
           no danger fearing.

The fair and noble Hilda   soon heard the wondrous tale,
Whereat the kindly maiden   did loudly thus bewail:
" My father, if he comes hither,   soon will make such slaughter,
That none e'er knew the sorrow   that will be felt by many
           a wife and daughter.

" We 'gainst that can guard us,"   answered the knight Irold:
" However he may bluster,   I would not take of gold
A mountain's weight in barter,   that day when foes are mated,
Could I see my uncle Wâ-te   near wild Hagen come,
           with anger heated."

Then the lovely maidens   began to wail and mourn.
The ship was tossed and rolling,   now by the west wind borne,
With warriors filled and crowded,   near to Waal, the river.
They there, in heavy fighting,   soon found a blood-stained
           resting-place forever.

Wâ-te bade that Hilda   on board a ship should stay.
To guard the queenly maiden,   while near the shore it lay,
On every side all hastily   men their shields were bearing:
To keep a watch o'er the ladies,   there were on board a hundred
           warriors daring.

Ready now for battle   were all who to the strand
Had brought the lovely Hilda   from her Irish fatherland,
Whence they the maid had stolen,   to her father Hagen's sorrow.
Many, sound and healthy,   must sorely fear for their lives
            before the morrow.

Hettel was soon heard shouting   and calling aloud to his men:
" Be on your guard, brave fighters!   Who never gold did gain,
To him it shall be measured,   in handfuls, without weighing.
Let this be not forgotten, —   that now your Irish foes you may
            be slaying."

Bearing then their weapons,   down they rushed to the sand;
Stirred with warlike bustle   was all the Waalisch strand.
Thither to King Hettel   flocked his champions daring;
Friends as well as foemen   soon towards the self-same spot
            were faring.

Now had Hagen also   reached the sandy shore,
And men at him were hurling   the spears they bravely bore:
Those upon the seashore   well their lives then guarded
From the stormy Irish onset;   but wounds yet all the more
            their bravery rewarded.

How seldom would **a father**   have wished to send his child
Where sparks of fire, all-glowing,   were struck by foemen wild
Forth from hardened helmets,   in sight of many a maiden!
To have sailed with these roving fighters   did now at last
            the lovely Hilda sadden.

By turns they smote each other   with heavy spears and long :
Altho' themselves they guarded   beneath their bucklers strong,
Yet wounded thro' their hauberks,   they were gashed and bloody ;
And soon with flowing life-blood   the waters' depths were
                            deeply stained and ruddy.

Then to his trusty liegemen   Hagen called aloud :
The sea gave back his shouting, —   truly his strength was good, —
He bade them help to land him,   their wounds by them unheeded ;
Glad were they to do it :   thereby were spears in many
                            hearts imbedded.

Hagen now drew nearer,   not far was he from the sand ;
His sword it clattered loudly ;   Hettel, near at hand,
Was standing by the water,   on the seashore waiting :
There, with daring followers,   deeds he did that praise
                            should aye be meeting.

Hagen, wild with anger,   leaped into the wave,
And to the shore he waded.   Then on that warrior brave
Came a shower of lances ;   like snowflakes falling thickly,
Fast they fell around him,   shot by the Hegeling foemen,
                            thronging quickly.

Then from the clash of sword-blades   a mighty noise arose.
Those who would slay wild Hagen   soon beneath his blows
Were seen to reel and stagger.   Hettel, the noble fighter,
Drew near to Hilda's father ;   at this the maiden wept, with
                            tears most bitter.

It was indeed a wonder,   as we the tale have heard,
So strong and brave was Hagen,   that Hettel, the Hegeling lord,
Before him held his footing.   As soon as, wildly fighting,
They had reached each other,   their helmets rang beneath
                     the heavy smiting.

But not so quickly ended   was yet the stormy fight.
Soon was Hettel wounded   by brave King Hagen's might:
Wâ-te the old of Sturmland,   with his kin, to Hettel hasted,
With Irold, too, and Morune, —   knights as good as foemen's
                     lands e'er wasted.

Now came the brave old Fru-te   and Wâ-te with his throng:
Knights there were a thousand, —   the press of them was strong.
Hettel's Hegeling kinsmen,   well their weapons plying,
Wounded many foemen;   on every side stretched low,
                     the men were lying.

After bravest fighting,   now had reached the land
The followers of Hagen;   then crowded to the sand,
After his friends so faithful,   a host from Ireland's borders.
Soon were helmets shattered: grimly they fought to win
                     the maids from their warders.

Hagen saw then near him   Hettel, the youthful knight:
Many strong and stalwart   were shorn of strength outright,
Both by those from Daneland   and the Hegeling lieges:
Now to meet wild Hagen   every one old Wâ-te loud
                     beseeches.

Then, by his strength, King Hagen   broke thro' the crowd a path,
And with his sword hewed boldly ;   well he wreaked his wrath,
Because his much-loved daughter   from him by craft was taken ;
Coats of mail lay fallen :   the wrongs of Hagen hate in him
                                        did waken.

He might not quench his anger   with the sword alone ;
By the thrust of his heavy long-spear   soon were overthrown
Many a knight most daring :   never the tale was given
By these unto their kinsmen,   of how in the stormy fight
                                        their luck had thriven.

Now came Wâ-te quickly,   the knight well born and good ;
Soon of his well-loved kinsmen   he saw the flowing blood,
Under the slash of broadswords,   out of their armor dripping :
Of those who would have helped him,   five hundred wounded men
                                        in death were sleeping.

Everywhere were gathered   friends as well as foes,
All in uproar minged ;   a mighty din arose.
Wâ-te and wild Hagen   rushed on each other madly,
Whoe'er could shun their pathway   of all the risk he had fled
                                        was thinking gladly.

Hagen laid on Wâ-te   many a heavy blow, —
Well his strength he wielded.   Their helmets were aglow
With fiery sparks outflashing, —   like to brands they glittered ;
Each cleft the other's helmet,   and ever still, each other's blows
                                        they bettered.

The ground beneath was trembling   with aged Wâ-te's stroke:
Scarcely could the maidens   of his onslaught shun the shock.
Now the wounds of Hettel   his faithful friends were binding;
He then began to ask them   where his cousin Wâ-te he could
                       be finding.

With Hagen, "of kings the Devil,"   he found old Wâ-te soon:
The skill of him of Sturmland   to guard himself was shown:
Brave were both these warriors,   and oft the tale was spoken
How Wâ-te the bold and Hagen   in hardest strife had each
                       his anger wroken.

Hagen's spear was broken   erelong on Wâ-te's shield:
Well in the fight he bore it,   and strength enough did wield.
Ne'er on the field of warfare   did blows of men fall thicker,
Even of bravest warriors;   Wâ-te scorned to flinch,
                       or seem the worker.

Hagen cleft the head-piece   of Hettel's brave old man,
The trusty, daring Wâ-te,   till blood from his helmet ran,
From out his wounds fast flowing.   Now the wind blew colder,
For eventide was nearing;   the struggling throng in fight
                       but grew the bolder.

Wâ-te gave back in anger   each grim and deadly blow,
Making the blood, like tear-drops,   on Hagen's breast to flow;
Strokes he gave his foeman,   until the sword-blade glittered
On the bosses of his helmet;   daylight before his darkened
                       eyesight flittered.

Wounded, too, was Irold,   Ortland's champion brave.
Though many there lay dying   from the wounds that Hagen gave,
Yet the blows of Wâ-te   still did Hagen batter.
Sorely wept the maidens   when of so many swords they heard
the clatter.

Now, in fear and sorrow,   Hilda, the maiden fair,
Cried unto King Hettel,   and begged of him to spare
Her father from old Wâ-te,   the fight so grimly waging.
He called for his standard-bearer,   and bade him lead his men
.where the strife was raging.

Then the kingly Hettel   right well and bravely fought;
Soon he found old Wâ-te,   to whom no joy it brought:
Then Hettel called to Hagen: " Let hatred hence be driven;
So shall it raise your honor,   if now our friends no more
to death be given."

Hagen shouted loudly, —   fell indeed was his mood, —
" Who bids that we be parted?"   Then cried the warrior good:
"I bid it, I, King Hettel,   the Hegelings' lord and master,
Who for the Lady Hilda   sent my friends so far, from you
to wrest her."

Then spake the lordly Hagen: " Since first to me 't was told
How you to win my daughter   showed yourself so bold,
This to your name with warriors   shame has ne'er been doing;
Clever was the cunning   to which your winning of my child
is owing."

Hettel then sprang nearer,   as oft by one is done,
Who thinks to stop the fighting.   Grim was the mood yet shown
By the bold and aged Wâ-te;   but he and Hagen yielded:
Then with all his followers   Hagen stepped back, nor longer
                         his weapon wielded.

Now the lordly Hettel   his helmet laid aside;
A truce was loudly called for   by all, both far and wide;
'T was said by Hilda's father   there was an end of fighting:
For many a day, the maidens   had heard no tale their ears
                         so much delighting.

The men took off the armor   which they in fight had worn,
And now at last they rested.   Many then must mourn
For wounds, in warfare given,   whence the blood was welling;
But many lay there also   who never more on thoughts of war
                         were dwelling.

Then stepped forth King Hettel   and near to Hagen stood,
And thus he spake to the warrior: "Since I well have wooed
Your lovely daughter Hilda,   't is fit that you allow her
To wear the crown beside me: my many well-bred knights
                         will fealty show her."

Then Hettel sent for Wâ-te,   of whom he was in need;
For many years now ended,   of him it had been said
That he from some wild woman   had learned a leech's cunning:
Wâ-te, forsooth, was skilful   to heal deep wounds and stanch
                         the life-blood running.

Wâ-te laid by his weapons;   his wounds he first had bound.
Herbs that were good for healing   by him were quickly found;
He had a box full costly,   that in it held a plaster.
Now the fair Queen Hilda   besought his help, and at his feet
she cast her.

She said, " My dear friend Wâ-te,   my father heal, I pray;
For this, whate'er you ask me,   I ne'er will say you nay;
And help his warriors also,   who in the dust lie bleeding,
And show your skill to his liegemen   who stood by him, when
he their help was needing.

" Nor must you be forgetful   of those of the Hegeling land,
Who were friends to Hettel;   wet with their blood is the sand
On which they now are lying,   as if a rain were falling:
Sorrowful tales of their fighting   for me there ne'er can be
an end of telling."

Then spake the aged Wâ-te: " Their wounds I cannot heal, —
In that I will not meddle,   until as friends they feel
Each unto the other, —   Hagen brave and knightly,
And Hettel, my lord and master;   till then shall I withhold
my skill most rightly."

The high-born maiden answered: " This I may not dare
To ask of the king, my father;   his tears I did not spare,
And now have not the boldness   to bring to him my greeting;
Both he and all his kinsmen   I fear would now my love with
scorn be meeting."

Then 't was asked of Hagen :   "My lord, may this now be,
That it would not stir your anger   your daughter here to see,
The youthful, queenly Hilda?   If you for this are willing,
She will come most gladly,   and soon your many wounds will
help in healing."

"Gladly will I see her,   whatever she has done ;
To me will she be welcome :   why should I her disown,
Here in a land of foemen,   nor take her greeting kindly ?
To me and to my daughter,   King Hettel must atone for deeds
unfriendly."

Horant, the knight from Daneland,   led her by the hand,
And with him went brave Fru-te,   to where the king did stand ;
One maiden only with them   looked on Hagen wounded.
For friends did Hilda sorrow,   though Hettel's love for her
was all unbounded.

On Hildeburg and Hilda   when Hagen now did look,
Then, from his seat upspringing,   thus he quickly spoke :
"Welcome be thou, my daughter,   Hilda, most noble lady !
I cannot leave unspoken   the greeting warm which I to give
am ready."

His daughter he allowed not   the care of his wounds to take ;
While Wâ-te these was binding   he bade the maids step back, —
The youthful high-born ladies.   Wâ-te's wish was the stronger
To heal her father quickly,   that so his daughter there
might weep no longer.

Healed with plants and herbage   and many a far-sought weed,
From all his pain did Hagen   feel himself now freed;
They eased his hurts with plaster,   and when again the maiden
Turned to see her father,   she found him well, with aches
                         no longer laden.

Wâ-te, the healing-master,   made haste, — no time he lost;
He hoped to gain such riches   among this wounded host,
That scarce could they by camels   be carried to his dwelling.
A skill so great and wondrous   never, that I have heard,
                         have men been telling.

First he healed King Hettel,   the lord of the Hegeling land;
Then all he saw there wounded   he helped by his skilful hand.
Those in the care of others   still with pain did sicken;
But they, when nursed by Wâ-te,   were turned to life, tho' they
                         by death were stricken.

There would they no longer   let the maidens stay.
Hagen said to Hilda: " Elsewhere must we to-day
Find us rest and shelter;   while others must not idly
Leave the dead thus lying,   who burial scarce can wait,
                         here scattered widely."

Hettel begged King Hagen   with him to his home to go;
Though loath, to this he yielded,   as soon as he came to know
That he, the king of the Hegelings,   of many lands was owner:
Hagen then with his daughter   went with him to his home,
                         and there had honor.

The youthful knights were singing,   as they left the field.
Happy then were the living;   but, never to be healed,
They behind were leaving   three hundred dead and dying,
The rich and poor together,   slashed with the sword,
                     and pitifully lying.

Then the war-worn fighters   through the land went home;
All who there were dwelling   were blithe to see them come:
But the kinsmen of the warriors   who in death lay sleeping
Were slow their hearts to gladden;   they for kindred slain
                     long time were weeping.

Hettel and Hilda with him   took their homeward way.
Many, bereft of fathers,   sorely wept that day,
Whose after life was happy.   The mighty Hettel later
Crowned the fair young Hilda;   by this the Hegeling name
                     became the greater.

Hettel now had thriven, —   his suit he well did gain.
Old and young together   with swords at court were seen,
As were the guests of Hagen   who from the ships came kindly.
The wedding of his daughter   was highly praised by Hagen,
                     now grown friendly.

Then with what great honor   to the bridal seat was led
That high-born, lovely lady!   Moreover, it is said
That full five hundred liegemen   then at court were knighted.
Fru-te the wise from Denmark   to guard King Hettel's wealth
                     was thought well fitted.

The riches of King Hettel   by Hagen now were seen ;
The tale had erst been told him   by many of Hettel's kin,
That over seven princedoms   well his sway had thriven.
All the poor there with them   were home in gladness sent,
and lodgings given.

Hettel gave rich clothing   to Ireland's warriors brave ;
Bright-red gold and silver,   and horses, too, he gave.
The whole they scarce could carry,   as they homeward wended :
Thus good friends he won him,   and this for Hilda in highest
praises ended.

Upon the twelfth day's morning   they left King Hettel's land.
The horses bred in Denmark   led they out on the sand ;
Each his mane, thick hanging,   down to his hoofs was shaking.
The guests from afar were happy   that they King Hettel's
friendship had been making.

Grooms and also stewards   with Hagen then did ride,
With cup-bearers and carvers.   Ne'er, in his greatest pride,
In his home and kingdom,   had he been served so truly.
The crown was worn by Hilda,   and Hagen's heart with bliss
was brimming fully.

Food as well as lodgings   they found upon their road ;
On Hagen and his followers   all men their care bestowed :
So to their homes most gladly   they the tale did carry
Of how the friends of Hettel   in showing them all kindness
ne'er were weary.

Hagen greeted Hildeburg,   and clasped her in his arms ;
He said, " Watch over Hilda   for the love your bosom warms.
So great a throng of followers   at times a woman dazes ;
Care for her so kindly   that of your worth all men
shall speak with praises."

" My lord, that will I gladly :   to you has much been told
Of the woes that with her mother   I bore in days of old ;
And I for years my friendship   for her did never loosen ;
Her for miles I followed   ere for a lover you by her
were chosen."

Hagen bade the others   their way to court to take ;
Never then could the maidens   an end of weeping make :
Now by the hand he took them,   and to Hettel they were given ;
He asked for them his kindness,   since from their homes they
sadly had been riven.

Then said he to his daughter :   " So well the crown now wear,
That neither I nor your mother   the tale shall ever hear
That men ill-will do bear you.   High your lot has raised you,
And you of blame were worthy,   if when men spoke your name
they never praised you."

Low bowed to the king wild Hagen,   and kissed his child again.
Neither by him nor his followers   ever more was seen
The kingdom of the Hegeling :   too far away was their dwelling.
Back to his home in Ballian,   in his trusty ships, King Hagen
soon was sailing.

When he had reached his castle,   and sat with the queen alone,
The mother of fair Hilda,   Hagen was free to own
That none to win his daughter   more fitly could have pleaded ;
And if he had yet others,   he fain to the Hegeling land
would send them to be wedded.

Hilda for this gave praises   to her master, Christ the Lord :
" That I of my dear daughter   such happy news have heard
Fills my heart with gladness,   and with bliss o'erflowing.
How fares it with her followers,   and Hildeburg, who long
her love was showing ? "

Then spake the kingly Hagen :   " Now in their land and home
All of them are happy ;   great hath our child become ;
Ne'er, with us, were her maidens   clothed in such fine dresses.
There we now must leave them :   for her were many breast-
plates hacked to pieces."

Tale the Ninth.

HOW GUDRUN WAS SOUGHT BY SIEGFRIED.

WE speak no more of Hagen.   A word may now be told
     About King Hettel's kinsmen :   they who land did hold
Ever owed him fealty   for these and for their castles ;
To court they all came often   when Hettel and Hilda sent
                              to call their vassals.

Wâ-te went to Sturmland,   Morune to Nifland rode ;
Horant, prince of Denmark,   led his warriors good
To Givers, by the seashore,   where as lord they held him ;
There their homes they guarded,   and many, far and wide,
                              their master called him.

With mighty sway in Ortland   Irold had his seat ;
Its lands he held of Hettel ;   so, as a vassal meet,
Near and far to serve him,   his duty was the greater :
The king was brave and worthy ;   and ne'er for a lord of lands
                              was known a better.

If ever in any kingdom   Hettel heard them speak
Of a fair and well-born maiden,   her he sought to take
Into his home and castle,   as handmaid to his lady :
Whatever Hilda wished for,   to help wild Hagen's child
they all were ready.

The king, with his wife beside him,   was happy on the throne ;
Their life was ever blissful.   To all in the land 't was known
That better far and dearer   than all on earth he thought her.
Never by all his kinsmen   a lovelier could be found,
where'er they sought her.

Within seven years thereafter   Hettel, in stormy fight,
Thrice to his foes gave battle.   They who, day and night,
To wrong his name and honor   did their utmost gladly,
Now by the knightly Hettel   found themselves brought low
and chastened sadly.

His castles he did strengthen,   and peace he gave to his land,
As well a king befitteth :   such were the deeds of his hand,
That never in any kingdom,   when his name was spoken,
Was it said he was faint-hearted.   The praise of all did well
his worth betoken.

While, with name so worthy,   Hettel held the throne,
Wâ-te, the man of wisdom,   never left undone
His duty to his master,   to see him three times yearly ;
Truly he was faithful,   far and near, to the lord
he held so dearly.

Horant, the lord from Denmark,   to court not seldom rode;
Costly gems and clothing   on the maids he there bestowed,
With gold and silken raiment,   meet for women's wearing:
He from Daneland brought them,   and to all who wished
                 was he of gifts unsparing.

The service true and steady   that the liegemen of the king
Gave to the lordly Hettel   honor to him did bring.
Praised was he for knighthood   more than any other:
This Hilda also furthered,   a queen herself, and child
                 of a queenly mother.

Hilda, Hagen's daughter,   children two did bear
Unto her lord, King Hettel: to bring them up with care
His faithful friends were bidden.   Soon among his vassals
Were the tidings bruited   that an heir no more was lacking
                 for his lands and castles.

One became a warrior,   Ortwin was his name;
To Wâ-te he was trusted.   It was the teacher's aim
That he from early boyhood   should his thoughts be turning
To all things good and worthy;   to be a trusty knight he thus
                 was learning.

The very comely daughter   of Hilda and the king
Was called Gu-drun the lovely: from the land of the Hegeling
To Denmark she was carried,   to be in her kinsmen's wardship.
Thus they helped King Hettel,   and this they never felt to be
                 a hardship.

When the maid grew older,   her shape became so fair
That neither man nor woman   to praise her could forbear:
Far from the maiden's birthplace,   all her worth were telling.
Gu-drun her kinsfolk called her,   in the Danish land
             where now she had her dwelling.

That age she now was reaching   when, had she been a man,
A sword she might have wielded.   Many a prince was fain
To wed the lovely maiden,   and sought her love and favor;
But many came a-wooing   who soon their hopes must lose,
             and win her never.

However fair was Hilda,   Hettel's lovely wife,
Yet was Gu-drun more lovely,   and fair beyond belief;
More fair than the early Hilda,   erst to Ireland carried.
Above all other women   Gu-drun was praised, ere yet the maid
             was married.

Her father scorned to give her   to the king of Alzabé;
When he heard he could not win her   to him 't was a sorry day.
He held himself most highly   for all his kingly graces,
And thought there could be no one   whose deeds, like his, were
             worthy of men's praises.

Both brave he was and daring,   and from the Moorland came:
He was known afar and widely,   Siegfried was his name;
A king was he full mighty   over vassals seven.
He sued for Hilda's daughter,   such tales of her lofty worth
             to him were given.

He, with his faithful liegemen   from far Icaria's strand,
Won many costly prizes   there in Hettel's land:
His strong and doughty warriors,   in sight of ladies seated
Before King Hettel's castle,   in games of knighthood often
there were mated.

When Hilda and her daughter   passed the hall within,
Before the house of Wigaleis   there rose a mighty din
From warriors of the Moorland,   who, all boldly dashing,
Rode in the sight of the women;   oft of spears and shields
was heard the clashing.

Never could knight in tilting   better in this behave.
A friendly will she bore him,   and oft kind words she gave,
Though he was brown to look on,   and in hue was dusky even.
He for her love was yearning,   yet for a wife she ne'er
to him was given.

This pained him beyond measure,   and truly he was wroth
That he from far had ridden,   yet gave she not her troth.
To burn the land of Hettel   then did he threaten madly:
His followers from Moorland,   when now his hopes were lost,
were mourning sadly.

From him was the maid withholden   by Hettel's lofty pride;
And now their loving friendship   was ended on either side.
Then swore the Moor that never   he his hate would slacken,
And that the grudge he bore him,   whate'er befell, should
never be forsaken.

Then from the land of the Hegeling   rode they all away.
When many years were ended,   there came at last a day
When by a knight most worthy   was bitter sorrow tasted ;
Then the foes of Herwic   did him the worst they could,
                             nor in it rested.

Tale the Tenth.

HOW HARTMUT SENT TO WOO GUDRUN.

Now in the land of Normandy   the tale was widely told,
  That never fairer maiden   did any man behold
Than was King Hettel's daughter,   Gudrun, the high-born lady.
A king, whose name was Hartmut,   to her then turned his love,
                      to woo her ready.

Gerlind, Hartmut's mother,   her wish to him made known,
That he should woo the maiden ;   her word he followed soon.
First they sent for his father,   when they of this had spoken ;
He bore the name of Ludwig,   and in Norman lands he wore
                      the kingly token.

Then the aged father   rode to see his son.
Of the end that he was seeking   had Ludwig knowledge won ;
But when to him he hearkened,   and learned his wishes wholly,
Evil he foreboded,   yet still the youth's fond hopes
                      upheld he fully.

"Who tells you," said King Ludwig,   "she is so very fair ?
Tho' she all lands were owning,   the home is not so near,
Wherein the maid is dwelling,   that we should go a-wooing ;
If we sent our men before us   to ask her love, their task
                     they would soon be ruing."

Then did Hartmut answer :   "For me 't is not too far ;
Whene'er the lord of a kingdom   no pain or toil doth spare
To win a wife and riches,   he gains a life-long blessing.
My wish, I pray you, follow ;   let men be sent, that they
                     my suit be pressing."

Then spake his mother, Gerlind,   of Normandy the queen :
"Letters must now be written ;   let clothes, the best e'er seen,
With gold, to those be given   upon your errand speeding ;
They, too, must learn the roadways   that towards the home
                     of fair Gu-drun are leading."

Then spake again King Ludwig :   "Know you not full well
That Hilda, the maiden's mother,   did erst in Ireland dwell ?
And know you not what happened   to many a one who sought her ?
Her kin are proud and lofty,   and now will scorn the love
                     we shall have brought her."

Then young Hartmut answered :   "Tho' with a warlike band
I afar must seek her,   over sea and land,
That shall I do most willingly :   my heart to her is given,
And never will I rest me   till I for Hilda's daughter
                     happily have striven."

“ Gladly will I help you,”   King Ludwig then did say :
“ Let this now make you happy ;   erelong, upon the way
I’ ll send twelve sumpter-horses   bearing silver treasure ;
That when they hear our errand,   our wealth and worth they
may more rightly measure.”

By Hartmut then were chosen   sixty men, to send
To woo the fair young maiden,   and help to him to lend ;
With food and clothing also   well were they outfitted,
And on the road well guided :   Ludwig was wise, and was
in this foresighted.

When everything was ready   that soon the men would need,
Then were letters written,   sealed, and given with speed.
Both by brave young Hartmut   and his queenly mother.
Then from home they started ;   so proud a throng there never
was another.

Fast they rode and steadily   for many a day and night,
Until the land they sought for   came at last in sight,
And they might tell the errand   they were thither bringing.
Long was Hartmut waiting,   while love and care were
in his heart upspringing.

Over land and rivers   they took their toilsome way,
As far as in days a hundred   a pasturing herd may stray,
Until the land of the Hegelings   lay before them stretching.
Their steeds were worn and weary   ere they gave the letters
they were fetching

At last they far had ridden,   and to the sea had come,
Upon the shores of Denmark :   sadly they long did roam,
Before they reached the kingdom,   and its lord did know them ;
Now they begged for guidance,   and men were bid the nearest
                           way to show them.

The news was given to Horant,   the knight well-bred and bold ;
Now asked the errand-bearers,   and the truth to them was told,
About King Hettel and Hilda,   and all they had been hearing.
They saw the men of Hettel   coming in throngs, their shields
                           and weapons bearing.

Horant, lord of Daneland,   then to his liegemen spake,
And bade for the errand-bearers   a safeguard now to make,
And that the men of Hartmut   should be by them well guided
To the court of his lord, King Hettel ;   they grudged no toil,
                           and well his bidding heeded.

When thro' the Hegeling kingdom   the heralds took their way,
So lordly was their bearing,   that often men did say :
" These folk are rich and mighty,   whatever they are seeking."
The news to the king was carried,   and soon to him all men
                           the tale were speaking.

To all the guests from Normandy   were lodgings given there ;
The king now bade his liegemen   to wait on them with care.
He knew not yet their errand,   and why to him they had ridden :
But on the twelfth day, early,   young Hartmut's men before
                           the king were bidden.

An earl there was among them;   how well his breeding showed!
Upon their clothing also   were praises high bestowed;
They rode the best of horses   on which men e'er were seated,
And before the king they gathered,   in fairest guise, that
                       well they might be greeted.

The king gave kindly welcome,   as also did his men,
Until their wooing errand   was unto him made plain:
Then were they ill-treated,   and knew the king's hard feeling.
I ween the mighty Hettel   to grant young Hartmut's wish
                       would ne'er be willing.

One who in that was skilful   to the king the letters read;
But he was greatly angered   that they to court were led
By the good and upright Horant,   a knight so brave and noble;
And, had they not his friendship,   they had not left the king
                       without more trouble.

Then spake to them King Hettel: "No good to you 't will bring
That you were sent a-wooing   by Hartmut, your lord and king.
To pay for this full dearly   you may well be fearing;
Your kingly master's wishes   both I and Lady Hilda are wroth
                       at hearing."

One among them answered: "Hartmut makes it known
That much he loves the maiden;   and if to wear the crown
In Normandy she deigneth,   before his friends there living,
That he, a knight all spotless,   will rightly earn the love
                       she shall be giving."

Then quoth the Lady Hilda:　"How can she be his wife?
A hundred and three of his castles　his father held in fief,
Within the land of Cardigan,　from Hagen, my noble sire;
It ill becomes my kinsmen　to be King Ludwig's vassals,
　　　　　　　　　　　　　　　　or owe him hire.

"Ludwig dwelt in Scotland,　and there it erst befell
That a brother of King Otto　did wrong to Ludwig deal:
Both were Hagen's vassals,　and of him their lands had taken;
And thus my father's friendship　for him was lost, and hate
　　　　　　　　　　　　　　　　instead did waken.

"Say you now to Hartmut　she ne'er his wife shall be.
Your lord is not so worthy　that he to boast is free,
That he doth love my daughter,　and she doth not disdain him;
Bid him elsewhere be looking,　if he be fain a queen for his land
　　　　　　　　　　　　　　　　to gain him."

The heralds' hearts were heavy;　't was not for their good name
That they, for miles full many,　in sorrow and in shame,
Back to their homes in Normandy　this news must carry sadly.
Hartmut, as well as Ludwig,　was vexed that they herein
　　　　　　　　　　　　　　　　were foiled so badly.

Forthwith to them said Hartmut:　"Tell me now the truth,
The grand-daughter of Hagen　have you seen, forsooth?
Is the maid, Gudrun, as lovely　as men have here been saying?
May God bring shame to Hettel,　that he my suit with such
　　　　　　　　　　　　　　　　ill-will is paying!"

Then the earl thus answered : " This can I truly say, —
Whoe'er shall see the maiden must feel her charms and sway;
Above all maids and women, her worth is past the telling."
Then quoth the kingly Hartmut : " To live without her ne'er
shall I be willing."

Whereon his mother, Gerlind, sadly thus did say,
With tears her lot bewailing : " My son, oh, lack-a-day !
Alas that e'er the heralds to win the maiden started !
If we at home had kept them, e'en to this day had I been
still light-hearted."

Tale the Eleventh.

HOW HERWIC SENT TO SEEK GUDRUN
AND HOW HARTMUT CAME HIMSELF.

HARTMUT left his wooing   to wait for many a year.
Soon a tale was bruited   ('t was true what men did hear)
Of one whose name was Herwic,   a king as yet but youthful:
Often his worth was spoken,   and men yet speak of him
                              with praises truthful.

He began his wooing,   trusting the lovely maid
Would take him for her lover;   long his hopes he fed,
And much he toiled to win her,   both with love and riches:
But tho' the maid was willing,   her father, Hettel, he in vain
                              beseeches.

Though Herwic long was striving,   and men to seek her rode,
Yet was his wooing slighted;   for this his wrath he showed.
The heart of proud young Herwic   by heavy care was fettered;
Freely his love he gave her,   and thought a life with her
                              could not be bettered.

There came at length a morning   when it to them befell
That in the Hegeling kingdom   both knights and maids as well,
With many lovely ladies,   his coming never fearing,
Before them saw bold Hartmut;   Hettel could not believe
                     he 'd be so daring.

From this did endless evil   soon come upon the land:
These guests high-born and worthy   were yet an unknown band;
Hartmut and his kinsmen   their host's goodwill were sharing,
And he the hope still harbored   that the maid would yet
                     the crown with him be wearing.

Now before Queen Hilda   by ladies he was seen
To stand with lofty breeding,   and with a stately mien.
There the proud young Hartmut   wore a look so knightly,
That he the love of ladies   well might ask, and 't would be
                     granted rightly.

Well-grown was he in body,   fair he was and bold,
Kind as well as lordly.   Why I ne'er was told
Had Hettel and Queen Hilda   from him withheld their daughter,
When he had thought to woo her;   wroth was he to be scorned
                     when now he sought her.

Of her his heart had longed for   he now had gained the sight;
There oft were stolen glances   between Gu-drun and the knight.
He made it known to the maiden,   by speech from others hidden,
That he was young King Hartmut,   and from the Norman land
                     had lately ridden.

Then she told her wooer   the pain to her it gave ;
And tho' she wished he ever   a happy life might have,
Yet from her father's kingdom   she begged him now to hasten,
For in the land of Hettel   was his life at risk, and this
                             would never lessen.

She looked on him so kindly   that now her heart was warned
That he should stay no longer,   for here his suit was spurned.
Friendly was she to Hartmut,   who her love so wanted,
But his hopes she little heeded,   and while he wooed, not much
                             to him she granted.

At last her well-bred lover   from Hettel's land must go ;
He bore upon his shoulders   a heavy load of woe :
To wreak his wrath on Hettel   would he now be choosing,
Yet feared he, if he harmed him,   that he the maiden's love
                             would then be losing.

'T was thus the daring Hartmut   the Hegeling kingdom left ;
Much he felt of sadness,   though not of hope bereft.
He knew not yet the ending   of his wooing of the maiden ;
For the sake of her, thereafter,   were helmets cleft, and many
                             sorrow-laden.

When he had reached his kingdom,   and home again did turn,
Where dwelt his father and mother,   Hartmut, grim and stern.
For war with Hettel longing,   began to make him ready.
Gerlind, the old she-devil,   at all times spurred him on
                             with hatred steady.

Tale the Twelfth.

HOW HERWIC MADE WAR ON HETTEL,
AND HOW GUDRUN WAS BETROTHED TO HIM.

WHAT more befell young Hartmut   we now forbear to say.
Upon the brave King Herwic   a weight of sorrow lay,
As great as that of Hartmut,   for love of the high-born lady.
He, with all his kinsmen,   to woo Gu-drun, as best they might,
made ready.

Near her he was dwelling,   and there he held his land.
A thousand times tho' daily   he should send to ask her hand,
Ever would his wooing   be met with scorn and flouting;
But though he now was thwarted,   later on her, as his wife,
he was fondly doting.

The king forbade him longer   to woo Gu-drun, his child;
Then sent he word in anger   that never would he yield:
Hettel should see him coming,   with men and shields, a-wooing;
And this to him and Hilda   would evil bring, that they
would long be ruing.

Whose rede it was I know not,   but thrice a thousand men,
Showing thus their friendship,   were soon with Herwic seen.
By them against the Hegelings   harm erelong was plotted
For the sake of the lovely maiden   he fondly hoped would be
to him allotted.

Those who came from Sturmland   the tale would not believe·,
To those from Denmark also   none the tidings gave;
But Irold, lord of Ortland,   soon the word was hearing
That now the daring Herwic   for warlike ends to Hettel's home
was faring.

When 't was known to Hettel   that Herwic, fearing naught,
E'en now the land was nearing,   and followers with him brought,
Then asked he of his kinsmen,   and of the queen, his lady:
" What say you to the tidings ?   I hear that guests to our home
have come already."

She said: " What can I answer,   but that 't is well and right,
When one such deeds is doing   as befit a worthy knight,
Tho' good or ill it bring us,   praise should they be earning.
Can aught amiss befall him ?   Herwic is wise, and aye for honor
yearning."

His queenly wife said further: " Yet must we beware,
That he may bring no burden   unto our kinsmen here.
This have many told me, —   't is for the sake of your daughter
That he with many warriors   has come into your borders,
o'er the water."

Hettel with his kinsmen   had waited a little too long:
The wrath of young King Herwic   now had waxen strong.
In the cool of the early morning,   he, with followers daring,
Reached King Hettel's castle,   and later with his men
the strife was sharing.

While yet the men were sleeping   within King Hettel's halls,
The watchman from the castle   down to them loudly calls:
" Up from your rest now, quickly !   Arm yourselves and listen !
Foes from abroad are coming !   E'en now, on their way, I see
the helmets glisten."

From off their beds upsprang they,   no longer dared they lie ;
Whoe'er there was among them,   in rank or low or high,
Must bear a heavy burden,   for life and honor caring.
Thus the young King Herwic   strove for a wife,
the storm of warfare daring.

Hettel and Queen Hilda   had now to the window come :
Men they saw with Herwic,   brought from a far-off home
Among the hills of Gâleis,   where they had their dwelling ;
These the mighty Morunc   in Wâleis knew, and oft of them
was telling.

The foes were seen by Hettel,   thronging towards the gate.
Well Gu-drun's brave father   must fear to meet their hate,
As they were rushing onward,   tho' high his heart was swelling :
Much they roused his anger,   but them his burghers helped
erelong in quelling.

Armed to guard the castle were a hundred men or more;
Hettel himself fought boldly, goodwill for this he bore.
His lieges all were doughty, but yet they could not save him;
Hard were the blows for Hettel, that in the fight the brave
young Herwic gave him.

Upon his foeman's helmet whizzing blasts, fire-hot,
Were struck by the daring Herwic. The many blows he smote
Gu-drun now saw with wonder, her eyes upon him feeding:
He seemed a knight most worthy, and love she felt, e'en though
her heart was bleeding.

Hettel bore his weapon grimly 'gainst his foe;
Of strength no less than riches he had, in truth, enow:
But soon he did unwisely, he pressed on him too nearly,
And those within the castle saw the fight between them
all too clearly.

The sore-beleaguered dwellers the gates would gladly shut;
But now their losses told them that this would nothing boot:
Friends as well as foemen near the gates were thronging,
And great was the hope of Herwic to win the maid for whom
his heart was longing.

Hettel then and Herwic against each other dashed,
In sight of all their followers; flames shot out and flashed
On the bosses of the bucklers which they both were wearing:
But little while it lasted, ere knowledge of each other
they were sharing.

When Hettel saw in Herwic   a warrior so proud,
And one so truly daring,   he cried to all aloud:
"Should any here forbid me   that I with him be friendly,
He knows the knight but little ;   deadly wounds he hews,
                    in mood unkindly."

Gu-drun, the lovely maiden,   looked on, and heard the din.
Luck is round and rolling,   like a ball, I ween ;
And since to end the fighting   to her it was not given,
She hoped that, when 't was over,   her father and his foe
                    would find their strength was even.

She then began to call to him,   from out the palace hall :
" Hettel, my noble father,   behold how blood doth fall,
From out the hauberks flowing !   Everywhere about us
The walls therewith are spattered !   A neighbor ill is Herwic,
                    and harm hath wrought us.

" If you would grant my wishes,   you now will be at peace ;
Give rest to heart from anger,   and let your fighting cease,
Till I can ask of Herwic,   and he to us be telling,
About his land and kingdom,   and where his nearest kinsmen
                    have their dwelling."

Then said the proud young Herwic :   " Not yet may peace begin,
Unless without my weapons   I your love may win.
If rest a while be granted,   the knowledge you are seeking
I then will give you freely,   and of my kinsmen will to you
                    be speaking."

Now, for love of the maiden,   the strife did they forego.
Then shook they off their armor,   each battle-weary foe,
And bathed in running waters,   from rusty stains to free them.
They soon were cheered and rested,   and none could grudge
                     in happy mood to see them.

A hundred knights with Herwic   went from the field to find
Gu-drun, the Hegeling maiden,   still wavering in her mind.
She, with other ladies,   gave him welcome kindly ;
But the worthy, high-born Herwic   hardly dared to think
                     their wishes friendly.

The fair and comely maiden   showed the guests their seats ;
The bravery of Herwic   erelong with love she meets :
His high and noble breeding   earned him kindest greeting.
'T was thought Gu-drun and Hilda   should grant his suit,
                     without a longer waiting.

To the ladies then spake Herwic :   " I oft have heard it said
That you of me speak lightly,   and think me lowly bred :
Your scorn may bring you sorrow,   after all my striving ;
The rich may from the poorest   a blessing gain, the while
                     with them they 're living."

She said : " Where is the maiden   who could behold with scorn
A knight who strove so bravely,   or from his love could turn ?
Believe me," said the maiden,   " I do not hold you lightly ;
Never maid more kindly   has looked on you, or prized
                     your worth more rightly.

" If now my friends and kindred   leave for this will give,
Even as you wish it,   with you I will gladly live."
Then with fondest glances   he her eye was seeking:
In her heart she bore him,   and owned the truth to all,
no falsehood speaking.

The brave and happy Herwic   begged that he might dare
To woo the fair young maiden.   Now to grant his prayer
Were Hettel and Hilda ready;   but first must they be knowing
Whether Gu-drun, their daughter,   was glad or sorry for the
kingly Herwic's wooing.

Herwic was quick in learning   how kindly was her mood:
And now the brave young warrior   before the maiden stood,
In shape as fair and comely   as if the hand of a master
On a white wall had drawn him: while there he stood her love
but grew the faster.

" If you your love will give me,"   he said, " most lovely maid,
Then shall my truest worship   to you be ever paid;
Throughout my lands and castles   to you there shall be given
My kinsmen's faithful service,   and ne'er shall I repent
that thus I 've striven."

She said: " I give you freely   the love for which you pray;
By all your toils and daring   you well have earned to-day
That you and all my kindred   foes shall be no longer.
Now none can make me sorrow,   and every day our bliss
shall grow the stronger."

Then they sent for Hettel: thus ended was the fight.
Soon came he to his daughter; and many a faithful knight
Followed the king, their master, who unto him had ridden
From all the Hegeling kingdom. Thus to the strife a long
                 farewell was bidden.

Now when Hettel's kinsmen their wish for this did speak,
Then asked he of his daughter if she would gladly take
Herwic, the knight so noble, who in his heart had set her.
Then said the lovely maiden: "There's not another I could
                 love the better."

They then betrothed the maiden at once to the knightly king,
Who in his land would crown her. This did gladness bring
To him, and sorrow likewise: ere many years were ended,
And she to him was wedded, good knights in stormy fight
                 their lives defended.

To take the maiden with him Herwic now was fain;
But this her mother grudged him: thereby much woe and pain
Came upon him later from foes as yet unheeded.
The king was told by Hilda that longer time ere she be
                 crowned was needed.

They thought it best for Herwic to leave the maiden there,
While he with other women might pass the time elsewhere,
And wait to wed the lady until a year were ended.
This learned the men of Alzabie: to wait so long for her
                 young Herwic ill befriended.

Tale the Thirteenth.

HOW SIEGFRIED MADE WAR AGAINST HERWIC.

SIEGFRIED, king of Moorland, called for all his men ;
　　Ships were soon made ready, wherever they were seen ;
Then with food and weapons to load them it was bidden,
For war against King Herwic : from all but faithful friends
　　　　　　　　　　　　　　his thoughts were hidden.

A score of wide, strong barges bade he to be made.
I ween they liked it little to whom the king now said
That forthwith unto Sealand to fight must they be faring ;
And he would thither hasten as soon as, winter o'er,
　　　　　　　　　　　　　　springtide was nearing.

Eighty thousand warriors soon to him had come ;
Of fighting men in Alzabie none were left at home.
Then swore the Moorland princes for war to make them ready ;
Some of these still lingered, others to follow with the king
　　　　　　　　　　　　　　were speedy.

Then against the Sealands   the threat of war he made.
This roused the wrath of Herwic,   who well might him upbraid;
To earn the hate of Siegfried   wrong had he done him never.
His marches and his castles   he bade his men to guard,
now more than ever.

Then he said in sorrow   to friends who came in haste
That foes would burn his castles,   and his lands lay waste:
All he could give his liegemen,   that he held but lightly.
They took their wages gladly;   that war would bring them
riches, hoped they rightly.

About the gladsome May-time,   there went across the sea
Warriors out of Alzabie,   and eke from Abakie.
Onward came they proudly,   as tho' the world's end seeking;
Many now trod boldly   who in the dust their rest would soon
be taking.

Into the land of Herwic   they cast the burning brand.
Then all whom he could gather,   and all his friends at hand,
Rode to the field with Herwic.   Thro' war-storms grimly driven,
They with their lives must bargain   for gold and gems
and silver to them given.

To him, the king of Sealand,   great ill erelong was wrought.
A stalwart foeman was he: Aha, how well he fought!
He made the land the richer   with the dead there lying:
The old in fight grew youthful: the strong were slain,
who recked not yet of dying.

Long the fighting lasted,   till thickly lay the dead:
Then to the brave King Herwic   came at last the need
To flee into his marches,   for life he there was turning;
All his lands lay smoking: of this to Gu-drun, his lady,
                         sent he warning.

Now to the land of Hettel   men at his bidding went:
Many tears and bitter   they shed when they were sent
To find the great King Hettel,   and the tale to him to carry.
They were not long in showing   unto the king their plight
                         so hard and dreary.

Tho' sad in mood he found them,   a welcome kind he gave,
Such as far-off wanderers   and homeless friends should have.
He asked if from their homesteads   they were hither driven,
When foes their lands had wasted,   and all their marches had
                         to flames been given.

Then to him they answered: "In sorrow did we leave:
The faithful men of Herwic,   from early morn till eve,
Sell their lives full dearly,   and well his gifts are earning;
They fight for name and honor: for this at home are many
                         women mourning."

Then to them said Hettel: "To my daughter make it known;
Whatever she shall wish for   at once shall that be done.
If she for vengeance calleth   for the wrongs he wrought you,
We then will help you gladly,   and pay him back the ill that he
                         has brought you."

Before they yet had spoken   unto the fair young maid,
Already of her sorrow   her friends had taken heed.
The lady had been longing   to see the heralds hourly;
Them in haste she sent for,   the loss of land and honor,
                    mourning sorely.

When they came before her,   they found the queenly maid
Sitting sad, and weeping, —   faithful love she had;
She asked them of her lover,   and how they leave had taken,
And if he still was living   when they of late had land and home
                    forsaken.

Then answered one among them: " We left him sound and well;
But since the day we saw him   we know not what befell,
Or how the men of Moorland   may his home have wasted:
Mischief they had done him,   neither from fire and plunder
                    had they rested.

" Listen, high-born maiden !   my master's bidding heed:
He and all his warriors   are now in sorest need.
To lose both life and honor   they are fearing daily;
And now my lord, King Herwic,   sends to beg your men
                    to his help to rally."

Gudrun, the lovely maiden,   then from her seat upstood;
The wrongs that had been done her   she to her father showed:
She said her men were slaughtered,   and her castles wasted,
And told her father, Hettel,   that to ride to Herwic's help
                    she would he had hasted.

Then in her arms she pressed him,   her eyes with weeping wet:
" Help, O dearest father !   My woes are all too great,
Unless your many liegemen,   with ready hand, are willing
To help my good friend Herwic :   none else can end the strife,
my sorrow healing."

" That will I leave to no one,"   the king did freely say ;
" I will haste to help King Herwic,   and wait not many a day.
As well as I am able,   I will end your sorrow :
I will call for the aged Wâ-te   and many other friends,
before the morrow.

" He will bring from Sturmland   all the men of his lands ;
And when 't is known by Morunc   how ill with us it stands,
Fighters full a thousand   to bring will he be speedy.
Our foes shall find out quickly,   that under helmets we
to march are ready.

" Horant, too, from Denmark   shall bring upon the way
Of men full thrice a thousand :   nor will Irold stay ;
But he will raise his banner,   and hasten to the slaughter.
Then, too, thy brother Ortwin   will come, and all will earn
the blessing of my daughter."

The heralds soon went riding   whom the maid did send.
Her friends far off were living,   but all who help would lend
To heal the maiden's sorrow   would honor great be earning ;
Knights would she warmly welcome :   for this erelong the more
to her were turning.

Hilda, the maiden's mother,   unto her daughter spake:
" Whoe'er is quick to help you,   and now his shield shall take
To follow with your warriors   when they to war are faring,
Whate'er we gain by fighting   he shall, in truth, henceforth
                      with us be sharing."

Then the chests were opened;   men to court soon bore
Whate'er therein was lying,   of fighting-gear a store,
Fast with steel well studded;   then the knights were laden
With armor white as silver: this made glad the heart
                      of the queenly maiden.

To full a thousand warriors   were given clothes and steeds:
Out of stalls men brought them,   as oft the horse one leads.
When, along the highways,   men to the fight go riding.
Of all the king's good horses   they left but very few at rest
                      abiding.

When from his queenly lady   the king his leave did take,
Both Hilda and her daughter   began to weep for his sake;
But on the knights forth riding   gladly they were gazing.
And said: " May God in heaven   so help the fight that men
                      may you be praising."

After they all were gathered   without the castle gate,
Youths were there heard singing,   hoping for plunder great.
Each thought, by hardest fighting,   to win himself much riches:
But far must they yet be riding,   for long the way to their
                      master's foemen stretches.

On the third morning early   came, at break of day,
The very aged Wâ-te   with a thousand to the fray;
And from the Danish kingdom,   as the seventh day was dawning,
Came Horant with four thousand,   to whom the fair Gu-drun
                        had sent her warning.

From out the Waalisch marches   Morune thither rode;
He ever fought for the ladies,   for the love to them he owed.
Twenty thousand warriors   he brought, — for nought he tarried:
These were all well-weaponed,   and happily rode, while help
                        to the king they carried.

The queenly maiden's brother,   Ortwin, the youthful knight,
Brought across the water,   to help her in the fight,
Forty hundred warriors,   or even a number greater:
Were it known to the men of Alzabie,   well might they have
                        feared to meet him later.

Before they yet could help him,   to Herwic and his men
The strife had now gone badly,   his luck began to wane:
To him and all his followers   was evil sore betiding;
Altho' they struggled bravely,   his foes too near his castle gate
                        were riding.

Great mishaps to Herwic   from Siegfried's kin arose;
For now the gates of the castle   were shattered by their blows.
False friends had made it easy,   and boasts too loudly spoken:
If e'er to such one trusteth,   it worketh him no good,
                        and his hopes are broken.

Now 't was told to Herwic,   men fast for help had gone.
The foes from fight ne'er rested,   by anger driven on;
From early morn to even,   they oft to the strife were bidden:
But now the friends of Herwic   on every side drew near,
nor long lay hidden.

When this the men of Karadie   did learn, they well might fear
That now two kings against them   in the fight should share:
For them it was unlucky   that Hettel now was leading
His many fighters thither;   he from afar had come, to Herwic
speeding.

Friends were they to each other;   so both would meet the foe.
These, the men from Moorland,   bold themselves did show:
One saw by all their bearing   they would from none be flying;
Those who with them struggled   by hardest toil must their
reward be buying.

Wâ-te, the very daring,   with all his knights had come;
Gu-drun, the lovely lady,   had called him from his home
To help her lover, Herwic,   and a host had ridden hither:
Whate'er might now befall them,   later full happy rode they
thence together.

Although their foes were heathen,   from out the Moorish land,
They might not back be driven: one well might understand
That in any earthly kingdom   they were the best and boldest.
To all who came to meet them   they gave a sorry welcome
and a shelter coldest.

Herwic, king of Sealand, his loss would now make good
Upon his foes from Alzabie. For this must flow the blood
On either side of many; to friends and kin were given
Wounds full fast and heavy: to bear his own was hard
        for Hettel even.

When they had come together of whom I spoke before,
Bringing all their followers, gladness they knew no more;
On them were ever resting heavy care and sorrow
For what the night might bring them. They thought:
      " How shall we live to see the morrow? "

Thrice with the Moorish foemen they strove on the stormy field,
While peace was given the castle, as knights are wont to yield.
Again with sword and spear-shaft they the strife would settle:
Peace not yet they wished for, but wounds the more they got
       in hard-fought battle.

Nor Herwic's men nor Siegfried's yet would leave the fight;
They to the last had struggled, and many a bravest knight
Upon the field lay wounded, or in death was sleeping.
This was told to the women, who now began a wild, unmeasured
        weeping.

How well the daring Wâ-te in battle-storm did fight!
Strong was he and skilful, and oft the aged knight
Gave to the foe heart-sorrow, by all the ill he wrought him:
Ever to fight with his warriors, by the side of the boldest
       and best, his wishes taught him.

Horant, too, from Denmark,   brave was he enough !
Beneath his hand were shattered   helmets strong and tough:
Ne'er by him 't was forgotten   to wear his armor shining ;
Ill he wrought to many,   and oft the ranks of his foemen
                           he was thinning.

The quick and fearless Morunc   boldly stretched his hand
Ofttimes beyond his buckler,   and oft the fight he gained.
To shun the king of Moorland   ne'er would he be seeking ;
Upon that king, so mighty,   he the wrath of Herwic now was
                           wreaking.

The great and doughty Hettel,   when that his daughter fair
Had sent to beg her father   in Herwic's fight to share,
That peace at last might follow,   fought for him not idly :
If life were dear to any,   't were best to shun King Hettel's
                           borders widely.

Bravely strove King Herwic   on the field and at the gate ;
None than he fought better.   His head was often wet,
Beneath his armor dripping,   with sweat that fast was oozing.
In death were many deafened ;   they who would crush him must
                           their lives be losing.

Wigalois, the faithful,   great ill to many wrought.
Sir Fru-te, too, from Daneland,   with knightly prowess fought:
The thanks of all his fellows   he should of right be sharing ;
He strove where the fight was stormy,   and none e'er knew
                           an aged knight so daring.

The lord who came from Ortland,   Ortwin, brave and young,
Showed the hand of a warrior;   it was on many a tongue,
That never man in warfare   bore himself more boldly:
Wounds he gave the deepest,   and this by none was ever told of
                         coldly.

For twelve long days of fighting,   earnestly they strove.
The men led on by Hettel   oft their spear-shafts drove
Thro' their foes' light bucklers,   as close they met together:
The fighters proud from Moorland   sorely rued the day that
                     brought them thither.

Upon the thirteenth morning,   ere early mass was said,
With sorry heart spake Siegfried: " How many here lie dead
Of all our bravest warriors!   In his lofty wooing
The king of Sealand also   here to himself has evil great
                       been doing."

Then to the men of Karadie   made he known his will,
To a stronghold to betake them,   there their wounds to heal:
They, with those from Alzabie,   were earnest to go thither;
Right glad were these far-riders   that all in death might not
                      be found together.

Then to a sheltering castle   to turn they all began,
Where onward, fast beside it,   a wide, deep river ran.
While they were thither riding,   fleeing away from danger,
They were still seen fighting   with those who ne'er would yield
                     their homes to a stranger.

Now against King Hettel   the king of Moorland rode:
Well might one believe it,   his former warlike mood
Was but a slight beginning;   he soon a foe was meeting
Who many of his kinsmen   with deep and deadly wounds of late
was greeting.

Hettel, he of the Hegelings,   and Siegfried, the Moorland king,
There unto the struggle   all their strength did bring;
Shields were hacked to pieces   by the swords they wielded:
The mighty lord of Moorland   to the castle fled, nor to him
of Daneland yielded.

Camps by the men from Denmark   for themselves were made:
Then the beleaguered warriors, —   it cannot be gainsaid, —
E'er many days were over,   with care were burdened sadly;
However good their shelter,   all would then have been at home
more gladly.

Thus the boastful fighters   were by the focman's hand
Fast held within the stronghold;   nor was their knightly band
Now able to give battle,   although for this yet longing.
Their castle well they guarded,   as best they might, wherein
they now were thronging.

Tale the Fourteenth.

HOW HETTEL SENT TIDINGS FROM HERWIC'S LAND.

HETTEL then sent tidings,   to still their fears at home.
  To the fair and high-born ladies   men with news did come,
That unto the old and youthful,   throughout the stormy fighting,
Good luck had aye befallen;   and now, with hope must they
                              for them be waiting.

He bade his men to tell them   how Siegfried was besieged,
While he with all his followers   war against him waged,
To help the lord of Sealand,   loved by Gu-drun, his daughter;
That all, as they were able,   daily fought for her, and for him
                              who sought her.

Hettel's queen, fair Hilda,   the hope began to have
That luck would follow Herwic   and all his warriors brave;
And, as their worth befitted,   all might well be speeding.
Then said Gu-drun: " God grant it,   that they our friends may
                              back in health be leading."

By Wâ-te's men from Sturmland,   the foes from Alzabie
And all who came from Moorland   were kept away from the sea ;
Sadly must they tarry   within the sheltering castle :
In Wâ-te and in Fru-te   foes they had with whom they ill
                                              could wrestle.

Loudly swore King Hettel   the castle ne'er to leave ;
That he and all his followers   still to the end would strive,
Till those to him had yielded   who now the Moor befriended.
Unwise had been their inroad,   and this for them one day
                                              in sorrow ended.

Meanwhile the spies of Hartmut,   whom he had thither sent,
Tho' little good they looked for,   from the Norman border went ;
Ever to learn what happened   they a watch were keeping,
And from the stormy warfare   they hoped that Hettel might
                                              no gain be reaping.

Now they saw that Siegfried,   the Moorland king high-born,
Was kept within the castle,   besieged both eve and morn ;
Thence could he sally never,   and this he knew with sorrow ;
His lands so far were lying,   he little help from them
                                              could hope to borrow.

The Norman errand-bearers,   sent forth their watch to make
By Ludwig and young Hartmut,   to them now hastened back :
The happy news they carried,   and soon at home were giving,
That Hettel, the king, and Herwic   were busy now, in warfare
                                              ever striving.

To them the lord of Normandy   thanks for the tidings gave,
And asked them : “Can you tell us   how long those foemen brave,
The men from the land of Karadie,   will in Sealand tarry,
Fighting ’gainst its warriors,   till they, their wrongs avenged,
of war are weary ?”

One of them made answer :   “The truth you now may hear :
There they yet must linger   more than another year.
Never from their stronghold   will the Hegelings free them ;
They there so well are guarded,   that on their homeward way
none e’er shall see them.”

Then the knight of Normandy,   the daring Hartmut, spake :
“This frees my heart from sorrow,   and hope in me doth wake !
If they are now beleaguered,   then are we well befriended ;
We must to Hegeling hasten,   ere Hettel’s fight with Siegfried
shall be ended.”

Ludwig and young Hartmut   had both the selfsame mind, —
Had they ten thousand fighters   whom they at once could find,
Gu-drun they might lay hold on,   and to their home might carry,
Before her father, Hettel,   came back again from the land
where he did tarry.

Hartmut’s mother, Gerlind,   earnestly gave thought
To wreak her wrath on Hettel,   that he to harm be brought,
Because her dear son Hartmut   he shamefully had slighted.
She wished the aged Wâ-te   and Fru-te might be hanged,
for the help they plighted.

Then spake the old she-devil : " Good knights, your hire behold !
If you will now ride thither,   my silver and my gold,
That will I give you freely, —   but women shall not share it.
I care not if Hettel and Hilda   shall rue their wrong, and
ne'er again will dare it."

Quoth Ludwig, Hartmut's father :   " We from our Norman land
Forthwith must make an inroad :   soon will I have at hand
Twenty thousand fighters   whom I for war will gather ;
With these it will be easy   to seize Gu-drun, and bear her
from her father."

Then spake the youthful Hartmut :   " Might ever this betide,
That Hilda's lovely daughter   I here should see my bride,
I would not take in barter   for that a princedom fairest ;
Then might we here together   pass our lives, each one
to the other dearest."

Busily his followers,   hour by hour, gave thought
How they could do his wishes.   A host King Ludwig brought
To lead against the Hegelings ;   well were they outfitted.
How should Hilda know it,   that soon thereby her welfare
would be blighted ?

The wife of Ludwig also   helped them as she could.
For this she plotted ever,   that fair Gu-drun be wooed,
And, as the bride of Hartmut,   to Normandy be carried ;
She did her best most busily   that the maid one day should
to her son be married.

Ludwig said to Hartmut,   his well belovéd son :
" Think well, O knight most worthy,   no toil we now must shun,
Until our foes are mastered   and from their lands are driven.
Reward the guests who help us ;   to our men at home by me
                         shall gifts be given."

These they soon were sharing,   all and every one.
Never yet in Suabia   gifts so rich were known,
Of steeds for war or burden,   saddles, and shields fair shining ;
I ween they were gladly given :   Ludwig ne'er before such
                         thanks was winning.

Quickly all made ready   to start upon their way.
Sailors were found by Ludwig ;   skilful men were they,
Who the deep sea-pathways   knew, and well could follow ;
Hard must they be toiling   to win their wages high
                         upon the billow.

Now, in seemly measure,   fit were they to go.
Throughout the lands and highways   soon the news did grow
That Ludwig and young Hartmut   home and land were leaving.
They yet would see much sorrow,   when they erelong their
                         Hegeling foe were braving.

When to the shore they had ridden,   ships were floating there,
That workmen well had builded,   the knights away to bear ;
Gerlind's gold and riches   had made them strong and steady.
Nor Wâ-te the old nor Fru-te   of this knew aught, nor were
                         for their coming ready.

With three and twenty thousand   they sailed the waters o'er.
Now for Gu-drun young Hartmut   a weight of sorrow bore:
This, before his followers,   to hide he was not earnest;
He hoped to meet King Hettel,   and him to overcome in strife
the sternest.

As yet they knew not fully   how they his land could reach.
To the sons of many a mother   the raid did sorrow teach.
Near to the shores of Ortland   the rolling billows bore them,
Before 't was known to Hettel: now Hilda's castle rose
in sight before them.

The warriors led by Hartmut   were still twelve miles away;
Yet had they come already   over the wide, deep sea,
Unto the land of the Hegelings,   and to its shores so nearly
That castles, towers, and palaces   in Hilda's town they all
could see most clearly.

Ludwig, king of Normandy,   bade that on the sand
They now should drop the anchors;   he then gave word to land
To all his men together,   and bade them do it quickly:
They now had come so near them,   they feared the Hegeling
bands would gather thickly.

Then bore they up the weapons,   with shields and helmets good,
That they had with them carried   over the heaving flood:
They to fight made ready;   yet they at first bethought them
To send through the land their runners,   to learn if friendly
helpers might be brought them.

Tale the Fifteenth.

HOW HARTMUT CARRIED AWAY GUDRUN.

Now at Hartmut's bidding   heralds quickly rode
    To where the queenly Hilda   and her daughter dear abode.
To them his word they carried,   that if to wed the maiden
They should think him worthy,   her and her mother both
                         it well might gladden.

If she her love would give him,   as he had asked before, —
Ofttimes his heart was heavy   for the love to her he bore, —
That he would ever serve her   so long as he was living,
And many lands wide-reaching,   held of his father, would to
                         her be giving.

But if she would not love him,   she then would earn his hate;
He asked of her that kindly   she his love would meet,
So that he to his fatherland   his lovely bride might carry
Without a fight or struggle.   To hope for this brave Hartmut
                         ne'er was weary.

Did she gainsay his wooing,　Hartmut sent this word :
" I will not be bought with silver,　albeit a heavy hoard,
To leave in peace her kingdom ;　she yet shall give me heeding.
I will show Gu-drun, fair maiden,　brave knights enough, to be
　　　　　　　　　　for her eyes fine feeding !

" Further, good errand-bearers,　this say to her from me :
I ne'er will leave her borders　to sail on the wide, deep sea ;
Better will I think it　to be hewn in pieces even,
Unless the Hegeling maiden　will follow me hence, to me
　　　　　　　　　　in wedlock given.

" But, should she scorn me wholly,　and never my bride will be,
Then me, with my daring fighters,　riding here she will see.
Before the Hegeling castle　I will then leave lying
Twenty thousand warriors,　on both sides of the roadway, dead
　　　　　　　　　　or dying.

" Since by the craft of Wigaleis　King Hettel has been led,
And by the aged Wâ-te,　hither our way we 've made
Into the Hegeling kingdom,　time and toil thus spending ;
For this shall many be fatherless,　and glad shall I be
　　　　　　　　　　of the whole to make an ending."

Those sent forth by Hartmut　fast on their way did ride,
For he bade them wait no longer.　They came to a castle wide,
By name ycleped Matelan ;　therein was Hilda dwelling,
And with her was her daughter,　the maid about whose charms
　　　　　　　　　　all men were telling.

With them sent Hartmut also   two earls of wealth and name,
Who with him out of Normandy   over the waters came.
He bade them see Queen Hilda,   and kindly to bespeak her ;
To pledge to her his friendship,   and say that his goodwill
                       would ne'er forsake her.

Of her they must ask her daughter,   for him who in his mind
So high had ever set her,   above all womankind :
In worthy love he wooed her,   and she would rank be taking
That for aye would make her happy ;   to do her will she ne'er
                       would find him lacking.

To the maiden's waiting-women   the news was quickly told,
That from out the land of Normandy   a band of wooers bold
Hither rode to Matelan,   and for Gu-drun were suing :
Hilda hushed the tidings,   for now Gu-drun in fright the tale
                       was ruing.

Queen Hilda's faithful warders   opened soon the gate ;
Those who had ridden thither   need no longer wait ;
They to come in were bidden.   The gate was thrown wide open,
And the men sent there by Hartmut   into Matelan rode :
                       no ill to them did happen.

They quickly told their wishes,   to see King Hettel's wife.
It was not yet allowed them ;   they who should guard her life,
And to the king must answer,   at first had this forbidden :
They never left uncared for   Hilda the queen, and eke Gu-drun
                       the maiden.

At last the men of Hartmut   into the hall were led.
To them the queenly Hilda   kindly greeting made,
As did Gu-drun the lady,   with fair and lofty bearing;
But she, the high-born maiden,   love for Herwic in her heart
               was wearing.

Altho' they felt unfriendly,   yet drink they gave to the men
Ere yet they told their errand;   freely then the queen
Bade them to be seated   before herself and her daughter.
She begged them then to tell her: " What boon to seek had
               brought them o'er the water ? "

All the men of Hartmut   before their seats yet stood,
As well-bred men beseemeth,   and errand-bearers should.
Then they told the ladies   what they would there be doing, —
That for their master, Hartmut,   they for the fair Gu-drun
               had come a-wooing.

The high-born maiden answered: " Of this I nought will hear, —
That with the young King Hartmut   I the crown should share,
Before our friendly kinsmen,   and troth to him be plighted:
The name of the knight is Herwic   whose love shall never
               by myself be slighted.

" To him I am betrothed;   me he chose for a wife,
And him for myself I have taken.   Ever, throughout his life,
All of good I wish him   that can henceforth befall him:
Ne'er, till my days are ended,   will I ask the love of another,
               or my lord will call him."

One of them then answered: "This warning Hartmut gives:
If nay shall be your answer,   before three days, if he lives,
Against great Matelan castle   you shall see him leading
All his knightly followers."   Smiles at this were the maiden's
                            face o'erspreading.

Their leave they would be taking,   and hasten on their way,
Those two great earls so haughty;   but Hilda bade them stay.
Altho' she ne'er had known them,   of gifts she was not chary;
But yet they would not take them,   for crafty men were they,
                            and in truth were wary.

At those sent there by Hartmut   Hettel's followers sneered,
And said, their scorn and anger   they very little feared:
If to drink the wine of Hettel   they were, in truth, unwilling,
Then this warning gave they: that they their cup with blood
                            would soon be filling.

When they had heard this answer,   back to the shore they went
Whence they had been by Hartmut   upon their errand sent.
He then ran forth to meet them,   to ask how they were treated,
And what had them befallen,   and how his courtship by Gu-drun
                            was greeted.

Then one of them thus answered: "This to us they said:
The high and queenly maiden   a lover long has had,
For whom, beyond all others,   love in her heart she is feeling:
If you will not taste their wine-cup,   they soon will fill to you,
                            your life-blood spilling."

"Ah, woe is me!" said Hartmut,   when he this answer heard;
"My heart is full of anger,   with shame I hear your word!
Never men more friendly   shall I need, till I am dying,
Than those who now will help me."   Straightway his men
                       upsprang, on the shore then lying.

Ludwig now and Hartmut,   with their men, set out for war;
Their banners high uplifted   in pride and wrath they bore.
These from Matelan castle   were seen afar to shimmer:
"Cheer up!" then said the maiden;   "Herwic and Hettel come!
                       their weapons glimmer!"

But Hilda saw the standard   bore not King Hettel's mark:
"Ah, woe shall now betide us   before this day grows dark!
To seek Gu-drun are coming   foemen grim and daring;
Many a well-made helmet   their blows shall hew before
                       the night is nearing."

Then her friendly Hegelings   thus to Hilda spake:
"If those led on by Hartmut   to-day an onslaught make,
Wounds we then must deal them,   and show we are the stronger."
Queen Hilda then gave bidding   to shut the castle gates,
                       and wait no longer.

But the men of brave King Hettel   followed not her hest;
They who the castle guarded   thought to fight their best.
They bade that now their banners   to the shafts be fastened;
King Hettel's daring followers,   to slay his foes, from out
                       the castle hastened.

The bars that should be lowered,   to keep the foemen out,
Were left, in over-boldness,   and the gates not fully shut,
Since from Hartmut's foreguard   they little harm foreboded.
But when they pressed in boldly,   then came the rest, who
                         ever on them crowded.

A thousand men or over   stood before the gate;
These, their swords upbearing,   the fight did there await.
A thousand more with Hartmut   now came thronging thickly;
They then from their steeds alighted,   and back to the rear
                         they sent their horses quickly.

Spears in hand they carried,   with points full keen to cut.
Who could shun their onset?   With heavy wounds they smote
Those who the castle guarded,   in their pride o'erweening.
Just at the hour came Ludwig,   with his Norman knights,
                         as the fight was now beginning.

Much the women sorrowed   as Ludwig nearer rode:
The banners o'er them floating   well and proudly showed
The fearless foe oncoming;   beneath each standard flocking,
Three thousand now came boldly,   tho' sad on their homeward way
                         they might yet be looking.

Before the walls beleaguered   the guards were a busy band:
Never hardier fighters   were seen in any land
Than were the faithful warders   in Hettel's castle dwelling;
Their blows they were thickly dealing,   and Hartmut's men
                         their strength were quickly feeling.

Ludwig, Hartmut's father,   the Norman king, was seen
From hardened rims of bucklers   to strike a fiery sheen :
Truly, great was the bravery   that now his heart was swelling ;
His friends and followers also,   in the bloody game, were bold
beyond all telling.

When they who the castle guarded   hoped for rest and peace,
Then their daring foemen   did nearer to them press,
Led by him of Normandy :   the youthful Hartmut's father
Grudged no toil to help him ;   and this from that day's fight
one well might gather.

Now the trustful warders   began in truth to mourn,
That they, 'gainst Hilda's bidding,   had their care forborne, —
The hest of the wife of Hettel,   the high and worthy lady.
For this their shields were shattered,   and many a life
was lost, in fight too ready.

Ludwig now and Hartmut   on the field had met,
And, holding speech together,   learned that, striving yet,
Queen Hilda's men were seeking   the castle gates to fasten ;
Then, with shields before them,   to bear their flags within
they all did hasten.

Rocks were hurled from the castle,   and many spears were thrown,
But the foe it hurt but little,   and his daring lessened none.
Little thought was given   to the dead around them lying :
With heavy stones down beaten,   many bold besiegers there
fell dying.

When Hartmut and King Ludwig   came within the gate,
Many, badly wounded,   from them their death-stroke met.
For this the lovely maiden   began to sorrow sorely ;
Now in Hettel's castle   the woe they wrought was growing
greater hourly.

Then the king of Normandy   was glad enough, I ween,
When to the halls of Hettel   he could lead his men,
Bearing well their weapons :   soon his banner fluttered
Over the roof of the castle.   Hilda at this her sorrow
loudly uttered.

Greatly do I wonder   what might these guests befall,
Had now the grim old Wâ-te   been there, and seen it all,
The while the men of Hartmut,   with Ludwig, brave and daring,
Thro' the halls were rushing,   and from her home the fair
Gu-drun were tearing.

Both Wâ-te and King Hettel,   if to them that day
A warning had been given,   would stoutly have barred the way ;
They their foemen's helmets   with swords would so have riven
That back to their homes in Normandy,   without Gu-drun, would
they have soon been driven.

Now within the castle   were all in saddest mood ;
So men to-day might sorrow.   Whate'er the foemen would,
There did they lay hands on,   and took from out the dwelling.
Rich grew Hartmut's followers, —   you well may trust that I
the truth am telling.

Then came the bold young Hartmut   where he Gu-drun could see,
And said: "Most worthy lady,   you erst looked down on me;
But now both I and my followers   think of your kin so little,
We will not seize and hold them,   but slay and hang them,
so the strife to settle."

Then said the maiden only: "Alas! O father mine,
Had you of this been knowing,   that I, a child of thine,
One day from out your kingdom   would thus by foes be stolen,
Never to me, poor maiden,   such woe and sorry shame had here
befallen."

Then was the gold and clothing   borne out by the robber band:
Forth they took Queen Hilda,   led by her snow-white hand.
Matelan's goodly castle   they would have burned up gladly;
For what became of the dwellers   the Normans never cared, nor
thought of sadly.

But Hartmut now had bidden   that it should not be burned.
To leave the land he hastened,   and home again he turned,
Before 't was known to Hettel,   who with his men was lying
Within the Waalisch marches,   and there against his foe
his strength was trying.

"Leave your stolen booty!"   to his men young Hartmut said;
"At home my father's riches   will I give to you instead:
Thus o'er the watery pathway   our sail will be the lighter."
To Gu-drun the hand of Ludwig   brought a heavy wrong,
and woe full bitter.

They overthrew the castle,   the town with fire they burned;
From it the best was taken;   with wealth they homeward turned:
Two and sixty women   thence with them they carried,
And many lovely maidens.   With heartfelt woe was queenly
Hilda wearied.

How were they filled with sadness   to leave the wine behind!
Now did the queenly mother   a seat in the window find,
And looked upon her daughter,   from home in sorrow turning.
Many a stately lady   the Normans left in tears, and
bitterly mourning.

Weeping now and wailing   was heard on either hand;
No one there was happy,   when from the father-land
The foe with Hilda's daughter   and with her maidens hasted.
Many, now but children,   for this, when men, to work them woe
ne'er rested.

Those who were seized by Hartmut   down to the shore he took;
All their lands were wasted;   their homes went up in smoke.
Now his hopes and wishes   happily were granted:
Both Gu-drun and Hildeburg   he with him carried off, —
the prize he wanted.

Well he knew that Hettel   was many a league away,
And war was grimly waging;   no more would Hartmut stay.
Yet from the Hegeling kingdom   no whit too fast he speeded,
For word was sent by Hilda   to Hettel and his friends, that
much their help was needed.

How mournful were the tidings   before the king she laid! —
That in his home and castle   his knights were lying dead,
Or else were left by Hartmut   now with death-wounds bleeding;
That foes had seized his daughter,   and with her many maids
                 were homeward speeding.

She said: "Now tell King Hettel   that I am here alone;
Evil hath me o'ertaken,   and now, with pride o'ergrown,
Our mighty foeman, Ludwig,   back to his land is faring;
A thousand men or better   lie at our gates, and the pains
                 of death are bearing."

Quickly then went Hartmut,   and, ere three days were o'er,
On board his keels was ready;   these the plunder bore,
As much as they could carry,   whate'er his men had stolen.
The men of brave King Hettel   were dazed and stunned by all
                 that had befallen.

What further did betide them,   who in truth can tell?
Loud on the ear it sounded,   as they shifted the flapping sail,
And away from the Hegeling kingdom,   unto an isle forsaken,
They their barks were turning;   the name of Wulpensand — or
                 shore of the wolves — it had taken.

Tale the Sixteenth.

HOW HILDA SENT TO HETTEL AND HERWIC TO ASK THEIR
HELP AGAINST HARTMUT.

THE fair and queenly Hilda,   with all her will and mind,
   Gave her thoughts now wholly   trusty men to find
To bear the tale to Hettel.   Her heart indeed was riven
By the wrongful deeds of Hartmut,   and food for tears he
                              to her eyes had given.

To Herwic and her husband   she bade that it be said
That foes had seized her daughter,   that many knights lay dead ;
And she was left in wretchedness,   lonely and forsaken ;
That all her gold and jewels   the Normans on their way had
                              with them taken.

Quickly rode the heralds   and through the land they went:
The queen in greatest sorrow   these on their way had sent.
Upon the seventh morning,   they came where they were greeted
With the sight of beleaguering Hegelings   who before their
                              Moorland foes were seated.

Oft in knightly matches   strove they every day,
And one might also hear them   at many a game and play,
That they might not be weary   who the siege were keeping;
Some at a mark were shooting,   and others strove in running
                     and in leaping.

When by the Danish Horant   errand-bearers were seen
Who to the land were coming,   thither sent by the queen,
Then said he unto Hettel :   " With news for us they 're riding ;
May God in kindness grant it,   no ill to those at home is now
                     betiding ! "

The king himself went forward,   and met them where they stood.
He said, with seemly bearing,   to them in their sorry mood :
" Brave knights, I give you welcome   here to this far-off border.
How fares it with Queen Hilda ?   Who sent you here ? and who
                     is left to guard her ? "

Said one : " Your lady sent us ;   to you for help she turns :
Wasted are your castles ;   your lands the foeman burns.
Gu-drun from thence is carried ;   her maidens, too, are taken :
Never can your kingdom   from all these woes and ills again
                     awaken.

" This must I say, moreover,   we are in straitest need ;
Now of your men and kindred   a thousand there lie dead ;
And into far-off kingdoms   have foes your riches carried ;
Your hoard of wealth is scattered :   it shames good knights
                     that thus your lands are harried."

The king then bade them tell him   who these deeds had done.
One among them answered,   and their names to him made known :
"Ludwig was one, the Norman ;   with many knights he fought us ;
Hartmut, his son, was the other :   't was they the inroad made,
                        and havoc wrought us."

Then King Hettel answered :   "To Hartmut I would not give,
For his bride, Gu-drun my daughter ;   for this he now doth strive
To waste with war my kingdom.   I know his lands are holden
Of Hagen, her mother's father ;   to woo her should his rank
                        not him embolden.

"To our beleaguered foemen   we nought of this must tell,
And to our friends but whisper   the ills that us befell ;
We then must call our kinsmen   hither to be hasting.
Worse could never happen   unto good knights at home,
                        from warfare resting."

Herwic then was bidden   to Hettel forthwith to go :
Hettel's friends and kindred   and his men were sent for, too.
When now these knights so worthy   their way to him had taken.
They found their king and master   dark in mind, and of
                        every hope forsaken.

Then said the lord of the Hegelings :   "To you I make my moan ;
And, trusting in your friendship,   my sorrows must I own :
The queen, my Lady Hilda,   has sent to give us warning,
That the men of the Hegeling kingdom   are ill bestead, and
                        bitterly are mourning.

“ My lands with fire are wasted,   and my castle broken down ;
Ill our walls were guarded   while we from home were gone :
Foes have seized my daughter ;   my kin in death are sleeping ;
My trusty men are slaughtered   to whom I left my land
                         and name in keeping.”

Herwic now was weeping,   in his eyes the tear-drops stood ;
Wet were the eyes of Hettel,   and fast they overflowed :
So it was with others,   at seeing them thus weeping ;
Every one was sorrowful   who, near the king, his faith to him
                         was keeping.

Then said the aged Wâ-te :   “ Further of this say nought.
For all the woe and losses   these friends to us have brought,
Soon will we repay them,   and we shall yet be gladdened ;
Ludwig’s kin and Hartmut’s   shall at our hands for this
                         erelong be saddened.”

Hettel asked in wonder :   “ How can that be done ? ”
To him old Wâ-te answered :   “ ’T is best that peace be won
Now with the king of Moorland,   with whom we yet are warring :
Our men, who here besiege him,   to seek for fair Gu-drun we may
                         then be sparing.”

Wise was the aged Wâ-te,   the words he spake were meet :
“ To-morrow morning early,   let us with Siegfried treat ;
And we ought so to bear us   that he shall well be knowing
That, should we not allow it,   he with his men can ne’er
                         be homeward going.”

Then said the daring Herwic: " Wâ-te has spoken right ;
To-day must you be thinking   how, with the morrow's light,
You all before the foeman   may show a warlike bearing :
It gives me pain that women   should make us leave our siege,
            and hence be faring."

Then they got together   horses and clothes with speed ;
Unto the words of Wâ-te   they readily gave heed.
When the day was dawning,   they again were striving
'Gainst those from Abakia.   Great praise for this were all
            to them soon giving.

On every side, with banners,   they to the field did throng ;
Many, sound in body,   there were slain erelong :
Wâ-te's men from Sturmland   " Nearer ! Nearer ! " shouted ;
But those they would o'ermaster   were quicker yet in fight,
            and nought it booted.

Soon the knightly Irold,   over the edge of his shield,
Called out, " Men of Moorland,   to peace with us will you yield ?
King Hettel bids us ask you,   will you this be choosing ?
Your lands so far are lying,   that you your goods and men
            will else be losing."

Siegfried, lord of Moorland,   answered to him thus :
" Would you for peace have pledges,   then win the fight o'er us ;
With no one will I bargain   for aught my name may lessen :
If you think to overcome us,   you will the more by this
            your losses hasten."

Then spake the knightly Fru-te :   " If help to us you 'll give,
And pledge your word to do it,   your stronghold you may leave
And go from my master's kingdom,   without more bloody fighting."
The Moors from Karadia   on this stretched forth the hand,
their faith thus plighting.

There came to strife a stand-still,   this I for truth may say.
The glad and happy warriors   met that selfsame day ;
Those who erst were foemen   their help to each other granted.
They both had quenched their hatred ;   to fight the Normans
now was all they wanted.

Then to Siegfried of Moorland   at once King Hettel told
All the heavy tidings   that he in his breast did hold ;
He pledged to him his friendship,   so long as he was living,
If Hartmut's foul misdoing   now to repay, his help he would
be giving.

To him the lord of Alzabie,   the Moorish Siegfried said :
" Knew we where to find them,   they should our coming dread."
The aged Wâ-te answered :   " I can show you nearly
Their path across the water :   and we perhaps on the sea
may meet them early."

Then to them all spake Hettel :   " Where can ships be sought?
And, if I wish to harm them,   how bring my wish about ?
I might at home make ready   within their lands to seek them,
And there, when I had found them,   my anger for my wrongs
should quick o'ertake them."

To him then said old Wâ-te :   " In this I can help you still ;
God is ever mighty   to do whate'er he will.
I know within these borders   now are lying near us
Well-made ships full seventy ;   filled with food, these barks
from the sands will bear us.

" In them have wandering pilgrims   sailed the waters o'er :
Their ships, whatever happens,   we must seize upon the shore ;
The pilgrims must be willing   that on the sand we leave them,
Until our Norman foemen   make good our wrongs, or we again
shall brave them."

At once old Wâ-te started,   no longer would he wait ;
A hundred knights went with him,   the others lingered yet.
He said he came for buying ;   what could the pilgrims sell him ?
For this men died thereafter,   and, for himself, but sorry luck
befell him.

On the shore he found the pilgrims, —   this I know is true, —
Fully thirty hundred,   I ween, and better, too.
To fight were they unready,   and could not rouse them quickly :
Nearer came King Hettel,   and with him led his men,
now crowding thickly.

Their goods the pilgrims guarded,   yet Wâ-te sent on shore
All that he had no need for,   of silver and clothes a store ;
But the food was left on shipboard,   so old Wâ-te chooses :
He said he should come hereafter,   and would reward them well
for all their losses.

Sadly mourned the pilgrims,   for sorest was their need ;
But for all they said old Wâ-te   cared not a crust of bread :
The bold, unyielding warrior,   stern and never smiling,
Said : " Both ships and flatboats   they to leave to him
must now be willing."

Hettel recked but little   if ever they sailed again
Over the sea with their crosses :   then he took of their men
Five hundred at least, or over,   the best they had among them ;
Of these to the Hegeling kingdom   few came back, from the death
that overhung them.

I know not whether Hettel   atoned for his evil deed
Done to these poor pilgrims,   that made their hearts to bleed,
And, in a far-off kingdom,   rent their band, to their sorrow.
I ween the God in heaven   saw the wrong, and his anger showed
on the morrow.

King Hettel and his followers   met with a kindly breeze,
And now their way were taking   quickly across the seas ;
Seeking for their foemen,   they sailed far over the water,
Wherever they might find them,   longing to show their wrath,
and bent on slaughter.

Tale the Seventeenth.

HOW HETTEL CAME TO THE WULPENSAND IN SEARCH OF HIS DAUGHTER.

LUDWIG, king of the Normans,   and Hartmut, too, his son,
　　Now, with all their followers,   far away had gone,
And on a lone, wild seashore,   after their toil, were resting.
Though many there were gathered,   yet little happiness they then
　　　　　　　　　　　　　　　　　　　　were tasting.

'T was on a broad, low island,   hight the Wulpensand,
That now the brave King Ludwig,   and they of the Norman land,
Shelter for men and horses   had found unto their liking;
But a doom to them most woful   erelong must come, instead of
　　　　　　　　　　　　　　　　　　　　the rest they were seeking.

The very high-born maidens,   torn from the Hegeling land,
Had been led out, and wandered   along the barren sand;
So far as 't was allowed them   to show their feelings freely,
They who had been stolen   in sadness wept before the foeman
　　　　　　　　　　　　　　　　　　　　daily.

Fires upon the seashore   were seen on every side ;
The men from far-off Normandy   were thinking there to abide.
Gladly with the maidens   would they seven days have rested,
And there have made them lodgings ;   but every hope of this
                                 erelong was blasted.

While on this isle forsaken   Hartmut now must stay,
Loth were he and his followers   the hope to put away,
Which till now they fostered,   that they for rest might tarry
Throughout a week in the shelter   whither they the maidens
                                 fair did carry.

It was from far-off Matelan   that Ludwig and his band
The fair Gu-drun had taken   unto this lonely strand ;
Nor felt they now uneasy   lest to their hidden dwelling
Wâ-te them should follow,   and never harm from him
                                 were they foretelling.

Now saw King Ludwig's sailors,   tossing on the wave,
A ship with sails the richest.   To the king they warning gave ;
But when 't was seen by Hartmut,   and others with him standing,
That on the sails were crosses,   they said these must be
                                 pilgrims, bent on landing.

On the waters floating   three good ships were seen,
With new and well-made flatboats ;   they bore across the main
Those who on their clothing   never yet wore crosses,
Their love to God thus showing.   The Normans must from them
                                 meet heavy losses.

As they the shore were nearing,   one on the ships might see
Helmets brightly shining.   No more from care were free
King Ludwig and his kinsmen,   and harm their fears foreboded :
" Look there ! " then shouted Hartmut;   " with grimmest foes of
mine these ships are loaded."

The ships were turned so quickly   that now men loudly heard
Rudders strained and cracking,   held by those who steered.
Both the young and aged,   who on the sea-sands rested,
Were indeed bewildered   when to spring on shore the foeman
hasted.

Ludwig and young Hartmut   their shields in hand now bore.
For them it had been easier   to reach their homes once more
If they had not too freely   their rest on the island taken :
They had falsely reckoned   that Hettel had now no friends,
and was all forsaken.

Ludwig called out loudly   to all his trusty men,
(He thought it child's play only   that he before had seen,)
" Now with worthy foemen   must I, at length, be striving !
He shall be the richer   who 'neath my flag his help to me
is giving."

Soon was Hartmut's banner   raised upon the shore.
The ships had now come nearer;   with spears the Normans bore
To reach the foe were easy   from where they now were waiting :
I ween the aged Wâ-te   was ready with his shield, the foeman
meeting.

Ne'er before so grimly   did champions guard their land.
Boldly the Hegeling warriors   nearer pressed to the strand ;
Soon they met the Normans   with sword and spear, undaunted ;
Blows they freely bartered :   such bargains cheaply given
                                     no more they wanted.

Everywhere the Hegelings   sprang upon the shore.
After a wind from the hill-tops   was never seen before
Snow so thickly whirling   as spears from hands that threw them :
Though they had done it gladly   idle it were to shun the strokes
                                       that slew them.

Thick fly the spears on both sides :   the time but slowly goes,
Till they on the beach are standing.   Quickly on his foes
Sprang the aged Wâ-te,   just as they were nearing ;
His mood was of the grimmest,   and soon they saw what mind
                                       he now was bearing.

Ludwig, king of the Normans,   then at Wâ-te ran,
And hurled a spear well sharpened   against the brave old man.
The shaft, in splinters shattered,   high thro' air went crashing,
For Ludwig drove it bravely ;   soon to the fight came Wâ-te's
                                       kinsmen dashing.

With a heavy stroke, old Wâ-te   Ludwig's helmet cut ;
The edge of the sword he wielded   the head of his foeman smote,
Who beneath his breastplate   a shirt of silk was wearing ;
(In Abalie 't was woven ;)   were it not for this, his end he must
                                       be nearing.

Hardly from him could Ludwig   with life and limb go free;
The spot he would fain be leaving,   for Wâ-te was ill to see
When he was roused to anger,   and to win the day was trying:
Struck by his hand were many,   who, brave in warfare, now
                                    on the field lay dying.

Irold and young Hartmut   each on the other sprang:
On either side their weapons   on the foeman's helmet rang;
Throughout the throng of fighters,   all could hear it loudly;
For bold in war was Irold,   and Hartmut, too, was brave, and
                                    bore him proudly.

Herwic from the Sealands,   a warrior strong and good,
Could not reach the landing,   but leaped into the flood,
And in the waves was standing,   up to his shoulders hidden.
Soon to his cost was he learning   how hard a task it is
                                    to win a maiden.

They the shore who guarded   their foemen thought to drown
While in the waters struggling.   Shafts at them were thrown,
And many on them broken;   but they, their foes now seeking,
Soon the sands were treading,   and many a knight his wrath
                                    on them was wreaking.

Ere they had reached the shoreland,   one saw the watery flood
Dyed by the killed and wounded,   in hue as red as blood;
Everywhere, so widely   the reddened waves were flowing,
One could not shoot beyond them,   how far soe'er he might
                                    his spear be throwing.

Heavier toil and losses   heroes never found,
And never so many warriors   lay trampled on the ground :
Enough were they for a kingdom   who lay, unwounded, dying.
The Normans who o'erthrew them,   on all sides too, I ween, in
death were lying.

It was to save his daughter   that there King Hettel fought,
And all his kinsmen with him.   On every side were wrought,
By him and those who helped him,   havoc and bitter sorrow.
Dead on the Wulpensand   were many bodies found before
the morrow.

Unto their lords all faithful,   they strove upon the sand, —
Alike the men of Normandy   and they of the Hegeling land.
Warriors brave from Denmark   fought with matchless daring ;
He ne'er should wait their onset   who much for his welfare
or his life was caring.

Morune and with him Ortwin   boldly held their ground,
And for themselves won honor ;   nowhere could be found
Men who greater slaughter   wrought, with hearts undaunted :
The heroes twain, with their followers,   gave full many wounds,
with spears well planted.

Proudly the men from Moorland,   as I have heard it said,
When from their ships they landed,   the way to the foemen led.
Hettel hoped, in his struggle,   help from them to be gaining,
For they were daring fighters :   one saw the blood beneath
their helmets raining.

How could he who led them   have braver or bolder been?
That day he dimmed with life-blood   many breastplates' sheen;
Siegfried it was, unyielding   in storm of battle ever.
How could the Danish Fru-te,   or even Wâ-te the old, have
                                  shown them braver?

Thickly hurled were lances,   hither and thither thrown:
Ortwin, with his followers,   in hopeful mood came on;
Helmets that day he shattered,   blows upon them dealing.
Gu-drun was bitterly weeping: her women, too, were deepest
                                   sorrow feeling.

The strife, on both sides, lasted   throughout the livelong day;
Longing to reach each other,   they crowded to the fray.
There to knights and warriors   must the fight go badly,
Where the friends of Hettel   to win his daughter back
                                   were striving gladly.

The evening sun sank lower;   and for King Hettel now
His losses grew the greater.   King Ludwig's men, I trow,
Did their best in fighting,   but could not flee the slaughter;
Their foes they wounded deeply,   and guarded thus Gu-drun
                                   from those who sought her.

The strife began at morning;   by night alone 't was stopped,
And steadily had lasted;   they ne'er their weapons dropped.
The old and young together   gained no shame in fighting.
Now the brave King Hettel   forward pressed, the king
                                   of the Normans meeting.

Tale the Eighteenth.

HOW LUDWIG SLEW HETTEL, AND STOLE AWAY IN THE
NIGHT.

HIGH in hand their weapons   Hettel and Ludwig bore, —
    Well had they been sharpened.   Soon each knew the more
Who was now his foeman,   such strength they both were showing.
Ludwig slew King Hettel ;   and out of this our mournful tale
                                        is growing.

When the lord of Matelan   upon the field lay slain,
Soon 't was told to his daughter :   loudly then began
Gu-drun to mourn her father,   so did many a maiden ;
Not one could stop her wailing :   friends and foes alike
                                        were sorrow-laden.

Soon as the grim old Wâ-te   the death of the king did know,
He cried and roared in anger.   Like to the evening glow,
Now were helmets blazing,   beneath the strokes quick given
By him and all his followers,   who by their loss were unto
                                        madness driven.

However hard their fighting,   how could it bring them good?
Drenched was all the island   with many knights' hot blood.
Not yet the Hegeling warriors   to think of peace were ready;
Away from the Wulpensand   they only wished to bring Gu-drun,
their lady.

In stormy fight the Waal men   bewreked the death of the king;
To many a fighting Ortlander   and hard-pressed Hegeling
Those who came from Denmark   of friendship gave a token:
Soon these knights so daring   found in their hands their
trusty weapons broken.

Now to avenge his father   Ortwin bravely strove:
Faithful to him did Horant   and all his followers prove.
Night the field had darkened,   the light of day was failing;
Then were given to many   wounds from which the life-blood
fast was welling.

Soon, in the dark, on Horant   a Danish follower sprang;
The sword that he was holding   loud on the armor rang:
Thinking he was a foeman,   Horant at once upon him
Wrought most bitter sorrow: a deadly wound by that warrior
brave was done him.

When Horant saw that his kinsman   beneath his blow lay dead,
Then he bade that his banner   be borne with his own o'erhead.
The voice of him who was dying   told whose life he had taken
With his hand so rashly;   sorely he mourned the friend
who never would waken.

Loudly called out Herwic :   " Murder here is done !
Since we can see no longer,   and daylight now is gone,
We all shall kill each other,   friends and foes together.
If this shall last till morning,   two may be left to fight,
                         but not another."

Where'er they saw old Wâ-te   on the stormy fighting-ground,
No one there was willing   near him to be found ;
No welcome, in his madness,   was he to any giving :
Many a foe he wounded,   and laid on the spot that he would
                         ne'er be leaving.

'T was well the foes were sundered   until the break of day ;
On either side the foemen   near each other lay,
Wounded to death or slaughtered.   Fast the light was waning,
Not yet the moon was risen,   and the Hegeling foe the field
                         were nowhere gaining.

The warriors grim, unwillingly,   to the strife now put a stop ;
The hands of all were weary   ere they gave the struggle up :
But, when the fight was over,   they near each other loitered.
Wherever fires were burning,   for each the other's shields
                         and helmets glittered.

Ludwig then and Hartmut,   lords of the Norman land,
Talked aside together.   Then to his faithful band
Spake the elder warrior :   " Why be longer staying
So near the brave old Wâ-te,   who all of us is madly
                         bent on slaying ? "

The wily king then bade them: " Lie low, and be not seen,
With your heads upon your bucklers: you then must make a din;
And so the men of the Hegelings   my plan will not be knowing, —
That, if I now can do it,   I with you all may hence
unseen be going."

Ludwig's men and kinsmen   did as he had said:
They upon their sackbuts   and trumpets loudly played,
As if they, by their prowess,   the land had gained them wholly.
Ludwig now to his followers   showed his crafty plot
and cunning fully.

Then were heard, on all sides,   mingled shouts and cries;
But wailing from the maidens   was not allowed to rise:
All who would not stop it   were threatened death by drowning, —
To be sunk beneath the waters, —   if they were sobbing heard.
or loudly moaning.

Whate'er was owned by the Normans   now to the ships was ta'en:
The dead were there left lying,   e'en where they were slain.
Friends were lost to many   who, seeking, could not find them:
So few there were still living,   that many an empty ship
was left behind them.

Thus unbeknown and slyly,   sailed away o'er the main
The men of the land of Normandy;   great was the women's pain
From kinsfolk to be sundered,   and yet to hush their weeping.
Of this the men knew nothing   who now upon the Wulpensand
were sleeping.

Before the day was dawning,   well were on their way
They whom the Danish warriors   had thought that morn to slay.
Then Wâ-te bade that loudly   his war-horn should be sounded ;
He was in haste to follow,   and hoped erelong to fell them,
deeply wounded.

On foot and on their horses,   the men of the Hegeling land
All were seen together,   flocking o'er the sand,
To fight the fleeing Normans ;   never in this they rested.
Ludwig with his followers   already far upon their way
had hasted.

Many ships lay empty,   and clothing there was found ;
All about the Wulpensand   't was scattered o'er the ground ;
Many weapons also   were seen, with none to bear them.
They had overslept their going,   and never to harm their foes
could they come near them.

When this was told to Wâ-te,   with anger he was torn :
How for the death of Hettel   he bitterly did mourn !
And that on Ludwig's body   his wrath he was not wreaking !
Helmets there lay shattered ;   for this must many a woman's
heart be aching.

How gloomily and sadly   now, in angry mood,
Ortwin was bewailing   the loss of his warriors good !
He said : " Rouse up, my fighters !   we may perhaps o'ertake them
Before they leave these waters ;   not far from shore we yet
in flight may check them."

Willingly old Wâ-te   would his bidding do:
Fru-te the winds was watching, to learn which way they blew.
Then said he to his kinsmen: "What helps it though we hasten?
Mark what now I tell you: the thirty miles they 've gained
               we ne'er can lessen.

"Moreover, we of fighters have not here enough
That we in aught can harm them, e'en should we now set off:
Scorn me not," said Fru-te, "and to my words give heeding;
What more to say is needful? Your foes you cannot reach,
               howe'er you 're speeding.

"Bid that now the wounded upon the ships be laid;
Then on the field of battle let search for the dead be made,
And bid that they be buried upon this strand forsaken,
So friends may rest together; this good at least from them
               should not be taken."

All, standing there together, wringing their hands were seen.
For this one sorrow only, would their lot have hapless been,—
To lose the youthful maiden, Hilda's lovely daughter.
How, when they saw her mother, if home they went, could news
               so sad be brought her?

Then to them said Morunc: "Would there were nothing more,
Beyond our own sad losses, for which our hearts are sore!
Small reward will be given for the news we home shall carry,
That Hettel dead is lying: far from Hilda fain would I
               longer tarry."

Then went the warriors searching   for the dead upon the sand.
Those they knew were Christians   who lay upon the strand,
As the Sturmisch Wâ-te bade them,   were all together carried;
Then both the old and the younger   chose a spot whereon
                            the dead were buried.

Then said the knight, young Ortwin :   " Let us bury them here ;
And thought must we be taking   to build a church full near,
That they be not forgotten,   while this their end is showing.
For it shall all their kinsmen   give of their wealth, each one
                            his share bestowing."

Then spake the Sturmisch Wâ-te :   " In this thou well hast said ;
We now should sell the horses   and the clothing of the dead,
Who on the shore are lying ;   so, since their life is ended,
Shall many poor and needy,   with the wealth they left,
                         be holpen and befriended."

Then asked the warrior Irold,   if foes who there lay dead
Should also now be buried,   or if wolves should on them feed,
And hungry ravens tear them,   that round their bodies hovered ?
Then to the wise they listened ;   none of the dead were left
                         on the field uncovered.

When now the fight was over,   and all were free from care,
Hettel, their king, they buried,   who for his daughter dear,
Upon this barren seashore,   e'en unto death had striven.
To others who had fallen,   whate'er their land and name,
                         was burial given.

First, the men from Moorland   each by himself they laid;
The same was done for the Hegelings   found among the dead;
Unto the Normans, also,   gave they graves allotted:
Alone was each one buried,   if Christian he were or heathen,
                     it nothing booted.

Until six days were over,   busy were they, at their best,
And never time were finding   (for the warriors took no rest)
To ask for dead and dying   the grace of God in heaven,
For sins of which they were guilty;   that they for their
                     misdeeds should be forgiven.

Saying mass and singing   were later heard on the strand.
Never was God so worshipped,   in any other land,
For the dead in stormy fighting.   Wherever men were lying
With their death-wounds smitten,   holy priests they brought
                     to shrive the dying.

Many there did tarry   to care for the churchly men.
A deed of gift was written,   wherein it could be seen
How of land to the brothers   three hundred hides was given.
Far and wide 't was bruited,   that well a godly house was
                     builded, and had thriven.

All who there were mourning   the loss of friends and kin
Gave of their wealth a tithing,   women as well as men,
For weal of the souls of any   whose bodies there lay buried.
The cloister soon was wealthy,   by the yield of three hundred
                     hides, through toil unwearied.

Now may God in his keeping   have those who there lie dead,
And the holy men there dwelling.   Those then homeward sped
Who still upon the Wulpensand   were left among the living ;
After all their sorrows,   they reached their fatherland,
                  no more in warfare striving.

Tale the Nineteenth.

HOW THE HEGELINGS WENT HOME TO THEIR OWN LAND

THE kinsmen of King Hettel   upon the sands had left
   Many in death's fast keeping;   never knights bereft
Their homeward way had taken,   hearts so sorry bringing.
Thereafter lovely women   for this, with weeping eyes,
                      their hands were wringing.

Ortwin, the knight of Ortland,   who to the fight had come,
After such shame and losses,   back to fair Hilda's home
Feared to bring these tidings,   his mother dear to sadden.
She there was waiting daily,   hoping her men would bring
                      Gu-drun the maiden.

Wâ-te, fearing sorely,   rode to Hilda's land;
The others dared not tell her   of the loss on the Wulpensand.
Ill in the storm of fighting,   his strength her men had warded;
Not lightly her forgiveness   he hoped to gain, who thus her
                      lord had guarded.

When the word was spoken   that Wâ-te near had come,
At once were men faint-hearted.   Erewhiles when he came home,
Back from the war-field riding,   it was with war-horns braying.
This he did at all times;   but now they all were still, and
nought were saying.

" Woe 's me!" said Lady Hilda,   " what sorrows must we fear?
The men of the aged Wâ-te   shattered shields now bear;
Slowly step the horses,   with armor heavy-loaded.
Some evil has befallen.   Oh! say what harm to the king
is now forboded ? "

When thus the queen had spoken,   but little time had passed
Ere to the aged Wâ-te   crowds came up in haste,
Who of friends and kinsfolk   tidings now were seeking.
Soon a tale he told them   with which the hearts of all were
well-nigh breaking.

Thus spake the Sturmisch Wâ-te :   " Your loss I may not hide,
Nor falsehood will I tell you;   all in the fight have died."
The young and old together   at this with fear were stricken.
Ne'er was a throng more wretched;   no other woes could one
to theirs e'er liken.

" Alas! my bitter sorrow! "   said King Hettel's wife.
" From me my lord is sundered,   who there laid down his life,
The great and mighty Hettel!   My pride, how is it fallen!
Lost are child and husband!   Gu-drun I ne'er shall see,
from me forever stolen."

Then both knights and maidens   with sharpest woe were torn;
Their sorrow knew no healing.   Loudly the queen forlorn
Was heard, throughout the palace,   for her husband mourning.
"Ah, wretched me," cried Hilda,   "that now to Hartmut's side
                         the luck is turning!"

Then spake the brave old Wâ-te: "My lady, end your moan:
Home are they coming never,   but when to men are grown
The youths within our kingdom,   sad days will have an ending;
To Ludwig and to Hartmut   the like we'll do, our wrath
                         upon them spending."

Then quoth the weeping lady: "Alas, that I must live!
Whatever I am owning   I would most gladly give
Could e'er my wrongs be righted.   If but this were granted,
That I, poor God-forsaken,   might see Gudrun again,
                         naught else were wanted."

Old Wâ-te spake to Hilda: "Lady, weep no more.
'T is best that we be sending,   before twelve days are o'er,
To gather all your warriors,   who will help you gladly
To plan a raid on the foeman;   so with the Norman will it yet
                         go badly."

He said: "My Lady Hilda,   list to what befell:
Erewhile I took from pilgrims   nine ships, and then set sail:
These should again be given   to those we ill have treated;
That when new strifes we're waging,   a better luck to us may
                         then be meted."

The weeping Hilda answered :   " 'T is best that this be done;
Ever is it fitting   that men for misdeeds atone.
To steal the goods of pilgrims   is a sin not lightly shriven :
For every mark we 've taken,   to them three marks of silver
shall be given."

The ships were brought to the pilgrims,   as the queen did say ;
Not one there was among them,   when they sailed away,
Who left a curse behind him.   For wrongs they found a healing ;
And for Hilda, Hagen's daughter,   they harbored, when they left,
no bitter feeling.

Upon the morrow early,   thither to come was seen
Herwic, the lord of Sealand ;   soon he found the queen
Weeping for her husband,   who in death was lying.
She gave the knight a welcome,   with hands she ever wrung, and
deeply sighing.

Seeing the lady weeping,   then, too, to weep began
The young and lordly Herwic ;   soon spake that well-born man :
" Their lives not all have given,   who help to you are owing,
And who would gladly grant it ;   though many by their death
their love were showing.

" My arm shall never falter,   nor heart from care be free,
Till Hartmut feels my anger,   who stole the maid from me,
And dared from home to tear her,   death to many dealing :
Soon will I ride to his borders ;   then will I seize and hold
his lands and dwelling."

His men, though filled with sorrow,   rode towards the town,
Flocking to Matelan castle.   The queen her hope made known
That, whatsoe'er might happen,   their fealty would not weaken ;
And, though the worst befell them,   that she by them would never
                     be forsaken.

To her the men from Friesland   and those from Sturmland went,
And from the Danish kingdom   were warriors likewise sent ;
The knights of Morunc also,   from the land of Wâleis riding,
Thither came with the Hegelings,   to where the fair Queen Hilda
                     was abiding.

Forthwith there came from Ortland,   Ortwin, Hilda's son ;
Then mourned they, as was fitting,   his father dead and gone.
Soon were all the warriors   aside with their ladies speaking,
And talking of the inroad   the fighters strong one day
                     would thence be making.

Then said the aged Wâ-te :   " This can never be
Till those who now are children   fully-grown we see,
And worthy to be swordsmen.   Then, their fathers mourning,
And of their kinsmen mindful,   gladly will they with us
                     to war be turning."

Queen Hilda then made answer :   " To wait for this were long :
Meanwhile Gu-drun, my daughter,   held by foemen strong,
Must in a far-off kingdom   be kept in bondage bitter ;
And I, poor queen and mother,   shall know no bliss, and my heart
                     will ne'er grow lighter."

Then said the Danish Fru-te :   " The maid we cannot free
Until once more your kingdom   shall full of warriors be.
Then, for the struggle ready,   we hence shall ride, unfearing ;
And so upon our foemen   shall work the greatest ill with blows
unsparing."

To this Queen Hilda answered :   " That day may God soon give ;
But I, unhappy woman,   a weary life must live.
Whoe'er of me is mindful,   and of Gu-drun, poor maiden,
Him will I trust most fully,   knowing his heart for us with care
is laden."

They now their leave were taking ;   to them the lady spake :
" May he be blest and happy   who thought for me shall take.
'T is right that you, brave warriors,   to fight for me are ready ;
Meanwhile for the coming inroad   do all you can, and therein
be you speedy."

Wisely then spake Wâ-te,   the warrior old and good :
" Lady, we should be felling   trees in the western wood.
Since we to fight have chosen,   our hopes upon it staking,
The men of every princedom   should forty well-built ships
for us be making."

" I too will bid," quoth Hilda,   " that near the deep sea-flood
Twenty ships be builded,   strong, and firm, and good ;
And have them fully ready   — my hest shall well be heeded —
To bear my friends and kindred   to where they for the fight
will soon be needed."

Siegfried, lord of Moorland,   while their leave they took,
With kind and seemly bearing,   thus to the women spoke :
" You have to tell me only   when our time to wait is ending ;
To sail shall I be ready,   nor need you then for me
                     be further sending."

Then to the sorrowing women,   before they spread the sail,
The friendly guests, now leaving,   bade a kind farewell.
The hearts of knights and maidens   deep in woe were sinking ;
Yet warlike deeds they plotted   of which their Norman foes
                     were never thinking.

When they at length had ridden   back again to their land,
Sadly they mourned their losses :   then to the Wulpensand,
For the sake of the dead, did Hilda   bid that food be taken
To the priests for them there praying.   The queen was wise,
                     the dead were not forsaken.

There she bade to be builded   a minster fair and wide ;
A house for the sick, and a cloister   built they at its side,
Near where the slain were buried.   In many a land one heareth
Its name, and of those there fallen :   ' The church of Wulpensand '
                     is the name it beareth.

𝕮ale t𝕙e 𝕮wentiet𝕙.

HOW HARTMUT WENT HOME TO NORMANDY.

NO further will we tell you   of how with these it fared,
Or how the cloister-brothers   their life together shared.
Now to the tale of Hartmut   we ask you all to listen ;
How he with many maidens,   high-born and fair, unto his land
                                            did hasten.

After the fight was ended,   as I have told before,
For many there was sorrow   for the bitter wounds they bore :
Many who had fallen   on the stormy field lay dying :
Children bereft of fathers   bewailed them soon with tears
                                            they ne'er were drying.

With heavy hearts the Normans   were wafted o'er the flood ;
Every night and morning   many a warrior good
Felt ashamed and sorry,   thus from the sands to be driven ;
So felt the old and the youthful,   although in all things else
                                            they well had thriven.

They came to the Norman borders,   unto King Ludwig's land.
It was a day of gladness   to all the sailing band,
To see at last their homesteads   and thither to be steering.
Then said one among them :   " These are Hartmut's towns that we
are nearing."

Helped by kindly breezes,   soon they reached the shore.
Now the men of Normandy   happy hearts all bore,
When to their wives and children   they again were coming ;
Long had they been fearing   that they must die, while they
afar were roaming.

When now the glad King Ludwig   did on his castles look,
Thus the lordly Norman   to Gu-drun, the maiden, spoke :
" See you that palace, Lady ?   In bliss you may there be living :
If you to us are kindly,   our richest lands will we to you
be giving."

Then the high-born maiden   thus made her sorrow known :
" To whom should I feel kindly,   when kindness none have shown ?
From that, alas ! I 'm sundered,   and in my hopes am thwarted ;
Nothing I know but hardship,   and all my weary days
I spend sad-hearted."

Then answered her King Ludwig: " Throw off this sorry mood,
And give your love to Hartmut,   a knight both brave and good.
Whatever we are owning   to give you we are willing ;
With one who is so worthy   blest may you live, and lofty rank
be filling."

Then spake Hilda's daughter: " Why leave me not in peace ?
Rather than wed with Hartmut   death would I dread far less.
That he should be my lover   by birth he is not fitted ;
To lose my life were better   than take his love and as
his bride be greeted."

When this was heard by Ludwig,   filled with wrath was he ;
Quick by the hair he seized her,   and flung her into the sea.
Straightway the daring Hartmut   his ready help then gave her ;
He sprang at once to the maiden,   and from the whirling waves
his arm did save her.

Just as the maid was sinking   Hartmut reached her side ;
Had not her lover helped her   drowned were she in the tide.
Her yellow locks well grasping,   then from out the water
With his hands he drew her :   else nought from death had spared
Queen Hilda's daughter.

Back to the ship did Hartmut   bring the maiden fair ; —
Rough ways to lovely women   Ludwig did not spare.
Dragged from out the water,   she in her smock was seated ;
How full was she of sadness !   Never before had the maiden
thus been treated.

Then all her friends together   wept for the lovely maid,
None could there be happy ;   for what could be more sad
Than to see the king's own daughter   handled thus so roughly ?
The thought to them was rising :   " To us they now will bear
themselves more gruffly."

Then said the knightly Hartmut: " Why drown my hoped-for wife,
Gu-drun, the lovely maiden,   dear to me as life?
If any but my father   so foul a wrong had done her,
Sore would be my anger,   and I from him would take both
life and honor."

To him King Ludwig answered: " Ever free from shame
Have I till age been living,   and still a worthy name
And rank among my fellows   will hold till life is ending.
Bid now Gu-drun, your lady,   that she no more her scorn on me
be spending."

Now unto Queen Gerlind   errand-bearers came,
Who, in mood most happy,   bore in Hartmut's name
Words of love and honor,   as from her son was fitting.
He asked a friendly welcome   for his many knights who on the
shore were waiting.

They bore from him the tidings   that he across the wave
Had brought the Hegeling maiden,   to whom his love he gave
Ere he had looked upon her,   and for whom he still was pining.
When this was heard by Gerlind,   a happier day on her
was never shining.

Then said he who told it: " Lady, you now should ride
To the sea before the castle,   where yet the maid doth bide,
And give her, in her sorrow,   your love and kindly greeting;
You and your daughter, Ortrun,   should haste to the shore,
the homeless maiden meeting.

"Likewise, riding with you   down unto the flood,
Should go both maids and women,   and also warriors good.
Her you will find in the harbor   who from home was riven;
Both to the maid and her followers   a welcome kind by you
                     should now be given."

Then Queen Gerlind answered :   "That will I gladly do ;
'T will make me richly happy   King Hettel's child to know,
And to find that, with her maidens,   she has come to tarry.
Well I know that Hartmut   will soon be blest, when he the maid
                     shall marry."

Then she bade that horses,   with saddle-cloths, be brought.
Ortrun, the youthful princess,   was happy in the thought
Soon in her father's kingdom   to see Gu-drun, the maiden,
If this might truly happen ;   for the speech of all was with
                     her praises laden.

Then out of chests were taken   of all the clothes the best
They knew therein were lying,   to be worn to meet the guest.
Soon the knights of Hartmut   to don the clothes were bidden ;
Erelong a throng of followers,   gaily bedight, from Gerlind's
                     halls had ridden.

Upon the third day early,   women as well as men,
All who there had gathered   before Gerlind, their queen,
To give the maidens welcome,   were ready and outfitted ;
Out of the gates they crowded,   and on their steeds not long
                     in the court-yard waited.

The Normans now with the women   had into the harbor come:
The booty they unloaded   that they would carry home.
All unto their birthland   back had come right gladly;
Gu-drun and her band of maidens,   alone of all, demeaned
              themselves but sadly.

Now the brave Sir Hartmut   led her forth by the hand.
If she had deemed it fitting,   this she had not deigned;
Yet the poor child, in sorrow,   took his love but coldly,
Altho' he showed it warmly,   and worship more had done
              freely and boldly.

With her went sixty maidens   who over the sea had come:
One saw, as he beheld them,   how that all from their home
Came with proudest bearing.   They erst high rank had taken,
In other lands and kingdoms;   their hearts were heavy now,
              of bliss forsaken.

The sister of young Hartmut   between two barons rode;
Now to Hilda's daughter   a welcome warm she showed:
Ortrun, Ludwig's daughter,   her eyes now wet with weeping,
Kissed the homeless maiden,   while she her fair white hands
              in her own was keeping.

Then the wife of Ludwig   to kiss her, too, was fain,
But to the youthful maiden   the thought was full of pain.
Thus she spake to Gerlind: "Why come you here to meet me?
Loath am I to kiss you,   and neither can I bear that you
              should greet me.

" 'T was by your own ill-doing   that I, poor wretched maid,
Have known no home nor dwelling ;   heart-sorrow long I 've had ;
My lot, alas ! is shameful,   and will, I fear, grow harder."
Then Ortrun strove to soothe her,   and did her best that with
                 love Gu-drun should reward her.

One by one she greeted   the maids on every side.
Now rose a wondrous shouting ;   men flocked from far and wide :
Upon the pebbly sea-beach   stakes for tents were driven ;
With silken ropes were they fastened ;   to Hartmut and his men
                 was shelter in them given.

To bear the goods from the seaside   the folk were all astir.
Gu-drun, fair maiden, sorrowed,   and pain it gave to her
To see that all around her   the Normans were so many ;
Unless it were to Ortrun,   she never showed a friendly mood
                 to any.

The maidens on the seashore   must all the day abide.
With tears their eyes were flowing,   whatever others did ;
Dry were they but seldom,   their cheeks were pale with sorrow :
Hartmut tried to soothe them,   but their sadness lasted yet
                 through many a morrow.

To hold Gu-drun in honor   was Ortrun ever stern,
And, e'en if others wronged her,   with love to her did turn :
She in her father's kingdom   strove to make her merry,
But, far from friends and kindred,   often the poor young girl
                 was sad and weary.

To the Normans home was welcome,   as indeed was right;
They boasted much of the booty,   both churl as well as knight,
Brought from the Hegeling kingdom,   as they home were turning.
What welcome glad all gave them   who ne'er to see them hoped,
                 albeit yearning!

Soon as Hartmut's warriors   from all their toil were free,
And they were fully rested   from off the stormy sea,
They quickly left each other,   for their homes in many places:
While some their hands were wringing,   smiles were seen to
                 brighten others' faces.

Then did Hartmut also   turn away from the shore,
And to a stately palace   the fair Gu-drun he bore.
Henceforth the youthful maiden   must tarry there far longer
Than she to stay was minded,   and there her woe and pain
                 grew ever stronger.

When now the high-born maiden   sat in Hartmut's hall,
Where his men should crown her,   then he bade them all
To be forever faithful,   and their goodwill to show her;
So would she not forget them,   but would enrich whoe'er
                 should kindness do her.

Then spake the mother, Gerlind,   old King Ludwig's wife:
" When will Gu-drun be ready   to share young Hartmut's life,
Our youthful prince so noble,   and in her arms to fold him?
Of her his rank is worthy,   and ne'er will she be sorry
                 for her lord to hold him."

Gu-drun to this had listened,   the wretched, homeless maid;
She said: " My Lady Gerlind,   't would make you sad indeed
If you must take in wedlock   one who the lives had wasted
Of many friends and kinsfolk;   by toil for him your life were
                                   ever blasted."

" This shall no one hinder,"   to her then said the queen ;
" Gainsay his will no longer,   let your love for him be seen,
And on my head I pledge you   that rich shall be your guerdon :
If to be a queen you spurn not,   you of my crown shall bear the
                                   happy burden."

Then said the sorrowing maiden: " That will I never wear;
Of all his wealth and greatness   you the tale may spare.
Your son, the knightly Hartmut,   my love can ne'er be winning:
Unwilling here I linger,   and hence to go I day by day
                                   am pining."

Then the youthful Hartmut,   who of the land was lord,
Was angry with the maiden   when he her answer heard.
He said: " If, then, to wed her   the lady granteth never,
So, also, to the fair one   shall my goodwill and love
                                   be wanting ever."

Then the wicked Gerlind   to Hartmut said, in turn :
" Ever the young and thoughtless   from the wise should learn.
Now leave to me this maiden,   let me for her be caring,
And I so well shall teach her   that she will quickly drop
                                   her lofty bearing."

"That will I grant you gladly,"　Hartmut answering said;
"Whate'er from this may follow,　to you I give the maid,
To have in your good keeping,　as suits her rank and honor;
The maid is sad and homeless;　lady, 't is right that kindly
care be shown her."

So Gu-drun, the fair one,　when Hartmut went that day,
Was left unto his mother,　and given to her sway:
But Hilda's youthful daughter　Gerlind's guidance hated;
She could not brook her teaching,　and never her dislike
for this abated.

Then to the lovely maiden　the old she-devil spake:
"If you will not live happy,　then sorrow you must take.
You have to heat my chamber;　yourself the fire must kindle;
See, there is none to help you,　nor may you hope your toil
will ever dwindle."

The high-born maiden answered:　"That I well can do;
Whatever you shall bid me,　in all must I yield to you,
Until the God in heaven　at last my wrongs has righted.
Never my mother's daughter　the fire upon the hearth ere this
has lighted."

Said Gerlind: "As I 'm living,　to toil must you begin,
As never queenly daughter　to do before was seen.
To be so proud and headstrong　I will make you weary:
Before to-morrow darkens,　your maidens you must leave,
and ne'er be merry.

" You hold yourself too highly,   as I have heard it said ;
For this shall work most toilsome   soon upon you be laid.
This pride and froward bearing   must be by you forsaken ;
Your lofty mood will I lower,   and all your hopes will very
quickly weaken."

Then went the wicked Gerlind   to court, in anger wild ;
She said to her son, young Hartmut :   " Hettel's wilful child
Scorns both you and your kindred,   and ever at us is sneering :
Would we had never seen her,   if we such talk from her
must now be hearing."

Then spake unto his mother   Hartmut, the knight so brave :
" Pray treat the maiden kindly,   howe'er she may behave :
So, for the care you show her,   my thanks will you be earning.
Greatly have I wronged her ;   it well may be that she my love
is spurning."

Then said to him old Gerlind :   " Whate'er by us is done,
In mood she is so stubborn   that she will yield to none.
Unless we treat her harshly   she ne'er, as you would have her,
Will come to you in wedlock ;   this must we do, or else
to herself must leave her."

Then to her thus answered   the worthy Norman knight :
" Good lady, show her kindness   henceforth in all men's sight,
Now for the love you bear me :   such care I beg you give her
That from her love and friendship   the king's fair daughter
may not bar me ever."

Then his devilish mother,   with anger brimming o'er,
To the throng of Hegeling maidens   quickly went once more.
She said: " Make ready, maidens,   and to your toil betake you,
To do what you are bidden ;   the task to each that's given
ne'er forsake you."

The maidens then were sundered,   and soon from each other torn ;
They saw not one another,   and long must live forlorn.
Those who once so worthily   lofty rank were taking,
In winding yarn were busied ;   while they sat at work
their hearts were aching.

Some her flax were combing,   others for her must spin ;
Ladies of lofty breeding,   whose pastime it had been
On their silken clothing   to lay, with skill unsparing,
Gold and gems most costly,   these for her now heavy toil
were bearing.

The first in birth among them   at the court was kept ;
Water she must carry   to the room where Ortrun slept :
To wait upon that lady   the high-born maid was bidden ;
By name was she called Hergart ;   her lofty birth was nought,
she still was chidden.

Among them was another,   brought from Galicia's strand ;
The griffin her from Portugal   had borne to a far-off land.
She to the Hegeling kingdom   with Hagen's child was carried,
From over Ireland's borders ;   now with the maids in the
Norman land she tarried.

She was a prince's daughter, who castles owned and lands ;
The fire must now be lighted by her, with fair white hands,
While in the room well heated Gerlind's ladies rested.
For all the work she was doing no thanks on her by them
                            were ever wasted.

Now you well may wonder to hear her sorry plight.
For Gerlind's lowest wenches she drudged both day and night ;
Whatever task they set her, to do must she be willing.
It helped her not with the Normans that she at home a lofty
                            rank was filling.

The work was mean and shameful that they were made to do
For seven half years and over, — this is all too true, —
Until the young Lord Hartmut, when three wars were ended,
Had come again to his kingdom, and found the maids
                          at work, and ill-befriended.

To see again his loved one Hartmut deeply yearned ;
But when he looked upon her, the truth he quickly learned,
That she good food and lodging of late had seldom tasted :
For choosing to live rightly, 't was her reward to be
                            with sorrow wasted.

When forth she came to meet him, to her young Hartmut said :
" Gu-drun, most lovely maiden, what is the life you have led
Since I, with all my warriors, my lands and home was leaving ? "
She said : " Such tasks they set me, 't was sin for you, and
                            shame to me 't was giving."

Then outspoke young Hartmut: " Why has this been done,
Gerlind, my dearest mother? Your love she should have known;
When with you I left her, her lot you should have brightened,
And all her heavy sorrows you should for her within my land
                         have lightened."

His wolfish mother answered: " How could I better teach
King Hettel's ill-bred daughter? 'T was bootless to beseech,
Nor could I ever bend her, to make her leave her jeering:
She scorned both you and your father and kindred, too:
                     to this should you give hearing."

Then again spake Hartmut: " Much wrong we 've done the maid.
Slain by us, her kindred and many knights lie dead;
While from the lovely maiden her father we have taken,
Slain by my father, Ludwig, and now with thoughtless words
                       her woes we waken."

Then answered him his mother: " My son, 't is truth I say;
If we Gu-drun, proud maiden, for thirty years should pray,
If she with brooms were stricken, or with rods were beaten,
Your wife we ne'er could make her; hopeless it is the wayward
                       maid to threaten."

She farther said to Hartmut: " However, since you bid,
I 'll gladly treat her better." But still her mind she hid,
And Hartmut never knew it; erelong Gu-drun would find her
Harsher yet than ever; and now the maiden's wrongs
                       could no one hinder.

Then went again old Gerlind   to where Gu-drun then sat,
And said to the Hegeling maiden,   in her wrath and hate :
" 'T were best you now bethink you,   or else, my fair young maiden,
You with your flowing tresses   must wipe the stools and
                             seats, with dust thick laden.

" Then the room I sleep in,   mark what now I say,
You, to do my bidding,   must sweep three times a day ;
You carefully must warm it,   and keep the fire well burning."
Said she : " That do I gladly,   rather than take a lover
                             I am spurning."

Whatever she was bidden   the willing maiden did ;
No work of hers she slighted,   nor should for aught be chid.
For seven years, full-numbered,   in a land far over the water,
The maid was toiling wearily,   and none did hold her
                             as a kingly daughter.

The years had long been running,   and the ninth was coming on,
When Hartmut to bethink him   wisely had begun,
That indeed 't was shameful   that he no crown was wearing ;
And for himself and his kinsmen   't was right the name of king
                             he now were bearing.

After heavy fighting,   Hartmut, with his men,
Bearing the prize of bravery,   riding home was seen.
He hoped the love of the maiden   would now to him be granted ;
For, more than any other,   he the fair Gu-drun for his
                             true love wanted.

When he reached his homestead,   he bade them bring the maid.
His evil mother, Gerlind,   allowed her to be clad
In meanest clothing only: Gu-drun but little heeded
The youthful Hartmut's wooing;   steadfast and true, no love
from him she needed.

To him his friends then whispered,   that, whether glad or no
For this might be his mother,   he never should forego
To bend the maid to his wishes;   and must his care be giving
That so he might with the lady   for many a happy day in love
be living.

To the ladies' room he hastened,   when thus his kinsmen spoke,
And there he found the maiden;   her by the hand he took,
And said to her: "Fair lady,   love me now, I pray you,
And sit as queen beside me;   my knights and men shall worship
ever pay you."

Then said the lovely maiden: "For this I have no mind;
For while the fiendish Gerlind   to me is so unkind,
The love of knights, tho' worthy,   I can long for never.
To her and all her kindred   henceforth am I a bitter foe
forever."

"Sorry am I," said Hartmut;   "to you will I make good
The hate my mother Gerlind   to you so harshly showed;
As for both of us is worthy,   your wrongs shall now be righted."
The high-born maiden answered: "I trust you not; your word
need ne'er be plighted."

Then said to her young Hartmut,   the lord of the Norman land:
“ Gudrun, most lovely maiden,   you well must understand
Mine are these lands and castles: to none may you betake you;
Who is there here would hang me   if, ’gainst your will, I now
my own should make you ? ”

Then said King Hettel’s daughter: “ That were a deed of shame:
Of aught so wrong and hateful   never did I dream.
It would be said by princes,   should they the tale be hearing,
That one of the kin of Hagen   in Hartmut’s land a harlot’s name
is bearing.”

Then did Hartmut answer: “ What care I what they say?
If only you, fair lady,   do not say me nay,
A king my men shall see me,   and you my seat be sharing.”
Then said the maid to Hartmut: “ That I should love you
be you never fearing.

“ Well you know, Sir Hartmut,   how with me it stands ;
And all the wrong and sorrow   I met with at your hands,
When far from home you carried   me whom you had stolen,
And, wounded by your warriors,   my father’s men erewhile
in death had fallen.

“ Well known to you ’t is also,   — for this I mourn again, —
How my father, Hettel,   was by your father slain.
Were I knight, and not a woman,   he durst not come before me
Unless his weapons wearing.   Why wed the man who from
my kindred tore me ? ”

For many years now bygone,   it ever was the way,
No man should take a woman,   and have her in his sway,
Unless they both were willing.   Much praise for this is owing.
Gu-drun, the homeless maiden,   her father's loss still mourned,
                     with tears o'erflowing.

Then spake to her in anger   Hartmut, the youthful knight:
"Whatever may befall you,   I reck not for your plight;
Since now you are not willing   to wear the crown beside me,
You 'll have what you are seeking,   your meed you 'll daily earn,
                     nor need you chide me."

"That will I earn most gladly,   as I have done before,
Though for the men of Hartmut   the hardest toil I bore,
And for Queen Gerlind's women.   If God my wrongs forgetteth,
To bear them I am willing;   but heavy is the woe that me
                     besetteth."

Still they sought to soothe her: first to the court they sent
Young Ortrun, Hartmut's sister,   whose looks all kindness meant;
'T was hoped that she and her maidens,   now by friendly dealing,
Would bring Gu-drun, poor lone one,   to bear towards them all
                     a better feeling.

Then to his sister Ortrun   Hartmut freely spake:
"Wealth I will give you, sister,   if kindly, for my sake,
To me you will be helpful,   and bring Gu-drun, fair lady,
Soon to forget her sorrows;   nor o'er her woes to brood be
                     ever ready."

Then spake the youthful Ortrun,   the Norman maiden fair:
"To help both her and her maidens   shall ever be my care,
Till they forget their sorrows: I bow my head before her,
And I and mine will hold her   even as our kin, and watchful
love spread o'er her."

Gu-drun now said to Ortrun: "My hearty thanks you win,
That you, with kindly wishes,   would see me sit as queen,
By the side of Hartmut,   while with pride I'm gladdened:
For this my trust I give you,   but homeless, none the less,
my days are saddened."

Tale the Twenty-First.

HOW GUDRUN MUST WASH CLOTHES ON THE BEACH.

THEN to Gu-drun they offered   castles strong and lands :
  Of these would she have nothing.   So, upon the sands,
She must wash their clothing,   from early morn till even.
Great ill this wrought for Ludwig,   when he with Herwic in the
                              fight had striven.

First, Gu-drun was bidden   to leave her seat, that soon
She, the high-born maiden,   should go with fair Ortrun ;
They bade that she be merry,   and wine with her be drinking.
The homeless wanderer answered :   " To make me queen you never
                              need be thinking.

" Well you wot, Lord Hartmut,   whate'er your wish may be,
Betrothed am I to another,   and am no longer free.
That I one day shall wed him   has with an oath been plighted ;
Until by death he 's taken   I will not wed with any man
                              e'er knighted."

Then spake the lordly Hartmut: "You only waste your breath;
By nought shall we be sundered   unless it shall be death.
In friendship with my sister   you should now be living;
Your hardships she will lighten,   and will, I know, her love
to you be giving."

Fain to think was Hartmut   that her unyielding mood
Might now by this be softened;   he hoped, whatever good
Should e'er befall his sister,   the maiden would be sharing:
Thus for both he trusted,   that a happy life erelong would them
be cheering.

Gu-drun soon greeted kindly   many a friend and maid.
Ortrun sat beside her;   her hue grew rosy-red
With eating and with drinking,   ere many days were ended.
Enough was always ready: still the poor girl her mood
ne'er wisely mended.

If Hartmut thought to greet her,   and spoke in friendly mood,
How little did it cheer her!   She o'er her woes did brood,
That she and all her maidens   in a far-off land were bearing.
Soon, against young Hartmut,   of harsh and angry words
she was not sparing.

So long a time this lasted,   the king at length was wroth;
He said: "Gu-drun, fair lady,   as good am I in birth
As is the young King Herwic,   who now you think is fitter
Than I to be your lover: too much you jeer at me, with words
most bitter.

"If you would leave your sorrow,   for both of us 't were gain.
It wounds me out of measure   when any gives you pain,
Or seeks your heart to burden,   or in your wish to cross you :
Though now you are unfriendly,   to be my queen I yet would
                                  gladly choose you."

Then young Hartmut left her,   and straight his men he sought.
He bade them to be watchful   of ills that threatened aught,
And well to guard his kingdom;   for he the while bethought him,
So sorely was he hated,   't was much to fear some harm would yet
                                    be wrought him.

The cross and wicked Gerlind   for her hard tasks did set ;
She on a seat but seldom   any rest did get.
Erst 'mong princes' daughters   men were wont to greet her,
As for her was rightful ;   now with the scorned and lowly
                                    they must meet her.

To her, in mood unfriendly,   the old she-wolf then spake :
"Now Queen Hilda's daughter   I a drudge will make ;
Although her evil feelings   seem so strong and steady,
We yet shall see her toiling   as ne'er before to do has she
                                    been ready."

Then said the high-born maiden :   "To work with all my might,
With hand and heart, I 'm willing ;   in this, both day and night,
Will I be always busy,   and every hour be striving ;
Since ill-luck begrudges   that I among my friends should
                                    now be living."

The wicked Gerlind answered :   " Now daily to the beach
You my clothes must carry,   there on the sands to bleach.
You must for me and my maidens   be washing and be drying ;
And that no one find you idle,   your work with care you ever
                          must be plying."

Then spake the high-born maiden :   " Wife of a mighty king,
If they will only teach me   the way to wash and wring,
And how to cleanse your clothing,   to do it I am willing.
Bliss no more I look for;   still greater woe my heart must
                          yet be filling.

" Bid them now to teach me,   and I will gladly learn ;
So high I do not hold me   that I the task should spurn.
Thus shall I be earning   the food I here am eating ;
Nought I say against it."   The poor Gu-drun her lot
                          was wisely meeting.

Then by a washerwoman   clothes to the sands were brought,
And how to wash and dry them   the maiden now was taught.
Much at first she sorrowed,   and by the work was flurried,
Yet was she spared by no one.   So was the fair Gu-drun
                          by Gerlind worried.

Before King Ludwig's castle,   she gained a skilful hand ;
For knights who there were dwelling   within the Norman land,
None could be more helpful,   their clothing better washing.
Loudly mourned her maidens   to see her toiling where
                          the waves were dashing.

One there was among them   who was also a great king's child;
The wailing of the others   was to hers a whisper mild.
This work so mean and lowly   went to their hearts too nearly,
As they saw the high-born lady   drudging on the shore,
                      both late and early.

Then with love true-hearted   Hildeburg made moan:
" Well we all must rue it —   to God may this be known —
Who in this Norman kingdom   erst with Gu-drun were landing;
No rest ought we to hope for   while on the sea-beach washing
                      she is standing."

This was heard by Gerlind,   who in anger spoke:
" If on the toils of your lady   with such ill-will you look,
The work shall you be doing,   and her place be filling."
" That would I do right gladly,"   said Hildeburg, " if only you
                      were willing.

" For the love of God Almighty,   Gerlind, my lady queen,
Let not this great king's daughter   toiling alone be seen:
A crown, too, wore my father,   yet work would I be doing;
Let me with her stand washing,   whatever good or ill we may
                      be knowing.

" It fills my heart with sorrow,   I feel her woes my own.
Once the greatest honor   to her by God was shown:
Her forefathers and kindred   were kings, and none were higher;
Though now her work is lowly,   to toil with the maiden
                      I shall never tire."

Then said the wicked Gerlind: " This oft will bring you pain :
However hard the winter,   still in snow and rain
My clothes must you be washing,   altho' cold winds are blowing ;
So will you be wishing   that you the warmth of heated rooms
were knowing."

Unwillingly she waited   until the night drew near ;
From this Gudrun the high-born   gained at last some cheer.
Then into her bedroom   went Hildeburg in sorrow ;
There they wept together   for the work that they must do
upon the morrow.

Then the Lady Hildeburg   said to her in tears :
"The woes that you are bearing   my heart with you now shares ;
I begged the old she-devil   no more alone to leave you
Upon the sea-sands washing ;   with you I 'll bear the burden,
and my help will give you."

The homeless maiden answered :   " May Christ your love reward,
That you with so much sorrow   of all my woes have heard.
If we may wash together,   the days will be the brighter,
And time will seem far shorter,   and on our hearts the shame
will weigh the lighter."

Soon as her wish was granted,   down to the sandy shore
The clothing then she carried,   gladness to know no more.
There must they wash in sorrow,   whatever was the weather ;
Whate'er was done by others,   yet still these two must wash
and toil together.

When her throng of handmaidens   had time from work to spare,
Bitter was their weeping,   to see her standing there
Upon the sea-sands washing.   Loud were their moans and many,
Nor did their sorrow lessen ;   greater woe was never known
by any.

Long the toiling lasted, —   that is true enough ;
There must they be working   full five years and a half.
Clothes for Hartmut's followers   they must wash and whiten :
Ne'er were maidens sadder ;   their toils before the castle
nought could lighten.

Tale the Twenty-Second.

HOW HILDA MADE WAR TO BRING BACK HER DAUGHTER.

WE now will speak no longer   of the toil the maidens bore
For knights as well as ladies.   Queen Hilda evermore
Her thoughts to this had given   how to win back her daughter.
Out of the Norman kingdom,   whither from home the daring
                                   Hartmut brought her.

First were workmen bidden,   near to the deep sea-flood,
Of ships to build her seven,   strong, well made, and good:
With two-and-twenty barges,   broad, with both ends rounded.
Whate'er for them was needed   was quickly brought, and
                                   everything abounded.

Forty galleys also   lay upon the sea:
On these her eyes were feeding.   Longing great had she
To see the throng of fighters   who should soon be sailing.
She their food made ready;   for this the knights her praise
                                   were loudly telling.

The time was drawing nearer,   when now to cross the sea
No more should they be waiting,   who wished the maids to free,
That in a far-off kingdom   in hardest toil were living.
Now Hilda sent for her liegemen;   to those who called them
                        clothes she first was giving.

The day that she had chosen   was at the Christmas-tide,
When they must seek the foemen   by whom King Hettel died.
Forthwith to friends and kinsmen   Hilda gave her bidding,
That they to bring her daughter   back from the Norman land
                        must then be speeding.

Trusty men were bidden   by Hilda first to go
To Herwic and his followers,   that one and all should know
Of the inroad on the Normans   that she had sworn and plotted.
To many Hegeling children   this erelong an orphan's life
                        allotted.

The men sent out by Hilda   to Herwic rode in haste:
For what they then were coming   the king full quickly guessed;
Then went he forth to meet them,   soon as he saw them nearing;
Gladly them he greeted,   and soon from them Queen Hilda's wish
                        was hearing.

" Well you know, Lord Herwic,   our woe and plight forlorn,
And how the Hegeling warriors   to help the queen have sworn.
Yourself Queen Hilda trusteth   more than any other;
To none Gudrun is dearer, —   the homeless maid, long sundered
                        from her mother."

The well-born knight thus answered : " I know in truth too well
How Hartmut had the boldness   my fair betrothed to steal,
Because his love she slighted,   and hearkened to my wooing ;
For this Gu-drun, my lady,   her father lost, and still her lot
is ruing.

" My pledge and hearty greeting   bear to your lady good ;
No more the Norman Hartmut   by me shall be allowed
To hold so long in bondage   my own betrothéd maiden :
For me, of all, 't is fittest   to bring the lady home, our lives
to gladden.

" To Hilda and her kinsmen   this answer you may say :
When Christmas time is over,   on the sixth-and-twentieth day,
I will ride to the Hegelings,   three thousand fighters taking."
Then the men of Hilda   waited no more, but home their way
were making.

Now Herwic made him ready,   and to the strife gave thought,
With many faithful liegemen   who oft had bravely fought.
Those who to go were willing   he for war outfitted ;
Though wintry was the weather,   they to take the field
no longer waited.

Of help the widowed Hilda   sorely felt the need :
Soon to her friends in Denmark   she sent her men with speed,
To tell the knights and warriors   no more at home to tarry ;
For they to the Norman kingdom   must ride, to free Gu-drun
from bondage dreary.

They bore to the youthful Horant   this errand from the queen:
That he and all his kinsmen   were to her lord of kin,
And the sorrows of her daughter   should by them be heeded;
For death to her were better   than ever that her child
                to Hartmut should be wedded.

Then sent the knight this answer: " Unto Queen Hilda say,—
Though yet 't will cost to women   many a bitter day,
I still, with all my followers,   will help be gladly giving;
For this will be heard the weeping   of many a mother's child,
                in the land now living.

" I bid you now, moreover,   to say unto the queen,—
Ere many days are ended,   in her land will I be seen;
Tell her that my wishes   all to war are bending,
And soon ten thousand warriors   from out the Danish land
                will I be sending."

The men sent there by Hilda   of Horant took their leave:
They sped to the Waalisch marches,   and found Morunc the brave
With all his men about him,   a margrave rich and daring.
He gladly saw them coming,   and of a loving welcome
                was not sparing.

Then spake the knightly Irold: " Since now by me 't is known
That into the Hegeling kingdom,   before seven weeks are gone,
I with all my followers   am bidden to be riding,
For this will I be ready,   whatever luck be there for us
                betiding."

The news was spread by Morunc,   within the Holstein land,
That Hilda now was sending   for all her friends at hand ;
He said that all good warriors   must the field be taking.
To the Danish knight, brave Fru-te,   they also gave the word,
                 his help bespeaking.

The worthy knight, then answering,   his ready will did show :
" Back to her home will we bring her.   Thirteen years ago,
We swore the land of the Normans   should with war be wasted ;
'T was then the friends of Hartmut   stole the maid Gu-drun,
                 and homeward hasted."

Wâ-te, the knight from Sturmland,   to this at once gave thought,
How he might also help her.   Altho' he yet knew nought
Of the word that Hilda sent him,   yet he at once bestirred him ;
Of his knights a goodly number   then in haste he called,
                 who gladly heard him.

All of them were busy   with care for the coming war ;
Wâ-te the old from Sturmland   brought from near and far
Full a thousand kinsmen,   for the fight well fitted ;
With these he hoped that Hartmut   would soon be overcome
                 and be outwitted.

The sad and homeless women   in toil and pain were kept
By the cross and evil Gerlind :   but fewer wrongs were heaped
Upon the Lady Hergart ;   (this name to her was given :)
She loved the king's high cup-bearer,   and greatly hoped to be
                 a princess even.

For this fair Hilda's daughter   often sorely wept;
And Hergart, too, yet later   woe and sorrow reaped,
Because she ne'er with others   would their toils be sharing.
Whate'er to her might happen,   Gu-drun for all her ills
             was little caring.

Of the Hegelings none were idle,   as you before have heard:
Tho' many for all their toiling   would find but scant reward,
Yet all within the kingdom   their ready help were lending.
Now the knights were thinking   for the brother of Gu-drun
             't were best they should be sending.

Riders then went swiftly   into the land of the North,
And found in an open meadow   the youth of kingly birth,
Where by the edge of a river   many birds were flocking:
There with his trusty falconer   he showed his skill, and spent
             his time in hawking.

As soon as, riding quickly,   these by him were seen,
He said: "Those men now coming   are sent to us by the queen;
They come to give her bidding,   proudly hither hasting;
My mother thinketh wrongly   that we the war forget,
             and time are wasting."

He set his hawk a-flying,   and thence at once he rode.
Very soon thereafter   darkened was his mood;
For when the men he greeted,   and they their tale were telling,
He learned that the queen, his mother,   ever in tears her loss
             was aye bewailing.

She to the youthful warrior   sent her greeting kind:
In her wretched lot, she asked him   what might be his mind;
And asked how many followers   he could to the war be leading;
For from the Hegeling kingdom   they all to the Norman land
                         must soon be speeding.

Then Ortwin sent this answer: "Me dost thou rightly bid;
I from hence will hasten,   and bring from far and wide
Twenty thousand fighters, —   men both brave and daring;
These my steps will follow   even to death, their lives and
                         homes forswearing."

Now from every border   many warriors went
Riding to Hilda's kingdom,   for whom the queen had sent;
They vied with one another,   to win her praises striving.
Not less than sixty thousand   together came, their help for
                         Hilda giving.

On the river Waal Sir Morune   had upon the wave
Of broad-built ships full sixty,   strong to bear the brave
Who with the Hegelings sailing   would o'er the sea be carried,
To free Gu-drun, the maiden,   who sadly now among the Normans
                         tarried.

From out the Northland also   finest ships were brought,
With horses and with clothing,   as good as could be sought:
Decked were all the helmets,   the weapons glittered brightly,
Ready for the onset   bravely they came, in armor fair and
                         knightly.

Now by their shields men reckoned   how many there might be
Who to the Norman kingdom   would go the maid to free,
And to the great Queen Hilda   their help to give were ready;
They numbered seventy thousand;   gifts to all were given by
                     the queenly lady.

On all who there were gathered,   or to court who later came,
The queen, though ever mournful,   yet let her kindness beam:
She gave them hearty welcome,   and every one she greeted;
Wondrous was the clothing · that to the chosen knights
                     Queen Hilda meted.

The many ships of Hilda   were stored with all things well,
And early on the morrow   were ready thence to sail;
Seemly was the outfit   for her worthy guests who waited:
They chose not to be going,   while aught they lacked to meet
                     the foeman hated.

They put on board the weapons,   as was the queen's behest,
And with them many helmets   of beaten steel the best.
Hauberks white were given,   besides the ones in wearing,
For warriors full five hundred;   these she bade them take,
                     to war now faring.

Their anchor-ropes well twisted   of strongest silk were made:
Their sails both rich and showy   to the winds were spread;
These to the shores of the Norman   the Hegelings would carry,
Who back to Lady Hilda   would gladly bring Gudrun,
                     of waiting weary.

The anchors for the sailors   were not of iron made,
But of bell-metal moulded;   (so have we heard it said :)
They with Spanish brasses   all were bound and strengthened,
That loadstones should not hold them,   and so the sailors' way
> by this be lengthened.

To Wâ-te and his followers   the Lady Hilda gave
Many clasps and arm-bands.   This roused the strong and brave
To meet their death from foemen,   for the Hegelings fighting,
When they from Hartmut's castle   strove to wrest the maid,
> in bondage sitting.

Freely then and earnestly   Queen Hilda spoke her thought
Unto the men from Daneland :   " When you have bravely fought
On the stormy field of warfare,   I will reward you fitly.
Still my banner follow ;   that will show the way, and lead you
> rightly."

They asked of her, who held it ;   to this then answered she :
" He bears the name of Horant ;   a Danish lord is he.
His mother, Hettel's sister,   she it was who bore him ;
Let him by you be trusted ;   forsake him not in fight
> with foes before him.

" Never, my hardy warriors,   must you forget my son,
Young Ortwin, dear-belovéd,   to manhood nearly grown.
Of life the youth has numbered   twenty years already ;
If any risk should threaten,   to guard him well then let
> your help be speedy."

To this they pledged them gladly,   and all together said,
So long as they were with him   nought had he to dread;
If he their lead would follow,   those from whom he parted
Again unharmed would see him.   At this young Ortwin showed
himself light-hearted.

Soon the ships were laden   with goods of every kind,
And now to tell his wonder   none fit words could find.
They asked good Hilda's blessing   on the work now undertaken;
The queen then begged of Heaven   that they by Christ should
never be forsaken.

Many youths went with them   whose fathers erst were slain;
Now bereft, these brave ones   to right their wrongs were fain.
The women of the Hegelings   were mourning all and weeping,
Beseeching God in Heaven   to bring them back their sons
in his holy keeping.

But all this pain and sorrow   the warriors might not bear;
They sternly bade the women   their bitter wails to spare;
Then on their way they started   in gladness, shouting loudly,
And as they went on shipboard   all were heard to sing,
and set forth proudly.

After these daring sailors   had cast off from the land,
Many sorrowing women   did at the windows stand:
From Matelan's lofty castle,   never the watch forsaking,
Their eyes the sea-path followed,   as from the land the men
their way were taking.

A friendly wind was blowing,   and loudly cracked the mast;
They the sails stretched tightly,   and left the land at last.
The son of many a mother   went, for honor seeking;
Though this awaited many,   yet to gain it they must
                         toil be taking.

I cannot tell you fully   of all that them befell,
Save that the lord of Karadie,   who in that land did dwell,
With fighters came to help them,   the foeman never fearing;
He from home brought with him   ten thousand knights, all men
                         of strength and daring.

Where foes upon the Wulpensand   had met in deadly fray,
These knights from many a kingdom,   now, at this later day,
Chose the spot for meeting;   and here they came together:
A church had here been builded,   and old and young alike had
                         their gifts brought hither.

Now within its harbor,   to seek their fathers' graves,
Out of the ships here gathered   went many of Hilda's braves.
Bitter was their sorrow,   and anger keen did waken;
Hard would it be for any   who erst in fight the lives of their
                         friends had taken.

Unto the lord of Moorland   they hearty welcome gave.
Four and twenty broad-boats   he brought with warriors brave;
Food therein was laden   that might for all have lasted
Till twenty years were ended: to war with the Normans now
                         they gladly hasted.

When they to sail were ready,   they left the sheltering shore
To make their way o'er the waters;   but heavy toil they bore
Upon the wild sea-billows   before their sail was ended.
What helped it that their leaders,   Fru-te the Dane and Wâ-te,
them befriended?

A wind from the south was blowing,   and drove them out to sea.
The crew of warlike shipmates   from fear no more were free;
They could not find the bottom,   altho' they should be casting
Lengths of rope a thousand;   many sailors wept, their lot
foretasting.

Before the mount at Givers   soon lay Queen Hilda's host;
However good their anchors,   upon that gloomy coast,
Drawn by loadstones thither,   they a long time rested.
Their masts so tough and hardy   soon before their eyes
were bent and twisted.

When now the hopeless sailors   were weeping o'er their lot,
Thus spoke the aged Wâ-te:· " Anchors again throw out,
The strongest and the heaviest,   into the sea unsounded.
I've heard of many wonders   I would rather see, than here
on the rocks be grounded.

"Since, astray long sailing,   our lady's ships here lie,
And we so far are driven   across the darkling sea,
I now will tell a sea-tale,   that stirred my childish wonder,
Of how, near the mount at Givers,   a kingdom erst was built
by a mighty founder.

" Men there in wealth are living ;   so rich is all their land
That under the flowing rivers   silver is the sand ;
With this they make their castles,   and the stones are golden
With which their walls are builded.   In all the kingdom none
                       in want are holden.

" 'T was told to me, moreover,   (by God are wonders wrought,)
If one who by the loadstone   unto this mount is brought,
Here will only tarry   till the wind from the land is blowing,
He with all his kindred   may be forever rich when homeward
                       going.

" Let us our food be eating   until our luck shall turn,"
Said then the aged Wâ-te ;   " before we hence are borne,
Our ships that here are lying   shall with ore be loaded :
When this we home shall carry,   wealth shall we have that
                       no one e'er foreboded."

Then spake the Danish Fru-te :   " A still, unruffled sea
Shall never keep in idleness   the men now here with me :
A thousand times I swear to you,   no gold would I be seeking,
But rather away from this mountain,   with friendly winds, would I
                       my way be taking."

The Christian men among them   raised to Heaven a prayer ;
But yet the ships ne'er yielded,   strongly fastened there :
For four long days or over   all their hopes were thwarted ;
Sorely feared the Hegelings   that they from thence could
                       nevermore be started.

The clouds now lifted higher,   as the mighty God had willed ;
Then no more they sorrowed,   for soon the waves were stilled,
And from out the darkness   the sun was shining brightly.
A wind from the west was blowing,   and now the woes were o’er
                 of the wanderers knightly.

For miles full six and twenty,   past Givers’ craggy shore,
The ships at last were wafted.   By this they saw yet more
The work of God and his goodness,   in all the help then given.
Wâ-te with his followers   had been too near the rocks
                 of loadstone driven.

To smoothly flowing waters   they now were come at last :
Their sins were not rewarded,   and all their woes were past,
While fear from them was taken,   since God was not unwilling.
The ships that bore the warriors   straight to the Norman land
                 at length were sailing.

But soon among the sailors   arose again a wail ;
For now the ships were groaning,   and soon began to reel,
Tossed among the breakers   that overwhelmed them nearly :
Then said the brave knight Ortwin :   “ We now indeed must buy
                 our honors dearly.”

Outspake then one of the sailors :   “ Alas ! and well-a-day !
I would we were at Givers,   and dead near its mountain lay !
If one is by God forgotten,   by whom is he befriended ?
My brave and hardy warriors,   the roar of the blustering sea
                 is not yet ended.”

Then cried the knight, Sir Horant,   he of the Danish land:
" Be of good heart, brave fellows ;   I well can understand
This wind no harm will do us ;   from out the west 't is blowing."
This cheered the lord of Karadie,   on him and on his men
fresh hope bestowing.

Horant, the daring warrior,   up to the topmast climbed,
And the widely stretching billows   swept, with eyes undimmed,
Keeping for land an outlook.   They soon his call were hearing :
" Wait you now, unfearing ;   I see that we the Norman
land are nearing ! "

The word to all was given,   that they should lower sail :
Searching the waters over,   they saw far off a hill,
Lofty, and thickly wooded,   with groves and leafage shaded ;
Then old Wâ-te bade them   thither to bend their way,
and this they heeded.

Tale the Twenty-Third.

HOW HILDA'S WARRIORS LANDED IN SIGHT OF HARTMUT'S
KINGDOM.

BEFORE the hill they landed,   in sight of the leafy grove ;
Wary to be, and daring,   them did it now behoove.
First they dropped their anchors,   deep the waters under ;
In a lonely spot were they hidden,   where none could see,
                          nor at their coming wonder.

Then from the ships, to rest them,   they stepped upon the beach.
Hey ! what they had longed for   was now within their reach !
A stream of pure, cold water,   through the fir-trees flowing,
Ran down the wooded hillside,   upon the wave-worn knights
                          new life bestowing.

While the weary warriors   were resting and asleep,
Irold soon had clambered,   there his watch to keep,
Into a tree high-branching.   He then began to ponder
Which way they should be taking ;   and, lo ! the Norman land
                          he saw with wonder.

“ Now, my youths, be merry ! ”   thus cried the youthful knight.
“ My cares indeed are lightened,   for now I have in sight
Seven lofty palaces,   with roomy halls wide-spreading ;
Before to-morrow’s midday,   the land of Normandy shall we
be treading.”

Then said the wise old Wâ-te :   “ Up to the sands now bear
All your shields and weapons,   whate’er in fight you wear.
Let every one be busy,   and let the youths be hastened ;
At once lead out the horses ;   helmets and breastplates must
with straps be fastened.

“ And now, if any outfits   are not good to wear,
Nor meet for you in fighting,   to that I ’ll give my care.
The queen, my lady Hilda,   has sent with us already
Full five hundred breastplates ; these will we give to any
who are needy.”

Quickly were the horses   forth on the sea-beach led ;
And all the showy horse-cloths,   that should on them be spread,
Were by the men unfolded,   and laid on steeds in waiting,
To see which best beseemed them ;   and each then took the one
he deemed most fitting.

In leaping, and in galloping   up and down the shore,
They rode, and watched the horses ;   many, strong before,
Now were dull and sluggish,   nor longer quick at running ;
Too long had they been standing,   and Wâ-te had them killed,
as not worth owning.

Fires by the men were lighted ;   and good and hearty food,
The best that could be met with   so near the shore and flood,
By the tired and hungry wanderers   soon was cooked and eaten.
They had not hoped beforehand   that rest like this their
                          toilsome life would sweeten.

Throughout the night they rested,   till dawn of the coming day.
To Ortwin Wâ-te and Fru-te   each his mind did say ;
Talking aside on the seashore,   many a threat was spoken
Against their Norman foemen,   who into the Hegeling castle
                          erst had broken.

“ Men must we now be sending,”   to them young Ortwin said,
“ Who shall tidings bring us,   if they be not yet dead,
About my long-lost sister   and many a homeless maiden ;
For when on them I ’m thinking,   my heart is heavy, oft with
                          sorrow laden.”

Together they bethought them,   whom they hence should send,
By whom the news they wished for   might with truth be gained,
And who could tell them rightly   where to find the maiden ;
By them, too, must the errand   on which they came, from foes
                          be wisely hidden.

Then spake the youthful Ortwin,   who from Ortland came,
A faithful knight as any :   “ Myself for the search I name ;
The maid, Gu-drun, is my sister,   child of my father and mother ;
Of all, however worthy,   am I more fit to go than
                          any other.”

Then spake the kingly Herwic :   " I too will go with thee ;
To live or die I am ready,   seeking the maid to free.
To you she is a sister,   but to me for a wife they gave her ;
To her am I ever faithful,   nor for a day uncared-for
will I leave her."

Then quoth Wâ-te angrily :   " 'T is childish thus to speak,
Brave and chosen warriors :   such risks you should not seek,
And this for truth I tell you.   Spurn you not my warning ;
Should you be found by Hartmut,   you 'll on his gallows hang,
your rashness mourning."

To him King Herwic answered :   " Though good or ill betide,
Friends should aye be friendly,   standing side by side.
I and my friend, young Ortwin,   will ne'er the task give over,
Whatever shall befall us,   and search will make till we
Gu-drun recover."

When now upon this errand   both were bent to go,
They sent for friends and kinsfolk,   and did their wishes show.
They bade them to be faithful,   and said the oaths then taken
Must never be forgotten,   and they who went must never be
forsaken.

" Of your pledges I remind you,"   the youthful Ortwin said :
" If we, by foemen taken,   should be in bondage led,
You with gold must free us,   and so our bonds must loosen ;
Lands must you sell and castles,   nor ever sorrow feel that thus
you 've chosen.

"And, warriors brave, now hearken   to what we more will say ;
If foes our life begrudge us,   and us in fight shall slay,
Be not our death forgotten,   let it on them be wroken :
Your swords in Hartmut's kingdom   must make your daring there
                            be loudly spoken.

"This we further bid you,   my good and well-born knights :
E'en though, with toil the hardest,   every warrior fights,
Let not those homeless maidens   be by you forsaken ;
Until the strife is settled,   let not their hope and trust in you
                            be shaken."

Their faith then freely pledging,   each gave to the king his hand ;
And all the best among them   swore that home and land
They nevermore would look on,   but still afar would tarry,
Until again to their homesteads   they from the Norman land
                            the maids should carry.

All of them were faithful,   but yet were weeping sore ;
They feared the hate of Ludwig,   and ills for them in store.
That they could send no others   they were deeply mourning ;
And all were sadly thinking,   " No one now can death from them
                            be turning."

All day they talked together ;   it now was near its end :
The sun, that low was sinking,   thro' clouds its beams did send :
Erelong it sank o'er Gulstred,   and there at last was hidden.
Ortwin and Herwic tarried,   that night to go, by the
                            waning light forbidden.

Tale the Twenty-fourth.

HOW THEIR COMING WAS MADE KNOWN TO GUDRUN.

OF them we speak no longer;   we now will let you hear
   Yet more about the maidens :   how hope their lot did cheer
Who on a far-off seashore   must wearily toil at washing :
Gu-drun and Hildeburg   must wash all day on the sands
                where waves were dashing.

'T was the time of spring-tide fasting,   and at the noon of day.
To them a swan came floating;   thereat Gu-drun 'gan say :
" O bird so fair and lovely,   such pain for me thou art feeling,
That now thou hither speedest   from a far-off land, across
                the water sailing."

Then to her in answer   spake the friendly swan,
Although a God-sent angel,   in speech most like a man :
" Words from God I bring you;   if you for this be seeking,
Tidings I give of your kindred ;   of these, most high-born maid,
              would I be speaking."

When the lovely maiden   his speech so wondrous heard,
Scarce could she believe it,   that thus an untamed bird,
Now, within her hearing,   in tones like these had spoken.
While to him she listened,   it seemed that his words from
                              the mouth of a man had broken.

Then said the bird-like angel :   “ Hopeful you now may be,
Homeless, sorrowing maiden ;   gladness shall come to thee.
If you would hear of your birth-land,   listen while I tell you ;
From there I bring you tidings,   for God hath sent me, of your
                              woes to heal you.”

At this, Gu-drun, the fair one,   upon the sands down fell ;
Crossing her arms, the maiden   her lowly prayers did tell.
Then she said to Hildeburg :   “ God hath us in his keeping,
And help to us has granted ;   we now no more shall sorrow
                              know, nor weeping.”

To the bird then said the maiden :   “ Christ has sent thee here
To us, poor homeless maidens,   our heavy hearts to cheer ;
Good and trusted harbinger,   tidings tell yet other :
Is now Queen Hilda living ?   Of poor Gu-drun is she the
                              much-loved mother.”

The Heaven-sent bird thus answered :   “ This can I say to thee ;
Hilda, thy queenly mother,   in health did I lately see.
To search for thee already   her warriors she has banded ;
Such throngs no kin or widow,   seeking for friends, on foeman’s
                              shore e’er landed.”

Then spake the high-born maiden :   " Good tidings thou dost bear:
Be thou with me not weary,   still more I fain would hear.
Lives yet my brother Ortwin,   as king in Ortland dwelling,
And Herwic, my betrothéd ?   'T would gladden me could'st thou
this news be telling."

The bird-like angel answered :   "That can I gladly tell ;
Herwic and young King Ortwin   are both alive and well.
Upon the swelling billows,   that rose and sank unending,
I saw those knightly sailors ;   each with even stroke to his
oar was bending."

She said: " This tell me also,   if 't is known to thee,
Whether Morunc and Irold   are now upon the sea,
And hither come to seek me ;   the truth I fain would gather.
Gladly I would see them,   for they are kin to Hettel, who was
my father."

To her the bird thus answered :   " That can I tell you, too ;
Morunc, and with him Irold,   I saw, in search of you.
They to this land are coming ;   their help will soon be given
To fight for you, fair lady,   and many a helmet will by them
be riven."

Then spake the winged angel :   " I bid you now farewell,
And leave you in God's keeping,   for work awaits me still.
I overstay my errand   to linger here, yet speaking."
Then from their sight he faded,   and left the maidens' hearts
well-nigh to breaking.

Then said Hilda's daughter: " My sorrows none can know;
Much that I wished to ask thee, now must I forego.
For the sake of Christ, I beg thee, ere thou alone dost leave me,
Poor and wretched maiden, that freedom from my woes thou yet
wilt give me."

Before her eyes he floated, and once again he spake :
" Ere yet we two are parted, and hence my way I take,
If I in aught can help you, of that I will not weary,
And, since through Christ you ask it, to tell you of your kin
will longer tarry."

She said: " I fain were hearing, if thou the truth hast learned,
If Horant, lord of Denmark, his way has hither turned,
And with him leads his kinsmen ? They leave me here forsaken.
Knowing him brave and daring, I would my lonely lot
his care might waken."

" From Denmark sailing hither, Horant, your kinsman, comes :
He to war is leading his followers from their homes.
The banner of Queen Hilda aloft in his hand he is bearing :
'T is thus the Hegeling warriors now the Norman Hartmut's land
are nearing."

Gu-drun then asked him further : " This would I also hear :
Lives Wâ-te still of Sturmland ? If so, no more I fear.
We all might then be happy, if thou could'st this be telling, —
That under the flag of my mother he and the aged Fru-te
are hither sailing."

To her the angel answered: " Hither comes in haste
Wâ-te the old from Sturmland.   He in his hand holds fast
The strong and guiding rudder,   and Fru-te's ship is steering.
Truer friends or better   you ne'er need wish their swords
                     for you were bearing."

Once more the bird was ready   upon his way to go;
Then said the wretched maiden :   " I still am full of woe ;
And now to know am longing —   if life such bliss can lend me —
When I, poor homeless maiden,   shall see my mother's knights,
                     whom she doth send me."

The angel answered quickly: " Your happiness is near ;
To-morrow morning early,   will two brave knights be here.
Both are true and upright,   and falsehood ne'er will tell you ;
Whatever news they bring you   you well may trust, and never
                     will it fail you."

At last the heavenly angel   hence in truth must go :
From him the homeless maidens   sought no more to know.
In mind they ever wavered,   'twixt hope and fear still tossing ;
Where their helpers lingered   they could not know, yet trust
                     were never losing.

Lazily and slowly   they washed the livelong day ;
Of knights sent there by Hilda,   who now were on their way
From over the Hegeling border,   busily they chatted :
Gu-drun's good, faithful kinsmen   were by the long-lost maids
                     uneasily awaited.

Each day must have its ending;   to the castle now must go
The weary, homesick maidens.   They there must harshness know
From evil-minded Gerlind,   who their lives still harrowed ;
A day went by but seldom   that she scolded them not, nor still
                          their bondage narrowed.

Thus she spoke to the maidens :   " Who gave the word to you
That you might wash so slowly   my clothes and linen, too?
All the things I gave you   must be quickly whitened ;
'T were best that you be careful,   you else shall weep, and
                          for your lives be frightened."

Then answered her young Hildeburg :   " Our work we ever mind ;
Truly you ought, fair lady,   to be to us more kind.
We oft are almost freezing,   with water o'er us splashing ;
If only the winds were warmer,   we might for you far better
                          then be washing."

Grimly answered Gerlind,   and roughly them did twit :
" Whatever be the weather,   my work you may not slight.
Early must you be washing,   nor rest till night be knowing ;
To-morrow morn, at daybreak,   you from my room must down
                          to the beach be going.

" I ween you know already   that Holytide is near ;
Palm-Sunday soon is coming,   and guests will then be here :
If to ill-washed clothing   my knights shall then be treated,
Never in kingly castle   to those who washed have woes
                          like yours been meted."

Then the maidens left her ;   they laid aside, all wet,
The clothing they were wearing —   they better care should get.
All they had known of kindness   for them no longer lasted,
And soon for this they sorrowed,   for bread and water now
                         was all they tasted.

Now the downcast maidens   for sleep had sought their bed ;
But this was not the softest,   and each one, in her need,
A dirty shirt was wearing.   Thus was Gerlind showing
Her care and kindness for them,   on benches hard a pillow
                         ne'er bestowing.

Never Gu-drun, poor maiden,   on a harder bed had lain ;
All were tired with watching   till day should dawn again.
They had but broken slumber ;   I ween, they oft bethought them
How soon the knights were coming,   of whom the angel-bird
                         the news had brought them.

Soon as the morning lightened,   Hildeburg the good,
Erst from Galicia stolen,   at the window gazing stood ;
All night she slept but little,   but on her bed lay tossing.
She saw that snow had fallen,   and hope the heart-sick maid
                         was wellnigh losing.

Then spake the hapless maiden :   " To wash we now must go.
Should God not change the weather,   and we, in storm and snow,
To-day must stand a-washing,   before the evening cometh
We, all chilled and barefoot,   shall dead be found, while us
                         the cold benumbeth."

By hope they yet were gladdened,   e’en as they well might be,
That those sent out by Hilda   they ere night should see.
When the lovely maidens   upon this thought were dwelling,
It made them now more happy,   and lighter was the pain
                               their hearts were feeling.

Then said Hilda’s daughter: “ My friend, you should beseech
The stern, ill-minded Gerlind,   that on the pebbly beach
Shoes she will allow us ;   she may herself be learning
That if we go there barefoot   we soon shall freeze, and there
                               our death be earning.”

The maidens then went seeking   King Ludwig and his queen.
He, in sleep held fondly,   in Gerlind’s arms was seen ;
Both were sunk in slumber,   and the maids, their anger fearing,
Dared not them to waken :   erelong Gu-drun yet greater woe
                               was bearing.

The weeping of the maidens   by the sleeping queen was heard,
Who quick began to chide them   with many a surly word :
“ Why, you heedless maidens,   are you not to the seashore going,
There to wash my clothing,   and rinse them with clean water
                               o’er them flowing ? ”

Then said Gu-drun, in sorrow: “ I know not where to go,
For in the night has fallen   a deep and heavy snow.
That we by death be stricken   unless you now are willing,
Do not send us washing ;   to stand without our shoes will us
                               be killing.”

To her the she-wolf answered ; " That I do not fear ;
Now to the shore betake you, or weal or woe to bear.
If you be slow in washing, my wrath may you be dreading ;
E'en if you die, what care I ? " At this the hopeless maids
                     more tears were shedding.

Taking then the clothing, they went to the water's brink :
" Of this," said Gu-drun, " God willing, I will make you think."
Then, in the cold, barefooted, through the snow they waded ;
The very high-born maidens, forsaken in their woe, were worn
                     and faded.

Down to the beach they plodded, as was their wont before,
Bearing the clothing with them to the bleak and sandy shore.
They once more were standing, over the washing stooping ;
Ever they were thinking of their sorry plight, and sadly
                     were they hoping.

Often now, and earnestly, over the watery waste,
While they toiled and sorrowed, longing looks they cast ;
Still of those now dreaming sent by the queen to free them,
Who o'er the sea were sailing. The high-born maidens hoped
                     erelong to see them.

Tale the Twenty=Fifth.

HOW HERWIC AND ORTWIN FOUND GUDRUN.

AFTER they long had waited,   now saw these washers lone
  Two in a boat fast nearing ;   others were there none.
Then said the maiden, Hildeburg,   unto Gu-drun, the lady :
"These two are sailing hither ;   perhaps the friends sent here
                                     are come already."

She, full of sorrow, answered :   "Ah, woe is me, poor maid !
Although, in truth I 'm happy,   I yet am also sad.
If at the seaside washing   Queen Hilda's men shall see us,
Standing thus barefooted,   we from the shame of this
                                     can never free us.

"A poor, unhappy woman,   I know not what to do :
Hildeburg, my dearest,   your mind now let me know ;
To hide me were it better,   or shall I stay to shame me
When they shall find me toiling ?   Rather would I that they
                                     a drudge should name me."

Then said the maiden Hildeburg: "E'en how it stands you see;
A thing that is so weighty   you should not leave to me,
Whate'er you think the better,   your choice will I be sharing ;
With you I 'll stay forever,   both good and ill together with you
bearing."

Then from the water turning,   both fled away in haste ;
But now the boat of the sailors   had neared the land so fast,
They saw the lovely washers,   away from the seashore hieing,
And at once bethought them   that they for shame away from
the clothes were flying.

They called unto the maidens,   as they sprang upon the beach :
" Whither so fast are you fleeing,   fair washers, we beseech ?
We are far-off wanderers,   as well our looks are showing ;
Your linen may be stolen,   if you leave it here, and from us
in haste are going."

They kept their way still swiftly,   as if they heard it not :
But yet the boisterous shouting   had reached their ears, I wot.
The bold and knightly Herwic   too roughly bade them hear him,
For he not yet mistrusted   't was his betrothed that now
he saw so near him.

Cried Herwic, lord of Sealand :   " Maidens fair and young,
Tell us now, we pray you,   to whom these clothes belong.
We ask you in all honor,   by the faith to maidens owing,
Most fair and lovely ladies,   that back to the shore you will
again be going."

Gu-drun, the maid, then answered : " It were a shame, forsooth,
Since to the trust of woman   you give your pledge in truth,
Were I of this unworthy,   nor faith in you were showing :
To the shore we back will hasten,   although my eyes with tears
                            are overflowing."

They, in their smocks, came nearer ;   both with the sea were wet.
Before that time, the maidens   were always clean and neat ;
Now the wretched drudges   with cold and frost were quaking ;
Little of late had they eaten,   and with the March-like winds
                            were chilled and shaking.

The time had come already   for snows to melt away,
And, with each other vying,   the little birds, each day,
Again their songs would warble,   as soon as March was ended ;
But in the snow, and ice-cold,   the maids were found forlorn,
                            and unbefriended.

Stiff were their locks and frosted,   when they now drew near ;
However well and carefully   they had smoothed their hair,
It now was tossed and tumbled   by the wind so wildly blowing :
Hard bestead were the maidens,   toiling there, whether it rained
                            or was snowing.

The ice was loose and broken,   floating everywhere
Upon the sea before them.   The maids were filled with care ;
Pale were now their bodies,   e'en as the snow around them,
By their scanty clothes scarce hidden.   Sad was the lot
                            in which the knights had found them.

Then the high-born Herwic   a kind " Good-morning " bade
To the sad and homeless maidens ;   of this sore need they had,
For oft their keeper, Gerlind,   had them with harshness taunted.
To hear " Good-morning," " Good-evening,"   was now to the maids
                                        but very seldom granted.

Then said the youthful Ortwin :   " I beg you say to me
To whom belongs this clothing,   that on the sands I see ?
For whom are you here washing ?   You both are so comely showing,
Who can this shame have done you ?   May God bring low the man
                                        such outrage doing !

" So fair are you and lovely,   you well might wear the crown ;
If all that is your birthright   you now could call your own,
You would, in truth, be worthy   to be with ladies seated.
Has he for whom you are toiling   more such washers fair
                                        so foully treated ? "

To him the lovely maiden   in greatest sorrow spoke :
" Many he hath beside us   who fairer still do look.
All that you list now ask us ;   yet, with eye unsleeping,
One from the leads doth watch us,   who ne'er will forgive
                                        the talk with you we 're keeping."

" Be not at this uneasy,   but deign our gold to take,
And with it these four arm-bands.   These your reward we make,
If you, most lovely ladies,   of speech will not be wary ;
To you we give them gladly,   if of the truth we seek you be
                                        not chary."

"God leave to you your arm-bands,   albeit you we thank ;
Nought for hire may you give us,"   quoth the lady high in rank.
" Ask what you will, but quickly,   for we must hence be going ;
If we were seen here with you,   nothing but sorrow should we
then be knowing."

" We beg you first to tell us   who this land doth own ?
Whose are the castles also ?   By what name is he known
Who leaves you without clothing,   low tasks upon you laying ?
He may of his worth be boastful ;   that he doeth well no man
may now be saying."

To him Gu-drun thus answered :   " Hartmut is one of the lords
To whom these lands owe fealty.   His castles well he guards,
With Ludwig, king of the Normans,   who is Hartmut's father :
And many knightly vassals,   to keep their lands from foes,
they round them gather."

" Gladly would we see them,"   said Ortwin, the friendly knight ;
" Happy were I, fair lady,   if we could learn aright
Where, within their kingdom,   we might those kings be meeting.
We bring to them an errand ;   as henchmen of a king, we bear
his greeting."

Gu-drun, the high-born lady,   thus to the warrior spake :
" This very morning early,   ere yet they were awake,
I left them in their castle ;   in their beds they slumbered.
I know not if thence they have ridden :   their men, I think, full
forty hundred numbered."

Again King Herwic asked her :   " To us yet further tell,
Why is it such brave princes   in fear like this should dwell,
That they so many warriors   always should be needing?
Had I that band of fighters,   to gain a kingdom I would them
                                                      be leading."

To him Gu-drun thus answered :   " Of that we knothing know ;
And where their lands are lying,   that neither can we show :
But from the Hegeling kingdom,   although it is not near them,
They fear that harm awaits them   from foes who soon may come,
                                                      who hatred bear them."

Trembling, cold, and shivering,   the maids before them stood ;
Then the knightly Herwic   spake, in kindly mood :
" I would, most lovely ladies,   if we might be so daring,
And' if no shame it gave you,   that on the shore our cloaks
                                                      you would be wearing."

Hilda's daughter answered :   " May God your kindness bless ;
We cannot take your mantles,   but we thank you none the less.
No eye shall ever see me   manly clothing wearing."
If only the maidens knew it,   much greater ills would they yet
                                                      be often bearing.

Oft the eyes of Herwic   did on the maiden rest ;
To him she seemed most comely,   and her bearing was the best.
For all her heavy sorrows   sighs in his heart were wakened ;
And to one erst thought of kindly,   from him long taken,
                                                      he the maiden likened.

Then spake again young Ortwin,   who was of Ortland king :
" Can either of you ladies   tidings whatever bring
Of a band of homeless maidens   who to this land were carried ?
Gu-drun was one among them,   and gladly would we learn
                     where she has tarried."

To him the maiden answered :   " To me is that well known ;
A maiden throng came hither   in days now long bygone :
They to this far-off kingdom   by fighters bold were taken ;
And full of heavy sorrow   came these maids forlorn,
                     of hope forsaken.

" The maid whom you are seeking   I know," she said, " full well ;
I here have seen her toiling,   this for a truth I tell."
She was herself the maiden   who was by Hartmut stolen,
Gu-drun, Queen Hilda's daughter,   and all she told had erst
                     herself befallen.

Then spake the knightly Herwic :   " Ortwin, list to me :
If fair Gu-drun, your sister,   yet alive may be,
In any land whatever,   for us on earth still watching,
This must be that lady ;   ne'er have I seen two maids
                     so nearly matching."

To him then said young Ortwin :   " The maid in truth is fair,
But to my long-lost sister   no likeness doth she bear.
The days are not forgotten   when we were young together ;
Should I rove the whole world over,   so fair as she I ne'er
                     could find another."

When now Gu-drun, who listened,   heard the name of the man,
That his friend did call him Ortwin,   she looked at him again:
For she indeed were happy   if she were thus befriended,
And found in him a brother,   for then her cares were o'er
and her sorrows ended.

"However they may call you,   a worthy knight are you:
A man in all things like you   in days of yore I knew;
The name of Herwic bore he,   in Sealand was his dwelling.
If that brave knight were living,   to loose us from our bonds
he were not failing.

"I am one of the maidens   whom Hartmut's warriors stole,
And bore across the waters,   in thraldom sorrowful.
Gu-drun you here are seeking,   but need not thus have hasted;
The queenly Hegeling maiden   at last is dead, with toil
and hardship wasted."

The eyes of Ortwin glistened,   filling fast with tears;
Nor was it without weaping   that now King Herwic hears
The tidings to them given, —   that fair Gu-drun, their lady,
From them by death was taken;   at this their heavy hearts
to break were ready.

When both, before her weeping,   were seen by the homeless maid,
With eyes upon them fastened,   thus to them she said:
"It seems to me most likely,   by the mood that you are wearing,
That to Gu-drun, the maiden,   you worthy knights are love
and kinship bearing."

To her young Herwic answered : " Yes, for the maid, forsooth,
I shall pine till life be ended ; to me she gave her troth,
And to me, in wedlock plighted, with faithful oaths was given :
Since then, by the craft of Ludwig, her have I lost, by him
         from her birthland riven."

Then said the sorrowing maiden : " Your words would me mislead,
For men have often told me that Herwic long is dead.
No bliss on earth were greater, that God to me were granting,
Could I learn that he is living ; a friend to lead me hence
         were then not wanting."

Then said the knightly Herwic : " Upon my hand now look ;
Know you this ring I am wearing ? Mine is the name you spoke ;
With this were we betrothéd : to Gu-drun I am faithful ever,
And if you were my loved one, I would lead you hence, and
         would forsake you never."

Upon his hand then looking, a ring there met her sight,
Set with a stone from Abalie, in gold that glittered bright ;
Never her eyes had rested on one more rich or fairer.
Gu-drun, the queenly maiden, of this same ring had whilom
         been the wearer.

The happy maiden, smiling, with words her bliss did show :
" Of this I once was owner, and well the ring I know.
Look upon this I am wearing ; 't was the gift of my early lover,
While I, a gladsome maiden, still dwelt at home, nor stepped
         its borders over."

He, on her hand now gazing,   upon the ring did look ;
Then unto the maiden   the knightly Herwic spoke :
"That a queenly mother bore thee,   I see by many a token ;
After my heavy sorrows,   a blessed sight upon my eyes
has broken."

Then in his arms he folded   the fair and high-born maid :
For all they told each other   they were both glad and sad.
He kissed the maiden fondly,   how oft I cannot reckon ;
So, too, he greeted Hildeburg,   showing his love to both
the maids forsaken.

Then the youthful Ortwin   begged the maid to say
Whether to do her task-work   there was no other way
Than, standing by the seaside,   all day to wash the clothing ?
At this she greatly sorrowed,   and felt for her work the
deepest shame and loathing.

"Tell me now, fair sister,   where may your children be
Whom you have borne to Hartmut,   in his land across the sea,
That all alone on the seashore   to wash they thus allow you ?
If here a queen they call you,   the name you bear but little
good can do you."

Shedding tears, she answered :   "How should I have a child ?
No love could Hartmut kindle,   that I to him should yield ;
And well do all men know it   who near him here are dwelling.
Because I would not love him   I now must toil, and woe
my heart is swelling."

Then spake the knightly Herwic :   " We now can truly say
That we good luck have met with,   on our errand far away ;
And nought could have befallen   that for us were better.
It behooves us now to hasten   to free the maid from the ills
that here beset her."

Then said the knight, young Ortwin :   " That may never be.
Had I a hundred sisters,   I would sooner let them die
Than here, in another's kingdom,   to hide a deed of plunder ;
Stealing those from our foemen   whom they by stormy fight
from us did sunder."

Then spake the lord of Sealand :   " This do I greatly fear,
Should our search be known to any,   or if they find us here,
They then may take the maiden,   and her far hence may carry,
And never shall we see her :   't were best to hide the deed,
nor longer tarry."

Him did Ortwin answer :   " How can we leave in need
Her faithful band of maidens ?   So long a stay they 've made
Here in this land of foemen   that well may they be weary :
Gu-drun, my worthy sister,   should ne'er forsake her maids,
in bondage dreary."

To him then spake brave Herwic :   " Is this in truth your mind ?
Ne'er shall my well-belovéd   be left by me behind ;
To take the ladies with us,   e'en as we can, 't is better."
Him did Ortwin answer :   " Here to be hacked with the sword
for me were fitter."

Then said the downcast maiden: " What have I done to thee,
My dearest brother Ortwin ?   Never as yet in me
Was seen such ill-behavior   that I for that was chidden.
For what great sin I know not   am I, my lord, to make atonement
bidden ? "

" I do not thus, dear sister,   for want of love to thee ;
Thereby your band of maidens   I shall the better free.
Only as fits my honor,   hence will I ever take you ;
Herwic for your lover   you yet shall have, and ne'er
will he forsake you."

Gu-drun was heavy-hearted   as they went on board the boat ;
She said : " Woe worth my wanderings !   my sorrow endeth not.
He whom once I trusted,   must hope in him be shaken
That he will break my bondage ?   My bliss is yet far off,
and my faith mistaken."

In haste the daring warriors   turned from the shore away.
Gu-drun, the maid, heart-broken,   to Herwic called to stay :
" Of me you once thought highly,   but now you hold me lightly :
To whom, in my woe, do you leave me ?   Bereft of kin, to whom
can I trust me rightly ? "

" I do not hold you lightly ;   you are of maids the best.
My coming, queenly lady,   hide within your breast ;
Again, ere morning lightens,   these shores will I be treading, —
For this my troth I pledge you, —   eighty thousand followers
with me leading."

As fast as they were able   they hastened then away;
Never friends were sundered   more sadly than that day
Were these from one another;   (the truth to you I 'm telling.)
As far as their eyes could follow,   the maidens watched
       the boat away fast sailing.

Gu-drun, the queenly maiden,   her washing now forgot;
Betwixt her bliss and sorrow,   her toil she heeded not.
The harsh and wicked Gerlind,   the idle women spying
Standing by the seashore,   in anger stormed, that her clothes
       unwashed were lying.

Then said the maiden Hildeburg,   from Ireland, o'er the sea:
"Why do you let the clothing   here uncared for be?
The clothes of Ludwig's followers   still unwashed are waiting.
If this be known to Gerlind,   yet harder blows from her
       shall we be getting."

Queen Hilda's daughter answered: "Too proud I am, I ween,
That for the wicked Gerlind   I e'er should wash again.
Henceforth a toil so lowly   in scorn shall I be holding,
For two young kings have kissed me,   they in kindness me in their
       arms enfolding."

Then Hildeburg made answer: "Scorn not that I should teach,
Or that I now would show you   how best the clothes to bleach:
We must not leave them yellow,   but carefully must whiten;
Else do I greatly fear me   our backs with blows and stripes
       will well be beaten."

Then said old Hagen's grandchild: " At last my lot is bright,
With hope and gladness beaming.   If they my back shall smite
With rods, from now till morning,   I trow it will not kill me ;
But soon shall those who wronged us   know themselves the ills
                         they chose to deal me.

" These clothes I should be washing   down to the tide I 'll bear,
And fling them into the water,"   said the maiden fair ;
"Their freedom I will give them,   even as 't is fitting
That I, a queen, should do it ;   hence they may float away,
                         no hindrance meeting."

Whate'er was said by Hildeburg,   Gu-drun the clothes then took,
That Gerlind her had given ;   her task she would not brook,
But far into the billows   she threw them, strongly hurling :
I know not if ever she found them ;   they soon were lost to sight,
                         in the waters swirling.

The night was drawing nearer,   and the light began to wane ;
To the castle, heavy-laden,   went Hildeburg again.
Seven robes of finest linen   she bore, with other clothing ;
Gu-drun, young Ortwin's sister,   with Hildeburg went also,
                         bearing nothing.

When they had reached the castle,   the time was very late.
Before King Ludwig's palace,   standing at the gate,
They saw the wicked Gerlind,   watching there to meet them :
Soon as she saw the washers,   with words of bitter scorn
                         she 'gan to greet them.

Thus she spake in anger : " What does this gadding mean ?
Stripes upon your bodies you both have earned, I ween,
Thus upon the seashore, in the evening light, to wander ;
For me it were unseemly into my room to take you,
after loitering yonder."

She said : " Now tell me quickly, think you this is meet ?
You spurn the greatest princes, and show them nought but hate,
But linger yet, at nightfall, with low-born varlets flirting.
Would you be thought of highly, know you that this your own
good name is hurting."

The well-born maiden answered : " Why speak of me so ill ?
Never have I, poor maiden, had the thought or will
With any man to tattle, however dear I held him,
Unless it were a kinsman ; a talk with him I rightfully
might yield him."

" Say you I chide you wrongly ? Hush, you idle jade !
For this, to-night, I tell you, a reckoning shall be made.
To be so bold and shameless you then will dare no longer ;
Before with you I 've ended, your back shall feel that I
than you am stronger."

" In that will I gainsay you," said then the maiden proud ;
" Again with rods to beat me you ne'er shall be allowed.
You and all your kindred in birth are far below me ;
You may yet for this be sorry, if treatment so unseemly
you shall show me."

Then spake the wolfish Gerlind : " Where is my clothing left,
That, folded in your apron,   you thus your hands have wrapt;
Bearing yourself so idly,   now from toil thus turning ?
If I live a little longer,   another kind of work shall you
                          be learning."

King Hagen's grandchild answered :   " Down by the deep sea-flood
I left your clothing lying.   It was too great a load ;
I found the weight too heavy,   alone to the house to carry.
If never again you see them,   but little I care, the while
                          with you I tarry."

Then quoth the old she-devil :   " All this shall help you not ;
Before I sleep this evening,   bitter shall be your lot ! "
Then were tied, at her bidding,   rods from hedges broken ;
Gerlind would not give over   the training hard 'gainst which
                          the maid had spoken.

Then strongly to a bedstead   she bade them bind the maid,
And alone in a room to leave her,   where not a friend she had :
There should she be beaten,   till skin from bone was falling.
When this was known to her women,   they all began to weep,
                          and loud were wailing.

Then spake Gu-drun, with cunning :   " Now list to what I say :
If I with rods am beaten   thus shamefully to-day,
Should e'er an eye behold me   with kings and princes seated,
And I a crown be wearing,   to you a fit reward shall then
                          be meted.

"Henceforth for me such teaching   't were best you let alone;
Sooner the king I 've slighted   shall have me for his own:
Then as queen of Normandy   here will I be dwelling;
And when I here am mighty,   what I will do may no one
                              now be telling."

"Be this your will," said Gerlind,   "angry no more I 'll be:
E'en if a thousand garments   you thus had lost for me,
I would, in truth, forgive it;   well you will have thriven
If to my son, young Hartmut,   the Norman prince, your love
                              at last be given."

Then said the lovely maiden: "I now would take some rest;
This care and heavy sorrow   my strength doth sorely waste.
Send for the young King Hartmut,   bid him be hither speeding,
And say, whate'er he wishes,   that I henceforth will always do
                              his bidding."

Those who heard them talking,   straightway to Hartmut ran,
And to the youthful warrior   told the tale again.
Some of his father's liegemen   there with him were seated,
When word to him was given   in haste to seek Gu-drun,
                              who for him waited.

Then said the one who told him: "Give me now my fee;
Queen Hilda's lovely daughter   will grant her love to thee.
She bids you now to hasten   at once to her in her bower;
No longer are you hated,   for better thoughts she harbors
                              than of yore."

The high-born knight then answered : " To lie you have no need.
If true indeed were your tidings,   well should you be feed ;
By me would three great castles   and a hide of land be given,
With sixty golden arm-bands ;   while bliss thenceforth my days
                                       should long enliven."

Then said to him another :   " This tale, I know, is true ;
The fee should I be sharing.   At court they wish for you ;
Gu-drun, the maid, has said it.   To love you she is ready ;
And if in truth you wish it,   she in your land will be
                                       your queen and lady."

To those who told the tidings   his thanks young Hartmut gave ;
From off his seat, o'er-gladdened,   upsprang the warrior brave.
He thought that, in His kindness,   God this boon had done him,
And, with a heart now happy,   he sought the maiden's bower
                                       who love had shown him.

In garments wet there standing,   was seen the high-born maid ;
With eyes still dim with weeping,   greeting to him she said.
Forward she came to meet him ;   and now so near was standing
That he, in fondness turning,   her in his arms would clasp,
                                       towards her bending.

She said : " Not so, King Hartmut,   this you may not do ;
For men in truth would wonder   if they should look on you.
Nought am I but a washer :   in scorn would they be holding
You, a king so mighty,   if in your arms Gu-drun you should
                                       be folding."

“ This will I, Sir Hartmut,   freely to you allow,
When, by my crown, your kinsmen   me as a queen shall know.
No longer shall I scorn you,   when I that name am bearing :
For both will this be fitting ;   me in your arms to take
you may then be daring.”

Then, with all good-breeding,   he farther off withdrew,
And thus Gu-drun he answered :   “ Maiden fair and true,
Since now you deign to love me,   richly will I reward you ;
Myself and all my kinsmen,   whate’er you bid, will kindness
show toward you.”

Then said to him the maiden :   “ Such bliss I never knew.
If, after my weary toiling,   I aught may ask of you,
This first of all I wish for,   that I, poor wretched lady,
This night, before I slumber,   may have for me a restful
bath made ready.

“ And list to me yet further :   another boon I crave ;
’T is that my friendly maidens   I now with me may have.
Among Queen Gerlind’s women   you will find them, sad and weary ;
But in their room no longer   those toiling ones away from me
must tarry.”

“ Your wish I grant you freely,”   the young King Hartmut said.
Then from the room of the women   the many maids were led ;
With hair unkempt and streaming,   and scanty clothing wearing,
They to court betook them :   for them the wicked Gerlind
nought was caring.

Of these came three and sixty ;   on them did Hartmut look.
Then Gu-drun, the high-born,   with lofty breeding spoke :
" Behold, my lord, these maidens !   Is it your worth befitting
That they are thus uncared for ? "   He said : " No more shall they
                 the like be meeting."

Then spake the high-born lady :   " Hartmut, for love of me,
I beg that these my maidens,   whom here in shame you see,
May have a bath made ready.   Let now my word be heeded ;
You ought yourself to see them   decked in the comely clothes
                 they long have needed."

To her then answered Hartmut,   of knights a worthy one :
" Gu-drun, belovéd lady,   if clothes the maids have none
Erst by them brought hither,   when they their home were leaving,
To them yet other clothing,   the best in all the world, will I
                 be giving.

" Gladly would I see them,   with you, more fitly clad."
Then by those in waiting   baths were ready made.
Among the kin of Hartmut   chamberlains many were there ;
To help Gu-drun they hastened,   thinking that later she their
                 hopes would further.

Gu-drun and all her maidens   were by the bath made glad ;
Then the best of clothing   that any ever had
To all the homeless women   alike was freely given.
The lowliest one among them   might gain the love of a king,
                 if she had striven.

When they their bath had taken,   wine to them was brought;
In all the land of Normandy   none better need be sought;
And soon the weary maidens   the best of mead were drinking.
To Hartmut thanks were given;   to gain such praises how could
he e'er be thinking!

Soon the lovely maiden   was seated in the hall.
Gerlind bade her daughter   then, with her maidens all,
To don their clothing quickly,   the finest and most fitting,
If they Queen Hilda's daughter   wished to see, among her
maidens sitting.

At once the well-born Ortrun   clothed her in her best;
To seek Gu-drun then straightway   gladly did she haste.
The grandchild of wild Hagen   quickly went to meet her;
When they saw each other,   the happiness of both
was never greater.

Each one kissed the other,   'neath a band of gold on her head;
The hue of both was brighter   for the golden light they shed.
Each in her way was happy;   Ortrun's eyes were beaming,
To see the high-born washer   in finest clothes now clad,
so comely seeming.

The poor Gu-drun was blithesome,   as we have said before,
That soon her friendly kinsmen   she would see once more.
The maidens sat together,   with playful talk now gladdened;
Whoever looked upon them   might gain a happy heart,
however saddened.

" 'T is well for me," said Ortrun,   " that I have lived till now,
When as the wife of Hartmut   you here yourself will show.
To one who loves my brother   gladly will I give her
The crown of my mother, Gerlind,   that I of right should wear
                 did I outlive her."

" Ortrun, may God reward you,"   thus the maiden spake ;
" Whatever you shall bid me,   that will I do for your sake.
You have bewept so often   the sorrows I was bearing,
From you will I ne'er be sundered,   and every day shall you
                 my love be sharing."

Then with maiden wiliness   spake the fair Gu-drun :
" Now you ought, Sir Hartmut,   to send out runners soon,
Through all the Norman kingdom,   to give to friends your bidding,
As many as will hear it,   to come to your palace now, to see
                 our wedding.

" When peace is in your borders,   this to you I say,
Before your host of warriors   I will wear the crown one day.
How many he has who woos me   thus shall I be knowing ;
Then before your liegemen   myself and all my kin will I be
                 showing."

The maid in truth was crafty ;   from the castle on that day
A hundred men or over   did Hartmut send away.
So, when the Hegeling fighters   should for him be seeking,
Fewer foes should meet them :   for this was Gu-drun
                 their going thence bespeaking.

Then spake the old Queen Gerlind: "Now, fair daughter mine,
You two must leave each other; when another morn shall shine,
Then may you be together, with none your bliss forbidding."
She left Gu-drun, low bowing, and begged that God would her
　　　　　　　　　　　　　　　　　　in his ways be leading.

Then did Hartmut leave her. All hearkened to her word;
They gave to the maiden cup-bearers, and carvers at the board:
The high-born lady's wishes they bade should well be heeded;
Nor food nor drink she wanted: busy were they to bring her
　　　　　　　　　　　　　　　　　　　　all she needed.

Then spake one lovely maiden among the Hegeling band:
"When we on this are thinking, how from our fatherland
Our foes have brought us hither, to live unblest forever,
We still are bowed with sorrow; when in our homes, such woe
　　　　　　　　　　　　　　　　　　we thought of never."

She then began a-weeping, where sat her lady fair.
When this was seen by others who stood beside her there,
They felt yet greater sorrow their heavy hearts now filling.
All then wept together; but they saw their mistress,
　　　　　　　　　　　　　　　　　　fair Gu-drun, was smiling.

They thought that now forever they far from home must stay:
But their lady ne'er was thinking to bide so long away;
They would, ere four days later, their freedom all be knowing.
The time had come already to whisper to Gerlind that they
　　　　　　　　　　　　　　　　　　would soon be going.

Beyond her wont a little   to laugh had the maid begun ;
For fourteen years now bygone   she never bliss had known.
Of her glee the bad she-devil   quickly now was hearing ;
She gave the hint to Ludwig,   for care she felt, and anger
past all bearing.

She went at once to Hartmut,   and said : " Oh, son of mine,
List to the truth I tell you !   throughout this land of thine,
All within it dwelling   shall see both strife and toiling.
Why it is I know not,   the fair young queen, Gu-drun,
is now so smiling.

" I know not how it happened,   or how the news she heard,
But men sent out by her kinsmen   hither to come have dared.
Therefore, knightly Hartmut,   some way must you be choosing,
Lest, thro' the friends she looks for,   your worthy name and life
you may be losing."

He said : " Be not so fearful.   I grudge it not to the maid
That she, with all her women,   should for a time be glad.
All her nearest kinsmen   far from me are dwelling ;
What harm can they be doing ?   I need not guard 'gainst ills
they may be dealing."

Gu-drun, now over-wearied,   some of her maidens sent
To see if her bed were ready,   for she on sleep was bent ;
For a night at least her sorrow   she could now be leaving.
Then went with them most kindly   King Hartmut's chamberlain,
his service giving.

Youths of the Norman palace   before her bore the light;
On her they ne'er had waited   until that very night.
Thirty beds or over   now were found made ready;
Nice were they and cleanly,   meet for Gu-drun and many a
                                 well-born lady.

On them were pillows lying   from far Arabia brought,
With green, like leaves of clover,   and other hues, inwrought.
Bedspreads on them hanging   were sewed in strips most fairly;
And red as fire was shining   the gold mixed in with
                                 silken threads not sparely.

Beneath the silken bedspreads   fishes' skins were laid,
To make them thicker and warmer.   The fair and lovely maid,
Thither come from the Hegelings,   Hartmut would be wooing,
For he as yet knew nothing   of the harm to him that her
                                 friends would soon be doing.

Then said the high-born maiden: "To sleep you now may go,
All you that wait on Hartmut;   we, too, the same will do.
I, and my ladies with me,   one night at least will rest us;
For, since our coming hither,   freedom from hardest toil
                                 hath never blest us."

All who there were gathered   of Hartmut's knights and men,
The wise as well as youthful,   thence to go were seen;
They to rest then hasted,   the ladies' bower now leaving.
Wine and mead unstinted   to the homeless maids were others
                                 freely giving.

Then said Hilda's daughter :   " Now shut for me the door."
They barred the ladies' bedroom   with heavy bolts full four :
The room was shut so tightly   that what therein was doing,
However much one listened,   outside he nought could hear,
nor might be knowing.

Awhile they all were seated,   merrily drinking wine ;
Then said Gu-drun, the queenly :   " Dearest maidens mine,
You well may now be happy,   after your heavy sorrow :
Your friends I soon will show you ;   on gladsome sights
your eyes shall feed to-morrow.

" Herwic, my betrothéd,   did I this morning kiss,
And Ortwin, too, my brother ;   you now may think on this.
She shall soon be richer,   and care from her be taken,
Who shall well be mindful,   when night is over, me in the morn
to waken.

" You well shall be rewarded.   To us glad days are nigh :
And freely will I give you   castles strong and high,
And with them many acres ;   for these shall I be gaining,
If I the day shall witness   when, as a queen, I o'er my lands
am reigning."

They now lay down to slumber,   with hearts all free from care.
They knew to them were speeding   knights full brave to dare,
Who erelong would help them,   and their woes would lighten.
To see them they were hoping,   soon as to-morrow's sun the day
should brighten.

Tale the Twenty-Sixth.

HOW THE HEGELINGS LANDED NEAR LUDWIG'S CASTLE.

WE ask you now to listen   to a tale as yet untold :
   Ortwin still and Herwic   their way did onward hold
Until they found their followers   on the seashore standing.
Then ran these Hegeling liegemen   to meet them on the sands
                 where they were landing.

Them they gladly welcomed,   and bade that they make known
The news that they were bringing,   and freely all to own.
First they asked of Ortwin,   if he could them be telling,
If still Gu-drun were living,   and if in Ludwig's land
                 she now was dwelling?

The knightly Ortwin answered :   " Of this I may not speak
To each and all that ask it ;   the truth I will not break
Till all are met together ;   then shall you be hearing
All that our eyes there greeted,   when we to come near Hartmut's
                 walls were daring."

The word was told to others,   and soon a mighty band
Of warriors brave and knightly   around the two did stand.
Then to them said Ortwin: " Sad is the news I give you,
And, were my wishes granted,   gladly I 'd spare the tale,
for much 't will grieve you.

" List to what has happened,   for wonders now begin ;
Gu-drun, my long-lost sister,   I, in truth, have seen,
And with her also Hildeburg,   erst in Ireland living."
When he the tidings gave them,   they thought the tale he told
not worth believing.

All then said together :   " It is not well to jest;
For her we long have waited,   and now our time you waste.
We hoped from Ludwig's kingdom   you would bring her sooner ;
To Ortwin and his followers   belong the shame and blame
for wrongs still done her."

" Ask you, then, King Herwic :   he, too, has seen the maid ;
And he can also tell you   what wrongs on us are laid.
Could you, my friends, bethink you   of any shame that 's greater ?
We found Gu-drun and Hildeburg   upon the seashore standing,
washing in the water."

Soon were his kindred weeping,   all who there were seen.
At this the aged Wâ-te   right scornful was, I ween :
" Truly for women only   is such behavior fitting ;
Why you weep you know not.   This, in a knight, one never
should be meeting.

“ But if you are in earnest,   to help Gu-drun in her need,
The clothes that she has whitened   must you in war make red.
Erst white hands did wash them   for men who must be bleeding;
So you now may help her,   and soon the maid forlorn
                      be homeward leading.”

Then said the Danish Fru-te :   “ How can this be done?
How can we reach their kingdom   before our plan is known,
Before the men of Ludwig,   and Hartmut’s knights, are learning
That Hilda’s friends are gathered,   and toward the Norman land
                      at length are turning ?”

Then said the aged Wâ-te :   “ Hear what ’t is best to do ;
I trust before his castle   fitly to meet the foe,
If I may live to see him   there before me standing.
Brave knights, your rest now leaving,   soon on the Norman shore
                      must you be landing.

“ The air is fresh and gladsome,   the sky is broad and bright,
And, well for us it happens,   the moon will shine to-night.
From the sandy shore now hasten,   my warriors bold and daring :
Before it dawns to-morrow,   we King Ludwig’s stronghold
                      must be nearing.”

Then they all were busy,   when thus old Wâ-te spoke ;
Soon their clothes and horses   on board the ships they took.
All the night still sailing,   towards the land they hasted ;
And ere the morrow’s daylight,   before the castle, on the sands
                      they rested.

Hushed were all by Wâ-te,   throughout the warlike band,
As soon as they to rest them   lay down upon the sand.
To his water-weary followers   leave for this was granted ;
Their shields about them spreading,   on them they laid their
                             heads, for sleep they wanted.

" Whoe'er to-morrow morning   hopes to gain the fight
Must not," said the aged Wâ-te,   " oversleep to-night.
For the struggle now before us   we hardly can be waiting ;
As soon as morning lightens,   then, good knights, the foe
                             must we be meeting."

" Further I give you warning :   whoe'er my horn shall hear
Along the seashore sounded,   soon as it meets his ear,
Let him at once make ready   the foeman to be meeting.
When I shall blow at daybreak,   no longer then may any
                             there be waiting.

" When I again shall blow it,   let each to this give heed ;
Quickly let his saddle   be laid upon his steed.
Let him then be waiting,   till I see 't is daylight fully,
And the time has come for the onset ;   let none hang back, but
                             meet the struggle truly."

To do as Wâ-te bade them   their word they gladly gave.
How many a lovely woman   did he of bliss bereave !
For soon their dearest kindred   unto death were wounded,
Who now were only waiting   until the horn in the early
                             morning sounded.

"When you, my friends and kinsmen,   thrice my horn shall hear,
Then, seated on your horses,   must you your weapons wear;
Thus must you, brave warriors,   wait, your steeds bestriding,
Till me you see, well-weaponed,   under the fair Queen Hilda's
                         banner riding."

Now on the seashore weary   lay they, one and all;
Very near were they resting   to old King Ludwig's hall.
Altho' the night had fallen,   its towers they saw while waking;
The brave and fearless warriors   in stillness lay, no sound
                         or outcry making.

The early star of morning   now had risen high;
Then came a lovely maiden   unto the window nigh.
She there was gazing skyward,   to see when day was breaking,
That she might bring the tidings,   and rich reward from fair
                         Gu-drun be seeking.

Ere she long had waited,   there dawned on the maiden's sight,
With its wonted gleam on the waters,   the early morning light;
Then the sheen of helmets   and many shields there flittered:
Foes had besieged the castle,   and all the sands below
                         with weapons glittered.

Back then went the maiden   to where Gu-drun she found:
"Arouse, my queenly lady,   wake from your slumber sound!
The land is held by foemen,   who will these walls be storming;
We have not been forgotten   by those at home; our friends
                         come hither swarming."

Gu-drun, the high-born lady,   quickly sprang from her bed,
And, hasting to the window,   to the maid her thanks she said.
"For this good news you give me,   wealth shall you be earning."
After her heavy sorrow,   now for her friends Gu-drun was
                                     sorely yearning.

Rich sails were seen to flutter   near by upon the sea;
Then said the high-born maiden: "Ah, wellaway!   Woe's me!
Would that I ne'er were living!"   the wretched one was sighing:
"Many a doughty warrior   this day for me shall here
                                     in death be lying."

While thus she was bewailing,   nearly all still slept;
But soon was one heard shouting,   who guard for Ludwig kept:
"Be up, you careless warriors!   your arms, your arms be taking!
And you, my king of Normandy!   I fear that all too late
                                     you will be waking."

This the wicked Gerlind   heard, as the warder cried;
Then, while fast he slumbered,   she left the old king's side.
Up to the roof of the castle   then at once she hastened;
She thence saw many foemen,   and on her devilish heart
                                     great sorrow fastened.

Back again she speeded   to where she found the king:
"Awake, my lord, make ready   for guests who followers bring!
Now hem they in your castle,   and well may they be dreaded:
That smile of young Gu-drun   will cost your knights a strife
                                     as yet unheeded."

" Hush ! " then answered Ludwig,   " I will go myself to see ;
We must all be bravely waiting   for whatsoe'er may be."
Then looked he from his castle,   to see the foemen thronging ;
His eyes by guests were greeted,   on whom to look he never
                   might be longing.

Before his palace waving,   he saw their banners spread ;
Then said the old King Ludwig :   " Let some one go with speed
And bear this news to Hartmut.   I for pilgrims take them,
To sell their wares come hither ;   before my hall a market
                   would they make them."

Then they wakened Hartmut,   that he the tale might hear.
Outspoke that daring warrior :   " Let none be sad or fear.
I see full twenty princes   their blazoned banners bearing ;
I ween these foes are coming   to wreak the hate they long
                   'gainst us are wearing."

Tale the Twenty-Seventh.

HOW LUDWIG AND HARTMUT MET THE HEGELINGS.

ASLEEP still left he lying   all his faithful men.
He and his father Ludwig,   the twain, to go were seen.
And, gazing from the window,   they saw the throngs below them.
Quickly then said Hartmut: " Too near our castle-walls
                                        methinks they show them.

" I ween they are not pilgrims,   in truth, my father dear;
More like it is that Wâ-te   and all his men draw near.
He from Sturmland cometh,   the lord of Ortland bringing:
The men I see are like them,   as I know from the flag that they
                                        to the breeze are flinging.

" I see a brown silk pennon,   that comes from Karadé;
Before that flag is lowered,   many will rue the day.
On it a head is blazoned. —   as red as gold it glitters:
Guests so bold and warlike   we well can spare: their sight
                                        the day embitters.

"The Moorland king is bringing   full twenty thousand men,
Knights as strong and daring   as any I have seen;
To win from us great honor   methinks they now are craving.
There comes another banner,   that o'er yet other knights
                         its folds is waving.

"It is the flag of Horant,   the knight from the Danish land;
I see with him Lord Fru-te,   I know both him and his band.
And hither, too, from Waleis,   many foemen leading,
Morune now comes riding;   he, for the morning's fight, o'er
                         the sands is speeding.

"I see another banner,   on it a chevron red,
With sharpened spears within it;   for this shall many bleed.
Ortwin it is who bears it,   from Ortland hither faring:
Erewhile we slew his father;   no kindly thought to us he now
                         is bearing.

"There floats another banner,   whiter than any swan;
Blazons bright and golden   you well may see thereon.
It is our mother Hilda   who sends it o'er the water;
The hatred of the Hegelings   will soon be known by me
                         who stole her daughter.

"There I see uplifted   a flag outspreading wide;
Of sky-blue silk 't is woven.   The truth I will not hide;
Herwic bears this banner,   he in the Sealands dwelling.
Sea-leaves are shown upon it;   he soon on us his wrath will
                         here be telling.

"There Irold, too, is coming, —   this that I say is true, —
From Friesland leading many,   as well indeed I know,
With fighting men from Holstein,   warriors brave and daring.
A stormy fight is nearing ;   now in our castle all must arms
be wearing."

Then cried Hartmut loudly :   " Up, my faithful men !
If to these guests so warlike,   who 'neath our walls are seen,
It may not now be granted   to ride so boldly near us,
Then, before the gateway,   with sword-blows we must greet them,
and bravely bear us."

Then from their beds upsprang they   all who yet did lie ;
At once, to bring their war-gear,   loudly did they cry.
The call to guard their master   gladly they were hearing ;
Forty hundred warriors   showed themselves, their shining
armor wearing.

Ludwig and Hartmut with him   armed themselves for fight :
To the sad and homeless maidens   this was a sorry sight ;
These within the castle   uneasy hearts were keeping ;
They said to one another :   " Let him who smiled before
this day be weeping ! "

Quickly came Queen Gerlind,   old King Ludwig's wife ;
She said : " What will you, Hartmut ?   Would you lose your life,
With that of all your kinsmen   who here our lot are sharing ?
The foe will surely slay you,   if to leave the castle-walls
you now be daring."

The well-born knight then answered :   " Mother, stay within ;
You may not give your teaching   to me or to my men.
Spare your words for women ;   they mayhap will listen,
While they sit at sewing,   making their silks with gold
and gems to glisten.

" Now, mother, let us see you   send Gu-drun to wash,
As you did before, with her maidens,   where the billows dash.
You weened they all were friendless,   and had no kindred living ;
You yet may see, ere nightfall,   what thanks to us our guests
will yet be giving."

Then spake his devilish mother :   " I did it for your sake,
Thinking her will to bridle.   My bidding kindly take ;
Strongly built is the castle,   let now the gates be fastened ;
They then will gain but little   who on their toilsome way
have hither hastened.

" Full well you know it, Hartmut,   you bear the maiden's hate,
For you have slain her kinsmen :   your watch you must not bate.
It is not friends or kinsfolk   who at our gates are knocking ;
The proud and warlike Hegelings,   twenty to one of us, come
hither flocking.

"Of this bethink you further,   my well-belovéd son :
Bread we have in the castle   and wine for every one ;
Food will not be lacking   if here for a year we are staying ;
But if on the field you are taken,   our foes will you from
bondage ne'er be freeing."

Then to him spake further   old King Ludwig's wife:
" Ever guard your honor,   but do not lose your life.
Bid men to shoot with longbows   at the loop-holes standing ;
So shall wounds be given,   for which their friends at home
will tears be spending.

" Let slings with ropes be fitted ;   we then will meet the foe
By hurling rocks upon them :   knights we have enow.
Before with these new-comers   you your swords are crossing,
Stones will I and my maidens   bring in aprons white,
on them to be tossing."

Angrily spake Hartmut :   " Lady, get you gone!
Why do you seek to lead me ?   Is not my mind my own ?
Before my foes shall find me   within my castle hiding,
Outside I would die far sooner,   in fight with Hilda's men,
against me riding."

Then to him said, weeping,   old King Ludwig's wife :
" I gave to you this warning   that you might spare your life,
And guard yourself the better.   Whoe'er is seen this morning
Beneath your banner fighting,   rich gifts from us shall he
be fairly earning.

" Now arm ourselves," cried Gerlind,   " stand by my son in fight ;
Strike from your foemen's helmets   a glowing, fiery light.
Be always near your master,   to help him ever striving ;
Fitly these guests to welcome,   deep be the wounds that you
to them are giving."

Then to his men said Hartmut: "My mother's words are true;
If you to me are faithful,   and strive your best to do,
And this day, in the struggle,   to give your help are ready,
When fathers shall have fallen,   a friend I 'll be to sons
bereft and needy."

A thousand and a hundred   within King Ludwig's halls
Now were all well-weaponed.   Before from out the walls
Went any thro' the gateways,   they left the stronghold guarded;
Still within it posted,   five hundred warriors brave
the castle warded.

On four gates of the castle   the bolts were backward thrown:
Ne'er had they been opened   to a single spur alone.
Then with the youthful Hartmut,   outgoing at his bidding,
All with helmets fastened,   went thirty hundred followers
boldly riding.

The hour of strife drew nearer.   He of the Sturmisch land,
Wâ-te, his horn was blowing;   and loud across the sand,
For thirty miles or over,   men the blast were hearing;
The fighters of the Hegelings,   to flock to Hilda's flag,
their arms were wearing.

Once again he blew it: at this should all take heed,
That every knight among them   then should mount his steed,
And each his men should gather   to ride as they were bidden.
A knight so old as Wâ-te,   and yet so brave, to the fight
had never ridden.

The third time that he blew it,   he such a blast did make
That all the land was shaken,   and the sea a sound gave back ;
Almost from Ludwig's castle   the corner-stones were falling :
To raise Queen Hilda's banner   Wâ-te to Horant then was loudly
calling.

They feared old Wâ-te sorely,   none dared to speak aloud ;
A horse was e'en heard neighing.   Upon the roof now stood
Herwic's well-belovéd,   and saw the warriors daring,
Onward proudly riding,   to wage the fight with Hartmut,
nothing fearing.

Hartmut rode to meet them ;   he and all his men,
Bearing well their weapons,   to leave the gates were seen.
Those from the windows gazing   saw the helmets glisten
Of friends as well as foemen.   Hartmut not alone to the fight
did hasten.

To all four sides of the castle   the foes their banners bore ;
Bright in hue like silver   was the armor that they wore ;
The bosses of their bucklers   were seen to glitter brightly.
Much was Wâ-te dreaded ;   no lion grim and wild
were feared more rightly.

The fighters from the Moorland   were seen apart to ride,
And heavy shafts were hurling ;   splinters were scattered wide.
When with the Norman foemen   soon the fight did thicken,
Sharply from their weapons   and from their breastplates
fiery sparks were stricken.

The warriors from Denmark near to the castle rode.
There the mighty Irold six thousand fighters good
Up to the walls was leading, an onslaught to be making:
Brave and daring were they; sore ill from them erelong
was Ludwig taking.

Elsewhere, riding boldly, Ortwin his followers led,
No less than eighty hundred; sorrow and woe they made
For many of the Normans, and all the land they harried.
Gerlind and Ortrun weeping, watching the fight from the roof,
together tarried.

Then came Herwic also, betrothed to fair Gu-drun;
Through him full many a woman must come to sorrow soon,
When, for his heart's belovéd, he to the fight was springing.
Beneath the heavy weapons were heard the clattering helmets
loudly ringing.

Now came the aged Wâ-te, with warriors not a few;
Grim was he and fearless, as soon they all well knew.
His spear not yet he lowered as he to the walls came riding:
Sad was the sight to Gerlind, but other were the thoughts
Gu-drun was hiding.

Then came the Norman Hartmut, riding before his men.
E'en had he been Kaiser, never would he be seen
To bear himself more proudly. In the sun was seen to glisten
All his shining armor. His boldness on the field not yet
did lessen.

When he was seen by Ortwin,   the lord of Ortland's throne,
He said: " Will any tell us,   to whom this knight is known,
Who is the daring fighter   now against us turning?
He shows as bold a bearing   as if to win a kingdom he were
yearning."

Then said one among them: " 'T is Hartmut whom you see ;
There indeed is a warrior !   a daring knight is he.
The selfsame foeman is he   who erstwhile slew your father.
Where'er the strife is raging,   a bolder man than he
there 's not another."

Angrily spake Ortwin :   " Me for his wrongs he owes,
And must atone full dearly   before from here he goes.
The ills that he has done us   must he be soon undoing ;
Gerlind cannot help him   that he from hence may e'er alive
be going."

Down upon young Ortwin   Hartmut riding bore.
Altho' he did not know him,   deep he plunged his spur ;
His horse sprang forward widely,   against brave Ortwin driven.
Both their spears were lowered ;   fire on their armor flashed
from spear-strokes given.

No thrust against the other   did either leave undone :
The war-horse then of Ortwin   was on his haunches thrown ;
Soon, too, the steed did stagger   whereon was Hartmut seated :
They could not bear the onset   of kings who rushed together,
to madness heated.

High upreared the horses ;   a mighty clang arose
From clash of kingly sword-blades.   Thanks were due to those
Who the fight thus opened,   as knights beseemeth ever.
Brave were both and fearless ;   to shrink from one another
thought they never.

On both sides came their followers,   lowering their spears,
And bringing death to many ;   each his foeman nears,
And in the shock of the onset   heavy wounds was giving.
All of them were faithful,   and well for a worthy name
they now were striving.

A thousand 'gainst a thousand,   now the strife began
Of Hartmut's men with Wâ-te's,   each man against his man.
Soon by the lord of Sturmland   were they so badly treated
That whoso now came near him   never a second time with him
was mated.

Now were thickly mingled   of foes ten thousand men,
Among King Herwic's warriors ;   they came in anger keen.
Their mood it was so stubborn   that rather than be flying
Far from the field of fighting,   they on the ground would first
in death be lying.

A knight indeed was Herwic ;   what daring deeds he did !
Earnest was he in fighting,   that so the lovely maid
Might be to him the kinder.   But how could he be dreaming
The boon could e'er befall him,   that the eyes of fair Gu-drun
on him were beaming ?

Ludwig, king of the Normans,   and they of the Danish land,
Now had met together.   Ludwig bore in hand
His strong and heavy weapon ;   lordly was his bearing,
Yet he with all his followers   to come too far without
the walls was daring.

There, with his men from Holstein,   Fru-te, brave and bold,
Slew full many a foeman ;   of this could much be told.
Now, too, from the land of Waleis,   Morune, many slaying,
Before King Ludwig's castle   made rich the earth with the dead
he low was laying.

Irold, the youthful champion,   a knight both true and good,
Slashed thro' foemen's armor,   shedding their hot life-blood.
Under Hilda's banner   was Wâ-te's kinsman fighting ;
Many in death grew paler   as Horant thinned the crowd
he fast was smiting.

Now the young King Hartmut   and Ortwin met again.
Thicker then than snow-flakes   blown by the wind are seen,
The sword-strokes of the warriors   upon each other lighted :
Thus it was that Hartmut   once more by Ortwin on the field.
was greeted.

Gu-drun's young brother, Ortwin,   was bold and brave enow,
But Hartmut through his helmet   smote him a heavy blow ;
Over his shining breastplate   soon the blood was streaming :
The followers of Ortwin   sadly saw the flow, its brightness
dimming.

Great was the crush and uproar; hand to hand they fought;
Many wounds were gaping thro' rings of steel well-wrought;
Many a head had fallen beneath the sword-strokes given:
Death was like a robber, that from their kin the
                         dearest friends had riven.

Now saw the Danish Horant that Ortwin from his foe
A bloody wound had taken; then Horant bade them show
Who 't was that thus had wounded his master loved so dearly.
Hartmut at this was laughing, for both upon the field
                         had met too nearly.

Ortwin himself then answered: " 'T is Hartmut this has done."
Then Hilda's banner was given by Horant to one of his own;
Thinking thus the foeman he could harm the better,
And gain himself much honor: now he sought his foe
                         with boldness greater.

Hartmut heard around him a loud and stormy din.
On many of his warriors streams of blood were seen
Fast from wounds out-welling; down to their feet 't was flowing.
Then cried Hartmut boldly: "For this shall you atone,
                         and this be ruing."

Now he turned him quickly where Horant met his sight;
Then might one be seeing, so brave were both in fight,
How from their ringed armor sparks of fire were flying;
Blunted were the sword-blades which they on each other's
                         helmets fast were plying.

Hartmut wounded Horant,   even as he had done
Not long before to Ortwin ;   a ruddy stream full soon
Ran from out his armor,   at Hartmut's hand forth welling.
Strong indeed was his foeman ;   who now to win his lands
                                    could hope be feeling ?

Then in bitter struggle   many, on either side,
Saw their bucklers shattered,   tho' strong and often tried ;
Beaten were they and broken   by sword-strokes quickly given
By each upon the other.   Well to guard himself had
                                    Hartmut striven.

Now the friends of Ortwin,   and those of Horant, too,
Away from the field did lead them ;   and care did they bestow
To bind their wounds wide-gaping ;   no time for this they wasted.
Then again to the war-field   the knights both rode ; once more
                                    to the strife they hasted.

We now must leave them fighting   as bravely as they will.
Who the day was winning,   or whom his foe did kill,
Before King Ludwig's castle,   none could yet be saying.
Grimly strove the Normans ;   their foes, not less, for fame
                                    were strength outlaying.

Of all that there befell them   none may ever tell ;
But 't is not yet forgotten   that many a knight there fell.
On every side were sword-blades   heard together ringing ;
Foemen all were mingled,   the slow with those who quick
                                    in fight were springing.

Wâ-te stood not idle,   that can I well believe.
He bade farewell to many,   nor longer let them live ;
Cut down by him in the struggle,   were they before him lying.
Fain were Hartmut's kinsmen   to wreak their wrath for friends
who there were dying.

Now came Herwic nearer,   so the tale is told,
And led against King Ludwig   many a champion bold.
He saw that aged warrior   his weapons bravely bearing,
Where he with all his liegemen,   a wondrous host of foes
beat down, unsparing.

Herwic called out loudly :   " Can any one now tell
Who is that fighting graybeard,   who all his foes doth fell ?
Deepest wounds for many   there his hand is hewing,
With bravery so fearless :   women in tears will this erelong
be ruing."

When this was heard by Ludwig,   outspoke that Norman foe :
" Who in the midst of battle   seeks my name to know ?
I bear the name of Ludwig :   for Normandy I 'm fighting ;
Could I but meet my foemen,   them indeed would I be sorely
smiting."

Then spake to him King Herwic :   " This thou well dost earn :
Seeing thou art Ludwig,   with hate for thee I burn.
For us, upon the sand-drifts,   many knights thou wast slaying :
Thou slewest Hettel also ;   a warrior brave was he, beyond
all saying.

" Still further thou hast wronged us,   before thy day was done :
For this we still are mourning.   I for my loss have known
Heart-heaviness and sorrow :   thou hast my lady stolen
From me upon the Wulpensand ;   and many knights for her
in death have fallen.

" I bear the name of Herwic :   thou hast taken my hoped-for wife,
And again to me must give her ;   else to give his life,
With that of many a liegeman,   must one of us be willing."
Then King Ludwig answered :   " Too boldly thou in my land
in threats art dealing.

" Thy name, and this thy warning,   thou hast no need to tell ;
There yet are many others   from whom I took, as well,
Their goods and eke their kinsmen.   To trust my word be ready,
In this I will not falter ;   thou nevermore may'st hope to kiss
thy lady."

When they thus had spoken,   the kings no more did rest,
But sprang upon each other.   If either got the best,
To hold it was not easy ;   youths were forward pushing
Under both the standards,   and daring knights to help
their lords were rushing.

A fearless king was Herwic,   and long and bravely fought ;
But quickly Hartmut's father   the youthful Herwic smote,
Till he began to stagger   'neath blows by Ludwig given,
Who gladly would have slain him,   or would from out his lands
his foe have driven.

If Herwic's faithful followers   so near him had not been,
And given help so quickly,   never could he, I ween,
Have freed himself from Ludwig,   or left the field yet living ;
So well that aged warrior   to make young Herwic dread him
                 now was striving.

But help to him was granted,   his life he did not lose ;
And, neither stunned nor wounded,   he from his fall arose.
Then to the roof quick turning,   his eyes he now was raising,
To see if, 'mongst the ladies,   his heart's beloved had
                 on his fall been gazing.

Tale the Twenty-Eighth.

HOW HERWIC SLEW LUDWIG.

NOW said Herwic sadly :   " Ah, welaway ! Woe 's me !
    If fair Gu-drun, my lady,   my fall did lately see.
Should e'er the hour be coming   when I shall clasp the maiden,
And as a wife shall own her,   with blame and scorn shall I
                                        by her be laden.

" Sorely doth it shame me,   that now the gray old man
Thus has overthrown me."   Forthwith he bade again
His men to raise his banner,   and 'gainst King Ludwig bear it ;
Then rushed they on the foemen,   who might not flee the fight,
                                        but all must share it.

Ludwig heard behind him   an uproar loud and din ;
Then he turned him quickly,   and Herwic sought again.
Soon he heard on helmets   many sword-blows stricken.
Those who stood near Ludwig   well might dread the wrath
                                        that both did quicken.

They sprang upon each other,   and fast and well they smote;
Blows on blows loud sounded   the stormy field throughout.
Who can tell how many   now in death were lying?
The day was lost to Ludwig,   who there his strength with Herwic
                       would be trying.

Soon Gu-drun's betrothéd   reached over Ludwig's shield,
And smote him 'neath his helmet;   well his sword did he wield.
Him he sorely wounded,   and strength no more did leave him;
Grim death he there awaited   until King Herwic should
                       of life bereave him.

Then Herwic with his broadsword   smote the king anew;
At once the head of Ludwig   from off his shoulders flew.
Well repaid was Herwic   for his shameful overthrowing;
The king lay dead before him.   For this fair eyes must soon
                       be overflowing.

Ludwig's faithful followers,   after their king was slain,
His banner to the castle   thought to bear again;
But all too far from the gateway   they had now been straying:
From them the flag was taken,   and death must them erelong
                       with their lord be laying.

The watchman saw from the castle   how Ludwig lost his life;
Then was heard the mourning   of knights and many a wife:
Their king, so old and mighty,   they knew in death was lying;
Gu-drun and all her maidens   stood in the hall in fear,
                       and loud were crying.

As yet the Norman Hartmut,   knew nothing of the tale,
How that the king, his father,   and kinsmen young as well,
With many bravest warriors,   now in death were sleeping.
Then he heard from the castle   the shrieks and wails of those
            who there were weeping.

Now the knightly Hartmut   unto his followers said :
" 'T is best we hence withdraw us ;   how many here lie dead
Who in stormy fighting   thought our men to be slaying !
Now will we seek the castle,   and there until a better time
            be staying."

To him they listened gladly,   and followed where he rode.
Great was the work of slaughter   the field around them showed,
Where with grimmest foemen   they were closely warring ;
Freely had blood been flowing   beneath the hand of Hartmut
            and his followers daring.

" So well," he said, " have you helped me,   who my kinsmen are,
That all my lands and riches   gladly with you I 'll share.
We now will ride to my castle,   and there to rest betake us ;
Men the gates will open,   and wine for us will pour,
            and mead will make us."

Fallen knights full many   they left on the field behind :
Were these of the land the owners,   still with no braver mind
They then had met the onset.   Those for the gates now striving,
By Wâ-te and his thousand   were not allowed to reach
            the castle living.

He with a host of fighters   near the gates was seen,
When Hartmut with his followers   sought to come within;
They in this were baffled,   and their strength were wasting.
Those who the castle guarded   heavy stones from off the wall
                         were casting.

They hurled them down so wildly   on Wâ-te and his men,
Like hailstones they were falling,   with not a stop between.
Wâ-te recked but little   how many were dead or living,
Might he the day be gaining;   to this alone his thoughts
                         he now was giving.

Hartmut saw old Wâ-te   before the castle-gate.
He said: "Tho' from our foemen   our gains this day are great,
Before it shall be ended,   for this their hate they 'll show us:
Let now the strong be heedful;   dead must many lie
                         on the field below us.

"Fear and care it gives me   that many here are seen
Whom we must now be meeting.   Wâ-te with all his men
I see before the gateway,   there with sword-strokes hewing.
If he of the gate be keeper,   I look for little kindness
                         he 'll be doing.

"See for yourselves, my warriors,   the gateways and the walls
By foes on all sides girdled;   knight to knight there calls.
The roadways all are crowded,   whichever way we 're turning:
Gu-drun's good friends and champions   will spare no toil;
                         to win the day they 're burning.

" That you may know too truly,   as I see already well ;
Friends we must lose full many.   Howe'er it so befell,
Before the outer gateway   already see I waving
The Moorland foeman's banner;   lest they get in, a care
must you be having.

" Near to the second gateway   I see yet other foes :
I saw Lord Ortwin's banner,   as on the breeze it rose.
Gu-drun's young brother is he ;   fair women's smiles he 's seeking :
Ere he shall cool his anger,   beneath his blows will helmets
yet be breaking.

" Now see I, too, brave Herwic,   before the third gate there ;
With him seven thousand followers   upon the field are near.
He comes in guise most knightly,   to win his own heart's lady ;
On him are gazing gladly   the fair Gu-drun, and many
maids already.

" To hasten back to my castle,   the thought too late has come.
I know not where, with my warriors,   now to seek a home.
I see the stern old Wâ-te   before the fourth gate fighting ;
My many friends in the castle,   I fear indeed must long
for us be waiting.

" Fly from here I cannot ;   no wings for this have I ;
Nor in the earth can hide me,   whatever else I try.
Neither from the foeman   to the waves can we be turning :
Now, in our lot so wretched,   what best it is to do from me
be learning.

"Good knights of mine, now hearken;   there 's nothing left to do
But, to the ground alighting,   their hot life's-blood to hew
From out the ringed armor :   fear not the word I 've given."
Then, from their saddles leaping,   their horses back at once
                     from them were driven.

"Now on, brave knights and warriors !"   Hartmut called to all ;
"To the castle-gates press nearer,   whatever may befall.
I yet must meet old Wâ-te,   whether I live or am dying ;
To drive him from the gateway,   and from the walls, I will
                     at least be trying."

Soon, with swords uplifted,   rushing on were seen
The brave and youthful Hartmut,   and with him all his men.
He fell upon grim Wâ-te,   who met his coming gladly ;
Now their sword-blades clattered,   and many knights lay dead,
                     or wounded badly.

When Wâ-te saw young Hartmut   the onslaught on him make,
While Fru-te bore the banner,   in wrath old Wâ-te spake :
"I hear the swords loud ringing   of many pressing near us ;
I beg, dear cousin Fru-te,   let none come out from the gates ;
                     from that now spare us."

Then Wâ-te, wild with anger,   did on King Hartmut run ;
But he, so brave and daring,   the onset would not shun.
The sun with dust was darkened,   now from the struggle rising :
Their strength was unabated ;   still for good name they fought,
                     that both were prizing.

What helped it that of Wâ-te   men said he was as strong
As six and twenty warriors?　Though this was on each tongue,
Yet still to him young Hartmut　his knightly skill was showing:
Howe'er his foe was striving,   the Norman lord and his men
                     no less were doing.

A knight he was most truly,   and well indeed he fought;
Of the dead there lay a mountain　whom on the field he smote.
It was, forsooth, a wonder　that Hartmut had not yielded,
And died before old Wâ-te: grim was the wrath from which
                     himself he shielded.

Soon heard he, loudly shrieking,   old King Ludwig's wife;
Sorely she was mourning　the loss of her husband's life.
She said she would reward him　who felt his death past bearing,
And would Gu-drun be slaying,   with all the maids who there
                     her lot were sharing.

Then ran a worthless fellow,   to whom the fee was dear,
To where the Hegeling maidens　sat together near.
Then the hearts of the women　with many fears he loaded;
For the sake of gold to be given,   to take their lives he now
                     was sharply goaded.

When that Hilda's daughter　against her saw him bear
A sharp and naked weapon,   she well indeed might fear,
And mourn that, far from kindred,   she was thus forsaken.
Had not young Hartmut seen it,   the knave her head from her
                     would then have taken.

She so forgot her breeding   that now she screamed aloud,
As if in dread of dying;   great fear made wild her mood.
'T was the same with all her maidens,   there beside her seated,
From out the window gazing;   the ladies such behavior
                                        ill befitted.

At once the sound of her wailing   to Hartmut made her known;
And greatly did he wonder   what made her scream and moan.
Soon he saw a ruffian   whose sword was near to falling,
As if he meant to kill her.   Loudly now to him 'gan Hartmut
                                        calling:

" Who are you, low-born dastard?   For what reward or need
Do you affright these maidens,   and seek to strike them dead?
If you shall strike one lady,   I give you now this warning,
Your life shall quick be ended;   your kinsmen too shall hang,
                                        this very morning."

Back then sprang the rascal, —   his anger he did fear;
For now the youtful Hartmut   held his life not dear,
When to the homeless maidens   he his help was giving:
With care was he o'erladen,   while from grim death to free
                                        them he was striving.

Quickly then came Ortrun,   she of Norman lands,
The fair and youthful princess;   in woe she wrung her hands.
She to Gu-drun came nearer,   the stately, high-born maiden,
And, at her feet down-falling,   bewept her father's death,
                                        with sorrow laden.

She said : " Most queenly lady,   do not your tears forbear,
For all my many kinsmen   who death together share.
Bethink you, if you also   a father slain were weeping,
How you would feel, great princess.   My father slain I mourn,
in death now sleeping.

" Behold, most high-born maiden,   my woe and bitter need ;
How almost all my kinsmen   lie, with my father, dead :
And now the knightly Hartmut   is death from Wâ-te fearing.
If I should lose my brother,   bereft of kindred, nought could
life be cheering.

" Reward the love I 've shown you,"   said the Norman maid.
" Of all that saw your sorrow,   when none a tear did shed,
I then alone was friendly,   and had you in my keeping ;
For all the wrongs they did you,   I the livelong day for you
was weeping."

Queen Hilda's daughter answered :   " Thou wast indeed my friend ;
But yet this strife so deadly   I know not how to end.
Were I indeed a warrior,   and knightly weapons wearing,
I 'd stop the fighting gladly ;   and none to slay your brother
then were daring."

Ortrun was sorely weeping ;   she still the maid besought,
Until within the window   Gu-drun at length she brought,
Who with her hand then beckoned,   and begged that it be told her
If from the land of her fathers   knights had come who did
in friendship hold her.

Then the knightly Herwic   answer thus did make:
" Who are you, young maiden,   who news from us do seek ?
We are not the Hegelings,   whom you see so near you ;
We hither come from the Sealands.   Tell us, maiden, how we now
can cheer you ? "

" This do I beseech you,"   said the queenly maid :
" Sore has been the fighting ;   him will I thank, indeed,
Who now cuts short the struggle.   Me will he be cheering
Who from the hands of Wâ-te   will Hartmut free in the strife
that I am fearing."

Then asked the well-bred warrior   who from the Sealands came :
" Tell me, worthy maiden,   what may be your name ? "
She said : " Gu-drun they call me,   of Hagen's blood I own me ;
Altho' my birth was lofty,   of late but little love has here
been shown me."

He said : " If you, fair lady,   my dear Gu-drun can be,
Then faithfully to help you   gladness will give to me ;
For I, in truth, am Herwic ;   you for my own I have chosen,
And fain am I to show you   how you from bonds of sorrow
I can loosen."

She said : " If you would help me,   my good and worthy knight,
I trust that you will grant me   that what I ask is right :
To me these lovely maidens   their prayers are ever making,
That from the fight with Wâ-te   some friendly hand will
Hartmut soon be taking."

" That will I do right gladly,   dearest lady mine."
Then to his men young Herwic   called above the din :
" Now against old Wâ-te   let my flag be carried."
Herwic then pressed forward,   and none of all his men
behind him tarried.

To do the lady's bidding   hard it was for him ;
But Herwic called out loudly   to Wâ-te old and grim,
And said, " My dear friend Wâ-te,   to grant my wish be ready :
Let strife be ended quickly :   this is the prayer of many
a lovely lady."

Then spake in wrath old Wâ-te :   " Sir Herwic, get you gone !
Did I mind the will of a woman,   how should I do my own ?
If I thought to spare the foeman,   unasked I 'd do it even.
I will not do your bidding :   Hartmut to pay for his sins
must now be driven."

Herwic, for love of his lady,   on both the fighters sprang
Right fearlessly and boldly ;   loud the sword-blades rang.
Wâ-te was wild with anger,   and bitter pain it gave him
That, ere the foeman yielded,   Herwic from his hand should
dare to save him.

Then he smote King Herwic   a strong and heavy blow,
Ere he could part the fighters,   and quickly laid him low ;
Now rushed the men of Herwic,   and did from Wâ-te bear him.
Hartmut was seized and taken,   though Herwic and his knights
had sought to spare him.

Cale the Cwenty-Ninth.

HOW HARTMUT WAS TAKEN PRISONER.

WÂ-TE loud was storming;   then went he towards the hall
    That stood before the gateway.   On every side did fall
The din of sword-blades clashing,   of groaning and of weeping.
Hartmut was in bondage;   ill luck alone his liegemen, too,
                                         were reaping.

With him were also taken   eighty warriors brave;
The others all were slaughtered.   Hartmut his life did save,
But to a ship was carried,   and fast and long they kept him.
Not yet was sorrow ended;   greater ills must they know
                                         who now bewept him.

Though often from the stronghold   Wâ-te's men they drove,
Both with slings and arrows,   yet still he grimly strove,
And won from them the castle.   The heavy bolts were broken
That once the gates had fastened;   at this fair women wept,
                                         with fear outspoken.

Horant, the lord of Denmark,   Queen Hilda's flag now bore;
Him followed many warriors,   he might not wish for more.
Up to a palace tower   that high its walls was rearing,
Far above all others,   the Hegeling men the banner
                               soon were bearing.

As I have told already,   the castle now was won:
To those they found within it   grimmest deeds were done.
Great was the crowd on-pressing,   for booty to enrich them.
Then cried the stern old Wâ-te: "Where are now the sacks,
                               and youths to fetch them?"

Now was broken open   many a well-filled room;
Loud was the din and uproar   that from within did come:
But all were not like-minded   who the halls were thronging;
While wounds were dealt by many,   others for plunder searched,
                               for riches longing.

They bore so much from the castle,   as we have heard it told,
That such a heavy burden   two ships could never hold:
Richest silken clothing,   silver and gold, were taken,
To load the ships on the waters;   tho' much they took, yet much
                               must be forsaken.

Now within the castle   joy was all unknown.
To all the folk there gathered   the greatest wrongs were done;
Men alike and women   were slain who there were dwelling:
To children in their cradles,   even to them, the foemen death
                               were dealing.

Irold then to Wâ-te   thus his mind made known :
" Of harm to you these children   devil-a-bit have done.
They indeed are blameless,   nor hate to our kin were showing ;
For the love of God, I beg you,   spare the poor babes, some pity
                           now bestowing."

The aged Wâ-te answered :   " Thou hast the mind of a child ;
Tho' now in the cradle wailing,   say, wouldst thou have willed
That I should leave them living ?   As soon as they are older,
They never can be trusted ;   to trust a Saxon wild would be
                           no bolder."

Blood throughout the castle   flowed on every side.
Those who saw the slaughter,   how bitterly they cried !
Now the high-born Ortrun,   filled with care and sorrow,
Sought Gu-drun, kind maiden :   she feared yet greater wrongs
                           before the morrow.

Then, her head low bending   before the lovely maid,
She said : " Gu-drun, my lady,   have pity on my need,
And, in my sharpest sorrow,   leave me not forsaken ;
I trust me to your kindness,   or else my life will by your
                           friends be taken."

" Gladly will I shield you,"   she answered, " if I can ;
Ever to do you kindness,   and help you, I am fain.
I will gain for you forgiveness ;   no more for life be fearing.
Your maids and women also   must stand near me, my care
                           they, too, are sharing."

" This doth make me happy,"   the youthful Ortrun said.
With three and thirty maidens,   she was kindly kept and fed ;
Warriors two and sixty   there the ladies guarded :
If they should gain their freedom,   their keepers would be slain,
and thus rewarded.

.

The old and wicked Gerlind   ran to Gu-drun in haste ;
As if she were her bondwoman,   herself at her feet she cast,
Saying : " Most high-born lady,   thou alone canst save us
From Wâ-te and his followers ;   else will his wrath, I ween,
of life bereave us."

To her said Hilda's daughter :   " I hear you asking now
That I to you be friendly ;   how should I kindness show ?
Nought that e'er I wished for   to grant me were you willing :
To me you showed but hatred ;   and now my heart with hate
for you is swelling."

That Ortrun then was near him   Wâ-te became aware :
He his teeth was gnashing,   and straight up-stood he there ;
Now his eyes were flashing ;   his yard-wide beard was flowing ;
And all were sorely frightened,   and feared what the Sturmisch
lord would next be doing.

Over him blood was streaming,   with it his clothes were wet.
Tho' Gu-drun was glad to see him,   she had liked it better yet
If he, in mood less wrathful,   had come for her to greet him ;
Such fear they all were feeling,   I ween that no one there
was glad to meet him.

To meet her friend, old Wâ-te,   went Gu-drun alone;
Then said Hilda's daughter,   with sad and care-fraught tone:
" Welcome art thou, Wâ-te!   How glad would be my greeting,
If now these folk so many   no evil from thy hand should here
be meeting."

" I thank you, fair young maiden!   Are you Queen Hilda's child?
Who are these many women,   whom here you seek to shield?"
" This," said Gu-drun, in answer,   " is Ortrun, high in breeding;
I beg you, Wâ-te, spare her: her women here your wrath
are sorely dreading.

" Those there are wretched maidens,   from far across the sea,
Brought from the Hegeling kingdom   by Ludwig's men with me.
But you are wet and bloody;   do not come so near us:
For all your help we thank you,   nor in our woe do scorn
the love you bear us."

Wâ-te went on further,   and Herwic soon he found,
And with him youthful Ortwin,   as king in Ortland owned.
Irold was there and Morunc;   Fru-te had thither hasted:
None of these were idle;   many they slew, nor soon from
slaughter rested.

Quickly then came Hergart,   the lady of a duke,
And said: " Gu-drun, good lady,   on me with kindness look,—
On me, a wretched woman.   Forget not that we ever
Have been and are your handmaids;   and let me, lady,
lose thy friendship never."

Gu-drun in anger answered :   " Stand back, come not so near !
Whatever we poor maidens   of wrong have had to fear,
For all you wept but little,   and cared for it but slightly.
Not much do I care either   whether for you it now goes ill
or rightly.

" You still among my maidens   may linger, if you choose."
Now the stern old Wâ-te   looked round among his foes,
To find the wicked Gerlind,   whom he in wrath was seeking.
That devilish crone, with her women,   the kindness of Gu-drun
was now bespeaking.

Grimly then old Wâ-te   stood before the hall,
And said : " Gu-drun, my lady,   send down, with her maidens all.
The old and wicked Gerlind,   who made you wash by the water :
And with her send her kinsmen,   who in our land so many
knights did slaughter."

The lovely maiden answered : " Not one of them is here."
Then Wâ-te, in his anger,   went in and to her came near :
He said : " Now show me quickly   the women I am seeking :
Else shall they, with your maidens,   all alike in the grave
their home be making."

Wâ-te was sorely angry,   of this was she aware.
A wink of her eye then gave him   a lovely maiden there,
And he knew the old she-devil,   on whom her glance was turning.
" Tell me," he said, " Queen Gerlind,   for other maids to wash
are you still yearning ? "

Then by the hand he took her,   and dragged her thence away;
The while the wicked Gerlind   sank down in sore dismay.
Said Wâ-te, wild to madness: "Most lofty queen, I warn you,
Never again, at your bidding,   shall my ladies wash for you;
                         they now can scorn you."

I ween that when he brought her   without the palace gate,
All looked on to witness   what he would do in his hate.
Then by the hair he grasped her,   no one a whit he dreaded,
His wrath indeed was bitter,   and at once the evil queen he
                         there beheaded.

Loudly shrieked the maidens,   their fright at this was sore.
Back again went Wâ-te,   and said: "Who is there more,
Who to the queen owns kinship?   To me you now must show her;
However high she holds her,   I yet to earth her head
                         will quickly lower."

Sobbing then and weeping,   the child of Hettel said:
"Let these with me find shelter,   who now to me have fled,
To ask of me forgiveness,   here my love bespeaking.
This is the well-born Ortrun,   who with her Norman maids
                         my help is seeking."

Those who were forgiven   she bade stand further back.
Then, in mood unfriendly,   the angry Wâ-te spake:
"Where shall I find young Hergart,   now of a lord the lady,
Who here within this kingdom   to take the love of the king's
                         great lord was ready?"

None of them would tell him,   but he to her came near,
And said : " Were you the owner   of all this kingdom here,
Who could in you be looking   to see so proud a bearing ?
Ill have you served your lady,   here in the land where you
                          her lot were sharing."

Then all cried out together :   " Let her now go free."
But the aged Wâ-te answered :   " That can never be ;
I have the care of the women ;   behold my overseeing ! "
With a stroke he her beheaded,   while the maids in fright
                       behind Gu-drun were fleeing.

Now from the bloody struggle   there was a rest for all.
Then the brave King Herwic   came to Ludwig's hall,
Leading in his warriors,   with stains of blood upon them.
Gu-drun her welcome gave him ;   her love for him was shown,
                       and kindness done them.

Soon the knightly Herwic   his sword from his side unbound :
He then shook off his armor   into his shield on the ground,
And stood before the ladies ;   iron-stained was his body.
That day, for love of his lady,   he oft on the field had hewn
                       a pathway bloody.

With him came Ortwin also,   who was of Ortland king.
When Irold came with Morunc,   the clothes they off did fling
Worn outside their armor,   for they were over-heated.
They wished to see the ladies,   and hoped by them they would
                       be kindly greeted.

When now the Danish warriors   were both with slaughter spent,
They laid aside their weapons,   and before the ladies went.
Shields no longer bore they,   their helmets were unfastened;
A very loving welcome   to give to both the knights
                     Gu-drun then hastened.

Irold and Morunc with him   then most lowly bowed
Before the lovely maiden.   How well her bearing showed
That to see these guests so lordly   she was indeed most willing!
Right glad and happy truly   the child of the Hegeling Hilda
                     now was feeling.

Alike they all were thinking,   both lords and all their men:
"Since now we have the castle, —   the stronghold Kassiane, —
Of the land are we the masters,   and everything is ours."
Soon bade the aged Wâ-te   that men should burn with fire
                     the palace with its towers.

The Danish Fru-te answered: "That may never be;
In this my queenly lady   to live must now be free.
Bid that from out the castle   men the dead shall carry;
Then 't will be the better   for all our knights who in the
                     land shall tarry.

"Very strong is the castle,   wide it is and good;
Bid from the walls now everywhere   to wash away the blood,
That for a home the maidens   may not dislike it wholly:
Then the land of Hartmut   we will raid throughout,
                     and see it fully."

They did as Fru-te bade them,   for wise he was, in truth ;
They bore from out the castle   many who there, forsooth,
Were sorely slashed and wounded,   and many who were dying :
Then to the waves they carried   those who before the gates
in death were lying.

They to the sea intrusted   four thousand of the dead ;
This to them was toilsome,   but Fru-te thus had bade.
The work that they were doing   not as yet was ended ;
Then in Ludwig's castle   the maid Ortrun was held,
now ill-befriended.

Two and sixty warriors   and thirty maidens fair
With her were also taken.   Then said Gu-drun : " Forbear !
The maids are in my keeping,   my word to them I plighted :
Wâ-te may do as he wishes   with the knights he seized,
until my wrongs are righted."

Siegfried, king of Moorland,   found a welcome warm,
As should to knights be granted   after the battle-storm.
Thanks to that worthy warrior   were by the ladies given,
That he from the land of Karadie   so far had come, and so well
for them had striven.

To the care of the Danish Horant   they their foes did give
Who in the castle of Kassian   still were left alive.
To him was Gu-drun intrusted,   and all her maidens near her :
To her was he a kinsman ;   they so might hope that he
would kindness bear her.

Him they made the master   of forty towers strong,
And six wide, roomy dwellings,   that stood the shore along.
Over three rich palaces   to him was lordship granted,
And there Gu-drun, the maiden,   with him must stay, and nought
                         she ever wanted.

To guard their ships on the waters   others now they bade;
Then back to castle Kassian   Hartmut, the knight, was led
With many of his kinsmen,   who in the fight were taken;
There the Norman ladies,   seized with the knights, were held,
                         by hope forsaken.

They bade that care be taken   that none from them might flee;
A thousand of their brave ones   must the women oversee:
They, with the men from Denmark,   kept guard in many places.
Wâ-te, meanwhile, with Fru-te,   sought other foes, and shields
                         to hew in pieces.

Thirty thousand warriors   with them the war-path shared.
Fire was thrown on all sides;   flames now flashed and flared.
Throughout the land, the dwellings   everywhere were burning;
And now the brave young Hartmut,   sad at heart, his first
                         true woe was learning.

The warriors from Sturmland,   and they of the Danish land,
Broke down the well-built castles   on every hill and strand.
They took away more plunder   than foemen ever carried;
Many lovely women   the Hegelings seized, the while the land
                         they harried.

Before the friends of Hilda   came back thro' the wasted land,
Six and twenty castles   fell beneath their hand.
Happy went they homeward;   proud were they of their raiding;
Soon of those there taken   a thousand or more to Hilda

they were leading.

Throughout the Norman kingdom   was Hilda's banner seen,
Waving now unhindered;   back again her men
Bore it down to the sea-sand,   where they had left their lady.
Here would they stay no longer;   to seek their homes they all

were glad and ready.

Those who still were resting   within King Hartmut's halls
Down to their friends came riding   from out the castle walls.
Gladly both old and youthful   now each other greeted;
Then asked they of Denmark: "Youths, what luck in the raid

hath you awaited?"

To them King Ortwin answered: "We there have done so well
That I to those who helped me   my thanks must ever tell.
Our foes are well rewarded,   tho' sore has been the fighting,
For all the wrongs they did us;   a thousand-fold have we

ourselves been righting."

Then spake the aged Wâ-te: "Who best can tarry here
To guard for us this kingdom?   Bid now Gu-drun, the fair,
Come down again to meet us;   soon shall we be going
To Hilda's land of the Hegelings;   and what we bring we will

to her be showing."

Then said they all together,   both the old and young :
" To Horant and to Morunc   doth the warder's task belong ;
They, and a thousand with them,   here in this land must tarry."
'T was done as they had bidden ;   but those who went did many
a hostage carry.

When to go back to Hegeling   they now made up their minds,
Then to their ships they carried   goods of many kinds,
All they once brought with them,   and all they had of plunder.
Gladly they bore their booty ;   on this their friends at home
would look with wonder.

Hartmut now was bidden   to leave his father's hall,
With all his bravest warriors,   five hundred men in all ;
They now were held in bondage   who had in strife been taken,
And won from their foes thereafter   many a weary day,
of hope forsaken.

Ortrun took they likewise,   the fair and high-born maid ;
On her and on her maidens   a heavy woe they laid :
As they away from fatherland   far from friends were carried,
They well might know the sorrows   felt by Gudrun and her maids,
who with them tarried.

Those whom they had taken   they bore with them away.
The castles, overmastered,   henceforth must own the sway
Of Morunc and of Horant :   when they homeward started,
They left in the Norman kingdom   a thousand of their men,
all fearless-hearted.

" Now do I beseech you," to them young Hartmut spake,
" That in my father's kingdom my freedom I may take ;
If this to me be granted, I pledge my life and riches."
The aged Wâ-te answered : " Now in our hands to keep you
                     wisdom teaches.

" Why it is I know not, that 't is my nephew's will
To carry home young Hartmut, who him would gladly kill,
And take from him his riches. Even before the morrow,
Were only my nephew willing, I would see that his foe no more
                     in bonds should sorrow."

Then spake the youthful Ortwin : " What gain to us would come
If we should slay our foemen here in their land and home ?
Hartmut and his kindred may better things be hoping ;
Them will I bring to my mother, as well beseems a knight
                     to wrong ne'er stooping."

All their goods and riches down to the ships were brought ;
With gold and gems and clothing, and horses they were fraught.
Her whom they had sought for they were homeward bringing :
They who once went mourning now on their way were heard
                     in gladness singing.

Tale the Thirtieth.

HOW GUDRUN WAS BROUGHT HOME TO HILDA.

HOMEWARD the men of the Hegelings   gladly took their way;
    But many whom they carried   erewhile across the sea
Now lay dead and wounded;   these must they be leaving:
Three thousand men or over   were mourned by friends, who
                                tears to each were giving.

Now their ships went smoothly,   the winds for them were good:
Bearing home their booty   they came in happy mood.
How it was done I know not,   they sent on men before them
Unto the Hegeling ladies: of what had them befallen
                                they tidings bore them.

With all their speed they hastened, —   that I well can say, —
And reached at last their kingdom, —   I cannot tell the day.
Never a tale so happy   had Lady Hilda gladdened
As this that now they told her: Ludwig was slain, who long
                                her life had saddened.

She asked : " Still lives my daughter,   and all her maiden band ? "
They answered : " Herwic brings her,   his own, again to her land.
Ne'er to so brave a warrior   it hath befallen better.
Ortrun, too, they are bringing,   and Hartmut, her brother;
                          these in bonds they fetter."

" A happy tale you bring me,"   said then the well-bred queen ;
" My life with care and sadness   by them hath cumbered been.
If e'er my eyes behold them,   ill shall they be faring :
Through them have I much sorrow,   untold and openly, for years
                          been bearing.

" The news that you have brought me   a rich reward shall gain ;
For you my heart have lightened   of hopeless woe and pain.
Gold I give you freely,   and this I do most rightly."
They said : " Most noble lady,   to make us rich we need
                          your gold but slightly.

" Of the booty we have gotten   we 're bringing home so much,
You need not think us scornful   if your gold we do not touch :
Indeed, our boats are heavy   with shining gold they 're bearing.
Over all our riches   keepers we have, who well for it
                          are caring."

Then did Lady Hilda,   when she the tidings heard
That guests so dear were coming,   for food and drink give word ;
For stools and benches, also,   on which they should be seated.
She of all was thoughtful,   that they might feel that they
                          were fitly greeted.

Now at Matelan castle   none were idle found ;
Down on the sandy beaches   and on the level ground
Workmen quickly gathered,   who nought of toil abated
That fair Gu-drun and Herwic,   as them beseemed, should worthily
                 be seated.

I cannot tell you truly   if aught upon the sea
Of ill had them befallen.   Six long weeks it must be
Ere Ortwin's men saw Matelan   at length before them looming.
They brought with them their lady,   and many well-bred maids
                 with her were coming.

When now they reached their homeland,   this for truth we hear,
Their search and strife for the lady   had lasted full a year :
It was upon a May-time   their foes they home were bringing.
Their toils were not forgotten,   but, as they came, the strand
                 with shouts was ringing.

Soon as Matelan castle   now from the ships was seen,
Of sackbuts and of trumpets   loud began the din,
Of horns as well as fluting,   and drums that men were beating.
The ships of the aged Wâ-te   at last in a harbor good
                 their rest were meeting.

After these came also   Ortland's warriors brave ;
Then Hilda with her ladies   to them a welcome gave.
Out from Matelan's castle   she to the shore went riding ;
Gu-drun they saw was coming,   with well-bred maidens wont to do
                 her bidding.

Alighted from their horses,   and standing on the sand,
Were Hilda and all her ladies.   Then, leading by the hand
Gu-drun, the lovely maiden,   came Irold, proud and knightly.
Though Hilda well had known her,   yet now she knew her not,
                              nor others rightly.

Hilda, among the followers   a hundred women saw ;
She said : " I know not truly   which one from me should draw
A mother's loving welcome ;   unknown to me is my daughter :
I give to all my greeting   who here with her have come
                              across the water."

" This is your long-lost daughter,"   by Irold she was told ;
Hilda to her stepped nearer.   Could ever wealth or gold
Outweigh the bliss that filled them,   as each the other greeted,
And welcome gave with kisses ?   Now from their hearts had all
                              their sorrow fleeted.

To Irold and his kinsmen   kind greeting Hilda said ;
Then to the aged Wâ-te   a lowly bow she made.
" Welcome, knight of Sturmland !   bravely thou hast striven !
Who can e'er reward thee,   unless to thee both land and crown
                              are given ? "

He to the lady answered :   " To help you all I may,
For that am I most willing,   e'en to my latest day."
Then, for love, she kissed him,   and Ortwin thus she greeted.
Now came Herwic also,   with proud and worthy knights,
                              as him befitted.

Ortrun, the Norman maiden,   then by the hand he led.
Gu-drun besought her mother   kindly to meet the maid:
" Dear lady, greet with kisses   this good and high-born maiden;
Oft in my years of sorrow   my life with help and kindness
                         she did gladden."

" To none will I give kisses   who is to me unknown.
Who are this maiden's kinsmen?   What name doth the lady own,
That you should bid me kiss her,   and be so friendly with her ? "
He said: " Her name is Ortrun;   she from the Norman kingdom
                         cometh hither."

" Never shall I kiss her;   how can you ask for this ?
If I should bid them kill her   I should not do amiss.
Truly have her kinsmen   filled my life with sorrow;
They fed their eyes upon it,   and gladness all the while
                         from this did borrow."

Gu-drun to Hilda answered :   " Ne'er hath this lovely maid
The word to any given   that wrong on you be laid.
Bethink you now, dear mother,   would blame to me be owing
Should our men slay her kinsmen ?   To the luckless maid, I beg,
                         your love be showing."

Gu-drun in vain besought her,   until at last, with tears,
The maid now begged her mother;   then gave she willing ears,
And said: " I can no longer   see you sadly weeping :
If e'er the maiden helped you,   for this shall she, in my land,
                         her life be keeping."

Then the stately Hilda   kissed King Ludwig's child,
And greeted other ladies,   e'en as Gu-drun had willed.
Then came also Hildeburg,   from far-off lands brought thither,
Erst with her found washing.   Now, by the hand, Sir Fru-te
                        led her hither.

Then Gu-drun said further: " Mother, most dear to me,
Your greeting give to Hildeburg.   What better can there be
Than true and faithful friendship ?   Gold and jewels even,
Whate'er the kingdom holdeth,   to Hildeburg most rightly
                        should be given."

Then said to her Queen Hilda :   " To me it hath been told
How she both weal and sorrow   hath borne with you of old.
Never shall I sit happy   beneath the crown I 'm wearing,
Till I indeed reward her   for all the ills that she with you
                        was sharing."

At once she kissed the maiden,   and others, too, as well.
Then Hilda said to Fru-te :   " No shame for this I feel, —
That I have come to meet you   and those whom you are leading.
Good knights, you all are welcome   into the Hegeling land,
                        now homeward speeding."

As they with thanks were bowing,   and she her greeting gave,
Siegfried, king of Moorland,   drew nearer on the wave,
And with his warriors, shouting,   up to the beach was springing:
A merry song from Araby   were all, as best they might,
                        together singing.

Queen Hilda him awaited   till on the shore he stood.
Then to the lord of Karadie   a greeting warm she showed:
" Sir Siegfried, king of Moorland,   welcome to you is given ;
It ne'er shall be forgotten   how you to right my wrongs
have ever striven."

" Lady, if I have helped you,   to do it I was glad.
Now must I hasten thither   to where my home I've had
Since early days of boyhood,   ere I thence had ridden
To war against King Herwic ;   henceforth to strive with him.
it is forbidden."

Then they their ships unloaded,   and up they bore on the sand
The many things brought with them   into Queen Hilda's land.
The night was drawing nearer,   the air was colder growing :
The guests no longer waited :   to seek a shelter they in haste
were going.

Then with the guests Queen Hilda   rode up on to the plain.
Before great Matelan castle   huts and tents were seen
Bedecked with gold and shining ;   there the guests were seated
Upon rich seats made ready :   within the tents were all
most kindly treated.

Such wealth, at Hilda's bidding,   was brought up to the land,
That none need leave behind him   his pledge or bond to stand.
Never in giving freely   could any host be vying
With this most high-born widow :   no guest need wine or other
cheer be buying.

There the weary rested   until five days were gone.
The greatest care and kindness   unto the guests were shown;
But Hartmut greatly sorrowed—   no happiness it gave him—
Until the lovely maiden   begged Queen Hilda would in freedom
                        leave him.

Then Ortwin went with his sister   where Hilda had her seat.
She said : " My dearest mother,   never this forget, —
We must not reward with evil   him who a wrong is doing.
Of your worthy name bethink you;   you should on Hartmut smile,
                        forgiveness showing."

She answered :   " Dearest daughter,   you do not ask aright :
I at the hands of Hartmut   the greatest ills have met;
He must atone in bondage   for all his wrongful dealing."
Then at the feet of Hilda   Gu-drun fell down, with sixty
                        maidens, kneeling.

Then spake the lady Ortrun :   " In freedom let him live;
To you will he be faithful,   for this my word I give.
Be to my brother friendly,   nor of your love be sparing;
'T will be to you an honor   if he again the kingly crown
                        be wearing."

His friends all wept together   that he in bondage sat,
Wearing chains so heavy;   their eyes with tears were wet :
Much they pitied Hartmut,   no more his kingdom swaying.
On him and on his followers   fetters fast and strongest
                        now were weighing.

Then spake to them Queen Hilda: " Leave your weeping now ;
Their chains will I unloosen ; they to my court may go :
But not to seek their freedom they their word must give me,
And with an oath must swear it, — not hence to ride unbidden,
nor to leave me."

Now the noble bondsmen were from chains set free.
Gu-drun then bade these warriors to bathe them in the sea ;
Then, in finest clothing, men to court must lead them.
Knights were they most worthy ; and so the more, good luck
did ever speed them.

There among the others Hartmut now was seen ;
Never a braver warrior or better knight had been :
E'en now, amid his sorrows, such a mien was he wearing,
It seemed as if a pencil had drawn him there, and a parchment
him was bearing.

Now on him with kindness did all the ladies look,
While he, their friendship trusting, greater boldness took.
Ill-will, that erst was borne him, none were longer feeling ;
It was by all forgotten what wounds they erst had been
to each other dealing.

Herwic now bethought him from the land of the Hegeling
How he might be going. He bade his men to bring
His clothing and his weapons, and on the horses load them :
When this was known to Hilda, to let them go no ready will
she showed them.

She said : "My good Lord Herwic,   I beg you longer stay !
All your love and kindness   a weight on me doth lay.
Not yet with my good wishes   may you hence be riding ;
Before you yet shall leave me,   there shall be high times
                           for the guests with me abiding."

To her Lord Herwic answered: "Lady, you know the way,
How those who send their kinsmen   to lands which others sway
Again at home to see them   are always greatly longing :
With pain our friends are waiting   until again they see us
                           homeward thronging."

Then spake again Queen Hilda: "Grudge not, I beg, to me
One happiness and honor,   for none can greater be ;
Herwic, king most worthy,   the boon now deign to give me,
That I, poor lonely woman,   may see my daughter crowned,
                           ere she shall leave me."

For this was he unwilling ;   but still she begged and bade :
Thereby those held in bondage   were soon from sorrow freed.
When now at last he told her   that to do it he was willing,
Then the Lady Hilda   was glad in heart, and rest of mind
                           was feeling.

Seats were made at her bidding,   yet more and better still.
Which many knights with honor,   near Hilda, soon did fill.
When came the high times merry,   that now were widely bruited.
To crown Gu-drun, the fair one,   King Herwic bade, for him
                           it now well suited.

Of those who him had followed there went away not one
Before at Matelan castle the high times were begun.
Then by Lady Hilda was clothing kindly given
To sixty maids or over : for praise and honor she had ever
              striven.

To full a hundred women clothing good she gave :
None of those were slighted, but all her care did have,
Who from their homes were taken ; these had clothes the rarest.
The gifts indeed were wondrous that Hilda gave, of queens
             the best and fairest.

Irold must guard the treasure ; to dwell in Hilda's home
That knight erelong was bidden, and quickly did he come :
Wâ-te, he of Sturmland, must carve the meat at table ;
They also sent for Fru-te, to come to her as soon as he
             was able.

Her cup-bearer she made him ; thereon thus spake the knight :
" That will I be most gladly, if now you think it right.
A fief you then will give me, with banners twelve to show it ;
Then am I lord in Denmark." Queen Hilda smiled, but never
             thought to do it.

To Fru-te thus she answered : " That gift is not for thee ;
For still your nephew Horant Daneland's lord must be.
You, in his stead, for friendship, must now our cup be filling ;
And, while he is with the Normans, kindly to care for him
             must you be willing."

The men and maids in waiting   all to their tasks were set:
Silken clothes were called for;   a hoard both rich and great,
In rooms and chests long treasured,   Queen Hilda bade them open.
These were brought by stewards,   and all the guests to them
                        were freely holpen.

Of these the very lowest   had clothing of the best.
If others than the Normans   were bidden to the feast,
Or why they called them thither,   I have no way of telling:
Full thirty thousand were they   whom there they brought,
                     in Norman lands once dwelling.

Clothes for all were wanted,   but where could these be found?
If e'en the wealth of Araby   any there had owned,
I ween he could no better   or finer clothes have given
Than now they shared so freely: that this should be, Gu-drun
                     her best had striven.

Soon as this lovely maiden   by the guests had now her seat,
She sent for her brother Ortwin,   and did his coming wait,
That she the word might give him   to be fair Ortrun's lover;
She, King Ludwig's daughter,   beside Gu-drun was seated then,
                     as ever.

Ortwin, lord of Ortland,   made haste to his sister's bower:
Him welcomed many a maiden   who sat with her that hour.
Then, from her seat arising,   by the hand she kindly took him;
And him aside then leading,   at the further end of the hall
                     she thus bespoke him,

Saying : " Dearest brother,   hear what for you is best ;
All that I shall tell you   comes from a faithful breast.
If you for bliss are hoping,   so long as you are living,
Then for Hartmut's sister   you must, as best you may,
henceforth be striving."

To her young Ortwin answered :   " Now think you this is well ?
I and her brother Hartmut   never as friends can feel ;
We slew their father Ludwig,   and, when to me she 's wedded,
Of him will she be thinking ;   then with her sighs I oft
shall be upbraided."

" You such love must show her   that for him she will not long.
If now this word I give you,   'tis from a love as strong
As I have had for any,   or e'er in my life was feeling.
Should she to you be wedded,   your bliss with her will
be beyond all telling."

Then said her knightly brother :   " If she to you is known,
And now you think the Hegelings   will her for a mistress own,
Gladly will I love her, —   a maid of such high-breeding."
Him Gu-drun then answered :   " You 'll ne'er a sorry day with her
be leading."

Of this he spoke to others,   but Hilda's word was nay ;
He told it unto Herwic,   to hear what he would say,
Who held it right and worthy ;   then to Fru-te speaking,
That friend would have him woo her,   " for many knights will she
your own be making.

"Soothed should be the hatred   that we each other bore;
Of how it may be ended,   I now will tell you more;
Then," said the Danish Fru-te,   whose word was ever heeded,
" Hildeburg, the maiden,   to young King Hartmut also
must be wedded."

The wise and upright Herwic   with faithful words thus spake:
" I deem it right and fitting   the maiden him should take;
When in the land of Hartmut   she is queen and lady,
A thousand lordly castles   to own her sway will there
be glad and ready."

Then to the high-born Hildeburg   Gu-drun the fair thus spake,
With words unheard by others: " Care for your weal I 'll take;
If I may well reward you,   my friend and playmate dearest,
For all the love you 've shown me,   soon in the Norman land
a crown thou wearest."

To her then said fair Hildeburg: " For me it were not well
To give my troth to any   who ne'er his love did tell,
Nor unto me, in fondness,   e'er his heart was turning;
Should we grow old together,   I fear between us oft there 'll be
heart-burning."

Her Gu-drun thus answered: " Give not a thought to that:
I soon will send to Hartmut,   and bid him answer straight
Whether he now would like it   if from his pledge I free him,
As well as all his followers,   and send him home, that his
friends again may see him.

" If he his thanks shall tell me, I then in turn will bid
That he by deeds shall show it, and shall my wishes heed.
I then will freely ask him if he will wed a maiden,
That I and all my kinsmen may him with love and friendship
           ever gladden."

To her they brought young Hartmut, king of the Norman land,
And with him came old Fru-te. Near her, on either hand,
Proud Hildeburg and Ortrun within her bower were sitting ;
If the lady's word they heeded, their many woes they both
           would be forgetting.

Hartmut, the son of Ludwig, went through the palace hall ;
To him a friendly greeting was given by one and all,
Alike both high and lowly from their seats arising.
None than he was braver ; no worth or greatness e'er in him
           was missing.

He by Gu-drun, fair lady, to seat himself was told ;
And neither of the others her greeting did withhold.
Then said Queen Hilda's daughter : " I beg you to be sitting
Near my faithful maidens, who washed with me for your knights,
           as was befitting."

" This in scorn you bid me, fair and lovely queen !
Whatever wrong was done you truly gives me pain :
'T was by my mother's wishes that this from me was hidden ;
To keep it from my father, and from his knights as well,
           were all men bidden."

To him the maiden answered :   " My wish I may not hide :
I now, in truth, Sir Hartmut,   must speak with you aside.
I and yourself, we only,   may hear what I am saying."
Hartmut then bethought him :   " May God now grant she is not
falsely playing."

No one else but Fru-te   allowed she to come near ;
Then the high-born maiden   said in Hartmut's ear :
" If you to me will hearken,   and do what I shall tell you
With ready heart and freely,   now of all your sorrows I will
heal you."

" Well I know your wisdom,"   then young Hartmut said ;
" Of aught that is unworthy   I need not be afraid.
My heart for nothing wishes,   unless to do your bidding :
Gladly, high-born lady,   to all that you shall say will I
give heeding."

She said : " My wish I tell you,   and now your life would cheer ;
I, and my kinsmen with me,   will give you a helpmeet fair.
To keep both land and honor   you may thus be seeking,
And of the hate we bore you   none shall evermore a word
be speaking."

" Who is it, say, fair lady,   that you for me will choose ?
Ere yet my love I give her,   life would I rather lose
Than ever that my kinsmen   her with scorn were eying ;
For me it were far better   that I in death upon the field
were lying."

"I will give your sister Ortrun,   the maid beloved and fair,
To be a wife to my brother,   himself to me most dear.
You must wed with Hildeburg,   of a king the well-born daughter:
Never a dearer maiden   you in the world could find,
where'er you sought her."

"If this indeed may happen,"   then young Hartmut said,
"And now your brother Ortwin   shall take that lovely maid,
My dear-loved sister, Ortrun,   and she to him is wedded,
Then I will woo fair Hildeburg;   thus hate will end, nor longer
shall be dreaded."

She said: "To this I've brought him;   his troth to her he gave.
If now 't would make you happy   your father's lands to have,
And again within his castles   that you should soon be living,
You well may wed with Hildeburg,   and there the queenly crown
to her be giving."

He said: "That pledge I gladly,   and on it give my hand;
As soon as the king of Ortland   shall with my sister stand,
And both the crown have taken,   then I, no more forbearing,
Will, with lovely Hildeburg,   among our men our lands
and fiefs be sharing."

When he his word had plighted,   then said the high-born maid:
"Now will I do gladly   a further friendly deed;
Unto the lord of Karadie   for a wife will I be giving
The sister of King Herwic,   that she with him may evermore
be living."

I ween that never hatred   was smoothed as now was done :
Brave knights who long were foemen   now became as one.
Fru-te, the lord of Daneland,   thought it right and fitting
Soon to send for Ortwin ;   also the Moorland king must them
                        be meeting.

When they to court were coming,   finest clothes they wore.
The news Gu-drun had told them   others to Wâ-te bore ;
To Irold, too, they gave it,   as soon as he came thither ;
This aside they talked of,   and fitting speech long time they held
                        together.

Then spake the aged Wâ-te :   " Peace we can never know
Until Ortrun and Hartmut   to Hilda, the queen, shall go,
And ask of her forgiveness,   down at her feet low bending.
Only if she allows it,   can we be friends, and hatred
                        have an ending."

Then spake Gu-drun, the high-born :   "This I can truly say :
To them is she not unfriendly ;   Ortrun wears to-day
Such clothes as by my mother   to me and my maids were given.
I 'll gladly gain forgiveness ;   in me they all may trust,
                        from home now riven."

Within a ring of maidens   Ortrun then they set,
And with her also Hildeburg,   of birth both high and meet :
Ortwin then and Hartmut   led them out to wed them.
" I hope," said Lady Hilda,   " that now, forever, we our friends
                        have made them."

When to his side young Ortwin   did the maiden Ortrun bring,
Lovingly and kindly,   he took a golden ring,
And this upon the finger   of her fair white hand he fitted.
Then far off were driven   the many woes that late her life
                      had greeted.

Hartmut around fair Hildeburg   then his arms did throw;
Each on the hand of the other   did a golden ring bestow.
The lovely maid was blameless,   and sorrow gave him never;
Of him and of fair Hildeburg   nothing their faithful hearts
                      thro' life could sever.

Then said Queen Hilda's daughter :   " Herwic, my lord most dear,
Say, does the land of your fathers   lie to us so near
That men could bring your sister,   if this by us were needed,
Here to my mother's kingdom,   that she to the lord of Karadie
                      may now be wedded ? "

To her King Herwic answered :   " This will I say to you :
Your men, if they will hasten,   in twelve days' time can go ;
But if any to your kingdom   the maiden would be leading,
Ill luck, I ween, awaits him,   unless with him my own
                      good knights be speeding."

Then answered Hilda's daughter :   " Your help, I beg you, grant ;
By doing this, of happiness   you nought shall ever want.
To your men both food and clothing   my mother will be giving ;
Only bring us the maiden,   that I may thank you, long as you
                      are living."

To her then said Lord Herwic :   " How can she be clad ?
The mighty lord of Karadie   a waste of my kingdom made ;
There he burned my castles,   and of her clothes bereft her."
Then said the king of Moorland :   " Her would I woo, if only
a smock were left her."

To bring the maid then Herwic   a hundred warriors sent ;
He bade his men to hasten   when on their way they went.
He begged that Wâ-te and Fru-te   would with them go riding :
This was to them a burden ;   but yet the worthy knights both
did his bidding.

With greatest speed they hastened,   both by day and night,
Until they found the maiden.   Wâ-te they feared would fight, —
'Gainst this did Herwic's liegmen   give their careful heeding.
Soon from her home the lady,   with four and twenty maids,
the knights were leading.

By Wâ-te they were guided   from the castle down to the sand :
Two ships they found, with row-boats,   lying by the strand ;
One of these they seized on,   and, helped by breezes blowing,
They fast away were sailing :   throughout twelve days they
to their homes were going.

When to the land of the Hegelings   they had brought the maid,
Many knights bethought them   over the sand to speed,
To meet the lovely lady,   and all with banners hasted.
They who had brought the maiden   had kept their oaths, nor
from the task had rested.

How could any maiden   a better welcome find?
Gu-drun went forth to meet her,   and gave her greeting kind;
Hilda, with many ladies,   to see the maiden hasted:
Nor came King Herwic's sister   all alone, though with fire
                                        her land was wasted.

She from home was followed   by full three hundred men.
Now when the kingly Herwic   his sister met again,
He, to show her honor,   rode forward, proudly dashing;
So did many others: loud were the shields of the knights
                                        together clashing.

Four kings both rich and mighty   rode to meet her there;
Thereon the knights 'gan wrangle   which of the ladies fair
Was loveliest and fairest.   Long their time they wasted,
For all alike were worthy;   on this at last their wordy war
                                        they rested.

The fair Gu-drun then kissed her   and those who with her came.
They walked along the seashore,   till a tent was seen by them,
With richest silken hangings;   while they stood thereunder,
What now to her should happen   gave to Herwic's sister
                                        greatest wonder.

Now the king of Karadie   forthwith to come they bade;
Then they asked the maiden: " Will you this man now wed?
Kingdoms nine most mighty   have for their master owned him."
With him were knights full many,   yellow in hue, now standing
                                        all around him.

His father and his mother   were not of faith the same ;
But him, so light in color,   one might a Christian name.
Like to gold, spun finely,   the hair on his head was lying :
She would choose unwisely   if she to him her love were now
                             denying.

She was slow her love to grant him,   as oft one sees a maid ;
But she to him was given.   The worthy knight then said :
"So well I like this lady,   from love I ne'er can free me.
Never will I leave her,   and as her husband men erelong
                             shall see me."

At last this knight and maiden   each their troth did plight :
Both of them scarce waited   till day should turn to night,
When, from others hidden,   they should their bliss be owning.
Soon, 'mid knightly warriors,   daughters of four rich kings
                        were hallowed for the crowning.

<h1 style="text-align:center">Tale the Thirty-first.</h1>

HOW THE FOUR KINGS WERE WEDDED IN HILDA'S LAND.

THEN the kings were hallowed,   as in days of yore;
   Also there were knighted   five hundred men or more.
Now in Hilda's kingdom   the folk high times were having;
It was at Matelan castle,   before the walls where the sea
the sands was laving.

There the fair Queen Hilda   to all fine clothing gave.
How, in the sight of ladies,   rode Wâ-te old and brave!
How Irold, too, and Fru-te   of Daneland, rode before them!
One heard the spear-shafts broken,   as these they lowered,
and in the onset bore them.

Lightly the wind was blowing,   but the dust was dark as night;
Yet to the maidens' clothing   the knights gave heeding slight,
Altho' 't was soiled and covered   with the dust thick flying.
Before the ladies seated,   riders bold in many a tilt
were vying.

Now at length the maidens   were left no longer there ;
They, with the queenly Hilda,   were led to a window near,
Where the daring champions   their eyes on them were feeding :
Beside the four betrothéd,   a hundred well-clothed maids
they were thither leading.

Many wandering players   there let their skill be shown ;
The best that each was able,   how gladly was it done !
When early mass was ended,   upon the next day's morning,
And God by them was worshiped,   knights of the sword again
to their games were turning.

Of uproar and of gladness   where could more be found ?
Of many tunes and singing   the halls gave back the sound.
Until four days were over,   there the high times lasted :
Well-born throngs were gathered,   nor oft the hours
in idleness they wasted.

An open-handed giver,   that day was Herwic seen.
He knew the wandering players,   who there had come again,
Were bent on growing richer,   and well for this were striving ;
Herwic meant, in kindness,   that all, while there, should gain
an easy living.

First the lord of Sealand   flung his gifts around
With willing hand so freely   that thanks from all did sound
Who saw his love and kindness,   or heard about it later :
In ruddy gold King Herwic   the worth of full a thousand
pounds did scatter.

Clothing, too, was given   by his friends as well as kin ;
Horses finely saddled   many there did win,
Who before not often   on such steeds had ridden.
When this was seen by Ortwin,   in giving then he would not
                         be outbidden.

He, the king of Ortland   finest clothes now gave :
Since then, if better clothing   knights did ever have,
Forsooth we cannot tell you, —   it never reached our hearing.
He and all his followers   stood bereft, erelong, of much that
                         they were wearing.

No one now could reckon   what store of clothing good
Was given by those from Moorland.   There fine horses stood,
Soon to be given also, —   such indeed is the saying :
Those who were to have them   for better never hoped, nor e'er
                         were praying.

All were now made richer,   both the young and old.
Then, too, was seen King Hartmut ;   nought would he withhold,
As though his home and kingdom   had not in war been wasted :
They saw him give so freely,   that greater love and kindness
                         none e'er tasted.

By him and his friendly kinsmen   who thither with him came,
And there were held in bondage,   how readily by them
Was given what was left them,   that any from them wanted !
By Hartmut and his followers   all that could be asked
                         was gladly granted.

Gu-drun, the lovely maiden,   a friendly will e'er bore
To Hildeburg of Ireland,   with whom, in days of yore,
To wash upon the sea-sands   the clothes she oft was bearing.
I ween no pains she slighted   that Hartmut's love her friend
might now be sharing.

Gu-drun then bade her steward   a hoard of goods to take
For those who shared her kindness.   Men of this would speak,
And say in wealth to give them   she would ne'er be wanting;
Heavy gold and silver,   and clothes, could she to all
her friends be granting.

Before his seat upstanding,   the Sturmisch lord was seen,
Clad so well and richly   that never king nor his men
Finer clothes or better   at any time were wearing.
None long time were waiting   who hoped that day his kindness
to be sharing.

Above all others, Wâ-te   gave such clothing there
That truly never better   a king was seen to wear;
With gold and gems it sparkled,   o'erhung with richest netting:
Such clothes with him he carried   when on his way to court
he was forth setting.

In every one of the meshes   lay a costly stone,
However one might name it;   thereby it could be known
That in the land of Abalic   the gems therein were fitted.
To Wâ-te and his followers   all gave the hand, and them
with thanks they greeted.

None of those there gathered,   who saw the clothes that day,
Could of the brave old Wâ-te   this truth indeed gainsay, —
That beyond the gifts of princes   his were far outreaching.
Of wealth he soon was master   who for these gifts his hand
                     was now outstretching.

Willingly did Irold   let them see his mind,
That he to none was grudging   gifts of any kind.
Good care of Hilda's riches   was Fru-te ever taking:
He was a faithful steward,   and long of him thereafter
                     men were speaking.

The high times now were ended,   and all their leave would take.
Then 't was allowed to Hartmut,   as well his worth bespake,
His peace to gain forever;   to this Gu-drun had brought him.
Then for their home they started;   each happier went than he
                     had erst bethought him.

With friendly love, Queen Hilda   bade them all farewell;
With her, Gu-drun and Hildeburg   went, with kind goodwill,
Far beyond the castle,   with all their maids-in-waiting.
There took they leave of Hartmut,   when he at last was on
                     his way forth setting.

A guard Queen Hilda gave them   across the land and sea;
Great was the host that Herwic   and Ortwin now set free,
Whom, long held in bondage,   they now were homeward sending;
Full a thousand followers   Hartmut brought to his land
                     when the war was ending.

Everywhere the ladies   one another kissed.
Many now were sundered   who long each other missed,
And nevermore thereafter   might again be meeting.
The high-bred Ortwin and Herwic   went with them to the boats
                 that for them were waiting.

Irold must be their leader,   while they did homeward fare.
Then by the king 't was bidden   that he the word should bear
To Horant, lord of Denmark,   how they the land were leaving:
Soon Irold to the warriors   guidance and guard unto
                 their homes was giving.

The time, or late or early,   in truth I cannot tell,
When they for their home in Kassian   did at last set sail.
The folk, now faring thither,   were nought but gladness showing:
After many sorrows,   God on them was fullest bliss
                 bestowing.

Irold said to Horant,   when he reached the Norman land,
That he by the king was bidden   homeward to lead the band.
" To leave to them their kingdom,"   he answered, " it is fitting,
They home have come so gladly;   I, too, to see my land
                 with pain am waiting."

Then they welcomed Hartmut,   and to him his land did leave:
But how he swayed his kingdom   I now no knowledge have.
With all his friends, then Horant   quickly homeward hasted,
And left the land behind them;   Denmark they reached,
                 nor many days they wasted.

There we now will leave them,   and only this will say:
That never from a wedding   homeward took their way
Happier knights and kinsmen   than now from there were going:
Only the men of Karadie   tarried still in the land,

                    their gladness showing.

Tale the Thirty-Second.

HOW THEY ALL WENT TO THEIR HOMES.

NOW with the friendly Hegelings   none would tarry more.
  Soon on the way to Alzabie   they Herwic's sister bore,
Shouting all for gladness   that they the maid were bringing ;
While, on their watery pathway,   with proud and happy hearts,
                              the knights were singing.

Queen Hilda gave, at parting,   a kind farewell to them.
Tho' rich were Herwic's followers   when first to her they came,
Yet gifts she gave full many   to them, when homeward faring.
When one is seen so lavish,   the name of a wonder-worker
                              is he rightly bearing.

Gu-drun then spake to her mother :   " May blessings on you be !
Mourn not for the fallen ;   by both my lord and me
Shall love to you be given :   no more you need be feeling
Heaviness or sorrow ;   your woes shall Herwic's kindness now
                              be healing."

To her Queen Hilda answered : " Dearest daughter mine,
If you would make me happy, henceforth must friends of thine
Come to the land of the Hegeling thrice to see me yearly;
Else must I greatly sorrow, and never can bear the loss
                                        I feel so nearly."

Then said Gu-drun, the high-born : "Mother, it shall be done."
At once, with smiles and weeping, and glances backward thrown,
She left the castle of Matelan, with many a friendly maiden.
Her sorrows now were ended : nought before did ever maids
                                        so gladden.

Hither men brought horses, saddled and fitly bred,
To bear her hence with her maidens ; these their keepers led :
Light were all the breastplates, and golden-red each bridle.
I ween the ladies wished not longer far from home
                                        to linger idle.

Many, with hair down-flowing, and decked with gold, rode there ;
Methinks from tears and sorrow none could then forbear,
Who must at last from Ortrun and from her maids be parted.
Should Ortrun be unhappy, Gu-drun would then be sad and
                                        heavy-hearted.

Ortrun, betrothed to Ortwin, then her thanks did give
To fair Gu-drun, the queenly, that she had granted leave
To hold the Norman kingdom to Hartmut, her knightly brother :
" Gu-drun, may God reward you ! my cares are gone, I ne'er
                                        shall know another."

To her mother Hilda, also,   Ortrun her thanks did say,
That she in Ortland's kingdom   the crown should wear one day,
Together with King Ortwin,   and there be called his lady.
Then said to her Queen Hilda   that she to grant her this was
ever ready.

Ortwin then and Herwic   each to the other swore,
With strong and steady friendship,   that they forevermore
Would sway with right and honor   the lands to them belonging,
And ever would be earnest   to seize and slay whoe'er
was either wronging.